HUNTER'S SALVATION

SHILOH WALKER

BERKLEY SENSATION, NEW YORK

THE BERKLEY PUBLISHING GROUP
Published by the Penguin Group
Penguin Group (USA) Inc.
375 Hudson Street, New York, New York 10014, USA
Penguin Group (Canada), 90 Eglinton Avenue East, Suite 700, Toronto, Ontario M4P 2Y3, Canada
(a division of Pearson Penguin Canada Inc.)
Penguin Books Ltd., 80 Strand, London WC2R 0RL, England
Penguin Group Ireland, 25 St. Stephen's Green, Dublin 2, Ireland (a division of Penguin Books Ltd.)
Penguin Group (Australia), 250 Camberwell Road, Camberwell, Victoria 3124, Australia
(a division of Pearson Australia Group Pty. Ltd.)
Penguin Books India Pvt. Ltd., 11 Community Centre, Panchsheel Park, New Delhi—110 017, India
Penguin Group (NZ), 67 Apollo Drive, Rosedale, North Shore 0745, Auckland, New Zealand
(a division of Pearson New Zealand Ltd.)
Penguin Books (South Africa) (Pty.) Ltd., 24 Sturdee Avenue, Rosebank, Johannesburg 2196, South Africa

Penguin Books Ltd., Registered Offices: 80 Strand, London WC2R 0RL, England

HUNTER'S SALVATION

A Berkley Sensation Book / published by arrangement with the author

PRINTING HISTORY
Berkley Sensation mass-market edition / July 2007

ISBN: 978-0-425-21632-3

BERKLEY® SENSATION
Berkley Sensation Books are published by The Berkley Publishing Group,
a division of Penguin Group (USA) Inc.,
375 Hudson Street, New York, New York 10014.
BERKLEY SENSATION is a trademark of Penguin Group (USA) Inc.
The "B" design is a trademark belonging to Penguin Group (USA) Inc.

PRINTED IN THE UNITED STATES OF AMERICA

10 9 8 7 6 5 4 3 2 1

This is for JR.
You asked for him—he's all yours.
Hope you enjoy him.

For all the readers who e-mailed me
asking if Vax was going to get a story.

For my husband, and my kids, always.
I love you all more than life itself.

CHAPTER I

"So, how is wedded bliss treating you?" Vax looked from Kendall to her husband, Kane, and grinned. "Have you gotten used to the ball-and-chain routine yet?"

Kendall flicked a peanut shell at him. She held a pilsner glass in her other hand and took a long drink before saying, "We keep the chains in the bedroom, darling. You ought to know that."

"Kendall, please. I don't want Rambo coming after me."

Kane looked at Vax and flashed a toothy grin. The eye-teeth looked a little longer than they had when Vax had first met him, but other than that, Kane looked pretty much the same. He had taken to the abrupt change in his life pretty damn well, but Vax wasn't surprised. Kane's being Changed into a vamp was the only way he and Kendall could have had a happy ending. Vax figured that if any-body deserved a happy ending, it was Kendall.

"Now, Kane isn't going to do that, are you, Kane?" Kendall snuggled up against Kane, resting her head on his chest. When he looked down at her, Kendall gave her hus-band an innocent smile and batted her lashes.

Kane leaned his shaggy blond head against the wooden slats that made up the back of the booth. His eyelids closed and he gave a faint smile. "Not right now. I'm enjoying the peace and quiet too much."

Quiet being a relative term, Vax hoped. The bar they were in was anything but quiet. The band was actually pretty decent, the singer crooning out his rendition of "Desperado." But even though they didn't sound like a bunch of cats fighting it out, they were not quiet. Kendall, Kane, and Vax were able to carry on a fairly normal conversation only because all three of them had superacute hearing. Everybody else in the bar had to raise their voices to be heard.

Vax knew that Kendall and Kane had just surfaced from a pretty messy job. A long one, too, if the look in her eyes was any indication. She seemed tired. Vax could sympathize.

Vax might be out of the game, but that didn't mean he'd forgotten it. He'd spent enough years doing the "defender of the innocent and helpless" bit to know just how exhausting and heartbreaking it could be.

He didn't know how she kept going. Kendall had been a Hunter for far longer than he'd been alive, and that could be measured in centuries now, not just decades. She'd been at this for several hundred years and Vax had left it behind him after fifty. He'd asked her once how long she'd keep fighting.

"Until I die or until there's no need left," she'd told him. Which meant until she died, because as long as the world kept spinning there was going to be in evil in it. Hunters faced down that evil and did what they could to level the playing field—a hard, thankless job.

But of the two of them, Kendall was the happy one. She was surrounded by evil, death, and despair, but she hadn't let it beat her. Vax had. He didn't fight the good fight anymore. He lived alone on his ranch, worked his land, cared for his horses—and he was lonely as hell.

Of course, the man at Kendall's side was definitely the main reason she was happy. Kane and Kendall, they'd saved each other.

Kendall glanced towards the dance floor and then back at Kane. "Enjoying the peace and quiet too much to get up and dance with me?"

Kane's lashes lifted. "Sort of." He reached over and trailed his fingers down the outside of her arm. "I'd rather dance once we get to the hotel."

She snorted. "That's not dancing, pal." Shifting her gaze to Vax, she lifted a brow. "How about you?" There was a wicked gleam in her eyes as she asked it.

Vax grinned as Kane stiffened in the booth, sitting up as straight as if somebody had swapped his spine for a metal pipe. "You aren't dancing with him, sugar."

Vax hid his smile by taking a drink. "I don't mind taking a turn around the dance floor, Kendall. For old times' sake."

As Kendall started to slide from the booth, an evil smile on her lips, Kane reached out and wrapped his fingers around her arm, locking her in place. Then he looked at Vax and narrowed his eyes. "Not a chance." Kendall stood up and Kane scooted out after her, sliding an arm around her waist.

Having gotten what she wanted, Kendall let her husband lead her out to the dance floor, leaving Vax alone. He reached over and grabbed a handful of peanuts from the tin bucket placed nearby.

As he cracked open a shell, a shadow fell across the table, and Vax lifted his eyes to the brunette standing there. Standing—hell, the way she was posed, she might as well be on the cover of a magazine. One glittery green strap of her tank top had slid off her shoulder. The emerald green matched the stones dangling from her ears, and as she shifted her stance, the hem of her top lifted enough for him to see a matching stone flashing in her navel. Her skirt was so low, he could see her hip bones jutting out over the band, and it was so damned short that if she bent over, Vax imagined she could get arrested for indecent exposure.

She smiled at him as she sat down across from him in the booth. "Hi." As she spoke, she leaned forward.

Whether it was to keep from having to yell too loudly or to treat him to a better view of her breasts, he didn't know.

Since she was going out of her way to treat him to the view, he went ahead and admired it as he popped a peanut into his mouth. "Hello."

"You look kind of lonely." She reached out and touched the back of his hand with a perfectly manicured nail and gave him a smile that showed perfectly white, straight teeth. "I hate seeing a man as sexy as you looking so lonely."

Vax decided she looked like a Barbie doll, with her perfect manicure, her perfect smile, her perfect breasts, and her perfect hair that fell halfway down her back. Plastic. A pretty piece of perfect plastic. Vax smiled a little to himself and leaned back against the booth. "And if I was an ugly-ass bastard, would it bother you to see me lonely?" he asked.

A blank look crossed her face, and he popped another peanut into his mouth while she tried to figure that out. She didn't for more than a second or two. "I love this song. Would you like to dance with me?"

Without even glancing at the crowded dance floor, he said, "Nope." He nodded towards the back of the club, where there was a long row of crowded pool tables. There were easily two dozen wannabe cowboys back there who'd love to impress Barbie. "I bet some of them guys would love to dance with you."

She flipped her hair back over her shoulder. "Boys. I came here looking for a man."

He wondered whether the chemicals used on her hair had started to affect her brain. She wasn't taking the hint very well.

Finally he decided to just spell it out for her. "Not interested, sweetheart. I just came to have a couple of beers and talk with my friends."

Her eyes narrowed and she stood up from the table, straightening her top and smoothing down the pathetic excuse for a skirt. "Your loss." She walked away with an exaggerated sway of her hips.

As the crowd swallowed her up, Vax reached for more peanuts.

His stomach rumbled demandingly, and he studied the scant menu that was glued to the table under the Plexiglas. He was debating between the burger or some buffalo wings when he heard it. None of the mortals could have heard, over the boom of music, the faint, almost strangled scream that ended abruptly.

By the time he hit the crowd at the door, he could see Kendall and Kane coming up behind them. Something rolled through the air, and the crowd parted around Kendall without even realizing why. He fell in behind the vampires. The second they got outside, Kendall threw a damper on the aura of fear emanating from her. "Such a handy little trick you have."

Kendall looked at Vax over her shoulder with a smile, but it looked strained.

The three of them trotted around the outside of the club, trying to find the source of the scream. Vax scented blood and magick. He swung to the east, along the farthest edge of the parking lot. They approached as one, Kendall pausing by the fallen body of a man. "He's alive," she murmured, pressing her hand to the gouges in his neck.

"Will he stay that way?" Kane was staring off into the darkness. Vax followed his line of sight but couldn't see as well as the vampires could in the dark. All he could make out were a couple of darker shadows.

"Yes. Just unconscious. Looks like he got his head bashed in." Kane didn't wait around to hear any more. He moved quickly to investigate whatever he'd seen in the shadows. Vax paused and crouched down by her side, studying the man's injured neck in the faint light. "The wounds are deep, but as long as he doesn't lose more blood . . ." Kendall's nose wrinkled and she looked up, her eyes seeking out Vax's. "What's that smell?"

It was faint. Vax just barely caught the scent, and it was oddly familiar. "Wait here."

She grimaced. "I'm not going anywhere until I get the bleeding to stop, darling."

Leaving her alone in the shadows, Vax approached the muffled sounds of fighting a block away. There was another body, but this one was moving. It was a woman clutching the shredded remains of her shirt together in front of her, whimpering and rocking herself. The panicked fear rolling off her hit Vax's shields like an avalanche. Bracing himself against it, he tried to sift through all the stimuli coming from her. He caught one random image, and it seemed as if all the fear was related to it.

It looked like a shifter.

Sort of. In a Hollywood-version-gone-wrong sort of way. A humanoid face covered in fur, the brow ridge more pronounced and the jaw elongated. The way a shifter looked for a split second as it shifted from human to animal. Limbs stretched out, as though somebody had replaced the bones with putty and jerked them all out of proportion. Vax had seen some scary-ass-looking creatures, but the wrongness of this image disturbed him.

Had she seen a shifter Changing? Could this stem from that random moment?

There was a scrabbling sound behind him and he whirled, flicking his wrist and dislodging his knife from the sheath he kept strapped to his forearm. It was eight inches long, slender, and made of pure silver. It was balanced for throwing, but he could also use it in a knife fight if it came down to it. He swung out with the knife, and it was the only thing that kept him from getting his throat ripped out.

He backpedaled away from the thing in front of him. As his back collided with a rusted-out work van, he stared.

It was the thing he had picked up from the woman.

It moved towards Vax, and he realized vaguely that it wasn't an *it,* but a *she*. He could make out the curve of breasts on her chest, and the fur on her torso started to thin out just under the rib cage. Her belly was practically hairless, save for a ribbon of hair that ran down to the pubic area before thickening and covering her thighs with a thick, coarse-looking pelt.

The eyes looked human. Vax found himself staring at her, almost dumb as his mind tried to process what he was looking at. The hair on her head could have passed for the hair he'd see on any woman, thick and shiny. And she was wearing an earring. Just one, a silver spiral that looked out of place against the darkness of her pelt.

She swung out towards him, and the sight of those deadly black talons flying towards his face snapped him out of his daze. He dove to the side, tucking his body into a ball and rolling away. He came to his feet and pivoted around. The wolf-woman turned towards him, studying him with her head cocked to the side. She opened a thin, lip-less mouth and spoke. Her voice was too garbled for him to understand, but the tightening in the air told him every-thing he needed to know.

Fire came hurtling towards him, and he swore. Drawing back his hand, he threw the knife. More magick shim-mered around him, but it ended abruptly as the knife planted itself in her malformed chest.

The fire had struck the Dumpster just behind him, and he dealt with that, using his own power to kill the flames. Smoke continued to rise from the Dumpster while he turned and approached the woman still huddled and whis-pering on the ground.

There was a faint sound behind him, and he turned to see Kane limping towards him. There were four furrows in the left leg of his jeans, and Vax could see blood welling from some nasty-looking gouges under the cloth.

"Was that a werewolf?" Kane asked, lines bracketing his mouth.

Vax looked back at the thing. The fur was slowly reced-ing into the woman's body, the limbs returning to a more normal length. In under a minute, all that remained was a human woman, her body covered with bruises and Vax's silver knife sticking out of her chest.

He drew it out and pulled a bandana from his back

pocket. After he'd wiped away the blood, he folded up the bandana and stuck it inside his jacket pocket. "I'm not really sure."

"You're not sure."

Looking up at Kane, Vax repeated in a slow voice, "No. I'm not really sure."

Hours later, the three of them were holed up in a hotel room.

Some mortal at the bar had seen a commotion and called the cops, so Kane and Vax had been forced to dodge the police, leaving Kendall there until the ambulance arrived. She fabricated a very believable-sounding line about how she had been trying to find the man she had come with when she stumbled across the bleeding man.

No, Officer. I didn't see anybody.

Yes, Officer, I'm sure I didn't hear anything.

Did I see anybody suspicious? Officer, it's Friday night. I've had a long week, and I was here trying to relax and have a good time.

Vax had been forced to burn the werecreature. Their kind couldn't go on an autopsy table, and considering that she'd died from a knife in the chest, that's exactly where they would have put her. Damn it all, though. He had a bad feeling about that thing. She felt unnatural. But now he'd never know why. Couldn't get too much from a scorched spot on the ground.

"You lie pretty well for a good little Irish Catholic," Vax said, glancing at Kendall as he continued probing at Kane's thigh. The gouges were the kind he would expect to see on somebody who'd been mauled by a were, but Kane was a vampire. They should have been healing better than this.

The edges of each furrow were an inflamed, angry shade of red. Fortunately Kane had stopped bleeding. Vamps could bleed to death—it just wasn't common. They healed too quickly, so in order to make one bleed out, it usually took a sustained series of injuries, making the vampire bleed from numerous places over a long period of time. It was usually faster to bleed them enough to weaken them, and then cut out the heart.

"Why isn't he healing?" Kendall was pacing the floor, her fingers fiddling nervously with the strand of black pearls around her neck.

"Not real sure, sweetheart," Vax muttered, distracted. The scent of magick had faded, so the cause wasn't anything that were had done to poison Kane.

"You're not real sure about anything tonight."

"Sure I am. I'm sure that the woman was something I've never seen before. I'm sure she used to be human. I'm also sure she was using magick and if I wasn't a witch myself, I'd be ash right now. Now shut up and let me concentrate." He probed the wound again, disturbed by the persistent slow bleeding.

Kane hissed out a breath as Vax pressed down on one of the gouges. "Damn it, you sick bastard. That hurt." He smacked at Vax's hand and said, "I thought witches were supposed to be better at this kind of thing. Your bedside manner sucks."

With a grunt, Vax muttered, "I'm a witch, not a nurse. Pipe down." Vax finally gave up looking for some plausible explanation as to why Kane wasn't healing. "This is going to hurt. Be still." He laid his hands over the wounds and called upon his weak Healing talent.

Kane's body jerked. From the corner of his eye, Vax saw Kendall move up, wrapping her arms around Kane's shoulders. Kane moaned, a tortured sound that made Vax feel guilty as hell. His hands fell away from Kane's thigh, revealing four shiny pink scars. He looked into Kane's dazed eyes and said, "Sorry. Healing isn't something I've ever been very good at."

"At least it healed." Kane's voice was hoarse, and he looked up at Kendall. "Get me some water, will you?"

After grabbing a cup from the bathroom and filling it from the faucet, she brought to Kane and sat down on the edge of the bed, cuddling against him. She looked at Vax, though. "You don't know what she was?"

"A shape-shifter gone wrong." That was his best guess, and it was no explanation at all. How had she gotten stuck between forms?

"She used magick. I felt it."

Kane spoke up. "I saw it. She used fire, man. Shape-shifters can't use fire."

Vax shook his head. "No. No, they can't. I smelled the magick at the same time I smelled blood. I don't understand it, though."

"Maybe she was a witch and she got bit?" Kane offered. He lifted the cup to his lips and drained it. When Kendall offered more, he shook his head. "Tastes like crap."

She stood up and dug some money out of her pocket. "I'll get a bottle from the vending machines. You need fluids."

Kane watched her leave before looking back at Vax. "So?"

Vax scowled and drove a hand through his hair. "That's not it. Most witches are immune to a werewolf's bite. The few who aren't—well, they just shift to wolf. They have no trouble shifting. This one, she looked like she was stuck between forms."

"She looked like something out of a nightmare," Kane said softly, staring down at his mauled leg. "What about a crossbreed? A witch got knocked up by a were? Were blood can pass through the genes just like other shifters, right?"

"Not often. God's way of controlling our numbers. The last thing this world needs is a bunch of weres roaming around that can control fire. You control it, it's a lot less likely to kill you. There just aren't that many crossbreeds. Very, very few offspring are born with the talents of both parents. Besides, she didn't feel . . ." Vax's voice trailed off as he tried to find words to describe it. Finally, he just finished lamely, "She didn't feel natural."

Kendall came back inside at that point. She had heard the entire conversation as she used the machine across the hall. "I felt that, too. Something just didn't feel right."

"Does evil ever feel right?" Kane asked, accepting the bottle from his wife and opening it with a flick of his wrist. After he drained half the bottle, he said, "I didn't feel anything."

"Takes time. You've only been a vampire a few years. Sensitivity to magick takes decades," Vax said shortly. In time, Kane would be as sensitive to magick, shifters, and weres as he was to the scent of blood. He'd learn to sense evil and all the subtleties within it.

Strong vamps could detect the presence of another predator, and Kane was definitely in that category. In a few decades, he'd know a shifter from a were and a witch from a psychic.

Well, he had a heads-up on the psychic one. Kane was one of few people with true psychic powers, the ability to sense thoughts without the use of magick as an aid. Wasn't the same as magick, any more than a shifter was the same as a werewolf. Werewolves *were* shape-shifters, but their powers were linked to the waxing and waning of the moon. All but the most powerful werewolf had to shift on the full moon. It wasn't a desire, but a need.

Shifters, though, weren't weakened by the moon's call. Some of them would feel it but they could control the desire to shift on a full moon. Weres couldn't. Whether it had something to do with being born a shifter versus made a were, nobody really knew.

Shape-shifters were born and they learned control from birth. Although weres could breed and pass the power on through the father's side, a natural were usually didn't come into the ability to shift until later in life.

Thinking about the were-witch-whatever they had faced was giving Vax a headache and pissing him off, and he wasn't in a good mood anyway. His stomach started rumbling again, and he realized he hadn't ever gotten around to eating anything at the bar. His most recent meal had been last night, and that wasn't good. Witches needed to eat more calories than mortals: their magick burned more energy, and going a day without food was just plain stupid. "Was there anything to eat in those machines?"

Kendall nodded. She was leaning against Kane again and kept touching him, almost as if assuring herself that he was fine.

"I'll be back in a second."

"Should we order a pizza?" Kane mocked as he watched Vax come back in a few minutes, his hands laden with bags of chips, beef jerky, and crackers.

Kendall rolled her eyes and smiled, shaking her head a little. "Witches have to eat more. They burn calories almost as fast as shifters and weres do."

"Learn something new every day." Kane watched Vax tear into a bag of sour cream potato chips, and he scowled. "I miss Lay's."

Vax smiled serenely and popped one into his mouth. He crunched down a little more loudly than necessary, and as he swallowed, he smacked his lips. "Yum."

"Jackass." But there wasn't much heat in it.

Vax watched as the other man lay back against the bed wearily. "If he isn't feeling more like himself after he feeds, take him to Excelsior. Have Kelsey or somebody take a look at him."

"I just fed last night," Kane drawled, not opening his eyes. "And don't you think we have a more pressing matter than your empty stomach and my lack of one? What about a witch who used some sort of shape-shifting spell?"

"Okay, that settles it. I think he belongs at Excelsior even if he does start feeling better," Vax said with a laugh. Excelsior was their training school. With Kane's age and background, it had been decided he wouldn't benefit too much from spending a full four years there, but apparently there were some things he still needed to learn. Instead of going to school, Kane was placed with Kendall. Kendall was one hell of a trainer, but that wasn't the same thing as a teacher, Vax figured.

"Am I missing something?" Kane asked when Kendall grinned a little.

The bag rattled as Vax dug out a few more chips. He ate them and washed them down with the soft drink. "Yeah, you're missing something, buddy. Shape-shifting spell." He laughed again and looked at Kendall. "Sweetheart, I realize it was decided that he wouldn't learn much of anything he didn't already know at Excelsior, but you do need to educate him on the basics."

Kendall laughed a little. "Apparently."

"What's so amusing?" Kane's voice was edgy and irritated, and when Vax looked at him, he saw that Kane had opened his eyes.

Returning Kane's glare with a grin, Vax said, "Kane, there are no shape-shifting spells. Witches can't shape-shift. As a matter of fact, there are very few actual spells— at least, the kind of spells you'd recognize as a spell."

"What, there's no way you can skin a werewolf and chant and dance around a fire so you can turn into a wolf?"

Vax cocked a brow. "I've never chanted in my life. And no, there is no way. Witches can't shape-shift any more than we can bring back the dead. We have power inside us and we learn how to harness it, how to use it to bring fire or to move objects by using the air elements. We can Heal. But we can't turn into animals."

"Okay, so a witch using a shape-shifting spell is out." Kane shrugged and took another swig from the bottle. He stared up at the ceiling, lost in thought. "I know that when a shifter and a witch mate, there's a fifty-fifty chance the offspring will inherit one of the gifts, or neither. Inheriting both is supposed to be extremely rare, right?"

Vax nodded. He knew the path Kane's mind was taking, and if he hadn't seen the thing, he would have assumed it was a logical path. But he had seen it—*not it, her. It* just seemed more appropriate. But there was no way that creature was the natural result of any union, whether witch, vamp, were, or alien mermaid. It just wasn't possible. He said so as he peeled the wrapper off a piece of jerky.

He bit into it without enthusiasm. He wanted a steak. Bad. Unfortunately the hotel they were holed up in didn't offer room service, and he wasn't leaving just yet.

Kendall replied, "Even if she was the child of a were and a witch, and that's not likely, but even if she was . . ."

Her voice trailed off, and Vax took up where she left off. "When I said unnatural, I meant unnatural. Maybe she was altered somehow."

"Altered? You mean, like, mutated?" Kane rubbed a hand over the healed scars on his leg. "This itches like a son of a bitch," he added, glancing towards Vax.

"Good. Means they are healing." Vax walked around the edge of the bed and crouched down, studying the wounds closely. "Some sort of mutation. I don't know, that's possible. We need to find out more. Once I know you're feeling better, I'm going to try and track her."

"Track her," Kane repeated slowly. "How can you track a corpse—actually, she's less than a corpse. She's ashes. What's left to track?"

With a faint smile, Vax replied, "There's always something to track. In this case, her magick. I'm going to try to track her magick."

TRY—yep, he tried to track her and failed miserably.

Back at the bar less than a day later, Vax sensed nothing from the witch/shifter. Even though she was dead, he should have been able to pick up some sort of trail to track, either the thing's scent or the taste of magick in the air.

He spent nearly two weeks trying to uncover more about the woman. But it was as if she had appeared out of nowhere, and now that she was dead, "nowhere" was going to remain off the map.

Chapter 2

THE honeysuckle was blooming.

Canton Cemetery was an old-fashioned one, nestled in a small valley behind Canton Christian Church. It was the kind with actual tombstones, and surrounded by a white-painted picket fence. The honeysuckle grew profusely in the summer months, covering the pretty white fence. One year, some of the men in the church had decided to cut down the honeysuckle, but the people who had loved ones buried there had argued, and now the honeysuckle was left alone, thinned out only when necessary.

The two sisters had always loved the scent of it. Jess had brought Myranda here for the past eight years, ever since they'd had to put their parents to rest.

Now— Jess closed her eyes against the tears that threatened to fall. Now she had to visit her baby sister here as well.

Randi had been the baby, younger than Jess by nearly ten years.

It just wasn't *right*.

Randi had been the golden girl, smart, sweet, funny. Full

of determination and drive, she had been born something special, and she would have become something special.

When most nineteen-year-olds were champing at the bit for some freedom, Randi had been content to stay at home and make the thirty-minute drive to the University of Indianapolis, instead of living on campus and partying. She'd been focused on her studies, dedicated to them. Randi would have graduated in one more year, nearly two years early.

But not now—now she was gone. Her life had ended before it had even really gotten started. But it was so much worse, knowing *how* she had been killed. Raped and killed, the entire sordid thing captured on video. The police had collected dozens of copies of the snuff film, but Jess knew there was no way to ever track all of them down.

Jess would have to live the remainder of her days knowing that any moment some sick pervert might be jerking off as he watched somebody choke the life from her baby sister.

"God, Randi, I'm so sorry," she whispered. Reaching out, she touched her fingers to the cool, soft pink surface of the marble headstone.

She was also going to have to live with the guilt— because she was the reason Randi had been killed. It had been a message to her.

Jess had been investigating a series of rape/murders that had been taking place in the city, and she'd been getting too close. Some reporters had a nose for a story. Jess had a little more. The sixth sense had served her well her entire life, and when she had first started investigating the serial murders, her gut had told her there was more going on than what they were seeing.

The cops had absolutely no clue, and her gut insisted they were looking in the wrong place.

Jess hadn't thought she was doing much better, but she must have been getting closer to something. Otherwise there was no reason to kill Randi.

I failed you.

Eight years ago, after they'd put their parents in the ground, Jess had promised she'd take care of Randi. That she'd protect her. She'd failed, and nothing would ever change that. Nothing would ever make it better.

Part of Jess wanted to lie down next to Randi's grave and die as well. She'd fallen into a depression so deep that death was the only thing that made sense sometimes. But a stronger instinct won out.

Finding them. Finding the bastards who had done this. Find them. Make them pay. Show them what real pain was.

Maybe after she did that, she'd join her sister.

Don't think like that, baby girl . . .

It was the ghost of her mother's voice she heard whispering through her head. Mom had done her best to teach both of her girls how to handle their gifts. One of the first things in controlling a gift was maintaining the emotions. Strong emotions, especially anger, shattered control, and Jess's hold was tenuous at best now. Her fury had all but shattered her control, but she couldn't find it in her to care.

Like her daughters, Leanne Warren had been gifted. She'd been psychic, and she'd passed her knowledge on to her daughters. She'd also taught them discipline. Her daughters had gifts that required utmost control.

Randi had been born Empathic. Vulnerable to emotions, Randi had mastered shielding around the time most kids were just mastering how to write their names.

Jess hadn't come into her gifts until she was a teen. She had a weak psychic sense, that sixth sense that helped her in her work. That wasn't the gift requiring control, though. It was the telekinesis. When things moved seemingly on their own, it freaked people out.

Every time Jess had slipped up, every time she had cursed the ability that made things go flying through the air, Mom had been there. *You can handle this, baby. We're never given more than we can handle.*

"You were wrong, Mom. I can't handle this."

She said the words out loud, and they seemed to echo through the empty cemetery. The wind blew through the trees, sounding oddly like a sigh. But the ghostly voice in her head stayed silent.

Jess brushed her fingers once more against the marble headstone, and then she rose to her feet. On her way back to the car, she passed by the fence and plucked a few honeysuckle blossoms. Still holding them in her hand, she climbed inside and shut the door.

Jess closed her hand around the blossoms, crushing them in her fist. As the scent of honeysuckle rose in the air, she just sat there and wept.

CHAPTER 3

Her screams haunted his dreams. The sight of her battered, broken body forever burned on the inside of his eyelids, so that every time he closed his eyes, he saw her.

Cora—

She'd been so sweet, so beautiful. So helpless. He'd loved her. More than his own life. And he should have stayed away from the beginning.

"You can't do this."

He reached out, threading his hand through her red-gold curls one more time.

"Vax, *please*! You love me, remember?" As she pleaded with him, tears sparkled in her sky blue eyes. Her heart was racing—he could hear it.

"Yes. I do love you," he murmured. "Shhhh . . ." He lowered his lips and kissed away the tears streaming down her cheeks.

"We can make it right, Vax. I know we can—you just have to help me."

"I will." He tipped up her chin and kissed her gently before guiding her head to his chest. He held her with one arm.

With the other, he drew the silver knife from his waist. *Am I really going to do this?*

As though he were watching it happen to somebody else, he saw himself raise the knife. Watched as he drove it into Cora's smooth, silky back. She arched against him, screaming. A little puff of smoke escaped her lips, and the scream ended in abrupt silence.

Vax came awake with the echo of that pain-filled scream sounding in his ears. He jerked upright in bed and stared into the darkness of the night, trying to breathe. His heart slammed against his ribs with a force that hurt. Air rattled in and out of his lungs, and his skin was cold, clammy with sweat. The sheets under him were damp and tangled.

He could still hear Cora screaming.

"Shit." He muttered the word as he flopped back onto the bed. He flung one arm over his eyes, but it did nothing to block out the pictures in his mind.

Ninety-six . . . It had been ninety-six years. And the dream still had the ability to do this to him.

"Cora . . ." He whispered her name, trying to bring an image of her face to mind. He couldn't, though. All he could see was blood.

"God, Cora. I'm so sorry."

DAWN hadn't even begun to tease the eastern horizon when Vax rolled from his bed. His gut felt raw; his throat was hot and tight, burning with the urge to empty his stomach. He swallowed bile down and stared at the hardwood floor between his feet as he waited for the nausea to pass.

It didn't pass completely, but it finally eased enough that he thought he could avoid puking on himself.

Ignoring the throbbing in his head, he pushed to his feet and grabbed the jeans slung over the end of his bed. Before leaving his bedroom, he pulled them up over his naked hips. In a concession to the chill in the air, he pulled on a threadbare black T-shirt and then headed for the kitchen.

Coffee wasn't going to settle his stomach any, but it might clear the cobwebs in his head and soothe the air a little. Especially if he used to it to wash down a couple dozen extra-strength aspirin. Before hunting down the aspirin, he set coffee to brewing. He finally found the bottle shoved in a cluttered junk drawer by the stove. As he popped the lid off with one hand, he grabbed a mug from a glass-fronted cabinet. Hot coffee sizzled on the burner as he pulled out the pot and filled his mug halfway.

He washed two aspirin down with coffee hot enough to scald his throat, and then he headed out to the back porch. The deck was huge, spanning the entire length of the house. Vax had built it with his own two hands one hot summer years ago. He'd planned on putting a hot tub off to the side, and maybe a fire pit, but then he'd lost interest. Pretty much summed up his entire life lately. He'd lost interest.

Depressing as hell, too, since he had a whole lot of years left in front of him. He already had a lot of years behind him, and most of them were bleak and empty.

Although he didn't look it, Vax had seen nearly two centuries pass. It was entirely possible that he'd see another two centuries before his body finally shut down on him. In another hundred years or so, he might start seeing lines on his face when he looked in the mirror, and the long pitch-black hair would eventually turn gray.

But it wasn't soon enough to suit him.

His life was empty and aimless, and had been for the past ninety-six years. He was going to spend whatever years were left to him empty and alone.

Sipping from the rapidly cooling coffee, he watched as the sun began to rise in the east. The sky bled from midnight blue to shades of purple and pink before finally settling into a clear, soft blue. The air remained chilly, though, even with the sun shining bright and clear.

Fall came hard and early to Montana. Although it was only early October, they'd already seen their first snow. He wasn't aware of the cold, though, until he felt a fuzzy warm weight settle around his bare feet. Looking down, he met a pair of warm, misty blue eyes that stared up at him with concern. He forced a smile as he reached down and rubbed the mongrel's head, scratching behind his ears.

He had found Wendigo a few years back, when he was just a puppy, shivering and near freezing. Part wolf, part husky, Wendigo and his littermates had been dumped by their owner on the roadside. Three of the pups had frozen before Vax had found them. The other two, he had found homes for. He'd planned on finding a home for Wendigo as well, but each time he did, the determined little thing escaped and found his way back to Vax.

After it happened the third time, Vax accepted the inevitable. He'd been adopted, whether he liked it or not. Vax would deny it if he was asked, but the mutt had worked his way into his heart. Kind of ironic. After a hundred years of making sure nothing got close to him, it was a big-eared, big-footed stray that found a way inside.

"How you doin', boy?" Vax crouched down in front of Wendigo. The dog took advantage of the moment to lean into his master, resting his head on Vax's shoulder and making soft whining noises in his throat.

"Don't worry about me." This time Vax's smile was a little more sincere. "I'm not going to disappear and forget to feed you." At least it wasn't very likely.

Rising, he headed inside, and Wendigo fell in step behind him. As Vax reached under the sink and pulled out the heavy plastic tub where he stored the dog's food, Wendigo started dancing around, rearing up on his hind legs and poking his cold nose against Vax's side.

"I swear, you'd think it had been months since you ate. I know I fed you last night." The evidence of said meal was still in crumbs around the dog's food dish. Vax dumped some kibble into the bowl and scooted it to the side so that Wendigo could eat while Vax cleaned up the dog's mess from last night.

He tossed the paper towels into the garbage can and put the food container away before he dropped down onto the floor next to Wendigo and rubbed the dog's back as he ate. Wendigo took a split-second break to look at his master, making that odd whining noise.

Vax smiled and tried once more to reassure the dog. "Don't worry, boy. I'm not going anywhere."

But not even a minute passed before he realized he just might be wrong. He was in the middle of pulling some eggs from the fridge when he felt it, that odd low-key burn in his spine. A call he hadn't felt for years, and a call he never wanted to feel again. It was there, though, strong and certain. It wasn't a fluke like the mess in Utah, either. This was a flat-out call and it was directed at him.

"I'm not in the game anymore," he said out loud. Not that there was anybody to hear him. Maybe he was just hoping he could convince himself to ignore it. Wasn't going to happen, though. It took him a whole day before he admitted he was wasting his time.

Somebody out there was in danger, and apparently it had been decided that Vax needed to play Hunter again.

You need to go home. . . .
Jess ignored the little voice in the back of her head as she shifted on the bar stool.

There was nothing to go home to. Randi was gone; her room sat empty. Jess couldn't even lose herself in her work. She couldn't concentrate on anything but her sister's face, the way they had beaten her on that fucking video.

There was no way she could do her job. Knowing that, she'd put in for a leave of absence the day after Randi had been killed.

Jess wasn't going to try to get back to her life until she found the ones who had ended Randi's. She'd spent the past four months tracking down leads, and finally she had a solid one. Going home was not going to happen.

You were always such a stubborn girl, Jess.

Was it disrespectful to tell your mom to shut up if she was just a ghostly voice whispering in your head?

Of course, Jess was trying really hard not to acknowledge her mom's presence. Acknowledging it meant she just might have to listen to the voice of reason that seemed to echo her mother's words. Acknowledging it meant that she might have to accept that it wasn't the voice of reason—but actually her mother.

So she just ignored it.

She'd started hearing her mother's voice the day Randi had died. Why her mom's ghost had shown up then, Jess didn't know. Didn't care. Before Randi's death, Jess had missed her mom so badly, she'd have given her right arm to speak with her again, even if it was just the ghostly little whispers. But now?

Now . . . Jess wished that voice would go away. Nothing her mother said would change her mind.

Jess didn't want reason right now. She wanted vengeance.

And she was close. Very close. She could all but smell the blood in the air. Her skin had been buzzing ever since she'd set foot in the club. The lower level of the club was open to the public, big on goth. The upper levels were for invited members only.

Jess hadn't expected to get invited up. She'd been happy just watching from the sidelines down below, hoping that he'd show up.

His name was William Masters, and when she'd seen him two weeks earlier, she had *known*. She'd spent the past two weeks getting every bit of information she could on him. It wasn't much.

He was the one who had raped Randi. The one who had killed her. Her first instinct had been to get her gun and blow his brains out. She had bought the Browning when she was researching a story about gun crime, and she had kept it, locking it up in the fire safe under her bed. Out of curiosity, she had learned how to shoot it, and still went to the firing range two or three times a year.

After Randi died, Jess had started going to the shooting range two or three times a week, and she'd gotten her hands on specialized bullets. Jess suspected she'd need one of those special bullets for this guy. He didn't feel right.

He was a monster. He was a rapist. He was a killer. But there was more than that. He made her skin crawl.

What was he . . . ?

Jess would find out. If she had to follow him twenty-four/seven, she'd figure it out. Her job might be a little easier if the bastard would show his damned face, but she could wait. He'd be here sooner or later.

Jess could wait.

So far, every man and the few women who had approached her had been rebuffed with a cool, impersonal smile. Jess had been watching this scene for a while now, even before Randi—*don't think about her now. . . .*

Jess had been studying the bondage scene since early summer in connection with a series of murders. The way the women had been treated prior to death smacked of somebody who took the dominance kick to a whole different level, and the way their bodies had been found, even more so.

While this wasn't exactly her scene, it wasn't one that was unfamiliar to her. Blending in was something she had a knack for—part of the reason she'd made such a good investigative reporter.

And that handy little talent hadn't ever come in so handy.

Thanks to her pale skin, the red wig she wore looked every bit as natural as her own pale blonde locks, and she had styled the wig into a tight topknot. She added a pair of nonprescription colored contacts, turning her green eyes blue. The final bits of her disguise included the clothes she wore, the makeup she'd put on using a heavy hand, and the black-rimmed glasses.

Since she rarely wore makeup and needed glasses only for reading, it was a pretty effective disguise. Jess hadn't even recognized herself when she'd looked in the mirror on her way out of the house.

So far, it seemed effective enough that she had blended into the club scene at Debach without a hitch.

Now if he would just show up.

A hot, burning tingle raced through her veins, and her fingers itched. It was a certain sign that she hadn't managed to extinguish her anger. Closing her eyes, she focused on taking slow, deep breaths and calming herself before the anger took over.

"Everything okay, ma'am?"

The voce was low and deep, too close for comfort, in her opinion, but she didn't edge away. But she wanted to. Badly. Lifting her lashes, she looked to the side and found a man standing there, wearing a suit that easily cost a couple of grand. He was good-looking, in a cold way, but he had dead eyes. Those eyes made something inside her start to hum, but there was no power coming from him.

A player in the game, maybe, but not one of the masters. She'd worry about pawns later.

Forcing a smile, she nodded. "Just fine, thank you."

"This is your first night up here?"

"Yes," she murmured, closing her hand around her glass of wine and shifting on her stool so that she could face the man in front of her—and get a better look at the other patrons. "Lovely place. So much more . . . elegant . . . than the scene downstairs."

He arched a pale brow. His hair was so blond, it was nearly white. Very blond—even paler than her own. "Yes. Well, the scene downstairs is for those who like to play with our lifestyle. Up here—this is for those who actually want to live it. Does that include you, Miss . . . ?"

"Ballard. Jennifer Ballard," Jess supplied, smiling a little more. She hoped it looked coy and secretive. Probably did, though the damned smile felt ridiculous on her face. "Games have their time and place."

"Don't they?" He held out a hand and Jess placed hers in its, maintaining her smile even when the chill of his flesh seemed to freeze her through and through. Definitely one of the pawns—he played his own sort of games, and he liked them. Games that involved a lot of pain, a lot of blood.

Her psychic sense wasn't that strong, but this was clear enough. There was a very real evil inside this man.

"My name is Nate. If there's anything you need . . ." His lashes lowered, and a smile curved his lips. "Anything at all, do let me know."

He lifted her hand to his lips. The press of his lips to the back of her hand seemed to burn her like acid. She wanted to go wash his touch away. Preferably in a vat of bleach. Instead she lowered her head in a nod and murmured, "Thank you."

Nate let go of her hand and looked at the man behind the bar. Jess had checked out the bartender earlier. Big and buff, with gold-streaked brown hair that looked a little too perfect to be natural, and muscles that gleamed under the soft lights. "This is Xeke, Ms. Ballard. Xeke, you take good care of Ms. Ballard, now. If you need anything or if you want him to show you around, just say the word."

The shirtless piece of eye candy nodded and looked at Jess, his lips curling in a smile that promised a world of pleasure. But for some reason, she suspected he'd rather dole out pain. And not the sweet kind that happened when the line blurred a little between pleasure and pain.

No. He wanted to give out real pain, and the more his partner screamed, the more he'd enjoy it.

She wasn't letting Xeke show her a damn thing about Debach.

O KAY, *that* one didn't belong here.

Didn't matter that she was wearing the right clothes. A tight black leather skirt that went down to her ankles, slit up the back nearly to her firm, round little ass. As she had taken a stool at the bar, the slit revealed more leather under her skirt, boots that went up and up. Her vest, yet more leather, zipped up the front, and she was either naked under it or wore a very low-cut bra. Vax was betting on the former.

She wore a thick band of hammered silver around her

right upper arm, drawing his eye to the well-toned muscles and the pale skin there. The thick red hair was twisted into one of those funny knots with two sticks poked through it.

Nothing about her clothing made her stand out from any other woman there.

But her eyes did.

She looked too wary, too watchful.

And pissed. Although most others wouldn't pick up on it, that woman was riding on a wave of fury. She'd be lucky if it didn't get her killed.

Vax Matthews studied the redhead with cynical eyes for a long moment before he filed away her face. One of several, an innocent who was way out of her league—he'd have his hands full making sure they didn't get hurt while he took care of the problem here.

Okay, *problems*. Only a couple, though. And he was irritated as hell that he'd felt the need even to address them.

It had been nearly two weeks since Vax had felt the call that took him away from his home. After speaking with his foreman, letting Jackson "Buck" Buckner know he'd be gone an unspecified amount of time, Vax had tossed a few essentials into a backpack and hit the road.

The road had led him to Indianapolis, Indiana.

Indianapolis was smack-dab in the middle of no-man's-land, as far as Hunters went. No Master had felt drawn here, so it was without formal protection. It was patrolled by Hunters on an irregular basis, when one of them felt the call.

Like the call that had led *him* here. Except he shouldn't feel the damned call. He'd left the Hunters behind years ago. Now if he could just convince whatever it was that kept sending him on these little rescue missions, he'd be a lot happier. Left to his own devices, all alone out on his ranch where he didn't have to deal with anybody.

Well, the ranch hands were always around, but most of them had grown up knowing the Matthews bunch were a weird group of people. It was a rumor that Vax had started when he'd first settled in the area nearly eighty years ago.

Every few decades, he disappeared and didn't return for years, long enough for a new "Matthews" to have grown up and matured, or for a long-lost relative to come home to claim the estate after the previous owner had passed away unexpectedly.

Wouldn't be too long before he had to disappear again for a while. Buck had been around nearly ten years. Vax was starting to see signs of age on his weathered face, which meant that sooner or later somebody might start to wonder why Vax hadn't done any aging.

But he couldn't even think about that problem until he'd solved this one.

Maybe he should just pass it on, tell somebody about the club and the general bad vibe he kept getting. It wasn't as if this was his life any more.

There were a couple of Masters in the general area. One in Chicago; one in Tennessee; and Excelsior wasn't that far. He could have just sent a message to any of those places, and the problem would be addressed. He could climb on his bike, and before he made it even halfway home, somebody else would be all over the club.

Except he couldn't ignore the burn in his gut any more than he could ignore the urge to breathe. "Should have just stayed home," he mused as he stared into his half-empty tumbler of whiskey.

It hadn't been that bad a few hundred miles away. Vax knew he could have ignored the call. Sooner or later, the need would reach for another Hunter, a willing one. As he had drawn closer to Indiana, though, the burn in his gut had gotten worse. By the time he'd hit Indianapolis, the burn was so bad that it was almost making him sick, and he knew he'd done the right thing by answering.

Walking by this club had been like feeling the cold finger of death run down his spine.

People had died because of somebody in that place. More would die. Unless someone acted.

And that someone, it seemed, would have to be Vax. Time was running short for at least one person in there.

The black stink of death clung to the place, and somewhere in there, death was ready to wrap her shroud around some innocent soul.

Or relatively innocent, considering what sort of club he was in.

It would happen tonight. He was the only Hunter close enough to act.

From the corner of his eye, he saw somebody staring at him, and he lifted his head, looking the man square in the eye. Muscle, plain and simple. Somebody hired to make sure no undesirables entered Debach. He wore a suit that cost close to two thousand bucks, easy, and Vax imagined that under normal circumstances the hired muscle was good at his job. He hadn't ever had to deal with somebody like Vax, though.

A slight smile curled his lips as their eyes locked. The guy had a head like a cinderblock, but still, it took only a minute to pierce through the dense shields. Vax wasn't psychic. He wasn't using psychic coercion to make the man walk away, and he wasn't brainwashing him the way a vampire would.

No, what Vax used was magick. Plain and simple. There was a flare of heat low in Vax's spine as he concentrated. The man's eyes glowed for one brief second. And then there was blankness. He turned around and walked away, his gait stiff, disjointed. He paused a few feet later, reaching up to rub at his temple. Some time late tonight, or early tomorrow, he would have vague memories of a dark-haired man who didn't belong in the club. He'd remember that he had been going to say something to him.

Just like the man at the door, and the woman who'd offered to get him a drink, a companion . . . Not one person would remember seeing Vax here until he was long gone. And not one of them would have a useful memory.

Once he'd taken care of whoever was in danger, Vax would make a quick stop by the security room and take care of the security tapes for tonight. It would be as though he'd never been there.

If his mark would just *move*.

So far he didn't know who he was here to save. He could sense power, but it was all tainted. Too often, places like these drew the young gifted. They often felt like they didn't belong, even if they didn't understand *why*. Eclectic lifestyles appealed to a lot of them, and usually they were safe outlets. But every once in a while, the darker things in the world used places like sex clubs or goth clubs as trolling grounds, looking for those gifted, unaware people.

But Vax sensed no young witch or shifter on the verge of coming into his or her power. He sensed no vampires, either. None of the people he'd seen so far had any unnatural sort of blackness lingering near.

Whoever death was looking for was hidden from Vax.

The only one that seemed to stand out to him was the redhead.

It could be her, he supposed. His eyes kept drifting back to her against his will. Could be her . . .

She wasn't exactly the kind of woman he usually went for. She was long and lean—he usually went for soft and curvy. Her eyes were cool and unreadable. For some odd reason, he couldn't feel anything from her, but he did have an odd, almost disconnected sense of grief. Something sad, angry, and full of pain.

Maybe it was that complicated mess that made him keep checking her out, or he might just be staring because he liked the look of her. Vax couldn't tell.

"Been out of the game too long," he muttered. He emptied his whiskey and tapped his finger against the edge of the glass as one of the female servers walked by. She wore nothing more than a dog collar around her slender throat, a white leather G-string, and a sweet, almost vacant smile. She took his glass, returned with a fresh drink, and left him without saying a word.

As she walked away, he caught sight of faint red stripes across her buttocks.

The only thing that kept him from exploding was the haze of sexual satisfaction he could sense inside her.

Whatever had been done to her had been consensual. So, as much as it bothered him, he would leave that one alone.

He was going to have his hands full dealing with the real problems. He didn't need to take ones on that were problems in his mind but not in the minds of those he'd try to rescue.

Damn, were there problems. Even after he dealt with the one in mortal danger, there were way too many victims in this place.

Vax had set one foot inside Debach, and that was all it had taken for his stomach to revolt. Visions had assailed him, women and men alike on their knees, blood running in rivulets down their torsos, whips slicing through the air, the heavy power that came from blood and sex.

And screams. People screaming. *Kids* screaming. Begging for help. Begging for release. Begging for pleasure. Begging for death.

It was warped, how deeply entwined pleasure, danger, pain, and death were inside these walls. Seeking one could mean attaining all. It should have had people running away screaming, but instead they were packed outside the door three and four deep, just *waiting* to get inside.

Most of them had no idea what they were getting into. Innocents came looking for some sort of thrill, and they got pulled into something too powerful for them to understand, and became so lost they might never find their way back.

Some of them had lost more than their innocence because of this place.

Some had lost their lives.

As Nathaniel Metcalf passed the bar, he met Xeke's gaze. He glanced towards the redhead with a cocked brow. Xeke's only response was a flicker of his lashes, but Nate had complete faith that Xeke would watch the woman.

She didn't belong here. Oh, she might be fun for the entertainment the club provided, but she wouldn't be the kind they could pay to be silent. It was in her wide-set blue eyes, in the way she lifted her chin and met his gaze head-on.

Nate wasn't sure what she was doing here, but they needed to get rid of her. The way she kept staring around, as though she was looking for something. What Nate really wanted to know was why she was on the upper level. Upper level was reserved for members and invited guests only.

She sure as hell wasn't a member, and if one of the regulars had invited her up here, that person needed a reminder on the types of people allowed in the upper levels. Most likely, that was what had happened, and Nate would have to deal with both her and the regular.

There was one other possibility, but Nate didn't think she fit the profile for the project, either. Nate didn't know precisely what the project was. He wasn't high enough on the food chain to rate getting details, but he didn't think she was meant for that.

The boss had people who trolled the club for one reason, and that was to sight out prospective subjects. When one was found, there was a protocol that was followed, and Nate would have been notified. So it didn't seem a likely prospect, but he couldn't rule it out.

Probably the best way to handle it was to have Xeke doctor her drink, and when she passed out, they could remove her. One of the others would have to do it. Xeke wouldn't be able to pass up the enticement she'd present, unconscious and helpless.

First, though, Nate needed to talk with the boss. Just to make sure the boss wasn't the reason she was here.

On rare occasions, for entertainment, the boss did bring in women who weren't like the kind they generally used. Hot anticipation flooded Nate's system as he contemplated that. If that was the case, he'd be in for some fun tonight. These women weren't selected just for individual patrons. They were for the fun and pleasure of all. Nate, being an employee, would have to wait his turn, but that wasn't so bad.

By the time they got to him, the women were so terrified and broken, they'd do anything. . . .

Leaving the public areas, Nate headed for the boss's office. Even before he reached the door, somebody had opened it for him. He didn't bother glancing at the naked woman who knelt in front of the desk.

As a trusted member of management, Nate was entitled to enjoy some of the pleasures offered to the club members, but not during business hours. His might be an unusual management position, but Nate fancied himself a businessman, and his pleasures didn't happen on the clock.

Well, not usually.

So instead of admiring her kneeling, naked, and bound body, he took the seat across from the boss and waited to be acknowledged.

The boss sat at a table off to the side. Another woman was bent over it, the pale white flesh of her buttocks striped with red welts. The boss was riding her so hard, the table beneath them was shaking. Her eyes were wide over the ball gag, and just as the boss shoved into her one final time, Nate watched her body stiffen and buck with an orgasm.

Under the fine linen of his trousers, Nate was erect, but when the boss pulled away from the woman and gestured towards her, Nate just smiled and shook his head. It wasn't a first-time occurrence. The boss had offered him women in such a manner before and would again. Usually Nate took what was offered, and happily, but not tonight.

If there were going to be games tonight, he'd wait. There was something to be said for anticipation.

A few minutes later, he couldn't help but grin.

Hot damn. There were going to be games.

The boss glanced towards the cameras as Nate explained his concerns about the redhead, but he didn't look at all concerned. "Yes, I know who she is. Do you remember the reporter who was nosing around about some former subjects, asking a lot of questions?"

Nate inclined his head. "Didn't we already address that?"

"Apparently she didn't take the warning."

Narrowing his eyes, Nate studied the redhead a little closer. She didn't look anything like the blonde who'd been nosing around, but if the boss said it was her, then Nate imagined it was. "You'd think after what happened to her sister, she'd leave it alone."

"Hmmm. That tactic doesn't always work, Nate. Maybe I should have handled this personally instead of passing it on to William. William gets so enthusiastic. That enthusiasm often overrules his common sense. It's entirely possible that killing her sister only pissed her off, and she won't care what happens to her." He smiled, and the smile nearly made Nate shiver in reaction. "At least, she *thinks* she won't care."

"Is there anything I need to do, sir?"

"No. She'll be dealt with tonight, once and for all. Right now there's nothing connecting her to us, so we need to take care of the problem immediately."

Dealt with. Nate didn't let his anticipation show as he asked, "Should I do anything to prepare?"

A cool, emotionless smile curved the boss's mouth. "No. The only thing you'll need to do later is clean up."

Excellent.

A COLD chill raced down Vax's spine, and he straightened in his chair, watching as the man from earlier approached the redhead. She shook her head when he spoke to her, but apparently her opinion wasn't of much concern. A big, hard hand closed around her upper arm, and as she was jerked from the bar, not one person batted an eyelash.

Vax still couldn't get much of a read on her, so he couldn't tell whether she was the one dancing at death's door. Instead of focusing on her, he focused on the suit. That man had so much darkness inside of him that it was sickening, and he had a murderous intent.

Going by what he picked up from the suit, Vax pegged the woman as the one he was supposed to protect.

The shirtless piece of muscle behind the bar watched as

she was dragged away, and there was a smile on his lips. Vax really didn't like the looks of that smile.

She planted her heels and twisted her arm, jerking back with a determination that probably would have worked on the average guy. Except Vax knew this man was used to having women fight him. He continued to pull her struggling body along behind him, heading for an unmarked black door. Vax slammed down his whiskey glass and shoved to his feet, following them.

The guy from behind the bar started towards him, but Vax didn't even pause. It took half a thought, and the guy collapsed to the ground. Several others were rushing towards them, but Vax reached the door before they got to him. He shut it behind him and locked it. Just ahead of him, he could see the redhead still struggling against Muscle Boy, arguing and insisting that he let her go. She could have been fighting with a rock wall for all the attention the man gave her.

Vax wasn't about to be ignored. "I don't think she's interested, pal."

NATE had a grip like a damned vise and she suspected there were bruises forming. But bruises would be the least of her concerns if Jess didn't get away.

The sophisticated man from earlier was gone, and in his place was an animal. As she stared up into Nate's eyes, all she could see was a ravenous greed that made her skin crawl.

How many times did Mom tell me that my damned nosiness would get me in trouble one day? she thought. For once she was aware of an emotion besides rage and grief, but fear really wasn't a welcome addition. Being afraid of anything had always pissed Jess off.

It added to the mess of emotions already inside her, turning into an unending spiral of fear, grief, and rage that built on itself as Jess bolstered her mental shields. Now wasn't the time to let anybody know how scared she was. Fear messed with her control, and she had to be in complete control if she wanted to make it out of this mess alive.

Jess didn't have her mom's strong psychic abilities and she wasn't an Empath like Randi had been, but she didn't need either of those gifts to know what was going on inside Nate's head. She could tell just by looking into his eyes, and what she saw there made her blood turn to ice. She had to get away from him, or she was dead.

Though death didn't seem that bad, she had a job to do first. Jess jerked her arm again and snapped out, "Damn it, let me go."

Nate just cast a bored glance her way.

"I didn't come here to get manhandled like *this*," she said. Maybe it was a misunderstanding. Maybe the guys just assumed the women wanted this—

Nate didn't even bother to look at her this time. But she could see a smile curving up the corners of his mouth. She didn't like that smile. It was almost as terrifying as that wolfish, hungry look she'd seen in his eyes.

"If you don't let go of me this second, you're really going to regret it," Jess said, snarling a little. She didn't like to use her gift when others could see, but it didn't look as if she had much of a choice right now.

Jess focused on the solid wooden door down the hall. That would do a decent amount of damage to Nate's hard head. But apparently she didn't need to do anything. Right as she started to open it with her mind, she heard a voice behind her.

Jess was convinced it was the sweetest sound she had ever heard.

Her assailant swung around. The grip Nate had on her arm had her spinning around with him, and Jess found herself staring at the newcomer. If she thought his voice was a welcome intrusion, then actually seeing him was double the pleasure.

Oh.

Oh. Wow.

Even though some bastard was forcibly taking her someplace she really didn't want to go, even though not one person had looked her way when Nate dragged her out of the bar, and even though she had come *thisclose* to having to use her talent to save her neck, the only thing she could think was . . .

Wow.

He looked like a warrior angel. Thick, raven black hair fell past his shoulders. There was a small braid at each temple. His face was strong, commanding, with high, arched cheekbones, a mouth that looked almost too soft, a squared chin. She could just barely see a glimpse of rawhide around his neck—some sort of necklace. His skin was a dusky gold color that she suspected he'd been born with. And his eyes . . . even from ten feet away, she felt the power of his eyes.

They were gray. Like the color of thunderheads, surrounded by thick, spiky lashes. They gleamed like jewels against the warmth of his skin. As she stared at him, mouth agape, those fantastic gray eyes began to glow.

Her skin crawled from the power she felt coming off him, and before she could stop herself, she muttered, "Shit."

Her soft gasp sounded terribly loud in the silent hall. The warrior angel looked at her briefly. Damn, but he was amazing. He didn't belong in here, wearing jeans and a faded, too-tight black T-shirt. He belonged on some mythical battlefield, carrying a sword in his hands.

The hand on her arm tightened, and the pain of it jerked her attention away from the warrior angel and back to Nate. "This is more trouble than you want to mess with, so just leave now," Nate said, his voice arrogant, confident— and oh so very wrong.

A faint smile appeared on the man's lips. In a calm, level voice, he said, "If you let go of her now, you might have two seconds to try to run for it."

Nate laughed. "Funny. You don't look like the stupid

sort. But you must be." Nate reached inside his jacket, and
Jess felt her heart freeze as he pulled a gun from inside his
jacket. "Too late now, buddy. Say good—"

That was as far as Nate got. The rest of his words were
lost in a strangled gasp. His grip loosened marginally, and
Jess jerked once more against his hold.

This time she got away. Arm throbbing and sore, stinging a little. She glanced down and saw that her arm cuff
was gone.

It fell from Nate's hand with a thud, but she never once
considered getting close enough to grab it. With wide eyes,
Jess stared at Nate. All the while, she backed away slowly,
one step at a time.

As she watched, Nate lost his grip on the gun, his fingers
going slack. It fell from his fingers and hit the floor with a
thunk. Oddly, though, Jess wasn't so worried about the gun
anymore. That gun could be cocked and loaded and
pointed at Jess, and it wouldn't be the most dangerous
thing in the room.

Jess knew, realistically, that there was magick in the
world. She hadn't run into it much—there had been a girl
in college who had a minor magick talent. And Jess
thought she might have seen a vampire one night when she
had been in New York City a few years back.

But she hadn't ever seen anything like this guy. Or felt
anything like him.

There was so much power inside him, it made her skin
feel tight. He had it banked down and shielded, in much
the same manner that Jess shielded herself, keeping all that
power under tight wraps. But with his using his power this
close to her, there was no way she could miss sensing it.

From what Leanne had told her daughter about witches,
Jess had expected a woman. She wasn't sure whether she
expected some old crone type or a New Age sort who
talked of auras and chakras. But she sure as hell hadn't expected a sexy, yummy-looking man with weird gray eyes.

There was no doubt in her mind, though, that he was in

fact a witch. He felt different from a telekinetic, and so did his power. She didn't know how to describe the power, but it felt wild and untamed. Mom had one time likened a witch's power to the elemental magicks that had filled the fantasy books Jess had grown up reading.

She couldn't describe the power, but she could sure as hell describe how she saw him using it. He seemed to have control over the air—he used it to form a dense, invisible hand that was choking the life from Jess's would-be abductor.

Nate's face was pale. That invisible hand had closed around his throat, and he arched up, straining against it, as he gagged and choked for air. Hell, Jess could *see* an indentation around the man's neck, whiter where it looked like fingers were digging into the flesh. Nate was clawing at the air around his throat, trying to break free.

Unable to stop herself, Jess looked back at Tall, Dark, and Delicious. His eyes weren't just glowing now. It looked as though streaks of lightning were shooting through them, while the gray swirled, alternating between light and dark.

The man's thundercloud gaze slid her way, and Jess swallowed the knot in her throat. She finally managed to suck in a breath of air, and as oxygen flooded her lungs, the burning in her chest receded a little.

"Get out of here," the man said softly.

If only . . . For half a second, she was tempted. This had gotten too weird, too fast. She was tempted to just leave— not the club, but everything. Leave it all behind. Maybe if she ran fast enough, she could leave everything behind.

"If only," she muttered. She shook her head. Running away wasn't an option. Since she couldn't run away, she wasn't going to leave, either.

But Jess had no plans to argue with that guy. He didn't have to know that the only way she was leaving would be if she found who she was looking for.

Or in a body bag, she thought grimly as she headed for the door.

She'd lie low until he was gone, and then she'd find her man. Then, and only then, would she think about leaving.

H E kept his senses partially focused on the woman, but the second the door swung closed behind her, Vax couldn't sense her anymore. That low-key aura of hers was peculiar. It had kept him from sensing that she was the one in danger, and it kept him from being truly aware of her presence unless he was practically on top of her.

On top . . . Even as the thought circled through his mind, he shoved it aside.

She was a puzzle. Vax couldn't feel her, not the way he should be able to. She was more like a person-shaped blank spot to his senses than like a living, breathing woman. Definitely a puzzle, but one he'd have to figure out later.

Once he took care of this mess, Vax would track her down. He'd have to. Although he hadn't been able to get beyond that aura, he knew it was her death he sensed. She wouldn't be safe until the threat was eliminated. Somehow, Vax doubted he'd be able to accomplish all of that in the next couple of hours.

As the door closed with a quiet snick, Vax called his magick back inside, and the air realigned and re-formed itself, becoming once more nothing but empty space and oxygen.

There was a hoarse gasping sound, and the man sucked in air as he collapsed to the floor. Closing the distance between them, Vax crouched down. The silver cuff lay on the ground, flashing at him. The dull, matte-black gun lay next to it. Vax picked both of them up and pocketed them before looking at the man who lay on his back, wheezing for breath.

He waited until the guy's eyes began to clear a little. Once Vax knew the man could see him, he smiled.

"Now . . . you and I are going to have a talk."

*   *   *

"I THOUGHT I told you to get out of here."

The voice was masculine and sexy, and it sounded pretty irritated. When Jess looked up and met his eyes, she saw the irritation hadn't been imagined. He looked ready to throw her over his shoulder and make sure she left.

Jess just shrugged and looked back to the employee parking lot. "I'll leave when I'm done."

"You think you're going to get action in a parking lot? Only thing you'll find out here would be drugs, sex, or trouble. And you can get sex in there without worrying you might get arrested."

Action? Jess snorted. The kind of action that happened here was the last kind that would appeal to her. Well, maybe not completely. She slid him a speculative glance. He'd look damn good in black leather. That would appeal to her. But she didn't see him going for it.

Focus, Jess. She looked back to the club and made herself think about the man in there that she was searching for. The rush of fury cleared her head a little, and she managed a derisive sneer as she said, "I'm not looking for drugs, sex, or trouble. I'm looking for a person, and I'll leave when I find him. Thank you for your help earlier. I'm fine now, and you can go."

The door to Debach opened, and she held her breath, hoping, but it wasn't the man she was looking for. It was Nate, if she wasn't mistaken. He wasn't walking out on his own.

She winced as two shirtless, muscle-bound thugs threw him to the ground. Through her binoculars, she could see he'd already been worked over, and instinctively she winced as they proceeded to kick the shit out of him.

"How much do you want to bet he's getting that beating because he let your pretty little neck slip away?"

Jess swallowed against the knot in her throat. "That's not my fault." She was damned proud of herself for not jumping. He hadn't made a sound as he approached her, and Jess had to admire his shielding. It was even more complex than Randi's had been, and Randi's shielding had been phenomenal.

Tall, Dark, and Delicious said, "That's not my point. My point is, if he's getting beaten because you got away, then somebody inside that club wants you pretty bad. Do you really need to hang around here?"

"Yes." She didn't even have to think about it. For all she cared, she could be getting that beating and it wouldn't change her mind. Between watching Nate getting his ass kicked and feeling the sexy witch at her back, Jess could hardly concentrate.

"Will you just leave? I didn't ask for a knight in shining armor, pal. I can handle myself."

"Is that right?"

His voice sounded odd. Turning, she looked up at him. Jess could just barely make out the glitter in his eyes. He was trying to use his magick on her. Jess realized it with a start as she felt something foreign pushing at the edges of her mind. For just a second, she felt herself giving in to it, felt exhaustion drop down on her like a curtain, weighting her down.

But then she shoved it off, focusing on the bridge of his nose, the line of his jaw, anything but the mesmerizing power of his eyes. Finally the pushing receded, and she relaxed a little.

A little *too much*. When his fist came flying towards her, she didn't see it until it was too late to do anything except stand there and get hit.

Vax caught her before she could hit the ground. She was slight. She felt a lot more delicate than he would have expected. She was long and lean, and delicate sure as hell didn't seem to fit her. Until he had his arms wrapped around her.

A lot of mortals had instinctive mental shields, but hers seemed to be a hell of a lot more than that. Dense enough that he couldn't penetrate them with his Empathy. He had barely tapped her, but using physical force on a woman was enough to turn his gut.

Hitting her and getting her out of harm's way was a sight better than letting her get caught around here. She might not care what they would do to her. Vax did, though. His brief contact with Nathaniel Metcalf had shown him enough to make him want to tear the man apart with his bare hands.

She had no idea about the kind of pain that lay ahead if they got hold of her.

He got her into the front seat of the shiny black BMW without looking at her face. He knew the car was hers. Even before he opened the door, her scent permeated it. Nothing flowery or perfumy, just the subtle aroma of lavender on her skin, mixing with the faint tropical scent in her hair. And under that, all woman.

Vax loved the way women smelled. Soft and warm. For the past few decades, losing himself in the warmth and softness of a woman's body had been the only times he truly felt alive.

He felt alive now. He didn't even have to touch her. She made his skin buzz and his blood heat. It wasn't something he really had time for, either. He wanted to figure out what in the hell he was here for, and then do it so he could get back home. He didn't want to take time to enjoy the long, slim redhead.

No matter how soft, how warm she'd feel next to him. He wanted to ignore it, but that was proving hard. Would have been easier if she had just left the damn club like he'd told her to.

Hanging around there wasn't the smartest thing to do, so staying translated to one of two things. She was either stupid, which he doubted, or very, very determined. He suspected the latter. There was an appealing strength to her long, lean frame, and he sensed the strength even more as he wrapped his fingers around her wrist, checking her pulse. Slow and steady.

Something weird, though. Even allowing from that low-key aura, he should have picked up something when he touched her. The instinctive natural shields mortals had wouldn't have mattered when he was touching her bare flesh. The briefest touch should have left her open for him to read, and he couldn't. It was like looking at a blank slate. Nothing there.

"Who are you?" he murmured. Better question might be, *what* are you. She was no witch, shifter, or vampire, but Vax began to suspect she wasn't exactly the average mule-headed mortal, either.

She was silent, her eyes closed, her lips parted as she breathed. Her chest rose and fell with each slow, steady breath, and Vax found himself staring at the subtle curves of her breasts. From his angle, he now knew that he'd been right earlier.

She was wearing absolutely nothing under the close-fitting leather vest.

"Damned pervert." He muttered it quietly and told himself he needed to stand up and walk away. He did, too. After a few more seconds of gazing at her.

Heat stirred in his blood, but it faded quickly as he looked back up at her face. The sight of the mark he'd left had a very sobering effect, like a bucket of ice dumped on him. There was a faint bruise blooming along the curve of her jaw. He swore under his breath and stood, slamming the door shut with a little too much force.

For now, she was out of harm's way, but he didn't think it would last long. Even if she didn't go back inside the club ever again, she was in danger.

So before she woke up, he had to figure out what in the hell he was going to do about her and the mess she'd gotten herself into.

"Decisions, decisions," he mumbled as he headed back towards the club. He didn't bother with the line in front. It was still ridiculously long, and he sure as hell wasn't forking over thirty dollars to get inside.

What he wanted to do was climb back on his bike and ride west, riding until he was about ready to pass out. Then he'd pass out, get up, and keep riding until he got back to the ranch.

But that wouldn't be the responsible thing to do.

The responsible thing would be to find out who wanted the woman dead, and why.

Vax blew out a breath and looked back towards the car. Doing that would probably require finding out *who* she was.

"Shit. Nothing is easy anymore, is it?"

CHAPTER 4

JESS came awake with a start, aware of the complete silence. It was the silence itself that had woken her up. Jess never slept without turning on the fan by her bed. She needed the white noise.

Her head ached, a distant, muffled sort of pain that tempted her to close her eyes. She felt achy all over, almost like she had the flu. All Jess wanted to do was bury herself back under the covers.

But she couldn't exactly figure out how she'd come to be under the covers. She had been in the parking lot, waiting for William Masters to leave Debach. It had been just a little too chilly for those clothes she wore. A leather skirt and vest just weren't conducive to skulking in alleys on cool autumn nights.

She had been thinking about getting the workout jacket from her gym bag, and that was the last thing she remembered.

Jess started to sit up, but only made it halfway before she sank back against her pillows with a moan. The pain wasn't so distant now. It was throbbing and swirling and making her head spin. Her belly roiled, and Jess had one moment to be glad it was empty. As usual, she hadn't eaten dinner, and that, for once, was good.

If she'd had anything in her stomach, she would have hurled it up right then and there.

Her head felt funny—and it was more than the pain. Everything felt all fuzzy and vague, and the harder she tried to focus her thoughts, the worse the pain got. The bed seemed to be calling out to her, singing to her about closing her eyes and going back to sleep. She wanted to go back to sleep, just close her eyes and sleep.

"Sleep," she mumbled, rubbing at her eyes.

She couldn't, though—there was something she had to do. Something she should have been doing. So instead of curling back under the covers, she kicked them off and sat up. She moved to the edge of the bed, gritting her teeth against the nausea roiling inside her.

Once it receded a little, she stood up. Her legs felt wobbly. "Shit," she muttered. Jess reached up and pressed the heel of her hand against one temple, and wondered what in the hell had happened last night. She hadn't eaten anything since the slice of pizza she'd had for lunch, but she was used to that. Had she drunk a little too much, maybe? Didn't feel like a hangover. Maybe she'd hit her head.

An image danced through her mind. Just the barest flash. A man. Stormy, compelling eyes. Her skin started to buzz, and Jess rubbed her hands up and down her arms. Goosebumps roughened her flesh, but she wasn't cold.

Another wave of nausea, and weakness rushed up at her. She battled it back. Making her way out of her bedroom, she managed to stumble to her desk. Dropping into the seat with a weak, shaky sigh, she flipped open the file folder sitting on top.

The sight of William Masters's image was like a cold splash of water. The cobwebs in her brain cleared, and even the pain receded. Fury burned inside her, and she shoved up from her desk so hard, the chair went toppling over behind her.

She'd been waiting for William. He had been to the club—she remembered seeing his car. Jess had been trying to catch him there for weeks, but he never showed up at the same time she did, and she couldn't just live in her car outside the club, waiting for him. When he had shown up, a rush of adrenaline had surged through her. Jess had planned on hanging around to see if she could learn more about him, and when he left, she'd follow him. Find where he lived.

After that, she didn't know what she'd do, but it was finally another step forward. Since she'd been stuck in a rut the past few weeks, she had been eager to take that step forward.

Then *he* had shown up. Tall and sexy, with eyes the color of thunderheads and more power than Jess had ever felt in her life. And the bastard had slugged her.

Vax felt it the minute his hold over her snapped.

It had been damned hard, almost impossible, to lay any kind of magickal compulsion in her mind. When she broke it, there was a backlash of power that set his head to throbbing.

She shouldn't have been able to break his compulsion that easily. Most people shouldn't have been able to break it, *period.* And definitely not as quickly as she had. Vax had his suspicions about how she had done it so easily, but he wouldn't be able to confirm them until he saw her again.

The night was cool and Vax was tired as hell, but instead of finding a hotel where he could crash for a while, he continued to sit on his bike out in front of her house. Several cars had driven by and he'd had to resort to magick to blur his presence. Last thing he needed was to have the cops sent out to investigate a suspicious character.

Suspicious character . . . He smiled faintly. Yeah, he would definitely strike most people as a suspicious character.

He watched as one by one all the windows lit up. First the upstairs bedroom. Her bedroom was simple and ultramodern, a platform bed covered with a black silk brocade comforter with a motif that looked vaguely Asian. The pattern was echoed in the two framed prints that hung over the bed, each with a different symbol. Peace and harmony, if he wasn't mistaken.

The walls were a rich, deep shade of red, and the plush carpet was snow white. It was almost stark in its simplicity, but it matched the classy redhead he'd seen in the club. He wasn't so sure about the blonde in the driver's license, though. She'd had a fake ID, a good one, in the tiny purse she'd carried. For some reason, she had been in disguise. An effective one—with that deep red wig and the black-rimmed glasses, she could have fooled him. He didn't fool that easily.

The redhead was identified as Jennifer Ballard.

The driver's license he found in the glove compartment with a picture of the blonde on it was issued to a Jessica R. Warren.

"Which one are you?" Vax murmured. Her shadow passed by the front window, and he leaned forward, bracing his elbows on the handlebars.

He wanted to know which name she called her own, but more, he wanted to know what in the hell had she been doing at Debach. It didn't seem to fit her, not that classy-looking redhead and not the lean, elegant blonde.

Of course, he didn't really get the bondage scene anyway. He knew enough to recognize when a club was run with the benefits of all in mind. Debach wasn't one of those. It catered to the pleasures of a select few. The images he'd gleaned from Nate had been disgusting, humiliating, and full of pain. The wrong kind of pain for almost everybody, including hard-core submissives.

Empathy could be one shitty ability, Vax thought, not for the first time. Especially when it made him feel this kind of shit. Pain was a turn-on for Nate. Vax had kept his contact with the man brief, but not brief enough. The sick fuck got a hard-on when he saw somebody beaten.

Nate fit in perfectly with the inner circle at Debach. The

air around that club was thick with blood, pain, and suffering. Vax knew there was a whole lot of wrong going on inside those walls, but with Miz Jennifer/Jessica's presence interfering, he hadn't been able to take much more than a cursory look around.

Her front door came flying open, and Vax leaned back in the seat, watching as she slammed it behind her. Her body language shouted that she was absolutely furious. But oddly enough, he still couldn't really get a good read on her. His skin should have been burning and stinging with the depths of the anger.

But he felt nothing.

Temper looked good on her. He had to admit it. Made her eyes glow and put some soft color to her high cheekbones. She jerked the door closed and locked it. She jammed the key in the lock so hard, Vax wouldn't have been surprised if the key snapped off inside. In the distance, he could hear another car, but he didn't bother blurring his presence this time. She came striding down the walk.

The moment she saw him, she froze. Only for a second, though. Her eyes narrowed, and she started towards him. There was a shadowed bruise on her jawline. Didn't look like she'd even bothered to try to cover it.

He looked away from it in time to see her fist flying towards his face. He could have moved. She was quick for a mortal, but not quick enough. Vax didn't bother, though. Her fist clipped him on the side of his face, and his head snapped to the side with the impact. If he hadn't had his weight braced, he probably would have toppled off the bike.

"Pretty damn strong for such a skinny thing," he said, turning his head and spitting a mouthful of blood onto the pavement. With his tongue, he touched the cut on the inside of his mouth.

"Well, I'd feel better if I'd knocked you unconscious, you son of a bitch."

"I'm sure you would."

Her chin went up, and Vax wouldn't have been surprised if she decided to slug him again. Instead she just curled her lip and sneered at him. "Didn't I tell you to leave me the hell alone?"

"If I'd left you alone to begin with, you'd be dead." He said it in a flat, cold voice, but if he expected it to slow her down or cool her fury, he was expecting too much. Most people tended to try to backpedal a little if they heard the word *dead*.

Not her. She just tossed her head and propped her hands on her hips. "So?"

The way she snapped out the short, simple word sent a cold, chilly finger down his spine. "So. You don't care if you live or die?"

"Yes, I care. I'd prefer death, thank you. I just want one thing before it happens, and you interfered tonight. Don't do it again." She jabbed her finger into his chest with each of the last words. She spun away on her heel.

Hell. *Tough little cookie, aren't you?* He couldn't help smiling a little. "Miz Warren . . . It is Miz Warren, right?"

She didn't even slow down. Jessica Warren continued right on walking across the street, her shoulders back, the shiny blonde locks bouncing up and down with each step.

"What happens if they kill you before you do that one thing?"

At his words, she came to an abrupt stop, her shoulders slumped. Vax threw his leg over the bike and dismounted, moving up on her cautiously. He lowered his shields again and tried once again to pick something up from her. There was nothing more than a distant sort of despair.

*I*F *I die before I make William Masters pay for what he did to Randi* . . . It wasn't something Jess had allowed herself to think. Destroying Masters was all she had left, and she wasn't going to fail.

But Nate hadn't been planning on taking her for a walk

in the park. Her gut told her that there had been more than bulky, muscle-bound bouncers waiting for her, wherever the hell he'd been taking her. In her gut, she knew there was more than just a beating waiting for her.

"I won't let that happen," she said, her voice low and steady.

"Sometimes things outside your control happen." His voice was low, sexy—and oddly comforting. It was the kind of voice that made a woman feel safe, the kind a woman would want to hear if she rolled over in the middle of the night after a bad dream—listening to that voice as she curled up against a hard, strong body while big warm hands stroked her back.

But at the same time, it was the kind of voice that made a woman think of doing all sorts of unsafe things. Like jumping tall, sexy strangers with deep, sexy voices.

Jess smiled bitterly. Jumping sexy strangers. Yeah, like that was going to happen. She didn't have the time or the energy for it. Jess was too tired, running on caffeine and nerves for too long.

Standing in the middle of the street, she turned her head and looked over her shoulder at him. *Sometimes things outside your control happen.*

Talk about ironic. Yeah, Jess knew things outside her control were going to happen. Losing her parents had been out of her control. Losing Randi had been out of her control. She refused to believe that avenging Randi was another one of those things.

"This won't be one of those things." Shrugging the rest of her emotional baggage aside, Jess headed for her car. It was late, yes, but maybe he was still there. Damn it, she was going to find him. He'd be at the club sooner or later, and when he was, she'd be waiting.

The cold air whipped around her legs. The leather skirt might as well be made of tissue paper for all the good it did in keeping her warm. As she stalked to the car, she wondered if she should grab some better clothes, but she'd wasted enough time.

A big, hard hand closed around her upper arm, and Jess spun, jabbing her finger into his chest. "Let go of me, jackass."

"You don't know what kind of trouble you're looking for."

This time, that low, sexy growl of a voice didn't make her all hot and bothered. It just made her *bothered*. As in, pissed. "Excuse me, but the blonde is just skin-deep. I'm not an idiot, and I know exactly what kind of trouble I'm looking for. *Let go*."

But he didn't.

Taking matters into her own hands, Jess focused on one of the decorative stones that Randi had used as a border for her flowerbeds. It was about the size of a chicken's egg. If Jess used enough force, her power could make it go in one side of the dude's head and out the other.

She settled for just clocking him on the temple and knocking him out cold. As he collapsed to the ground, his grip on her arm loosened, and Jess backed away. This time, she'd find a hiding spot out of the open.

"SON of a bitch."

Thirty minutes later, Jess sat on the roadside, staring into nothingness.

Masters had already left.

None of Jess's contacts had been able to unearth where the man lived. The address listed with the Bureau of Motor Vehicles was legit, but it was a family that lived there, not Masters.

Jess's only way of finding him was to wait for him at the club. Tonight she'd had vague plans of following him when he left. Now she'd have to wait until another night.

"Son of a bitch," she said again.

WHEN Jess walked into her kitchen the next morning, she wasn't terribly surprised to find that she had an intruder. During her sleepless night, she'd put two and two together and figured out why Tall, Dark, and Delicious was at the club. Once she had figured it out, she had to wonder what had taken so long. She'd known for months that something was off about the place.

The infallible Hunters should have been all over the place ages ago.

Jess knew about the Hunters. Nothing specific, but enough details to know that they *should* have been here. Mom had told her about the Hunters—paranormal cops, basically. Considering that the badness in the club had some sort of unnatural bent to it, it was right up the Hunters' alley. Or should be.

"Don't you have a job to do?"

A thick, straight black brow arched, and he leaned back in his chair, studying her with a probing gaze. "Excuse me?"

She just smiled. So what if it felt a little pissy. "How is your head?"

He lifted a shoulder in a shrug and said, "Considering that somehow you levitated a rock and plowed it into my skull, I guess it feels okay." There was just a shadow of a bruise on his temple, already nearly gone.

Witches really did heal fast, she mused. Then she shook her head and focused on the problems his presence could bring about. She wasn't giving up on Masters just because some Hunter appeared on the scene. Some big, sexy Hunter who had the most amazing eyes . . .

A little focus here, Jess? Tearing her gaze from the sexy Hunter with the sexy eyes, she turned away. She answered him in a cool, dismissive tone. "I didn't levitate it. It looks like you made yourself at home." There was a half-empty pot of coffee sitting on the warmer. He had poured himself a cup, and he was using her favorite mug, too. She could grab it. She liked using her mug when she drank her coffee at her table. But that wasn't an option. She'd have to wash it five or six times, and she would still find herself wondering whether it was him she was tasting on the cup, or the coffee.

Instead Jess took another mug from the cabinet and poured herself some coffee. "How nice of you to make yourself so comfortable," she said as she turned around to look at him.

He was either ignoring her sarcasm or didn't notice it. She was betting on the former. He took a sip from his mug and said, "If you didn't levitate it, how did it fly up off the ground and hit me?"

"It's called telekinesis. Surely the Hunters have seen telekinetics before." She arched her brows and smiled sweetly at him as his eyes narrowed. Her skin prickled and she suddenly had an idea how a gazelle must feel right before a lion took it down. Her heart kicked up its speed, slamming into her ribs so hard that it stole her breath. Her hands grew sweaty, and every instinct in her body was screaming at her to run away.

She didn't run, though. Instead she lowered her head and blew on the coffee. Faking bravado wasn't as good as actually being fearless, but it was a damn sight better than letting him know how unnerved she was.

"What?" His voice was soft and quiet. It shouldn't have sounded at all terrifying, but for some reason, she *was* terrified.

But Jess would be damned if she let it show. She might not be able to keep her heart from beating a mile a minute, and she couldn't keep herself from breaking into a cold sweat, but she could control her facial expressions and she could keep from backing away. She wanted to. Really badly. She wanted to back away—hell, screw that. She wanted to turn tail, run, and hide.

She didn't, though. She kept her face blank and her voice level as she replied, "You heard me. You all have been around for centuries, if I've been told right. Telekinetics are pretty rare, but not that rare. There's no way I am the first you've run into."

"That wasn't what I was referring to," he said. His tone was still as silky and as soft as before, but now there was an undercurrent of menace.

It struck Jess as maybe just a little ridiculous, and her fear retreated to normal levels. "Oops. Is your existence some top-security secret that I shouldn't know about?" She rolled her eyes and said dryly, "You may be able to live right under the nose of average mortals, but you can't expect the gifted ones to not know about you."

No. Vax didn't expect the gifted people to remain blissfully unaware of the creatures, those of the Hunter variety or otherwise, that shared their world. Gifted people sensed others, so why wouldn't they be aware of the Hunters?

Vax knew some of the gifted population didn't trust the Hunters. Most of that came from not understanding their purpose. The Hunters had been around for ages, going back so many generations their true origins were shrouded. They'd come together with one goal and that was to make sure that other gifted creatures—witch, vamp, shifter, or were—didn't try to turn mankind into their playthings.

He just hadn't expected *her* to know about them. He hadn't expected her to be anything other than the average mortal. Well, maybe not completely average. The telekinesis was a bit of a surprise—she'd flown right under his radar with that one. She was too damned nosy and too damned stubborn, and she had a mouth he really wanted to feel under his. But she was mortal all the same.

Thanks to the rock she'd pelted him with, though, Vax knew firsthand just how *not* average she was. A telekinetic. He hadn't met more than one or two people in his entire life who used pure telekinesis. Like psychic ability, it had nothing to do with magick and everything to do with a hyperrefined mental sense. All in the brain, as opposed to magick, which was in the heart and soul.

Magick used the elements of air, fire, and water.

Telekinesis used the power of the mind.

That could explain why Vax hadn't read her until it was almost too late to help. His strengths lay in reading the emotions, and like most psychically gifted people, she had probably learned to master her emotions when she learned to master her gift. They had to—emotions wreaked havoc on the control of somebody with psychic gifts. Poor control wasn't an option for somebody who could hurl objects through the air without even touching them. But he had met telekinetics before, and not one of them had been like her. She was like a blank slate.

He was silent for a moment as he tried to figure out how to handle her. Under normal circumstances, mortals who learned too much about the paranormal races were placed under a compulsion, their memories wiped.

If her shields were anything to go by, wiping her memories would work about as well as laying a compulsion. And he'd already tried that, with absolutely no success.

Vax suspected logic wasn't going to work, either. "If you know about the Hunters, then it probably won't surprise you to realize that there is a world of wrong going down in that club. You don't need to be there." Suspecting it wouldn't work and refusing to try were two different things.

"Oh, I beg to differ." Her voice was low and throbbing with passion as she said, "I have *every* reason to be there. I know just how much wrong is happening there. Believe me, Mister . . ." Her eyes narrowed on his face, and she scowled. "You know, you're sitting in *my* house, using *my* coffeemaker to make very bad coffee, and I don't even know who the hell you are."

Grinning at her, Vax sipped at the overly strong brew and said, "Where I come from, strong is the only way to make coffee." He sipped again before adding, "I'd bet you like it weak and watered down. Or do you prefer those iced foamy things like they sell at Starbucks?"

"Please." Jess shuddered in reaction. Sugary, icy mocha latte whatevers were definitely not how she preferred her coffee. But she did like to drink something that might leave her stomach lining intact. "And you still didn't tell me your name."

He debated on that for a minute, trying to decide whether he should give her the name he was currently using legally. Finally he gave her the name he'd been given years ago when he was still a child. "You can call me Vax." Even as he told her, though, he wondered why. Only a handful of people knew his real name. Why the hell had he chosen to tell a total stranger?

"And is that your first name, last name, or neither?"

He smiled at her over the rim of his coffee cup. "Take your pick."

Her pretty green eyes narrowed. He thought she was going to say something, but instead she just turned to the fridge and opened it. She took out a plastic bag full of bagels, and Vax watched as she popped one into the toaster. The scent of toasting bread drifted through the room, and accordingly his belly started to rumble. "Not much of a breakfast."

She glanced at him and shrugged. "I'm not much of an eater."

Shoving up from the table, he said, "That's okay. I am." He went for the fridge and opened it to find mostly bare shelves. No milk. No juice. A carton of eggs, a few veggies, and several different kinds of cheese. A few things of Chinese takeout that looked ages old, and some deli meats. "Man, you aren't kidding."

"Huh?" She gave him a puzzled look that quickly shifted to outright irritation as she watched him open one of the containers of Chinese food. He sniffed it and then he closed it and tossed it over her head. He heard it land in the trash as he reached for another one. "What do you think you're doing?"

Vax straightened and met her annoyed gaze with a smile. Mildly, he replied, "I'm going to make an omelet. I'm hungry, and I don't think a bagel is going to do much to fill me up."

"I don't think I offered you one."

Vax reached out, catching a thick lock of pale blonde hair. He gave it a tug before letting go. "That's okay. I don't want a bagel. You know, you ought to clean out your refrigerator a little more often than once a season. That moo shu was about to grow legs and walk out of your fridge."

She gritted her teeth, and he turned away to hide his grin. He grabbed eggs, a tomato, one of the hunks of cheddar, and the package of shaved ham. Whistling, he walked over to the stove and dumped the ingredients onto the counter before hunting down a skillet. From the corner of his eye, he could see her standing by the fridge and glaring at him.

She was irritated as all get out. He could tell just from the look on her face, the way she stood glaring at him, hands fisted on her narrow hips. But he couldn't sense anything from her.

"You know what an Empath is?"

"Yes." She spat out the word like she had something nasty in her mouth.

He finally found a skillet in a cabinet under the sink. Most of the counters were dusty. It didn't look as if she'd cooked in here for months. Odd, though. Most of the stuff was the high-end variety, and all of it looked like it had been put to good use. He sauntered back over to the stove and started searching for something to grease the skillet with. All he found was some low-calorie spray crap, but it was better than nothing. Well, at least he thought so until he smelled it. "This stuff smells like crap. Why the hell do people cook with it?" he muttered, reading the ingredient label.

"What would you prefer that I use? Lard?" Jess said with a saccharine smile.

"No. Butter or vegetable oil works just fine." He ignored her sarcasm as he greased the skillet and turned on the stove. As the skillet began to heat, he grabbed a bowl from a cabinet and began cracking the eggs.

"Since you know what an Empath is, I don't suppose you can tell me why I can't feel anything from you?" He spun around and braced his back against the counter, watching her as he started to beat the eggs. If he hadn't been watching her so closely, he would have completely missed seeing the surprise in her eyes.

"An Empath," she repeated slowly.

He crooked a brow at her. "Why are you surprised?"

Jess studied him intently. She had an insightful stare. He wondered what she saw when she looked at him. Not too much, he hoped. Vax didn't much care much for the thought that anybody might be able to read him easily.

Finally, she lifted her narrow shoulders restlessly. "I'm not sure. You don't seem the type to be an Empath."

Vax smiled bitterly. "Tell that to the people in charge of handing out gifts."

"There are people in charge?" she drawled. "I never realized that."

"There's got to be somebody in charge. How else did any of us end up as we are? Whether it's magick, intelligence, telekinesis . . . pretty green eyes . . ." He stared into hers and watched as a blush turned her cheeks pink. "Don't you think there's a master planner?"

"Nope. I think it's science, genes, natural selection. People like us end up different because of some sort of weird gene sequence. Gifts run in families—that adds up to something in the DNA. That means science to me." She shrugged dismissively and took a bite out of her bagel.

Vax turned back to the stove and poured the egg mixture into the hot skillet. As he washed the tomato, he said, "Natural selection doesn't have to be exclusive of a master design. When the weak die off, maybe it plays into that master design."

Blonde brows arched over her eyes. She stared at him for a minute and then turned away with a shrug. "Master design. Sort of like intelligent design?" she asked.

Vax smiled. "If you like."

"I also wouldn't have pegged you for a religious type."

Vax shrugged as he started dicing the tomato. "I'm not. I'm a faith type. Religion is for the masses—it can be a status thing, a comfort thing, or just a thing you do out of habit, but it isn't always because somebody believes. I believe. I define that as faith." He tossed the scraps into the garbage can before looking back at her. "You know, I've spent most of my life alone. It hasn't been the happiest one, but I'd say it's a sight better than spending my life thinking this is all there is."

Jess snorted. "This *is* all there is. You don't actually think good behavior is going to take you to some higher plane when it's all over, do you?"

"Good behavior." He repeated it slowly, a wide grin on his face. Then he started to laugh. "Good behavior isn't something I've ever been accused of. If, and that's probably a big *if,* I get to that higher plane, it will because of grace, not anything I've done."

"That seems kind of pointless to me."

Turning back to the skillet, he checked the omelet before adding the tomatoes. Going to work on the cheese, he said, "So does thinking that this is all there is. That everything you do, all the good or the bad a person does, that every choice you make in life is futile. I prefer to think that in the end, it actually means something."

She looked as confused as hell. "But if good behavior doesn't matter, why should you care?"

He checked the bottom of the omelet and turned the heat down a little before he turned back and looked at her. "Because it means somewhere along the way, I did something good with my life, good that maybe will make a difference to somebody else."

Her voice was soft. "You're a Hunter, aren't you? Something good is what you're all about."

"Once, maybe." And he missed it. Vax hadn't realized it until that very second, but he missed it. He missed knowing that he'd made a difference to someone or something. But he couldn't go back to it. He just didn't have the heart for it anymore.

Silence ensued, and Vax finished cooking the omelet, although by the time he finished it, he wasn't hungry. All the same, he carried the steaming mass of eggs, tomatoes, ham, and cheese to the table and sat down. He jabbed at it with his fork and said, "Want some? That bagel isn't much to work on."

She looked down at the bagel as though she'd forgotten

all about it. With a shrug, she said, "This is all I ever eat." She added in a wry tone, "But by all means, you go ahead. Enjoy my food."

"Somebody ought to."

Jess put down her bagel and leaned back in her chair. With a sardonic smile, she asked, "Are you here to discuss my dietary habits, or was there something you actually wanted?"

Running his eyes over her lean form, he mused that somebody should discuss her dietary habits, especially if that chewy piece of bread was her normal breakfast. But if Vax had learned one thing in his life, it was that women rarely appreciated a man's view on their diets. She was as slender as a reed. If that bagel and the contents of her refrigerator were anything to go by, she didn't spend nearly enough time enjoying one of the finer things in life.

A good meal.

He wondered how many of life's other little luxuries she robbed herself of. Taking a hike in the mountains. A horseback ride right at sunset. Lying beside a campfire and staring up at the stars. Sex.

He shrugged off that train of thought and focused on her question. He looked up and saw that, once more, she was staring at him with irritation written all over her pretty face. "You know, you never did answer me. I'm curious as to why I can't read you. But there is a more pressing matter at hand."

She stood up and strolled over to the sink. After she rinsed the plate and the cup, she turned around and propped her hands on her hips. Skinny hips. The hem of her shirt rode up just a bit, revealing a bare slice of skin. Her belly was flat and sleekly muscled. He wondered idly if the rest of her body was that toned. He had an urge to see, to run his hands over her long, slender body and see if her skin was as silky and smooth as it looked, to see if her body was as strong as he suspected it was.

Generally Vax liked his women with a little meat on them, some nice soft curves. But damn if she wasn't appealing. Heat began to pulse through his veins, pooling in his loins. As he stared into her eyes, his cock started to stiffen until he had to shift around in his seat to get a little relief.

Apparently she could read him as well as he *couldn't* read her. Because she started to blush. "I didn't peg you as the type to blush so easily, Miz Warren," he teased.

Instead of responding, she changed the subject. "What is the pressing matter?"

Vax shrugged. His interest wasn't going anywhere, and neither was her careful lack of a reaction to it. If the interest remained, he'd pursue it later. If not . . . well, it wouldn't be the first time he'd lost interest in something.

He cut into his omelet with his fork and popped the first bite into his mouth. After he'd swallowed, he took a sip of coffee and then he responded, "Debach."

"MAGICK, my dear friends, lies not in the heart and soul as so many have always thought."

William sat in his seat at Thomas's right hand, listening with a smile on his face.

Years of hard work, years of bloodshed, years of careful planning had led to this. Thomas had spent nearly a century on this research, preparing for this very moment. William could tell he was relishing every second.

As Thomas continued to speak, William turned and studied the images of various CT scans. Most of these people had absolutely no clue what they were looking at, other than brains.

Fools.

Only one of the brains came from a normal subject, one with no gift, no talent, no magick whatsoever. The other scans came from various subjects, werewolves, vampires, telepaths, Empaths, witches, and psychics. Psychics and vampires were proving the hardest to pin down, but William was content to let them go.

What mattered to him were the six images that belonged

to witches. Some had come into the power completely. Two of them were latent. They hadn't come into their power until after they'd been taken. It wasn't an unheard-of thing. Some mortals had magick in their blood, but it never manifested itself. They were born unknowing and lived their lives without ever having a clue that they could have been so much more. But on rare occurrences, those latent witches came into their talents as a result of some brutal, traumatic shock to the senses.

Like rape. Or torture.

It was something, that rush of power he could glean from them as they lay there struggling to live. The very weapon they needed to survive was within their grasp, but they didn't recognize it for what it was and couldn't control it. William did hate waste.

"Years of careful research and exhaustive studies have proven what I always suspected," Thomas continued, and William fought not to let his boredom show. The man was a brilliant scientist, dedicated and determined. But he loved to listen to himself talk. "Magick is a thing of the brain. We've discovered an interesting anomaly in witches—an overdeveloped frontal lobe. The frontal lobe controls creative thinking and—"

There was a mocking laugh. Leona Mackie stood and flicked a dismissive hand towards the scans. "What a load of rubbish," she said. She had a crisp British accent and still spoke like the Victorian chit she'd been when she had come into her power. She had just gotten married, and her brute of a husband had apparently scared the talent into wakening when he'd come to their marriage bed and raped her. "Magick is not science. *We* are not creatures of science. We simply . . . are," she finished with a dramatic flourish.

"My lady, I beg to differ," Thomas said gently. "There is no denying my results. Years of research back it up. We are indeed creatures of science. I can explain exactly what it is inside your pretty skull that makes you a witch, and I can tell you about the chemicals that spike during the full moon and cause weres to Change. I can tell you how the blood of a vampire mutates during his transition and why we need to feed on blood."

Leona sniffed delicately. She smoothed down the collar of her pink Chanel pantsuit, looking at Thomas with distaste. "I care not what makes me a witch. I care that I am a witch, that I have power mortals only dream of. That is all that matters."

William interrupted before Thomas could try to make Leona see the more practical side of his research. "Then perhaps you do not need to be here for this meeting. . . ."

She turned a pair of ice blue eyes on him and stared at him. Then, just like that, she was gone.

Thomas gave William a disgruntled stare. William shrugged. "Not all will understand the impact this could have, my friend. But others will much appreciate it. So why waste our time on those who choose not to open their eyes?"

"This is all very fascinating, I'm sure. But what does any of this have to do with us? Why shouldn't we go, just like Leona?"

William glanced at Thomas before looking towards the speaker. It was Paulo, a vampire who had seen more than six centuries pass, if William remembered correctly. "You would think that a creature as old as you would understand the ramifications of this information."

Paulo's black eyes narrowed to slits. "You'd think that a pup as young as you would show caution when speaking to a vampire as old as I am."

Smiling at the vamp, William said, "Oh, I did show caution. If I had been careless, I would have called you a stupid, shortsighted fuck."

Paulo lunged, and William rolled to the side. As he surged to his feet, he flung out a hand. Fire bloomed, and he hurled it towards Paulo. Just a millisecond before it would have touched the vampire's flesh, William snuffed it out. "Be careful, Paulo. Our research has revealed many, many interesting things."

As William turned to face the others, he found that all eyes were on him. He gave them a toothy grin as he lowered himself back into his seat and gestured towards Thomas. "Please, my friend, continue."

Thomas smiled and lifted a pointer from the desk, tapping the end against a small portion of the brain. "There is a chemical secreted, one that is unique to witches. Each paranormal creature actually has several physical anomalies unique to their race, but witches . . . This is the most interesting and the most versatile. We've learned that we can harvest the chemical. Injection into a host body causes a slight mutation of the frontal lobe within three days. Within a month, the frontal lobe has gone into a state of hyperdevelopment. Within six months, fifteen percent of our selected study participants started to show signs of latent magickal power. With the proper guidance, we can bring this latent magick to the fore."

Thomas fell silent, and William looked out at the group gathered at the conference table. "We can build our own witches—men and women that we hand select."

His sharp ears detected the harsh intake of breath from several of the living creatures, and even from one or two of the undead. Paulo studied the scans on the wall with renewed interest. "Build them from what?"

With a smile, William replied, "From our numbers. Any of our ilk who choose to undergo the process are welcome."

"Any of our ilk," Paulo repeated. And then he began to laugh, tipping his bald head back and laughing until tears streamed from his eyes. "You *are* a young fool. You cannot crossbreed a witch with a vampire. Or with a shape-shifter. We've *tried* to turn witches, and if they survive the bite, they rarely Change. The Change kills them."

"Usually, yes." It was Naomi who spoke, a tall, regal woman with hair the color of cinnamon, and yellow-green eyes. Those eyes remained the same whether she was in human form or in wolf form. "On rare occasions, a witch can survive the attempt to convert. But the witch's power cancels out our mark."

Thomas gestured towards William. "Here is living proof that we indeed can harvest our own breed of witches."

Holding Paulo's gaze, William lifted his hand and breathed into his cupped palm. As the warm air struck his hand, it ignited. William looked away from Paulo and studied the rest of his guests, tossing the fireball back and forth between his palms. "It is quite possible to forge both gifts into one creature. The Hunters have their own half-breeds. Some of us have faced them down a time or two. Many lesser creatures have fallen under the hands of such Hunters. It's very rare, but when you can force both powers inside one creature, each gift is enhanced by the other."

"For instance . . ." William studied the fireball. It didn't actually touch his flesh. He could barely feel the warmth from it right now. But as he cupped both hands around it and moved it closer to his chest, his flesh began to burn from its intensity. He pushed the fireball against his chest. The scent of burning cloth filled the air, and several people swore.

Paulo rose from his chair and moved closer, studying William with wide eyes. "Wolves burn under a witch's fire. Like a bonfire, they burn."

William smiled and crushed the fire into his chest. But instead of incinerating him as the fire would have done two or three years ago, it sizzled, flickered, and then extinguished itself. All that remained was the fading red spot on his chest, surrounded by the charred remains of his linen shirt. "Fire is little threat to me now."

He passed a hand through the air, palm down. Then he flipped it over, revealing a flaming orb. "Imagine the possibilities, Paulo."

"Oh, I am, wolf. Indeed I am." Paulo smiled, revealing a mouth full of crooked, dirty teeth. The only two clean, white teeth were his incisors. The man's hygiene in his mortal life must have been abominable, William mused. Of course, dentists weren't something found in the average fifteenth-century Spanish village. It was probably a miracle that the man had teeth left in his head when he died. The thought amused William, and he contemplated it for a brief second—toothless vampires.

Naomi moved closer, reaching out to touch his chest with her fingertips. "Amazing. Not one mark."

His body had already absorbed the faint red burn, and as she stroked his flawless skin, he smiled at her, meeting her odd yellow-green gaze.

Bu she didn't return his smile. Her hand fell away, and she stepped closer to the CT images. "You said fifteen percent. That, to me, seems a rather low number. What happened to the other eighty-five percent?"

"They died."

For a moment Naomi just stared at him. "You mean to tell me that this insane project of yours will kill the vast majority of the fools who agree to it? With the odds so stacked against them, why would any sane person agree to it?"

With a slight smile, William said, "I did not say that it was the process that killed them. Roughly forty percent of all participants do have fatal results. The remaining participants *do* successfully make the transition. However, they are . . . flawed."

Naomi's lips curved up in a cool smile. "Please explain what you mean by *flawed*."

Thomas stepped forward, resting a hand on William's shoulder. "Some have suffered slow mental deterioration, similar to Alzheimer's. Others had ministrokes that eventually culminated in a massive one."

"We do not have strokes." This came from Maurice. A diminutive vampire, he stood barely five feet tall, and he spoke with a faint lisp. With his too-pretty features and slight form, he looked more like a doll than like a creature of the night. But William knew just how bloodthirsty Maurice was. He had seen him in action. "Shifters and vampires are not human, Thomas. We do not suffer their weaknesses. Perhaps the witches do, but not us."

"On the contrary, Maurice." Thomas's eyes went vague, and William knew he was sifting through all the information he kept stored inside his computerlike mind. "Our immune systems repair injury too fast for most maladies to slow us down. However, for those who undergo the process and live, they seem also to have slowed immune response after the Change. Additionally, it affects the circulatory system, slowing the flow of blood and the speed of healing. This, I believe, is why some are having strokes. Those who fall victim to brain disease, I'm having a harder time pinpointing why."

"Because you are messing with nature, you fool." Naomi gave William and Thomas a mocking smile. "So, it can either kill them or turn them into vegetables. Tell me, Thomas, who does the diaper changing when they lose control of their bowels?"

Thomas glanced at William. William shrugged. "The end results of our research, regardless of success or failure, are too sensitive to risk letting them fall into the wrong hands. Successful transitions can handle this threat. Those who cannot are eliminated."

"So you kill them."

"I'd rather be dead than have to have some nurse wipe my ass." William shrugged. "Besides, we did have one creature who escaped the labs. She was a witch, and the process augmented her power. She hadn't learned to use it very well, and she did not tolerate the Change at all. When she escaped, we went after her, but she fell into trouble before we could bring her back and dispose of her. She was killed—we believe by Hunters, but we were unsuccessful in tracking her movements, so we cannot be sure. Her escape endangered the entire project. Now, when we see that a result is not what we would wish, we simply dispose of it right away."

"*It*. Like they are just pieces of garbage," Naomi said with distaste.

William didn't respond, just smiled faintly.

Naomi saw the smile and shook her head. "You are a cold, crude bastard, but, then . . . you always were." She took one long, last look at the scans. "It has possibilities, William. Too bad the risks outweigh the benefits." She left without saying another word. William didn't bother watch-

ing her go. He had known she would not want to try this
new game. Naomi was an unusual creature, for a werewolf.

She acted with caution instead of haste, and she never let
her arrogance get in the way of rational thought. Naomi
would never be one to assume that her power as a were
would see her through any and every obstacle.

But just as William had known he wouldn't be watching
Naomi through a piece of bulletproof glass as she transi-
tioned, he also knew that there were a great many shifters
and vampires who *would* count on their strengths to see
them through.

The door had just closed behind Naomi when Paulo
stepped up. He had a cocky grin on his face, although the
yellowed teeth in his mouth did detract a little from that
smile. "I have seen centuries come and go. You do not live
through six centuries if you are weak or a fool. This . . .
project will not kill me or drive me mad."

William suppressed his own smile as he looked towards
Thomas. "Excellent."

Paulo would count on his strength, but what he didn't
know was that the less desirable effects seemed to impact
the older creatures. The higher success rates were with
werecreatures still in their twenties or thirties, and vampires who had only been dead a few years. The younger the
creature, the more likely the chances for success.

Paulo was looking at a death sentence.

CHAPTER 5

I T was the soft scent of her skin that signaled to Vax he was no longer alone. He heard her footsteps a heartbeat later and turned to watch as she made her way down the alley towards him. She hadn't bothered putting the red wig on. Although she was still wearing black, it was no longer the *fuck me if you dare* getup. Instead she wore a pair of black boots with sturdy soles, slim-fitting black jeans, and a black shirt, topped off with a short black leather jacket.

Irritated, Vax turned his focus back to the club across the street. "I thought I told you that this was no longer your concern. The club isn't going to be open much longer, and the owners will be dealt with."

He saw her out of the corner of his eye and could see the determined look on her narrow face. It was dim in the alley, but he could still make out her soft green eyes, and there was no denying the low burn of rage simmering in them. "That's not really up to you, is it?"

"You're out of your league here, blondie," Vax said, his tone curt. Turning to face her, he jerked his head towards the club. "People in there get hurt, sweetheart. Hurt bad, and it's not the kind that a couple of days in the hospital will heal. I don't know what the hell your problem with the place is, but believe me, I'll— Oomph."

He looked down as she slammed something into his stomach. It was one of those expandable plastic file folders, and it was full. "You want to know what my problem is, look inside."

Automatically, he caught the file in his hand. He snapped the stretchy band that held it closed, and scowled. "I don't have the time or the patience for recreational reading, darlin'."

"My name is Jess. Don't call me *darlin'*, don't call me *sweetheart*, don't call me *blondie*. *Jess*." She curled her lip at him and gestured to the file. "I'll give you the Cliff's Notes version. In the past three years, there have been seven women abducted. None of them related by race, body type, hair color . . . nothing, except that they all attended *that* club in the months prior to their disappearances. Abducted from different parts of the city, different times of day. They are missing anywhere between six months to a year before the bodies turn up. The bodies are discovered within a day of death, or less. There are signs of brutal rapes before they are slowly and methodically beaten to death. Whoever held the women made sure they were cared for. There are no signs of starvation, no signs of abuse that took place over the months they were missing.

"There are, however, some very, very odd things. Needle marks, tracks, on their arms. They were practically turned into pincushions. But whatever was injected into them is something that can't be traced."

She stood there staring at the club, her arms crossed over her chest. In the faint light, he could see the silvery tracks of tears rolling down her face. When she turned to look at him, the grief he saw there was like a sucker punch straight to his gut. "I'd been working the story, off the record, since the fourth victim. When the fifth victim was found, my editor gave me the go-ahead to start on it officially. The fifth victim was the mayor's daughter."

She held out her hand, and he saw that she was holding another file. This one was slender, and he took it, tucking the other folder under his arm. He opened it to find a couple of crime-scene photos and a coroner's report. He didn't have to look at anything but the first picture to know that the girl had been brutalized.

Her face was left untouched and there was just enough of a similarity to make dread start a slow march up his spine.

"She's the latest victim, although the police don't entirely believe it. Her name was Randi. She was my sister." Jess's voice was husky and soft. "Randi didn't fit the profile at all. She had never been to the club. She wasn't kidnapped and held for months on end, but I know they killed her. The why of it is what I don't understand. It wasn't like I was even close to uncovering anything. But they didn't like my asking."

She turned away, walking halfway down the alley and stopping. She took a deep breath, her shoulders lifting and falling. Then a second one, like she was having a hard time breathing. The long ends of her hair brushed the base of her spine as she tipped her head back to stare up at the sky. "There was no warning. I had no chance to try and save her, because I didn't know they had grabbed her until it was too late. If . . ." Her breath caught in her throat, hitching a little. "Do you know that if I had even a tenth of Randi's gift, or my mom's, I would have known in time. I could have gotten to her. I could have saved her. I would have felt it in time to stop it, you see. But by the time I knew what they were doing to her, it was too late. She bled out while I was trying to find her."

Jess's head turned, and she held out a hand. Vax watched as a rock lifted off the ground and drifted over to her. "I can make rocks float. I don't ever have to get a ladder to get something down off a tall shelf. But I couldn't save my sister." She closed her hand around the rock so tightly, her fingers went white. A half sob escaped her, and she turned, the rock still levitating. Her hand fisted, and when it did, the rock hurtled through the air, slamming into the wall with a force that made the brick crumble.

When she looked back at Vax, there were tears in her eyes. "Her body was found in the park where we used to go with our parents. The night after she was found, I went home to find a note on my pillow. *Leave it alone or you can join her. We had a great deal of fun with her.* There was also a tape. They recorded it. Her rape, her beating, her murder. Now there's a snuff film out there with my baby sister on it."

"Fuck." Vax blew out a soft breath. "God, I'm sorry."

"So far the police have recovered dozens of copies, but they'll never get them all." Her green eyes shifted to a point over his shoulder, and he knew she was staring at the club. "The only face that ever showed up on the tape was my sister's. The guys, all you could see was their bodies. But I know who was behind it. I *know*. I want all of them dead, but the bastard in charge? Death isn't enough. I want him to suffer."

"Bloodshed won't bring her back," Vax said quietly. "It won't make it any easier for you to sleep at night."

"No." She reached up and pushed shaking hands through her hair. The eyes staring back at him were desolate. "But if I can find out why they were killing the girls, and stop them, *all* of them, then maybe I can live with killing my sister."

Looking into her haunted, heartbroken eyes, Vax said gently, "You didn't kill her."

A sad smile curled her lips. "Didn't I?"

Finally Vax felt a flicker of emotion from her. Pain—but it went too deep for such a simple word to describe it. By the time he'd acknowledged it, it was gone, and she'd locked her emotions down tight once more.

"No." Closing the distance between them, he waited until she looked up into his eyes before he finished. "You did not kill her."

Lowering her lashes, Jess turned her head aside. "Why don't we agree to disagree on that one?" She reached inside the jacket and drew something from an inside pocket. A picture . . . no, two of them. She rubbed them together between her hands as she started to pace.

"There's no real connection among the girls who've been killed, other than the fact that they hung out at Debach." She licked her lips, staring down at the two pictures in her hands. "The police couldn't find anything there, and the owners seem pretty much clean."

Vax glanced over his shoulder at the club. *Clean, my ass,* he thought idly.

Jess's next words mirrored his thoughts. "They may not *look* dirty, but something is up with those two, I'd bet my life on it. I don't have much information on the owners. There are two—there's a silent partner, Thomas Fitzpatrick. He immigrated over from Ireland fifteen years ago."

She handed him the first photograph. The blond man in the photo didn't looked familiar to him. There was a keen intelligence in his eyes, paired with an utter lack of conscience. Never a good combination. He also had that death white pallor common among vampires.

"He owns the club jointly with his partner. He seems to have the money in the operation—the other partner handles running the club itself."

As she handed him the second picture, she continued talking. Part of him wanted to tune her out, do something to make her go away. Even if it required something less than polite. He wasn't going to hit her again, but he had other weapons at his disposal. His magick hadn't worked on her before, but there had to be something, some sort of weakness in those thick defensive shields.

But another part of him remembered what it was like to lose somebody you loved, the gut-deep need to *do* something. Weary, he dragged a hand through his hair. There were reasons he didn't Hunt anymore. Reasons he preferred to be left alone. But he couldn't totally silence what was left of his conscience, no matter how hard he tried.

Physically, the guy in the second picture wasn't quite as nondescript at the first. His head was bald and he had a neatly trimmed goatee. Eyes of an indistinct color, average height, stocky build. It was the eyes that made him stand out, something that would make people remember him.

His eyes were cruel. Soulless and cruel. This guy walked down the street and, Vax bet, people cleared a path for him. He had that look about him, the kind that said, *You don't want to mess with me.*

Slowly, a grin curved his lips. A good old-fashioned dirty fight might just be the thing he needed. He could take out this guy and blow off some steam. Both problems solved, nice and easy. Flipping the picture around, he tapped it with his finger and asked, "Where can I find this one?"

For a second, Jess just stared at him. Then she fisted her hands on her hips and demanded, "Hell, if I knew that, you think I'd just be standing here? He's the one I've been trying to get to. And I *might* have been able to if you hadn't interrupted. He's not the easiest person to track down. He seems to come and go like magick. His name is William Masters. His face never showed in the tape, but he's the one who was using a knife on my sister. He was one of the ones who raped her."

"And you know that . . . how?"

Her voice shook with resolve as she said, "I just know." She reached out and took the picture back from him. She stared with hatred at the man in the picture. "I was going to try following him home. Then *you* showed up."

In a mild voice, Vax said, "You were going to follow him home." Like he was some guy that had sideswiped her, and she wanted to get his license plate. That alone could get a woman killed. But she was talking about following somebody she suspected of raping, beating, and murdering her little sister.

For a split second, he was surprised. It passed quickly, though. This woman had absolutely no survival instincts. "Darlin', it's a good thing I showed up. Sooner or later you'll get that through that pretty head of yours." He held up the second picture. "Mind if I keep this?"

She made no comment, so Vax just shrugged and tucked

it into his pocket. He was quiet for a moment as he tried to think of the words he needed to make her understand that she had to let him handle this. He didn't want to see those pretty green eyes staring lifelessly up at the sky.

"I understand how much it hurts, losing somebody. I've lost more than I care to think about. It hurts, and nothing will ever make that pain go away. But putting yourself into their hands? That's no answer. There's no reason for it."

"No reason?" she whispered. He started to walk away, and Jess stood there for a moment, staring at him, dumb-founded. He turned the corner at the mouth of the alley, disappearing from sight, and Jess was spurred into action. Running after him, she caught his arm in her hand. Her palm on the bare, bunched flesh of his bicep. His muscle jerked under her touch, and Jess felt as though she were trapped in a torrent of emotion.

"No *reason*?" She snarled it at him. "You have no idea what they did to her."

Vax stood there, staring at her with unreadable eyes. "I'll deal with the club. If he's part of it, I'll handle him. But he's more than just a rapist." He reached up as if he was going to touch her hair, and Jess batted his hand away. "He's something you can't handle."

Her eyes narrowed down to slits. Her head buzzed from that brief contact with his skin. And she felt like crying, screaming, or both. "Don't tell me what I can and can't handle. Don't tell me you'll *deal* with it. If you don't know what they are doing, you can't deal with it."

"That's my job."

"Screw your job." Jess closed the distance between them and reached up. She braced herself for the jolt as she snapped, "Deal with this." Then she cupped his face in her hands and dropped her shields. She knew enough about Empathy to know that his gift would do the rest. All she had to do was lower her shields—and think about what they'd done to Randi.

"See what they did to her, and then tell me there is *no reason*."

The images that haunted her endlessly were no longer just hers. She knew he was seeing them as his body stiffened, contorting as though he was trying to pull away from her. Tears streamed down her face. She couldn't make him feel her pain without her feeling it as well.

Randi had only been dead for a few hours when Jess was called in to identify her, and her sister's spirit had hovered for a couple of days before she passed on.

When Jess had touched Randi's broken body, it opened her mind to the horrors that had been Randi's last hours. How they'd beaten her. How they had toyed with her. How they had fed off her pain and laughed.

Jess had seen what Randi had seen, and as she relived it, she cried.

His eyes burned into hers, flickering and glowing. Jess was damned glad she wasn't psychic. She didn't want to know what he was thinking. Dealing with her own pain was enough.

"Don't tell me there is no reason," she said through gritted teeth. Then she peeled her hands away from him. Exhausted, she stumbled to the wall and fell against it, letting it support her weight.

Vax simply collapsed. He dropped to his knees in the middle of the alley. He stared straight ahead, seeing nothing but the memories that Jess had shared with him. The things that had been done to that poor girl were unimaginable. He found himself looking at up at Jess, speechless and more than a little sick.

With stark eyes, she met his gaze. "Now do you understand?"

"WHAT of Nate?"

William glanced at Thomas. "He's been dealt with."

With a scowl, Thomas sat back in his chair. "He was an excellent assistant, Will. You didn't have to kill him."

"He let her get away. That jeopardizes everything,

Thomas. Did you really think I'd leave him alive?" William studied the contents of the bar and finally settled on a bottle of Patrón. He selected a crystal tumbler from above the bar. "You can find another assistant easy enough."

Thomas scowled at him. "There was no reason to kill him."

"There was every reason. He didn't do what he was told to do, and because of it, that nosy reporter is still out there asking only God knows what." As far as William was concerned, the discussion was over.

"And we still have her to deal with, and one of my best men is no longer around to deal with her." Thomas sounded a bit pissed off.

Leaning back, William said, "And what would you have done?"

"I would have sent him after her. Again. With a little bit of backup. Once he had killed her, I would have killed him. Nice little murder-suicide deal with no loose ends that might unravel for us later. Xeke is particularly talented in that area. And he knows how to elude those who might bring us trouble."

For a second, William was a little surprised. Then he smiled and lifted his glass to his friend. "Why, Thomas. You are learning."

Thomas laughed. "Loose strings are never a good thing. I've a few years on you, remember. I may have my nose buried in reports, tests, and brain scans most of the time, but I am not a fool." He lifted his own glass, staring into the whiskey and brooding. "We still have to deal with the reporter. Why don't you send someone to her home?"

"More than a few years, slick." Nearly two centuries, easy. William had gone through the Change after being attacked by a were nearly fifteen years ago. The vampire had gone through his Change sometime in the early 1800s.

"Perhaps we could send Xeke." William scraped his nails over his carefully groomed goatee and murmured, "If you think he can handle it. I don't know. We can't have any more mistakes. Perhaps we should just see what happens. She'll be back here sooner or later, and I can deal with her. I'd rather not do it in the club. Not now. There's no telling who she might have told about the other night. We can't have her found anywhere near here. This can't be connected to us in any way."

William was a bit unhappy about that. She'd cost him so much trouble over the past few months that he'd been looking forward to taking some form of payment out on that long, sleek body. There was nothing to be done for it, though. She needed to disappear, far away from here. "There can't be another mistake on this. We don't have room for it."

Amusement lit Thomas's blue eyes. "You know, I am the doctor. You would think that I would be the one worried about a possible disruption in the experiments. Don't worry so, Will. The most she could do is tell the cops she has concerns about the club. Debach is very, very clean. There is nothing to link her sister to us. The police know the other women came to the club on occasion. But the police will find no other link, not from the girl, and certainly not to us. We were careful."

Disgusted, William replied, "You are not taking this seriously, as always."

"On the contrary, I'm taking it very seriously. However, we wouldn't be in this bloody mess if you hadn't killed her baby sister." His chilly smile revealed the pointed tips of his fangs. "That did nothing more than piss her off."

Leaning forward, William said, "Well, I don't recall you having any wonderful ideas on what to do about her. As always, you're too wrapped up in your research, your tests, and your subjects, while I handle the real world around us. You're so damned certain she can't cause trouble. I'm not. There *are* other people to be concerned about besides the police."

Thomas didn't look at all concerned. "There are no Hunters here, Will. That's why I chose this area. It's a dead zone as far as they are concerned. The closest established

Master is a minimum of three hundred miles away in any given direction." He tossed back the rest of his Scotch and rose to refill his glass. "However, I am not dismissing her as a possible threat. And I agree we should handle it. You know, I am curious to see exactly how the hormone works on one such as her. I don't think she's quite human."

William narrowed his eyes, studying the vampire thoughtfully. "She's no witch."

"No. Nor is she shifter or vampire. But there is something peculiar about her. I tried to read her the other night. And I cannot." Thomas tugged thoughtfully on his lower lip. "I simply could not read her."

"Strange." William rubbed a hand over his head, vaguely aware of the slight growth of stubble. He had just shaved his scalp clean a week ago, but it grew quickly. The hair was barely an eighth of an inch right now, but within a week or two, that scant bit would be nearly an inch long.

"Interesting. Her sister was such a pleasant treat—Empaths are so sensitive to pain and anger. Feeding on her fear was almost as sweet as her blood. I would imagine that talent runs in the family. I wonder what the sister's talent is." Thomas leaned back in his chair, a smile twisting his lips into a mockery of the expression. "You know, we should have held on to her for a little while. It would have been an interesting change to use her in some of my trials."

"Humans are a waste of time. We've already tried, remember?"

Thomas cocked a brow. In a cool voice, he said, "*I* have tried. I do not recall you working side by side with me in the labs while I carry on my work. I do not recall you volunteering to research, assist. Nothing until you decided you wanted to go through the process. However, for the record, yes, I know there were several human failures. But an Empath is not just the average human."

"Do you really think that Empathy is going to make her any different from the rest of the screwups?" William moved over the console and hit the button that would bring the screens to life. Ten images flashed into view on the console. Each of the transitioning chambers had a video camera set up just outside the bulletproof glass, keeping a constant record of what happened inside the cell. "We have more than enough failures. We know what works. We should stick with it."

The failures were an endless source of frustration for Thomas. This particular unit of patients was for a different branch of Thomas's experiments. Instead of using the natural chemicals from a witch and introducing them into a host's body, Thomas had turned the tables and was trying to introduce DNA harvested from a shape-shifter into a witch's body.

On average, more than ninety percent of the subjects were written off as failed experiments. They were either unaffected, or their bodies rejected the hormone and the adverse reaction killed them. Seemed like a waste of time to William, and he'd told Thomas he needed to give up on that project.

Thomas would not. Part of William understood why. The end results of the successful experiments were pretty damned amazing.

Like Dena.

Dena was a whore he had picked up in Calgary a few years ago, back when they first started down this road. With her big, plump lips and dark hair, she was a sultry piece of work. He knew for a fact that she knew how to put those lips to good use.

She was a witch of only mild talent, so mild she could barely even call herself a witch. She used her talent to help score the better johns or to sniff out drug deals so she could interrupt and steal some coke. In her former life, she had been a sad, pathetic waste. Well, except for her very skilled mouth.

Now though . . . now she was magnificent.

She'd sat in a cell for nearly six months before Thomas decided to do anything with her. The process itself took too damn long. Months, sometimes more than a year. The weaker people tended to die during the early months. Dena hadn't, and both of them had watched her transition with varying degrees of curiosity and exhilaration. Thomas had nearly a year invested in her when he administered the final dose. She had slipped into a coma, and William figured she was gone.

Thomas hadn't been so sure. He had maintained her body, feeding her through a tube stuck down her nose and making sure she was cared for. He had some highly skilled medical staff in the lab, and he rode hell on them to make sure his experiments were treated properly.

Of course, none of the nurses cared. They were all little more than zombies. Thomas had used some of the nastier talents some vampires had, eradicating their free will. His suggestions wore off in time, and he'd either plant the suggestions all over again, or kill the subjects and replace them.

After three months, Dena had emerged from the coma. William still remembered the blast of power he had felt coming from the lab. She'd opened her eyes, and her fury at still being held prisoner had triggered her first Change.

The entire process had been touch-and-go, but now William was glad Thomas had stuck it out with Dena. She'd survived the trials, but more than that, she had emerged from them much more powerful. Dena was unique. She intrigued him, and for several reasons.

That raw sensuality she possessed was only one of them.

So far, most of the creatures had only weak talents and couldn't even manage to shift. They had some of the strength and all of the hyperacute senses, but they couldn't shift. Worse, the experimenting left them pretty much insane. And not the psycho-killer type. That, at least, could have provided some amusement.

No, it generally left them useless and unfit for combat, little more than sniveling, whining waste heaps.

Dena was most definitely fit for combat. There had been one other female with serious potential, but she had escaped before they finished with her. The retrieval process had been interrupted by the damned Hunters.

Fortunately Dena didn't seem to be in a big hurry to try running away. Very fortunate, because she was one of the last subjects Thomas had success with. After another dozen witches had either rejected the DNA or emerged from the trials unchanged, Thomas was finally starting to see the futility of this particular project.

Damn good thing, because William was tired of getting rid of the bodies. Witches didn't burn the way shifters or vampires did. Disposing of the bodies in a way that wouldn't raise suspicion was paramount. Which added up to a serious pain in the ass for William.

Yes, Dena was a success. But anytime Thomas had tried his experiments on humans, he had not been even remotely successful. Many mortals died within minutes of receiving the harvested chemicals, but others might as well have been given injections of saline. No change, no effect at all. There hadn't been one single human who had shown any kind of promise.

Eventually Thomas had decided to let go of the failed experiments and focus more on the successes.

Since giving up on new specimens, Thomas had concentrated on Dena. Almost fixated—he seemed determined to understand why she had survived the transition and emerged so much stronger. He hadn't had much luck yet.

The only thing he did seem to be able to say with certainty was that females tolerated the transition better and had a higher survival rate.

He spouted a bunch of technical jargon that meant absolutely nothing to William. But he could definitely see why Thomas wanted to create more like Dena. She was a mean-ass, cocky little bitch with a thirst for blood. Predatory, sensual, and cruel, she was one of the sexiest things he'd ever come across.

"Elsa has spent a great deal of time training Dena lately," Thomas murmured from behind.

William had been so focused on her that he had forgotten about Thomas. He glanced over his shoulder and then looked back at Dena's image. "Has she?"

"Hmm-hmm. She's mastered fire. She's learning how to use her own sense of magick to sense others. It's rather amazing—she's gone from a penny-ante witch to this. She will be a force to reckon with. I also believe that with a little instruction, she will master her shape-shifting equally quickly." Thomas said it in a neutral tone, but William heard the unasked question clearly enough.

William wasn't much of a teacher, nor did he care to think of himself in that particular role. However, it might be best to get an idea of Dena's abilities. She had the power inside her. William sensed it. If she could master it, it would add that much more to their army. "I can give it a shot, work with her a little."

Right now, Dena was pacing back and forth along the clear, reinforced wall that made up the front of her cell. The camera was positioned just outside, far enough back that they had a bird's-eye view of the cell. And of Dena.

She wore a plain black tank top and nothing else. William could see the naked curve of her ass as she paced up the floor, and when she turned back, he could see the gentle sway of her braless breasts. The rooms were a bit chilly and her nipples were hard.

William liked it. He liked the entire package. Her tight, muscled ass; her long legs; her big breasts and nipples. There was plenty to like. Working with her could be a lot of fun.

She stopped and stared at the camera. William found himself staring at her image on the monitor in front of him. Her wide-spaced eyes looked black. She had straight, thick brows and a long sensual mouth. She rose up onto her toes and tapped the camera lens. "What are you doing in there?"

William rocked back on his heels, studying her. Behind him, Thomas chuckled. "I'm amazed at how her talent has grown. I can't understand why I can't duplicate these results."

"She's one of a kind, Thomas. That's why. She isn't just

the end result of an experiment." William leaned forward, staring intently at her image.

"Unique."

Vax rubbed his head. The lingering headache was nothing in comparison to what he had felt when Jessica Warren dropped her shields and made him feel the pain she lived with daily.

The diner was all but empty, and the waitress didn't seem to be in any hurry to stop by their table. It was as much privacy as he figured they were going to get. He doubted she was in any hurry to invite him back to her house, and he wasn't about to have this discussion out on the street.

"Where did you learn to shield?" Vax asked. She had closed back up again, hiding behind those impenetrable shields.

"My mother," she answered softly, without ever raising her gaze from the Formica tabletop.

"Did she train your sister, too?"

Another quick glance at him, and then she went right back to looking at the table. "Yes. Mom and Dad died a few years ago. Randi was born with her gift, and Mom started working with her as soon as Randi was old enough to talk. She had to. Randi couldn't leave the house, even as a baby, unless Mom shielded her."

"What about you?"

Jess shrugged, a faint smile on her face. "Mine came with puberty. Bad enough I got the acne and the hormonal bullshit, and was taller than most of the boys in my grade. But I had this little problem—I got mad or worried or embarrassed or nervous . . . things started floating around me. That sure as hell made me an extrovert," she drawled, her voice dripping with sarcasm.

Vax smiled a little. "I imagine. You certainly got it under control, though. I can't get a read on you at all."

Finally a real smile curved her lips, a thoughtful one. Her eyes took on a far-off look. "I had a good teacher."

"She must have been amazing." Little wisps of envy curled through him. He hadn't ever had that, a mom to miss. He'd never known her. He didn't know whether she'd abandoned him or whether she'd died having him. Either one was a likely possibility. He didn't know which of his parents had been white, which had been Native American. He did know that the stigma of being a half-breed bastard was one he would have lived with no matter what. Wouldn't have been easy on his mother, either. "You miss her."

"A lot." She leaned back in her chair and crossed her arms over her chest, finally meeting his gaze. Her eyes were troubled. "Mom would have been able to save her."

"You don't know that." Better than most, Vax understood the kind of guilt she must be feeling. It was the kind of guilt that turned to acid inside the heart and ate a person alive. Before she could say anything else, he added, "This isn't your fault. The blame lies with the men who took her, not with you."

She shrugged and shook her head. "Up here, I know that." She tapped her brow. Then she lowered her hand to her chest, covering her heart. "In here, it's a different story."

He knew all too well what she meant. He still hadn't forgiven himself for what had happened to Cora. Didn't know if he ever would. Abruptly, he changed the subject, tugging the picture out of his back pocket and studying it. "You said his name was William Masters. And the other . . . Thomas?"

"Thomas Fitzpatrick."

"How many victims?"

"That the police know of? Seven. But . . ." Her voice trailed off, and she turned her head to stare out the window into the night. "But I think there are more. These women who are missing—I think there are more. There was a spike in unexplained disappearances. The cases are all open, and although the cops won't admit it, they do suspect there is a link, at least among some of them. I think this goes a lot deeper than just the average run-of-the-mill psycho."

"How so?"

Now she started to squirm on her seat. "It's hard to explain," she mumbled. She put her hands on the table, spreading her fingers wide, curling them into a fist, then spreading them open again. "I felt something."

Vax began to speak, but the waitress moved in their direction. He looked down at his menu, but she didn't stop. She headed past them, and Vax heard a door open. As the waitress disappeared into the bathroom, he looked back at Jess with curious eyes. "Felt something or sensed something? You psychic, too?"

"Just barely." She shifted on the seat and reached for her water. She closed both hands around it, but instead of drinking it, she just stared into it. "It's more like just really good intuition. I tend to know when there are cops doing radar, and I can tell when somebody is lying to me. Comes in handy in my job, but that's about it. But something just felt wrong."

"Felt wrong when?"

She squirmed more. "Every time one of the victims was found. I went to see most of them in the morgue. When a body was found, I went to the crime scene. And I . . . felt something."

Something had better not mean what Vax suspected it meant.

Ten minutes later, though, Vax knew it did. Real magick wasn't something Jess had much experience with. Her mother was a psychic, her sister an Empath—she was familiar with psychic skills and with Empathy, but real magick was different. It felt different. Trying to explain magick to a psychic might be like trying to explain colors to the color-blind. Took a while for her to get it, but once she got it . . .

It was witch power she'd felt. Fading and weak, but there all the same.

He heaved out a sigh and pushed a hand through his hair. Across from him, Jess stared at him with unreadable eyes and asked, "So do you think I'm crazy?"

"Unfortunately I don't. Life would have been a lot easier if I could just write you off as a nutcase." He fell silent for a minute, turning everything over in his mind. "Do you know if any of the victims were drained?"

"Not one of them." Jess rubbed her hands over her face. "I checked. That was something that would have made sense. A vamp might keep a woman alive for a while, keep her clean, keep her fed until he got tired of her."

"You've put a lot of thought into this." She looked exhausted. There were lines of strain fanning out from the corners of her eyes, and she was so pale, he half expected to be able to see through her. She sat with her shoulders slumped, as though there were some invisible weight on her shoulders. He imagined there likely was.

Vax wondered when she'd last had a decent night's sleep.

A cynical smile curved her lips. "What else am I supposed to do?"

Instead of responding to that, he blew out a breath and shoved away from the table. He stood up and held out a hand to her. "Come on."

Jess glanced towards the waitress. "You haven't even ordered yet. I thought you were hungry."

With a sardonic smile, he drawled, "I am. But if we wait for her to take our order, we'll be waiting until doomsday. We've got work to do, so my belly will have to wait a while."

Vax suspected that if he found what he expected to find, his appetite was going to wither up and die. He had some protein bars stashed on his bike, so he'd just eat one of them on the way.

Once they were outside the diner, he told her where he wanted to go and she just stared at him for a moment. Finally she pushed her hair back from her face and shook her head. "Why are we going to the cemetery? Randi was the last victim, and that was months ago."

"It's not Randi's grave I need, Jess. And you don't need to go there, either. I get the feeling you're spending way too much time there. I need to visit the graves of the other women. And their homes."

She just gave him a puzzled look. "Why?"

"To see if they had any gifts," he replied.

Vax had a bad feeling that they would find most, if not all, of the women had been gifted. It might have made sense if they had been drained of blood. Blood from gifted people had a stronger kick. Some feral vamps preyed on witches for just that reason. But they weren't drained.

He doubted it was a witch, either. The only reason a witch would hunt other witches would be to steal their powers using blood magick. Witches who walked the blood path had ways of tapping into the energy of gifted people, whether they were mortal or otherwise, and using the power to enhance their own. But blood-path magick left a taint he would have felt. Hell, Hunters from a thousand miles away would have felt that. A bloody, violent death was what the blood-path demanded and during the time of death, a witch could steal the power. But it wasn't a subtle thing. They couldn't hide it.

So if it wasn't a vampire and it wasn't a blood-path witch, who was doing it? Why?

He had to agree with Jess. So far it didn't feel like random pointless violence. There had to be a reason. He'd have to find out why before he could kill the men responsible. If he didn't, somebody else might just take up where they left off.

That wasn't an option.

"I HATE being right." Vax slid her a sidelong look and added, "I also hate *you* being right."

They hadn't felt anything at the grave of Greta Sanders. Greta had been murdered five months before Randi Warren, and she'd been missing for four months before they'd killed her. Vax hadn't expected to feel much at her grave, with her being gone so long. That sort of aura hung around a dead body only so long before fading away.

Her home, though—that was a whole different story. There was enough power still lingering around to make his hair stand up on end.

A young couple lived there now. Vax could hear them—they had a new baby, and she wasn't happy. Through his shields, he sensed an upset stomach and suspected that the couple would be taking the baby to the doctor come morning. Right now they were both frustrated and exhausted.

He sensed the power under all of that, and it didn't come from the family living there now. They hadn't been there long enough. Even after nine months, Greta's power was still in the air.

"Right about what?" Jess had her hands tucked into the pockets of her jacket, and she hunched her shoulders against the cold.

He shifted so that he stood in front of her and blocked some of the wind. Watching her face, he said, "She was a witch."

"Ahhh . . . so?"

It was twilight, and the red and gold light gleamed against her pale skin. She looked entirely too touchable, Vax decided. She stood there glaring at him. Her hands were fisted on narrow hips, and Vax had the urge to replace them with his own. To pull her against him and cover that scowling mouth with his. His cock throbbed. *Like things aren't complicated enough,* he thought sourly. She was skinny and mouthy, and seemed to be irked with him 90 percent of the time. Not to mention he had known her for less than forty-eight hours.

There should be no reason for him to be this obsessed with her. Why the hell he couldn't stop thinking about seeing her naked was beyond him.

"So . . . whatever you felt when you went and saw her in the morgue, do you feel it here now?"

The scowl on her face faded and she turned around, staring across the street at the house. She shivered, but he suspected it had nothing to do with the cold. She licked her lips. He wondered what she'd do if he bent down and did the same thing, tracing the path her tongue had taken with his own.

When she nodded, he forced himself to focus on the problem in front of them. "Yeah. I can feel it," she told him. "They were witches. All of them. *Why?*"

Jess caught her lower lip with her teeth, and he saw the sheen of tears in her eyes. "Damn it, what the hell did I do?"

"You didn't do anything. You were trying to help. You were just . . . unprepared."

Her laugh was a harsh, almost-painful sounding bark, so bitter and angry. "I was unprepared. Fuck that. My baby sister is *dead*. Unprepared. Don't you think that's maybe a little too polite?" With every word, her voice got louder and louder until she was practically screaming at him.

Vax reached out and caught her arm, stepping close. "You want to scream, you're entitled. You want to cry, you've got more reason to do it than most people. But if you do it here, we're going to have problems. We have enough problems already."

For a second, he didn't know what she was going to do. He suspected she didn't, either. Then she turned her back on him, and he watched her slender shoulders rise and fall as she took a series of deep, slow breaths. "Yeah. I was unprepared. But it still doesn't make sense."

Jess frowned. She lowered her head, staring down at the brick sidewalk. The neighborhood was an old one, and the people here took a lot of pride in it. A person could see that from the way the people took care of their houses, how they maintained the out-of-date brick sidewalks, not to mention the homes themselves. Houses built back in the 1920s weren't exactly easy on the pocket.

She continued to stare at the brick sidewalk's elegant pattern as though she were trying to solve some puzzle hidden inside it. "It still doesn't make sense. They weren't drained. Raped, beaten, and murdered, but not drained. If somebody is seeking out witches, wouldn't it be because they want something? Like their blood? Or their power?"

"Maybe they want something else." She shook it off fast, that was for damn sure, Vax mused. Shook it off or locked it down. Sooner or later, she wasn't going to be able to do either one. She was blocking out the grief by dealing with the fury instead. Not the healthiest way to deal with a loss, but he couldn't think about that now.

There was a serious problem shaping up here, and she had some of the pieces.

Vax headed back down the sidewalk. By the time he'd mounted his bike, Jess had joined him. "Know where any of the others live?"

She climbed on behind him, resting her hands on his hips. "Yeah. It's a drive, though."

"Not like I got anything else to do." Over his shoulder, he slanted a look at her. "What about you?"

Jess just sighed. "Nope. Not a thing."

It was the sad, heartbreaking truth, too. Jess knew there was no way she could even try to get on with her life until they found out what was going on. Found out why they had killed Randi. A sweet, innocent college girl. It was senseless. Jess had to make sense of it, or she'd go insane.

If they had killed Randi as a warning to Jess, then making sense of it would mean exposing them. Finding out what they were doing, and making it stop.

Her gut went cold every time she drove by Debach, and it was worse when she looked at the picture of Masters. He was involved in something that he was willing to kill to keep hidden. As far as Jess was concerned, her only chance at vengeance was to uncover that something.

Absolution . . .

Vax started the bike, and she automatically tightened her grip on him. As the ghost of her mother's voice whispered through her mind, she buried her face in his denim jacket. She could feel the heat and strength of him through it, and it felt wonderful. Almost wonderful enough that she could block out Mom's words.

Is it vengeance you seek, or absolution, baby? What happened to Randi wasn't your fault.

It was. Jess remained silent. She hadn't argued with her mother's ghost yet, and she wasn't about to start now. There was no point. Jess was right, and she knew it.

She heard something sort of like a sigh, and then her mother's presence faded. Squeezing her eyes closed, Jess unconsciously squirmed closer to Vax and held on for dear life.

I T was late.

After spending nearly three hours riding around Indianapolis on a Harley, Jess's butt was sore and she couldn't walk quite right, either. "You haven't spent too much time on a bike before, have you?" Vax asked.

As she mounted the steps to her house, Jess scowled at him. "Yes, I have. It's just been a while."

"How long a while?"

"High school." And she sure as hell didn't remember being this sore then, but then she hadn't spent hours at a time on the back of Danny Cirelli's Honda. Cuddling up against her high school boyfriend while they headed for the movies was nothing like sitting behind Vax.

Of course, even if she had been riding just around the block behind Vax, there would still be no comparison. Bigger bike, sexy man—nope, no comparison.

She unlocked the door and stripped off her jacket as she went inside. Tossing the jacket across the back of the couch, she turned around and watched Vax as he stepped inside and closed the door. She toed off her shoes before reaching for the phone. "I'm hungry."

He quirked a brow at her. "You actually get hungry?"

Giving him a baleful stare, she punched in a number and asked, "You like pizza?"

A few minutes later, she had a large pizza on the way, half everything, half veggie. "Veggie is no way to eat a pizza," Vax told her.

"Neither is everything. You got any idea how many calories are in one slice of Sal's Special Supreme?" She padded into the kitchen, making a beeline for the refrigerator. She could feel him staring at her as she opened it and grabbed a bottle of water from inside. Before she could close it, a big brown hand caught the door, and she stood there trapped between the cool air blasting out of the fridge and the warmth of Vax's body.

"I burn calories pretty easy, so no, I have no clue. And I'm not real worried about it, either. I don't see death by heart attack in my future. You know, the contents of your fridge are seriously lacking. No beer. Nothing to munch on. Hell, I don't think I saw a single bag of potato chips." But he wasn't looking into the refrigerator. He was looking at her.

At her mouth, more specifically. Jess felt her skin start to buzz, her pulse kicking up a little at the heat she saw simmering in those thunderstorm eyes. "Ahh . . . pizza will be here soon," she said, trying to inch back a little. He just moved closer. Now she was trapped. She could move back and end up falling into the refrigerator, or she could stand there and feel the seductive heat of his body. It wasn't a hard to choice to make, although Jess suspected the wiser choice would have involved the fridge.

Vax reached up and caught a hank of hair in his hand. He held her gaze as he wound the long strands around his wrist. "Yeah, I know. Funny, though, I'm not really that hungry for pizza now."

Oooo-kay. There was no denying the intent in that statement, or the sleepy, heavy-lidded look to his eyes. Even though her hormones were clamoring, her knees were a little weak, and she was feeling a whole lot of heat, Jess pressed a hand against his chest. He eased back a little. Regret and misery went pretty well together, she decided. The loss of his heat caused a reaction inside her that was almost painful. Still, she didn't lower her hand. "This isn't a good idea, pal."

His hand came up, covering hers. She hadn't noticed it

before then, but he wore a simple silver band on the ring finger of his right hand. Then she forgot about the ring as he closed his fingers around her wrist and dragged her hand a little to the left, until it covered his heart. Under her palm, she could feel the quick, steady beat. "Why not? Other than the fact that there's a pizza boy due here in about forty-five minutes. Forty-five minutes is plenty of time . . . for now." His lids drooped, and Jess could feel herself giving in.

Just thinking about the things they could do to each other inside of forty-five minutes was enough to make her breathing kick up. He was entirely too sexy, with that thick black hair, that heavy-lidded look to his dark gray eyes, and that mobile, sensual mouth. Under his stare, she could feel everything inside her going hot and liquid. Her breasts ached, her hands itched to touch him, and she was dying to get a taste of him.

Everything inside her was clamoring, and for a moment it left her a little dazed, a little disoriented, even confused until she figured it out. She felt alive. Jess hadn't felt alive since she had stood over her sister's lifeless body.

Randi's face flashed through Jess's mind. The guilt that followed nearly choked her. Panicked, she shoved her hands against his chest and tore away from him. "I can't do this."

A warm hand came up, caressed the back of her neck. She tensed, ready to struggle, but he made no move to pull her back against him. All he did was watch her face as he gently massaged her neck. "You feel guilty."

"I *am* guilty," she muttered, her voice rough. "She's dead. Until I stop the men who did it, how can I even *think* about something like this?"

Vax laughed softly. He rubbed his hand up and down her back as he responded, "Because you're human, darlin'. It's how we are. The body doesn't always understand grief or the need for revenge. It just understands living." His hand slid down her back and cupped over one hip, then his other hand came up, sliding around her waist. He pulled her back against him. She tried to resist, but eventually she leaned back against him. "Feeling something isn't a betrayal to your sister, Jess. Let me make you feel something. . . ."

He lowered his head and nuzzled her neck. His teeth grazed her skin, and then he whispered into her ear, "Feel alive for a few minutes. . . . Just feel."

Oh, she was. She was feeling more heat, more hunger than she'd felt in such a long time. He felt good against her. Strong. Warm. Unable to help it, she slid her hands down and laid them over his. She thought about it—more than thought about it. She was tempted. So very tempted. "My life is a mess right now. It's not just losing Randi."

"Too much of a mess for this?" He placed his palm against her belly and spread his fingers wide. That simple, almost innocent touch felt achingly good. Too good.

"Definitely too much of a mess." And even if it wasn't, Jess wasn't sure she was ready to deal with the *this*. Not with this man.

He had *complicated* written all over him. All over the hard, sinewy planes of his body . . . in those amazing storm cloud eyes . . . *Focus, Jess.* "Look, I just . . . I'm a mess. Half the time, I don't know if I want to scream, cry, or beat something up."

He pressed his cheek against hers, and she could feel him smiling. "Sometimes *this* can help. Think of me as a security blanket. Or a punching bag," he teased. He trailed his fingers over her belly, along the waistband of her jeans, along one hip. "I can be gentle. Or not."

His hands tightened, and he fisted a hand in her hair, drawing it aside to bare her neck. Teeth raked over the exposed skin, a hot, erotic caress. The air seemed to shimmer with the violent heat of passion. "Whatever will make you feel better—I can give it to you."

That sexual promise was almost more than she could withstand. Even with all the nervous anxiety, grief, and confusion tangling inside her, she had to fight not to turn and press her mouth to his. "I can't handle this right now, Vax. Shoot, I can't handle *you*."

"Nothing to handle, unless you want to." He continued to speak with her in a teasing, gentle tone, and she suspected he was trying more to distract her than anything else. "I can do all the handling myself." Then he rubbed his hips against her butt, and she felt him, the hard, firm length of his cock. Okay, maybe he wasn't *just* trying to distract her.

A smile curled his lips. "Baby, I'm not looking for an all-out relationship. I'd say, considering what you're dealing with lately, that's not what you need, either."

A little miffed, but not sure why, Jess jerked her hand back and jabbed her elbow into his stomach. It was rock hard, and she suspected he only backed away because he felt like it. Her blow hadn't done a damn thing. "But some hot and sweaty sex is?" Jess refused to acknowledge, even to herself, how good the idea sounded.

"Never hurts."

"Maybe I don't do the casual sex thing, Vax. Hell, I don't even know your last name."

He stepped a little closer, and Jess realized she'd let him corner her again. Against the counter this time, and his hands came up, caging her in place. "You don't need to know my last name in order for me to make you scream. Matter of fact, you don't really even need to know my first name." He lowered his head and pressed his mouth to the side of her neck.

Jess felt that light contact clear down to her toes. He was right. She had absolutely no doubt that this man could make her scream. Even though she wasn't much of a screamer, she knew he could do it. And she was tempted. She was damned tempted. He was as hot and sexy as he was irritating. Okay. More. But still . . . "I'm not into casual, Vax. Okay?"

For a moment, she wasn't sure whether he was going to move. But then he did, stepping away and studying her with unreadable eyes. "If you're sure that's how you want to play, blondie. Casual is about all I'm good for."

"Ah, weren't you standing in here telling me about faith

and belief just this morning? Don't you have to write off casual sex as part of that?" Jess asked, slipping around him so that he couldn't pin her again.

He lifted one shoulder in a shrug, and Jess found herself staring at the way the T-shirt stretched over his muscles. His earlier words didn't make sense, and she looked at his face and said, "Huh?"

That cocky, cynical smile was on his face again, but this time it didn't reach his eyes. "I said . . . I have faith in something beyond this. But I don't have a chance in hell of seeing paradise, Jess. I fuck up and destroy everything I touch sooner or later. So I'll just find what little bit of paradise here that I can."

He turned away and left the kitchen.

I don't have a chance in hell of seeing paradise.

The strength sapped out of her legs, and she collapsed at the table, burying her face in her hands. Her body was screaming at her. Although she definitely didn't do casual, a quick roll in the sack with him sounded damned appealing.

In the sack. On the table or the floor. Up against a wall.

Jess also had a feeling that casual sex wasn't what she'd get if she got naked with Vax. Something about his eyes, about the way he looked at her. A woman would get in bed with him and come out with a little weak, a little sore, and a lot thankful. And addicted. Very addicted.

Jess wanted that. She *craved* it. If he had pushed, just a little, Jess had no doubt she would have given in. He probably knew that. Instead he had backed off.

What had he meant?

I don't have a chance in hell of seeing paradise.

The man had *hero* written all over him. Heroes bled for others. If they weren't the kind to make it into some cloudy, ethereal wonderland, then who did?

Finally Jess pushed herself to her feet and headed out of the kitchen. She halfway expected to find him gone, but she found him crouched in front of the fireplace, dropping a log onto the grate. "There are some matches on the . . ."

He glanced at her and smiled before he held his hand

over the logs. "That's okay. I think I got it." She jumped as the wood burst into flame. A little burst, but still, a burst all the same. The log crackled away, little red embers floating upward. "Wow."

His lips quirked. He drew his hand back and held it out in front of him. In his cupped palm, he held a dancing, spinning sphere of fire. "David Copperfield's got nothing on me." Lowering his head, he blew on the mass of flames, and it went out.

"Can you fly?" Jess drawled. She strolled into the living room, trying not to let him see how much he'd affected her. As she dropped down onto the couch, she could tell he already knew. It was there in those weird gray eyes. She wondered when he'd decide to press his advantage again.

"Not the way you mean."

Before she could ask him what he meant by that, he was gone. *Gone.* Like, poof. Except there was no smoke screen for him to disappear into. He was just *gone. "Holy shit."* Jess jumped up off the couch, her heart pounding out a drumbeat and her palms slick with sweat. "What the hell . . ."

Before she finished the sentence, he was back and holding an apple in his hand. Standing in the exact same spot he had been in before he disappeared. Okay. Some sort of illusion. He hadn't really disappeared. Some sort of illusion. That was it. "How did you do that?"

Vax shrugged. "I flew." He lifted the apple and took a bite out of it, his eyes bright with amusement.

Sourly, she thought, *I'm so glad I amuse you.* Out loud, she said, "That wasn't flying. That was disappearing. Or making me think you had. How did you do that?" If she hadn't been in her own house, she would have gotten up and started checking for trapdoors.

"Like I said, I can fly. Just not the way you mean." He sauntered over to her and reached out, putting his finger under her chin and closing her mouth with a snap. He moved away again with that same loose-limbed easy grace.

He moved like a cowboy. The thought popped into her

head from nowhere, distracting her from what he had just done. "Why don't you explain that to me?"

"Maybe some other time. Right now . . . we need to talk about what's been going on here."

Jess shook her head and said, "No. I think right now I need to know what I just saw. People can't just disappear like that." Jess would have started pacing, but he was standing close to the fire again, and it seemed he took up a hell of a lot of space. Her skin was still buzzing from earlier, and her gut was all tight with nerves from that little trick of his, so going near him wasn't an option.

"Normal people, no. You're right. But I'm not exactly normal, sweetheart."

"Would you stop calling me *sweetheart*?" she shouted. The sound of it surprised her. She turned away with a wince. Jeez. He got to her like nothing she'd ever seen. Deciding a little more distance would be a good thing, she moved behind the couch before she turned to face him.

"You sure as hell are touchy," he mused. Then he looked back to the fire, crouching down in front of it and staring into the flames. "Look, it's a complicated thing, and not one I understand particularly well. I just know I can do it. A few other witches have the ability, too. It's called *flying*. We don't disappear into nowhere. We leave one place, appear in another. I appeared in your kitchen and grabbed the apple." He lifted it and took another bite out of it before glancing at her.

No. Oooohhhh, no. "That isn't possible."

His voice was mild as he replied, "Well, some people would say it's impossible to move things with your mind, but you do it."

He had that tone of voice people used when they were explaining things to small children or to somebody who was very dense. Her eyes narrowed. She decided she didn't care for it at all. "There is scientific evidence of psychic ability. Disappearing into thin air, different story."

"What about fire?"

Her gaze slid to the roaring flames in her fireplace. "You know, you make my head hurt."

Vax laughed. "I've been told that a time or two. Come back over here and sit down. We need to figure out what's going on with these kidnappings, why the women are being held for so long before they kill them. And why *these* women."

CHAPTER 6

"I DON'T think she is ready for this."

Thomas stood in front of the cell, staring through the clear wall panel at Dena, watching as she lay sleeping. Or pretending to sleep. She knew they were there. Perhaps she could even hear them. They had yet to determine just how acute her senses had become, and William had been more interested in other things during his brief visits.

Like seeing whether she had the power to shape-shift before the full moon rose in the sky. Seeing how long it took to replenish the power the shifting took. Seeing whether she could use her magick while in wolf form.

She was definitely the most promising of all the current subjects. She had come through the transition intact, and she possessed the capabilities William and Thomas needed for success: violence, intelligence, and a complete and utter lack of conscience.

Most of the other subjects either would be terminated or Thomas would use them to conduct further tests. The man was ruthless when he was trying to unravel a mystery. And that was exactly what the failed experiments were to him.

Of the other nine occupied cells, there were three that were of importance to them.

A male, a young vampire whom they'd convinced to join the study just a few weeks out of his Change. He'd probably survive. He wasn't a powerful vampire and he wouldn't ever become a Master—he wouldn't ever have control over other vamps. But he would definitely come in useful. He had come through the transition remarkably intact.

The other two important occupants were women. The monitors showed them strapped to tables, their heads shaved bare. The straps were mostly just a precaution. These women were brain-dead. They had been the strongest witches the team had dared to grab, and they were currently being used to harvest more of the chemical. Thomas had been quite successful at developing a synthetic version, but he and William preferred to have some of the real stuff on hand just in case.

Unfortunately for the witches, harvesting it was a pretty damaging process. The surgery left them brain-dead. As long as Thomas didn't take too much too quickly, and as long as they continued to care for the witches' bodies, kept them hydrated and fed, they'd produce the chemical for some time to come.

Tubes had been inserted into their skulls. Thomas used those to harvest the chemical. The witches weren't the most attractive creatures, tubes running this way and that, their scalps bald and scarred. But their appearance was of no concern. Their worth lay inside those skulls.

William heard an annoying tapping, and he turned around to see Thomas standing before the computer. William recognized the disc Thomas was viewing. It was a recording of one of their subjects Changing. It was odd to watch—like watching himself shifting and then freezing just before the shift completed.

William didn't particularly care that the shift wasn't complete. The shifters still possessed the strength, the speed, and the animal instincts needed. Thomas wouldn't be happy, though, until he knew why the shifts were incomplete. William didn't give a damn about Thomas's happiness, but when Thomas wasn't happy, he was a serious pain in the ass.

"I still don't understand why their forms look so bizarre." Thomas frowned, ever the scientist. "Only a few of them have been able to shift at all, and not one of them has been strong enough to complete the full shift."

"Perhaps it is not a question of strength," William said with a shrug. "We are forcing their bodies to accept this new change. Perhaps a minor shift is all they will ever accomplish. If you want me to be honest, I don't give a flying fuck if they will ever run on four legs through the forest. I care for the soldiers you are breeding, ones that will be loyal to us."

Thomas turned away from Dena and focused on William. "As I said, this is not wise. Dena is little more than a child when it comes to her new powers. Sending her out could be her death, and I'd rather not lose the one successful specimen from this particular study."

Patting Thomas's shoulder, William said, "You worry too much. After all, this is just a mortal we are sending her after. If she can't handle one weak, foolish human, is she really any use to us?"

Thomas had no argument for that. As William went over to the keypad and entered his code, the vampire murmured agreement. He also added an additional word of warning. "We do need to be careful. If there is one wrong move, if she is seen by the wrong person, even once, it could lead them to us."

William slid a glance at him as he watched the doors to Dena's cell slide open. If she was as clever as he suspected, she'd find a way to the girl in a relatively short amount of time. "If you speak of the Hunters, I'm aware we need to stay under the radar. But they didn't have much luck tracking our escapee, now, did they?"

"That is because they killed her. If they had kept her alive and questioned her . . ." Thomas's voice trailed off, but the unsaid words came through loud and clear.

"She was a failure. We both know that. If she hadn't escaped, we would have likely eliminated her within a few days. She was caught because she was weak and stupid. Dena is neither."

"I don't know. I was stupid enough to get taken in by you." Her voice didn't match her body. With those sultry, deadly looks, she should have had a low, husky, telephone-sex kind of voice. Instead, it was high-pitched, with a shrill sort of Minnie Mouse quality. Not the kind of voice that was going to be forgotten. And it definitely wasn't the kind of voice a man wanted to listen to for very long.

She sauntered in, stopping in front of the bank of monitors. She tapped long, ragged nails against one, studying the two brain-dead witches. "Geez. And I thought I was getting a bad deal. Least I'm not one of those turnips strapped down." When she turned around, she had a nasty little smile on her red mouth. "I'm just a guinea pig locked in a cage."

William grinned. "Now, Dena, you're not a guinea pig. You're a wolf. Well, sort of."

Dena smiled, that same evil smirk. "Sort of a wolf. I *was* a witch. What the hell am I now? And why am I . . . whatever I am now?" She twined a thick lock of black hair around her finger and strolled up to William. She was a tall bitch, that was for sure. He was six feet even. Dena stood just a breath taller than he did. He could feel the heat of her body, smell her skin—she smelled female, wild, and very, very appetizing.

His cock got hard as he thought about just how appetizing. He imagined she'd be completely ruthless in bed. She'd want to dominate. He usually took women who were a little meeker, a little more mild. But he had a violent urge to strap her down and climb on, fuck her until she screamed, until some of that defiance faded from her eyes.

Her nostrils flared, and her gaze slid down. As she stared at the ridge tenting the front of his trousers, her smile widened. "Is that a rabbit in your pants?" she murmured. Her eyes lifted, and she held his gaze as she brushed the back of her hand against his penis.

William reached down to cover her hands with his, but her hand shifted and she grasped him through his pants. She tightened her fingers, squeezing to the point of pain. "It had better be. Because if you're happy to see me, then you're stupider than you look," she purred, squeezing tighter and tighter.

He smiled back and arched into her hand. "Not stupid, precious. And if you want to do it right, it would be more effective to put that stranglehold on my balls instead of my dick," he whispered. Lowering his head, he licked her lips and pushed his tongue inside her mouth.

She tasted as wild and dark as he'd expected. He traced his tongue over her teeth, lingering on the sharp points of her canines. Purposefully, he slid his tongue along the tips, feeling his tongue slice open. As blood flooded both of their mouths, Dena groaned and tore away from him. She stared at him, wide-eyed, as she touched her fingers to her lips. Then, in a blur of motion, she reached up and clasped her hands around his skull, jerking his mouth back to hers.

HE'D finally left. Jess lay in her bed, staring up at the ceiling and brooding. Sleep escaped her, but that was nothing new. Sleep was a rare luxury for her and had been for most of her adult life. On most nights, she averaged two or three hours and catnapped for the rest of the night. Just another one of her little neuroses. And it had gotten worse since Randi's death. Now, on most nights, she might get an hour. If she got more than that, she was grateful.

Even though her lids felt heavy, she knew she wouldn't be sleeping for quite a while. Normally when she knew sleep was going to elude her, Jess wouldn't bother staying in bed. There was usually something either annoying, stupid, or funny on TV—sometimes she could numb herself into sleep with a B movie marathon.

But tonight she was just too drained. She might not be able to sleep, but she could feel herself zoning out. If she got relaxed enough, she might just get some rest. So long as she didn't really think . . . about . . .

Jess drifted in a comfortable haze, not quite awake. Total sleep lay before her, yawning like a warm dark cavern. Maybe she might even dream. A nice hot dream featuring none other than—

It's always a scary thing to come into complete wakefulness and realize you're not alone. Even more so when one knows one *should* be alone. Jess didn't stiffen, or sit up, or even move at first. She continued to lie there, her senses attuned, as she forced herself to breathe softly and deeply. Her skin crawled, and she was so damned tense that she felt like she was going to snap into pieces.

As the silence continued, she rolled over onto her back, careful to keep her movements slow and easy, just like somebody would when she shifted in her sleep.

By the door. A shadow just a little darker than the others. Vax? She studied the shadow from under her lashes, and although the height seemed right, nothing else did. For one thing, the übersexy witch just didn't strike her as the type to stand in a woman's bedroom and pull the creepy watcher act.

For another—the glitter in the eyes was all wrong. She could just barely make out the eyes, and although they did glow, it wasn't the same kind of glow. More like a cat's eyes glittering in the dark. An *evil* cat. There was something malevolent about it. Terror had wrapped a fist around her throat, and she couldn't control the sudden, harsh intake of breath.

The eyes seemed to disappear, as though the thing had blinked. When they reappeared, it had moved closer. Whatever it was, the thing would know she was awake now. Waiting any longer wasn't going to do her any good. Jess squinted her eyes and braced herself, and then focused her mind on the light switch by the door. As light flooded the room, the shadow lunged.

She couldn't make sense of what she was seeing, but she didn't need to know what it was before she could act. Instinct kicked in, and she lifted her hands. The hand movements had nothing to do with the kinetic energy jolting out of her—they were just an intuitive thing, like she was trying to shield herself against the coming attack. The physical power that shoved back the intruder came solely from her mind.

The thing went flying through the air, and it crashed into her wall so hard that plaster cracked. Jess took advantage of it and rolled from the bed, kicking the sheets away so they wouldn't tangle around her. She said a quick prayer that her legs would support her as she shoved herself to her feet. Her knees wobbled a little, but her legs held. One look at the thing, though, almost turned her into a quivering, mindless mass of fear.

"Holy shit."

Jess felt as if she had been pushed into one of those B movies. The thing surged to its feet as though it had springs in place of muscle. The muscles were huge. It looked like the thing had basketballs rolling around under its skin. The thing was enormous, probably close to seven feet. Thighs the size of tree trunks; big, brawny arms; and meaty-looking hands. No, they were more like claws, Jess decided, longer than fingers, with at least three articulated joints in each digit, topped with wicked, curving black claws.

The nose looked oddly flat in the thing's face; the jaw jutted forward. It had golden eyes that were almost lost under the huge, protruding brow ridge. It looked like a cross between Michael J. Fox in the old eighties flick *Teen Wolf*, and a Neanderthal. A very, very hairy Neanderthal. So damned hairy, she couldn't see skin under the hair. And the hair looked thick, coarse, almost like a pelt.

Jess swallowed. The thing looked at her, and its lips spread in a grotesque mockery of a smile. At the sight of it, a cold, nasty sweat broke out over her body. But if she thought the smile was disturbing, it was nothing like the deep, rasping voice that came out of its mouth. "You're going to be more fun than I thought."

The voice was alien, like the sound from one of those voice distorters she'd seen in movies, rough and growling, squeezing through a throat that had been made for a human, not an animal.

The terror threatened to drown her, but she battled it down, refusing to let it take hold. She had learned how to deal with emotion, whether it was fear, excitement, terror, or anxiety. She could funnel it away and let it dissipate on its own, all without ever letting down her shields. Jess didn't let down her shields. She didn't trust herself or the power inside her. Anger played tricks, with a gift like hers. Fear played even worse tricks, and the chaos that came from it could hurt people.

But Jess suspected she had only one chance get out of this alive, and it wouldn't work if she kept her shields up. Hell, she didn't even know if it would work after she let them down.

The thing pushed to its feet, and Jess acted, lowering her shields and screaming out for Vax. She just prayed that he wasn't far, and that he heard her call.

As the monstrous vision in front of her leaped at her, Jess dove to the side and lifted her hand. The blanket from her bed wrapped around the thing, tangling around its face. She tried to use the few brief seconds she had to get out of the room, but huge obsidian black claws shredded the blanket. The heavy silk brocade made a hideous sound as it tore.

Caught between the door to the hall and the door to the bathroom, she faced down the monster. She figured the thing would expect her to run for the door to the hall, so instead she ran for the bathroom. Jess used her mind to shove the door closed behind her, and then she looked at the big window over the bathtub. Her parents had designed this bathroom from top to bottom, an anniversary present to each other.

It had been finished just a few weeks before they died— they only got to enjoy it a little. But one thing in that bathroom just might be Jess's key to living a few days longer.

The window opened and closed. Leanne Warren had wanted to be able to sit in the bathtub on a summer night with the window open so she could smell the honeysuckle blooming in the backyard.

The lock opened with a quiet snick, but Jess's control was shot and the window slammed up so hard, it nearly shattered the glass. As she climbed through it, the door opened with a crash. She didn't dare stop to look back. Clinging to the windowsill for the briefest second, she took a deep breath and let go. It was only fifteen feet, but when she landed, she ended up on her back with her breath knocked out of her.

She wasn't quite sure she'd be able to move, but the sight of the thing leaping through the window was one hell of an impetus. Scrambling to her feet, she took off running towards the back door. As she drew closer, she focused on the door and unlocked it with her mind. She ran inside. It swung closed behind her and locked.

Not that the lock would do much good. She could hear the thing behind her, could practically feel it. She could smell it—a curious odor that reminded her of a wet dog and ground-up, bloody meat.

Like most people with psychically based gifts, she found that the fear-induced adrenaline rush sharpened her abilities. As long as she could control the fear, it would help her. Her telekinesis would become stronger, and so would her weak psychic ability. The few seconds she'd let her shields down to scream for help, she had caught some random, chaotic thoughts, oddly human thoughts from the monstrous, bizarre-looking creature.

It was irritated—no, not it. *She.* There was something uniquely feminine about the monster's thoughts. Something intangible, something Jess couldn't quite put a finger on. She was irritated, in a hurry, and pissed because Jess hadn't been the easy target she'd been expecting.

Sorry I disappointed you, Jess thought, feeling a little manic from the desperation rushing through her.

But apparently that brief connection with the creature

wasn't the end. What came next was little more than a flash
of memory, but it was enough to make her blood go cold.
As if she were watching through the she-wolf's eyes, Jess
could see Thomas Fitzpatrick, striding down a long white
hallway, a long white coat flapping around his legs. He
held a clipboard in his hand, and as the woman watched,
he stopped in front of her, studying her with an oddly clinical stare. "You still can't make the full shift, can you?"

The woman made no response, just stared at Thomas
with disgust and frustration. She wanted *out*. She wanted
to run. She wanted to hunt. Feed. Kill.

The blood thirst in those thoughts was enough to make
Jess sick to her stomach, and she tried to rip herself out of
the she-wolf's memory. The flash wasn't done yet, though.

Thomas tapped his pen against his lips, cocking his head
as he studied Dena. "How did the moon feel last night,
Dena?"

Then he turned his head, calling down the hallway. As
footsteps approached, Thomas punched a button and a
clear-paneled door slid away. He stepped in—the woman
wanted to grab him and rip his heart out. But before she
could even lift a hand, somebody grabbed her.

The last thing Jess picked up from the woman's mind
was a needle, and how the woman struggled as it slid into
her arm, her very *human* arm. Jess felt a residual burn as
the poison pumped inside Dena's.

Poison—

Finally Jess was jerked out of the memory flash. Just in
time, too. She barely managed to duck the clawed hand
that came swinging at her head. Fear had dried the spit in
her mouth, and her heart was pounding so loudly, she figured the wolf-thing could hear it as well.

She took off running once more, dashing up the stairs.
She took them three at a time, and Jess still wasn't running
fast enough. She needed to get away. But she wasn't sure
she could make it to the car, and even if she could, that
thing could bust through the windows as if they were paper.

Her purse was by the bed, though. And inside it, her

Browning. If she could just make it . . . Jess rounded towards her bed and plowed straight into a rock-hard chest.
Big calloused hands closed over her upper arms and she
started to struggle, but the warm scent of his skin permeated her senses and she realized it was Vax.

"Oh, thank God," she whispered. She didn't have more
than a second to heave out a sigh of relief. She could hear
the thing behind her.

"There's a—" That was all she got out before Vax
shoved her away. *Far* away. Jess ended up skidding down
the polished wooden floors of the upstairs hallway on her
butt, stopping only when she crashed into the wall. Her
head flew backward, slamming into drywall. He'd pushed
her so hard, she felt like her teeth rattled in her skull.

She'd suspected that he had a lot of power inside that
long, sinewy body. But she hadn't realized just how physically strong he was. The animal-woman was probably close
to seven feet tall, but when she lunged for Vax, he met her
head-on. He ducked under one slashing claw, slid behind
her, and wrapped his arms around the thing's waist. He
twisted, taking the thing to the floor with him. He didn't stay
down long, but rolled to his feet. As he stood, Jess saw that
he was holding a wicked, long knife. It glinted in the faint
moonlight.

The creature surged upward, powerful muscles uncoil-
ing. The she-bitch looked at Vax and growled. Jess winced
as the deep noise reverberated through the air. Even if nobody had heard the window breaking, and that wasn't
likely, somebody would hear sooner or later.

They'd call the cops, and Jess couldn't even imagine trying to explain this.

But that particular worry was going to have to go on the
back burner for now. Jess felt something roll through the
air, and instinctively she dropped to the ground. She
wrapped her arms around her head, but from the corner of
her eye, she saw something neon blue arrowing through
the air, hurtling towards Vax. He swore, and there was a
huge crash, a noise she felt more than heard.

Jess turned her head a little more and saw Vax rising from the floor. She caught a glimpse of the wall behind him. It was blackened, smoke rising from it in delicate little wisps. *"Shit,"* Jess whispered.

That blue thing she'd seen did that. And it hadn't come from Vax. Reluctantly, she turned her head and looked at the she-wolf. She was looking at Vax, and her misshapen mouth was twisted in a bizarre smile. "Surprise," she said, her voice a deep, guttural snarl.

She lifted a hand. When Jess saw the spinning, writhing mass of fire in the she-creature's hand, everything inside her went cold with fear. *That's not right.* That *thing* was some sort of shape-shifter. Shape-shifters didn't have magick. Did they?

This one did. The fire went hurtling towards Vax, but it didn't strike him. It landed in front of him, and huge fiery pillars erupted from the gleaming wooden floor, surrounding Vax. Jess felt a scream building in her throat, and she scrambled to her hands and knees. She had a weird thought that she should do something to help, but what? Her father had been a sergeant in the local fire department, and he had drilled fire safety into their heads, including the need to always be prepared. Jess still kept a small fire extinguisher on each floor, but the small one she had under the bathroom sink wasn't going to do that much good.

It was all she had, though. She couldn't see the sink from where she sat, and she inched across the floor, hoping the she-wolf wouldn't see her. Stretching out on her belly, she saw the bathroom sink. It opened silently, and she stared at the extinguisher, watching as the small red canister slid out of the mounting bracket.

It cleared the frame and flew across the hall to her hand. Shoving to her knees, Jess climbed to her feet. She broke the safety seal. The tiny sound was horribly loud, and she winced, looking towards the thing.

The she-bitch wasn't looking at her, though. Quickly, Jess pointed the extinguisher towards Vax. She squeezed the trigger, moving closer. Foam went spraying out in front of her, but by that time she realized the fire was out. She ended up covering Vax with foam. He wiped the white muck away from his face and slid her a narrow look before looking towards the she-bitch.

From the corner of his eye, he could see the fire extinguisher in her hand, and Vax had to smile a little, despite the situation. He was splattered with white foam, and his eyes stung as he wiped it away.

He flicked the excess foam off and glanced at the strange-looking wolf creature. "You're good," he murmured. It wasn't fire he used. He simply forced his power inside of her and knocked her unconscious. Stepping over her still body, he added, "I'm better."

Holding out a hand to Jess, he helped her to her feet. She looked at him from head to toe, and as he tried to push his hair back, foam dripped from his fingers. Jess covered her mouth. As she muffled her laughter, Vax rolled his eyes. "You don't have time for this. Come on, we have to get out of here. As in, now. Somebody would have heard us."

It took less than three minutes for them to get out of the house, but it was still too much time. Lights from the neighboring houses were on, and as he carried out the unconscious wolf creature, he saw a couple of curtains flutter as though somebody was peeking outside.

Great. Now Jess's neighbors could tell the cops they'd seen a suspicious-looking character throwing something into Jess's trunk. "This is just too perfect for words," he muttered, but nobody was around to appreciate his sarcasm. Jess was in the driver's seat, staring towards him with wide, worried eyes.

Police would be here in just a few minutes, and they had to be far away.

He groaned under the were's weight as he shifted her in his arms. She probably weighed over three hundred pounds in this form. He should have forced her into human form before knocking her out. Would have been a lot easier to carry. But he didn't have the time to try that right now. He dumped her in the trunk and slammed the top down. He said a quick prayer that she wouldn't regain consciousness for a while, and then he ran around to the passenger door and climbed in.

Jess sat in the front seat, wearing nothing more than a skinny strapped tank top and loose lounge pants. Her purse lay on the floorboard, half of the contents spilled. She must have just thrown it inside when she climbed in. He slid inside, and the foam clinging to him smeared all over the butter-soft tan leather interior. "This is probably going to do a serious number on your leather."

Jess slammed the car into reverse. "Get me out of this alive. Help me find Masters. We'll be even."

She peeled out of her driveway, and he warned her, "Don't drive too fast. Your neighbors have already called the police."

Instantly she slowed down. By the time they reached the entrance to the classy subdivision where she lived, Jess was driving at a normal speed. They passed two squad cars on the way out, and she didn't so much as blink. "You handle stress pretty well."

She glanced at him. "You expect me to start driving all suspicious and secretive-like? Give them a reason to pull me over? I've got a werewolf in the trunk of my car. I don't think the average officer is equipped to handle it. Which means you and I need to get that thing away from here." Jess fell silent for a minute, and then she said softly, "I haven't ever seen a werewolf before. I didn't think they'd look like . . . that."

"They don't." Vax stared out the window, watching the streetlights turn into a blur as she sped up.

"That—you mean that wasn't a werewolf?"

"I'm not real sure what it was." Vax scrubbed his hands over his eyes before looking up and staring around them. "We need to get someplace isolated. Fast."

Jess nodded. "Does this mean you haven't ever seen that kind of thing before?"

"I have. Once."

The were in the back looked almost exactly like the one

he had run into with Kane and Kendall a year ago in Salt Lake City. He'd tried tracking it, but there was no path, nothing to track.

Kendall had checked with the Hunters and with the Council. A creature like that hadn't ever been seen by any of the Hunters. The only one he knew about was the one he'd killed last summer—and burned before they could learn a damn thing about her.

He felt Jess staring at him and turned his head to look at her, seeing an expectant look on her face. He cocked a brow at her. "What?"

"You going to expand on that a little? You saw something like that . . . once? Where? What is it? If she's not a werewolf, is she some other sort of shifter?" In the dim light coming off the dashboard, her face looked pale, her eyes dark, scared. But she was holding together.

When she'd called out to him, it had almost knocked him off his feet. It had been out of control, full of power and fear, and he was terrified he wouldn't make it in time. He knew it in his gut. He'd get there too late, again, and Jess—

"It didn't happen," he muttered. "Get it together." He looked over his shoulder towards the trunk, dread twisting in his gut. He'd made it, this time. But if they didn't find out what the hell these things were, how they'd come to be, there were going to be a lot of next-times and a lot of lives lost.

"She's a werewolf—just not a right one." The car slowed down and he looked back out the front, watching as Jess exited the expressway and took a smaller county highway. This late at night, it was empty, and from the looks of it, there was nothing much in the direction they were heading.

They were both silent for a while. The only noise came from the wind blowing through the open window. Their unwilling passenger was silent. Vax kept his ears tuned, and the only sound she made was an occasional growling little grunt. As Jess slowed down to make a left, he could just barely hear a faint, steady heartbeat.

"Where should we go?" Jess asked softly. "What do we do?"

Vax turned to look at her. Her eyes looked nearly black in the faint light and blood streaked from numerous little scrapes along her shoulders and arms. They needed someplace safe, someplace out of the way. "I don't know, Jess. I just don't know." He let his head fall back against the headrest and closed his eyes. "Give me a minute, okay? Just drive."

"What if she wakes up?"

"I'll deal with that when it happens."

CHAPTER 7

J ESS climbed into the car, her entire body aching. In her right hand, she held something more precious than gold: coffee, piping hot, so damned strong that it would probably eat away her stomach lining. The one sip she'd taken in the store had burned her tongue and sent energy zinging through her veins.

Pure bliss.

She jammed the keys into the ignition and shifted into drive. As she pulled out of the parking lot, she looked at her unexpected partner. She was a little disgusted at what she saw.

On her way into the gas station, she'd caught a brief glimpse of herself. Hair a fricking mess, bags under her eyes, and wearing her pajamas. She looked awful.

Vax, on the other hand, looked refreshed, as wide-awake as if he had climbed from bed after eight solid hours of sleep. At some point during the night, they'd stopped at a rest area and he'd run into the bathroom and cleaned off the foam.

He hadn't slept all night, and the black T-shirt had white

streaks left over from the foam she'd sprayed him with, and he still looked good enough to eat. Jess had a passing thought—what would he do if she pulled onto the shoulder, crawled over the console, planted her butt in his lap, covered that mouth with hers, and rubbed her body against his?

A grin tugged at her lips. If she had the energy, she just might have tried it. Screw the fact that he was a hell of a lot more complication than she was ready to handle. After the night she'd had, she was ready to forget about everything for a while.

Maybe even a long while.

If it weren't for Sleeping Beauty in her trunk, Jess would have seriously considered it. Almost as if thinking of her woke her up, Jess's unwilling passenger started to stir. Jess stared into her rearview mirror. The lights of the gas station were growing fainter, but not faint enough. If the wolf-woman got free, she could reach the gas station in minutes. The protective steel-and-bulletproof-glass cage where the attendant worked might help against robbers, but Jess didn't know if it would hold against the wolf-creature.

That thing could tear the woman apart.

Jess couldn't deal with any more blood on her hands. Fear made her mouth go dry, and she looked towards Vax as fists pounded against the trunk lid. "What do I do now?"

His eyes were grim. A chill raced down her spine as she saw the little lightning-streaky things shooting across the stormcloud irises. "Just keep driving as long as we can. She can't get much leverage back there, so it might take a few minutes to get out."

"Oh, well, that's a relief. We're buying a few minutes." Jess heard her biting, sarcastic tone and flinched. This was none of his fault. In a brusque tone, she said, "Sorry."

He didn't look at her, but a faint smile appeared on his lean, sexy face. It didn't quite reach his eyes, though, and even that faint smile disappeared quickly enough as another flurry of pounding sounded from the trunk. There was a horrendous shrieking sound, the sound of metal scraping against metal. Her trunk went flying up with a crash, and Jess jumped. Fists banged on the roof. When a dark, hairy hand slammed down on the windshield, Jess screamed. She was going to hate that when she thought back, she knew she would, but she couldn't stop it.

She swerved, trying to throw the wolf-woman off. "You got any ideas over there, hotshot?"

He had both hands planted against the dashboard, and his mouth was set in a hard, tight line. "Yeah, pull over before you kill us both."

Considering that her life was pretty much in his hands, Jess managed to keep her mouth closed. Just barely. She slammed on the brakes and spun the wheel. The car went into a controlled turn, slamming her against her door. If she hadn't been wearing her seat belt, she probably would have whacked her head on the glass.

The desperate, reckless move worked, though. She watched, a little dazed, as the wolf-woman went flying through the air. The car hadn't even stopped completely when Vax threw open the door. Jess saw silver glint as he went after the were. His knife.

Jess could hardly see a thing—it was so dark, just the thin sliver of a moon shining down on them. It didn't seem to affect the two fighting. She heard masculine grunts, animalistic growls, muffled cussing—then a sharp, yelping sort of cry. That weird magickal tension spiked in the air, and then Vax's voice: "Oh, no, you don't—" Vax's words carried across the night. Squinting her eyes, she could just barely make out the silver flash as Vax's knife cut through the night.

Part of her didn't want to leave the car, but Jess had to know what had happened. After she climbed out the door, she rubbed her sweaty palms against her legs. Walking over the dew-slick grass, she muttered, "What in the hell have you gotten mixed up in?"

A soft, warm chuckle came from her left, practically in her ear. She jumped and then reached out, slamming the heel of her hand against his chest. "Damn it, don't do that," she hissed.

"I'm pretty sure I tried to tell you before that you didn't want to get messed up in this." He cupped a hand around her arm. "Go back to the car."

Shaking her head, Jess tugged against his hand. "Is she . . . dead?"

He sighed. She felt the warm brush of his breath against her cheek. "Go back to the car, Jessica. Please."

Jerking her arm away, she said, "Don't call me Jessica." Turning her back to him, she started carefully making her way across the wet grass. She had to see. Maybe it was the reporter in her, or maybe it was just sheer nosiness. But she had to see.

"Don't get so close," Vax growled in her ear. He grabbed her arm again, guiding her to the left. Just then, the moon passed out from behind some clouds and she could just barely see the ground. A big, clawed hand was inches away. As Jess drew back, the hand lifted, slashing at the spot where she would have stepped.

"Ah . . . yeah. Good advice." Her breath wheezed out of her lungs, and she felt a little sick to her stomach. Those long, wicked claws, so close . . . one more step and the were could have grabbed her. It would take just a few seconds. If that thing got her on the ground, got her pinned, no amount of magick would save her.

"Can you make her change back to human?"

"I could. But I won't."

"Wouldn't it be safer?" At least in human form, the woman wouldn't have nails two or three inches long and sharp as razors. And those teeth—she could see the moonlight glinting off the wet, gleaming incisors. Jess narrowed her eyes. "Damn it, is she contagious?"

"Possibly." Now he sighed. A warm hand reached up, rubbing the back of her neck. "I really don't know, since I don't know what she is. But it would have to come from the bite. It's spread through the saliva. HIV is easier to catch than the were genes."

But that didn't make her feel any better. She'd seen the teeth in that thing's mouth. The wolf started thrashing around on the ground, and Jess jumped, moving back even farther. "What did you do to her?"

"Silver nitrate," he said quietly. She could feel the soft caress of his breath on the back of her neck. She couldn't quite stop the shiver that ran through her. Out of the corner of her eye, she saw his hand, and she cocked her head, studying the small vial he was holding. He tossed it up and then caught it before he slid it inside his jacket, out of sight. "She's not a powerful were. The nitrate will keep her from shifting."

"That won't keep her from running away."

"No. But being hamstringed will." There was no emotion in his voice as he said it. She wasn't going to ask for any more details on that one, Jess decided. "With the silver in her system, she can't shift. She'll need a healer to get it out of her bloodstream before she can change. The silver will also slow down her healing process." His voice was level, but she sensed a tension inside him, felt it in the undercurrents. He didn't like what he'd done.

"So this bought us a little more than a few minutes, then, right?" she asked, shifting on her feet so that she could see him but still keep an eye on the wolf lady.

He nodded. He cupped her cheek. "A day or two. Enough time for me to figure something out." He rubbed his thumb over her lower lip and gazed at her. For a second, she thought he was going to kiss her. Hot little ribbons of excitement wrapped around her belly, but then the moment passed, and he pulled away.

"Come on—we need to get out of here. Can you open the trunk?"

Jess stood off to the side and watched as Vax threw the wolf's huge, bulky body into the trunk. "Wow. So just how much can you lift?" Although the wolf was female, there was nothing delicate or soft about her. She looked damn heavy.

Vax slanted a look at Jess. "Beats the hell out of me," he responded. "I got better things to do than go to a gym." He touched a hand to the wolf's chest, resting it between the fur-covered breasts. He held it there a moment and then pulled his hand back. He rubbed it down the outside of his jeans, as if he was trying to wipe away something digusting. He forced the trunk door down, and it closed with a thunk.

"Yeah, I guess running around and saving the world is pretty good exercise." Apparently *very* good exercise. Unconsciously, her eyes traveled down over his body, lingering on the long, hard muscles of his legs. "You don't work out at all, huh?"

That faint half smile appeared on his face, and he reached up, toying with the ends of her hair. "I don't have time for that. And I don't run around saving the world. I stopped Hunting a long time ago. This is just . . . a thing."

"You don't run around Hunting. But you're a Hunter."

Lashes drooped low over his eyes. She felt his grip tighten on her hair, and he lowered his head, brushing his lips across her brow. "I am no longer a Hunter. Left it behind years ago."

"You're so damned confusing. If you left it behind years ago, then what are you doing here now?"

"Now?" He grinned. His teeth were a white flash in the darkness of his face. His other hand came up and curved over the back of her neck. "Right now I'm getting ready to kiss you."

And he did.

His lips felt warm, almost gentle as he pressed them against hers. He lifted his head, and she wondered if maybe he was going to let it go at that, with that one, almost chaste kiss. She swallowed and lifted her lashes, staring up at him.

Nope. He wasn't stopping there, not with that look in his eyes. His eyes were a deep, smoky gray, and he held her gaze as he reached up and threaded his hands through her hair. "You've got this thing about playing with my hair," she said.

He smiled, a slow, teasing curve of his mouth. Lowering his head, he pressed his lips to hers and murmured, "I can think of some other things I'd like to play with." Then he pushed his tongue inside her mouth, using his grip on her hair to bring her closer.

Jess hadn't ever been one for waxing poetically about anything. Although she enjoyed the idea of romance, it wasn't something she'd had much time for in life. She hadn't met too many people who'd been likely to change that, either. Hadn't ever felt the earth move just because somebody touched her.

At least not until now. It seemed as though the earth had opened up under her feet, but instead of falling, she went flying. Her hands came up, clutching at the front of his jacket. The strength went out of her legs and she sagged against him. If he hadn't wrapped an arm around her waist, she was pretty sure she would have collapsed to the ground in a hot, boneless puddle.

Jess hadn't ever felt so seduced by a simple kiss. Even though it didn't feel at all simple. He kept his hands where they were, one fisted in her hair, one curving over her waist. But every inch of her skin buzzed. She felt hot, her heart slamming away inside her chest, and deep inside, she ached. Throbbed. Damn it, she felt empty.

Vax pulled back, nipping at her lower lip. Jess leaned against him, sliding her arms up his chest and wrapping them around his neck. She couldn't get close enough. She could feel the thick, hard length of his cock against her belly, and she rubbed herself against him.

Noise intruded. A semi came roaring down the highway, and there was a thumping from within her trunk. Jess barely heard it, but Vax did. He eased back and she tried to follow him, her hands tangling in his hair. She felt him laugh, then heard him swear. "That's just my luck. *Now* you seem interested in listening to something other than your head."

Hands closed around her arms, moving her back, and Jess felt blood rush to her face as she sucked in a deep breath of cool night air. It cleared her head like a bucket of icy water, and she jerked her hands away from him as if she'd been scalded. Shit. She'd wrapped herself around him like a vine. She would have been perfectly happy if he had stripped them both naked and they had gone at it on the trunk of the car like a couple of teenagers.

Hell—she hadn't done this sort of thing even when she had been a teenager. Hadn't ever done this sort of thing. Sex wasn't a burning need for her, and she liked it that way. Burning was out of control. Jess hated anything that took away her control.

Vax wouldn't just take away her control. He would shatter it, destroy it completely and totally, and Jess didn't know whether she'd ever get it back. Careful not to look at him, Jess stepped back and ran her hands through her hair. Her voice was stilted as she said, "Shouldn't we get going?"

He opened his mouth to say something, but Jess turned away, walking around to her side of the car. As she climbed in, she sensed him moving towards the passenger side. She started the car and slammed it into drive. She pulled out onto the road, gravel flying behind her as she accelerated.

"Do you want me to say I'm sorry?"

Jess stared straight ahead. She was afraid that if she looked at him again, she just might pull back over and crawl into his lap. So what if they were on a public road? It was night. So what if there was a werewolf-thing in the trunk of her BMW? It wasn't too much of a threat this very second.

"Do you?"

Through gritted teeth, she growled out, "No."

His hand came up, cupping the back of her neck. She tensed up, mostly to keep from leaning into him. "You sure about that?"

She hunched her shoulders and tried to shrug his hand away. "Apologize for what?"

"For kissing you, maybe?" Then he leaned over the console and brushed her hair back. Vax pressed his lips to her ear and asked, "Or maybe it's because I stopped?"

I'm not answering that question on the grounds that I might embarrass myself. By stopping the car and demanding that he pick back up where he'd left off. Her common sense finally started to kick in, and a quiet voice in her head reminded her of why she hadn't let him kiss her before. He was too damned complicated, and Jess had a bad feeling she could fall for him.

Really fall—like the fall-in-love kind of fall.

Even if this wasn't the completely wrong time for it, even if she wasn't trying to track down Randi's killer, he was the completely wrong kind of man. He was a *witch*, for crying out loud. A Hunter. They didn't stay in one place, and they led lives that would make the life of a Navy SEAL seem dull.

She tried once more to pull away from his touch, and this time he let her, moving his hand away with one last, lingering caress. "You don't have to apologize," she said.

His tone was wry as he said, "But you'd rather I not do it again."

She finally dared to look at him, and saw that he was watching her with that faint, aggravating, sexy little smile. The kind of smile that told her he was going to do pretty much whatever the hell he wanted—and if he decided he wanted to kiss her again, he knew she wouldn't stop him.

"You're impossible," she mumbled.

"So I've been told."

T HANK God for gym bags.
     Jess always kept hers in the backseat in case she felt like hitting the gym. The billboard they had seen on the side of the highway had been like a message straight out of heaven.

Not because of the hot food, or the hot coffee, although the promise of caffeine had her nearly drooling.

Nope, the sign for the truck stop had been glorious because it had in big, bold yellow letters: CLEAN SHOWERS. As she climbed from the car, she was all but itching. Jess paused only long enough to reach under the backseat and grab something.

She slid it inside her gym bag, watching the back of Vax's head. He never looked her way as she slid the bag's strap over her shoulder. "I won't take too long," she promised.

Vax sat in the passenger seat with his eyes closed and his arms folded over his chest. He didn't respond, just lifted his lashes and glanced at her before closing his eyes once more. Covered with grime and sweat, she was so anxious to get clean, she practically started stripping in the middle of the very public hallway.

She took the bag inside the shower stall with her. Her clothes might get a little damp, but she couldn't let it out of her sight. The bag was waterproof, though, so she hoped she'd have dry, clean clothes to wear when she finished.

It was a lot cleaner than she'd expected, but at this point she wouldn't have cared how filthy the place, so long as it had running water. Not only did it have running water, but it had hot, pulsating streams of running water. She stood under the shower with her face upturned, letting the water beat some of the dust and dirt out of her hair before she shampooed it.

She felt just a little guilty. Vax wouldn't leave the car, or their reluctant passenger, even to use the bathroom, so he was missing out on the shower. She washed her hair and then grabbed the body wash and started scrubbing every last inch of her skin. She had dirt and grass stains smudged on her hands and arms from when she'd hit the ground. Until she'd looked in the mirror in the bathroom, she'd had no idea just how bad she looked.

And she'd gone into gas stations looking like this. She grimaced and rinsed off the body wash. "I bet that made an impression."

She knew she had felt grimy—she just hadn't realized how very grimy she was.

"You had other things on your mind." Like the werewolf in her trunk and the witch in her front seat. The most disturbing thing, though, was that the witch was bothering her a lot more than the werewolf was.

Jess hadn't realized just how absolutely wonderful clean clothes were until she was pulling on the black yoga pants she wore when she worked out. The sports bra and form-fitting black T-shirt followed, and then she finished towel drying her hair.

She tossed the ruined pajamas into the garbage can and repacked her gym bag. She left the bathroom feeling almost normal. Even a little hungry. The truck stop had one of those travel stores with anything and everything that a person who lived on the road might need.

Including clothes.

Considering how the guy liked to eat, she doubted the junk food that filled the store was going to do much for him, so she went to the café-style food area and bought him a twelve-inch meatball sub, a salad, some chips, and a couple of cookies. She grabbed some apples for herself and hit the clothes section. After finding some jeans that looked like they might fit Vax, Jess grabbed two pair and a plastic package of black T-shirts. There was a small selection of underwear, but for some reason she couldn't quite see him as the tighty-whitey kind of guy. She did grab some socks for him, though.

She ended up having to get a basket to carry everything to the front of the small travel store, but the cashier didn't so much as bat an eyelash. Jess figured they had a lot of people come through who had to buy everything but the kitchen sink from this place.

Vax looked a little surprised when she dumped the bag of clothes into his lap. "I figure once we get back on the road, we'll find someplace where you can change by the car without getting arrested for indecent exposure."

He smiled a little. "Thanks."

As she rooted through the bag for his food, she looked in her rearview mirror. "She making any noise?"

Vax shrugged. "Just a little. The silver's making her weak. She feels pretty groggy."

Jess arched a brow. "She tell you that?"

He tapped a finger to his temple and said, "She didn't

have to." He gave her an appraising look. "I'm kind of surprised you aren't picking up anything from her. I thought you said your psychic gift was weak. That wasn't a weak call I felt last night."

"It is. I was terrified last night—you know what terror does to psychic gifts." She handed him the plastic bag holding his sub and the rest of his food, and then she pulled her apple out of the bag. She set it on the console while she started the car and pulled out. She breathed a little more easily as they left the truck stop, and all those helpless, clueless people, behind them. Before taking a bite of her apple, she glanced at him. "I don't think I said thank you."

"Sure you did. When I was worried I might tear up your leather, you told me we could call it even if I got you through this alive." He grinned a little as he ripped the wrapper off his sub. "So you decided living isn't so bad, huh?"

"I can't get Masters if I'm dead," she said softly.

"You don't really want to die, Jess. There's too much life inside you."

At that moment, she could easily hate him. Life? She felt dead inside. She'd felt like this for so long. "Don't try to psychoanalyze me, pal."

He shrugged. "Didn't realize that was what I was doing. Just telling you what I see when I look at you." He was quiet for a few minutes as he polished off half of the sandwich.

"You handle yourself well. Hard to believe you're only human." He skimmed his fingers down her temple and mused, "Even if you do have something extra behind those pretty eyes. You're strong, you're smart. You also taste pretty damn good." He touched her mouth lightly, and Jess felt her heart skip a beat or two. "You've got the prettiest eyes. I don't like to think about seeing them lifeless."

Her throat felt tight. She opened her mouth to speak, but nothing wanted to come out except a couple of weird little hiccouping sounds. Okay, compliments hadn't ever impressed her much. How come one coming from him left her temporarily speechless?

Jess cleared her throat and was finally able to speak. "Would you stop acting like you found me standing on a chair with a rope around my neck?"

His hand settled possessively over the back of her neck, which didn't do much to help clear her clouded mind. "Just don't go using me as a means to an end, not if you don't plan on walking away from this." He squeezed lightly and then pulled his hand away.

Foil crinkled, and Jess watched out of the corner of her eye as Vax popped a potato chip into his mouth. He chewed slowly, his eyes staring straight ahead. "You know, I've been thinking. There are some people I need to talk to. We need to figure out what to do about our friend. They might be able to help."

Jess wasn't sure what he was talking about. "Friend?" Well, shit. She sounded bright. The weak thump on the trunk of the car jerked her back into reality. Back to the reality where she had a monster in her trunk that wanted to bleed her. "Oh." She heaved out a sigh and rubbed her temple. A vivid flash from the past night leaped before her eyes—obsidian black claws and cold, hungry eyes. "So what do we do? Are we going to drive and see them?"

"Well, since I'm not sure where they are, that wouldn't be very practical. We'll find a place to stay, then I'll track them down."

"What do we do until then?" If she could have taken the question back, she would have done it. His eyes dropped to study her mouth, and a wicked grin curved his lips. She could feel the blood rushing to heat her cheeks—and elsewhere. That grin of his had a bad effect on her. It made her feel too hot and too hungry. Dangerous. He could make her forget anything and everything. "Damn it, would you at least pretend to focus? Shouldn't we try to find out where she came from?"

"Hey, I am focused. I'm talented, blondie. I can focus on the problem we have in the trunk and still focus on you." Vax shrugged his shoulders, his attention shifting away from her. Irritation and frustration colored his voice as he said, "Besides, I've already tried that. The last time I saw a were like her, I spent weeks trying to track her and found nothing but dead ends."

There was another thump from the trunk, this one weaker. Still, for some odd reason, it formed a leaden weight in her belly.

The memory flash that Jess had picked up from the wolf-woman started to do a little tango through her mind. Thomas holding out a syringe as he stared at the woman in the cell and he said, *You still can't make the full shift, can you? How did the moon feel last night, Dena?*

Jess's mouth had gone dry. She swallowed against the knot in her throat and licked her lips nervously. "Maybe you didn't know where to start."

"That hasn't changed. I still don't know where to start. And I don't think *that* is going to help us." He shifted his gaze toward the trunk before leaning his head back and closing his eyes.

Dena. Her name was Dena. And whatever was going on with that woman had something to do with the syringe Thomas had been holding. Jess's belly felt queasy as angry little butterflies of anxiety started jumping around. She rubbed the back of her hand over her mouth. "I think I know where to start."

He flicked a glance at her. She didn't exactly feel that look was a vote of confidence. "Look, I'm sure you've got a whole smorgasbord of witches, vamps, weres, and whatnot. You can all get together and sit down in some dark, secret room, and brood over the fate of the universe. That's just fine. But . . ." Her voice trailed off. Damn it, why was she wasting her time? She was an investigative reporter trying to kill the man who'd killed her sister, and so far she hadn't been able to get even a good look at him.

This guy was a Hunter. He knew what he was doing.

She almost just shut up. Almost.

If that image she'd gotten from Dena was worth anything, Jess had a weird feeling they were in trouble. She made her voice sound a lot more certain than she felt. "Thomas."

He didn't say anything. The guy had a way of saying a thousand words with just one look. She bet those looks also tended to make people run off at the mouth. She was feeling a case of babbling coming on. In effort to keep the babbling to a minimum, she clamped her lips shut and drove.

*T*OUGH *little cookie, aren't you?*
         After she'd said that one word, just a name, Jess had fallen silent and continued to drive on down the small country highway like she didn't have a care in the world.

She had showered and changed at the truck stop. Her hair was still damp, and he could smell the faint tropical scent of shampoo. The pants she wore clung to her hips, butt, and thighs like a second skin, outlining her subtle curves. Despite what he had told her, he was having a hard time focusing on anything else. Although he knew he had more pressing issues at hand, the only one he could think about was how to find a way around this one—by pressing his body to hers and easing the hunger that burned through him.

From the trunk, he heard their passenger moving around sluggishly. She pounded once on the lid and then fell silent. Vax knew this wasn't going to last too long. It was just a matter of time, and they needed to be someplace a lot more secure before she woke up.

Which meant he really did need to focus on the job and not on how nice Jessica Warren's ass looked in a pair of snug black pants.

"Thomas."

When he spoke, she looked over at him, one pale blonde brow lifting.

"What about Thomas?"

Jess gave a short, concise explanation—he could see why the hell she'd decided to become a reporter. As she laid out the details of that little vision, she never once hesitated; her voice never rose, never changed rhythm. She seemed completely unaffected by it. She might as well have been giving a weather report. Vax, on the other hand, *was*.

Profoundly, disturbingly affected.

He knew she kept dismissing her psychic skills. But even if she did pick this up out of a rush of fear-induced adrenaline, her psychic ability wasn't one to be discounted. He blew out a breath and forced himself to think. Sounded like some sort of lab. And Thomas Fitzpatrick, was he a doctor?

"What was in the syringe?"

Finally her face showed some expression. The kind that displayed extreme sarcasm. "Gee, I don't know. I didn't think to ask while I was trying to pull myself out of her memories."

Vax hadn't realized just how much he had always relied on his Empathy to read people. Her shields were damned good. He got about as much off her as he'd get off a brick wall. That poker face of hers didn't help any, either. A little irritated, Vax draped an arm against the door, beating out a tattoo with his fingers. "Anything else?"

Jess shrugged restlessly. "No. Climbing inside somebody else's thoughts is a bit of a new experience. Mom and Randi were the only ones I've ever been able to pick up anything from, and then I usually had to be really close to them physically, or they had to be upset."

She turned her head, but not before he caught a glimpse of the sadness in her eyes. Her voice was muffled as she spoke. "Look, don't go reading much into this. I picked it up at random. I don't know why, and I don't know how reliable it is. It could just be a figment of my overactive imagination—I haven't ever woken up before in the middle of the night to find some monster in my room." She smiled sadly. "Mom and Dad used to tease me about my imagination. Mom would say that with my imagination, I ought to write a book. Maybe that's all it was, my imagination working overtime because a monster scared me out of my sleep."

"You don't really believe that."

She scowled. "No. No, I don't. I sure as hell wish I did, though."

He didn't blame her. "How are you so certain she's a monster?" Vax knew, but that was because he could feel the vibes coming off her. Their guest wasn't a happy camper. There was a gut-deep sense of rage inside the wolf-creature, and something that could only be described as evil.

Jess shivered a little, as if she were cold. The cool, implacable look on her face cracked, and he saw underneath, just for a second. Just long enough for him to see that she wasn't as unflappable as she wanted him to think. "I felt it when I took my little trip through her mind. Even before Thomas got his hands on her, she wasn't Girl Scout material. I think that's part of why they took her. But she's not the only one."

Silence fell. But it was a heavy kind of silence. Vax's mind spun back to the alley. Just hours ago. Jess had shoved a file at him, one full of images of women who'd been killed in terrible ways.

Not just women. Witches.

"The missing women."

Jess swallowed. Her hands tightened on the steering wheel. She glanced towards him, and he saw a world of fear in her eyes. "I'm afraid so."

CHAPTER 8

"Yuck."

Jess came awake with a jerk at the sound of the strange voice. She sat up in bed, her heart slamming against her ribs. She jumped out of the narrow cot, but the rough wool blanket tangled around her legs and she ended up fighting to get free of it instead of backing away from the voice.

When she finally kicked the blanket away, she had scrapped the idea of retreating.

The slender blonde standing in the doorway looked like a Kewpie doll—all curly blonde hair, big blue eyes, and peaches-and-cream skin. Her hair looked like one of those highlight jobs that cost a couple hundred dollars. People didn't have hair like that without chemical help, did they? Sunny gold, pale blonde, warm brown, all mixed together in a tumble of curls that fell past her shoulders.

She wore a worn-out sweatshirt that was probably three sizes too big and some of those skinny-legged jeans that didn't look good on 99.9 percent of the population.

Of course, they looked good on the Kewpie doll.

Jess decided right on the spot that she didn't like her. Both of them were skinny, but on this woman it looked good. She had that fragile, delicate look to her. Jess was too damned tall ever to look fragile or delicate.

"Who in the hell are you?" Jess demanded.

The woman arched her brows. They were the deepest shade of blonde possible without being brown. She stared at Jess guilelessly and said, "Me? I could ask the same of you. Vax, this isn't very smart, leaving her alone in here with *that*."

Vax appeared in the doorway, standing behind the cute little blonde. He had a look of irritation on his face. "Didn't I tell you to wait?"

The woman blinked, and then a smile canted up the corners of her mouth. "Why, yes. I believe you did." She continued to stare at Jess, head tilted to the side. A puzzled frown replaced the smile. "What are you?"

Jess reached up and scrubbed her hands over her face. It didn't help. She still felt half asleep. "Vax, what in the hell is going on? Who's the kid?"

"Nessa. *Move.*"

The blonde glanced over her shoulder at Vax and then sauntered into the small, ramshackle cabin. Who owned the cabin, Jess didn't know. They were about an hour west of Louisville, Kentucky, close to the Ohio River. They were supposed to be waiting for help. But this kid wasn't exactly the kind of reinforcements that Jess had been counting on.

"Vax."

He slanted a look at Jess and muttered, "Not now." He looked about ready to pull out his hair by the roots. He slammed the door closed behind him, stomping inside. His feet made heavy thudding sounds on the wooden plank floor, and he looked mad enough to spit nails.

"Call for help, and I get this," he mumbled under his breath. He shot the blonde a dark, evil look and then went over to the bathroom doorway. There was no door. Jess figured at one time there must have been. There were still hinges attached to the wall, rusted and old.

Dena lay in the bathtub restrained by the silver in her bloodstream and little else. Jess could take the small cabin. Even though it was so damned small that she and Vax kept bumping into each other, she could take it. She could take sleeping on the narrow cot, and she could take the faint fishy smell that hung in the air.

What she couldn't take was having to stay so close to Dena. Every time Jess closed her eyes, she saw the wolf-woman again, and those wicked, long black claws. Those soulless eyes. All of that hate, menace, and violence, re-strained by a chemical? It wasn't very reassuring. The sil-ver manacles on her helped, but not much.

Vax stared into the bathroom for a minute, then turned back around to stare at Nessa. The girl gave him a sweet smile and stretched out on Jess's cot. "You know, you really should show more appreciation, Vax." Her voice was prim. Mary Poppins kind of prim. She gave Vax an arch look, and he just scowled back

He closed his eyes. Jess got the feeling he was either counting to ten or praying for patience. Or both.

"I drive him insane." She said it in a conspiratorial voice and winked at Jess.

Jess smiled weakly. "Not a far drive, is it?"

Vax grunted. "Getting shorter by the minute." He braced a shoulder against the wall and glared at the blonde.

"Why don't you show me what's behind door number one," Nessa said, rolling to her feet. She hooked her thumbs in her jeans pockets and headed towards the bath-room. "I hope she doesn't look much worse than she feels. She feels all wrong to me."

"Brace yourself, beautiful. She's worse." Vax stepped into the bathroom, pressing against the wall to make room for a third person. Jess moved over to the doorway, cran-ing her head to see around him.

Both Nessa and Jess were outside the wolf's reach, but Vax wasn't. She-bitch struck out with one manacled hand, chains rattling. He jerked away, looking down at her with narrowed eyes. "Unless you want to lie there with that silver burning inside you for the next six months, you had better behave."

"Are you going to put her in time-out?"

Nessa was staring at Vax with wide eyes, a smile flirting with the corners of her mouth. He barely glanced at her. "Old woman, don't you have something better to be doing?"

Old woman? Jess looked back at the shorter woman. The kid didn't even look old enough to be out of college.

"I did. Then you called. I'd rather see what you're up to." She batted long, thick lashes at him, her smile turning flirtatious.

Vax winced, but Jess didn't see the look on his face. She was too busy trying to swallow the bitter jealousy that sprang to life as the woman moved around the table and rested a hand on Vax's back. There was an intimacy between them—Jess couldn't exactly describe it as sexual, but they knew each other. There was a bond there, no matter how irritated Vax appeared.

"I called Kelsey."

With a graceful shrug, Nessa replied, "Well, Kelsey wasn't there, now, was she?"

Vax opened his mouth but didn't say anything. He side-stepped out of the way as Nessa edged around him and peered down at Dena. The woman reached down and laid a hand in the middle of Dena's torso, just a little below the two small, misshapen breasts. Jess wouldn't have touched the she-bitch with a ten-foot pole, and she almost warned the girl, but Vax didn't looked worried.

"Oh my, Vax. She's a nasty one. You have a bad habit of finding trouble—I thought you were retired."

Disgruntled, Vax muttered, "Believe me, if I had any choice in the matter, I'd be home."

"Ah, yes. Your ranch. Such a lovely little spot."

Ranch . . . Jess could vaguely remember his mentioning a ranch. The knot of jealousy grew just a little bit bigger. She hadn't figured Vax was into the peppy, *young* teenaged type, but it looked as though Jess was off the mark. She could feel something bitter and rude burning on her tongue. She was just a millisecond from giving in to the ugly monster of jealousy when Dena struck out. Razor-sharp claws missed Nessa's chest as the small woman spun away, but just barely. When Nessa stopped, she looked down and held out her shirt, revealing two long, skinny tears in her sweatshirt where Dena's claws had shredded it.

"Was that really necessary?" Nessa asked. Her Mary Poppins voice was chilly as she glared at Dena.

From the bathtub, Dena snarled and bared her teeth at Nessa. She snapped her jaws together as if she were biting down on something. Jess was five feet away, and with Vax standing between her and the restrained wolf-woman, she was as safe as could be expected. But she still backed away.

Nessa, on the other hand, moved forward, leading with a short, straight-armed jab that caught Dena square on her malformed jaw. Jess heard the smack of flesh against flesh, and she winced reflexively as Dena's head flew back under the impact. Dena yelped a little but then looked at Nessa with hatred in her eyes.

"Not only are you an ugly mess, you're stupid as well," Nessa muttered, turning her back dismissively.

From the doorway came a new voice. "Agnes, love, please don't irritate it."

It was a deep, melodic voice, with a hypnotic accent that Jess thought was Scottish. Turning her head, she found that the voice belonged to a man every bit as intriguing as it was. He was big—that was the first thing she noticed. Too damned big for the small cabin. He seemed to dominate it, towering over everything and everyone. The deep red hair on his head was the second thing she noticed. Jess imagined a lot of women would sever an arm to have hair that color, but she had no doubt it was natural. He didn't strike her as the type who'd have the vanity to dye it.

He had deep blue eyes, the color of the eastern sky at twilight. Those eyes were currently fixed on the small blonde, filled with a mixture of amusement and exasperation.

Where the hell had he come from? The door hadn't

opened. There was one window, but it was too narrow for the likes of him. She turned to look at Vax, but if she thought he'd been irritated before, he was even more so now.

"What do *you* want?" Vax asked as he came out of the bathroom.

The giant gave a wide smile. "That is no way to speak to somebody you called for help. Where is this problem you spoke of? She smells . . . strange." He lifted his head, sniffing at the air. Jess wasn't sure how he could smell much of anything over the stink of cigarettes and old fish, but he did. He headed towards the bathroom and peeked inside.

He stepped a little closer to the tub and studied Dena with puzzled eyes. "I haven't ever seen anything like that." He looked back at Vax. "What is she?"

"A mess," Nessa said. Her nose wrinkled. Turning away with a shrug, she repeated, "Just a mess."

"You're so helpful." The giant took up the place that Vax had vacated, leaning against the wall.

Nessa smiled, but it didn't reach her eyes. Her eyes actually looked dull, almost lifeless. "I live to serve, Malachi," she said in a mocking tone.

As yet another woman stepped into the room, the look on the giant's face changed to complete and utter adoration. At that point, Jess just gave up trying to keep track of who was talking. She was tired. She was sore. She felt every little bruise and scrape she'd gotten during her mad dash to get away from the wolf-woman before the thing ripped her throat out. She wanted to go back to sleep, but it obviously wasn't going to happen.

The newcomer had red hair as well, but it was a sunny red-gold that looked like it belonged on a Pippi Long-stocking doll. She wore it in a fat braid that trailed halfway down her back, and as she moved to the bathroom, the giant caught her braid in his hand and jerked her head back, covering her mouth with his.

Damn.

The heat between them was hot and palpable, and when they parted, they looked at each other with an intimacy that made Jess squirm a little. There was such naked devotion on their faces, such love, it felt wrong even to be standing close to them while they shared the moment.

And for the second time in just a couple of minutes, Jess was overcome with a bout of longing so deep, it almost hurt. The woman rose on her toes and pressed her lips to the corner of the man's mouth and then looked at Jess. She smiled. It was a bright, open, friendly smile.

Great. Another peppy type. Just as vibrant as the curly hair trying to free itself from the long braid. Normally that sort of type irritated Jess. The cute blonde certainly did.

But there was something so warm, so friendly about the redhead that Jess couldn't help but smile back. When the woman held out a hand, Jess stepped forward and accepted it.

"Hi. I'm Kelsey. The big guy behind me is my husband, Malachi." She glanced out towards the slender blonde and smiled. "I've got a feeling that neither one of them bothered, so I'll introduce you to Nessa, our resident nutcase."

"Impertinent little brat." That came from Nessa.

There was something very strange about the way Nessa spoke. It wasn't just the proper, prim English accent. Looks aside, the woman sounded—old. Maybe not in years, exactly. Old-fashioned, mature, old-world . . . Jess wasn't sure of the right way to describe it. But with each passing moment, Nessa seemed less and less like the college coed that she appeared to be.

Kelsey moved around the table and slung an arm around Nessa's shoulders. "Awwww . . . I love you, too, Nessa."

Nessa rolled her eyes and then looked back at the table. "We have a bit of a mess on our hands, I am afraid." She glanced towards the bathroom and said, "Did you see Vax's little surprise? Nasty thing, isn't she? I'd wager he isn't going to stay and help us with it, either."

Vax didn't say a word. He actually looked like he'd rather not be here. He leaned against the wall, hands jammed deep inside his pockets and his mouth in a flat, unsmiling line.

"What is she?" Malachi asked. As he spoke, he turned his back to the doorjamb, standing so that he could see Dena and still look at the others. Dena snarled. There was something oddly challenging to it. Malachi narrowed his eyes and shoved off the wall, disappearing inside the bathroom. From where Jess stood out in the main room, she could see him. Dena struggled against her chains as the big guy moved closer. He bent low over the tub, and Jess said, "I wouldn't do that." She could just see those deadly black claws slicing through the air, ripping into flesh.

But the second the last word left her mouth, Dena started to whimper. Cringing, in fact. If the wolf-woman could have disappeared inside the yellowed bathtub to get away from Malachi, she would have.

Jess sort of understood why, too. Even though the guy wasn't looking at her, Jess had a sudden urge to cringe and hide herself. She even backed away, reaching out to wrap a hand around Vax's arm. He felt solid. Real. But she still couldn't get rid of the nasty taste of fear on her tongue.

"You vamps are handy bastards, but go easy on the bystanders, okay, Mal?" Vax shifted until he was standing behind Jess, but oddly, she felt a little more protected against that weird, irrational fear. Vax skimmed his hands up and down her arms, and with each slow, careful stroke, the fear bled away.

As the knot in her throat eased, Jess swallowed. Then she sucked in a lungful of air, staring at the man as he straightened over Dena's body. He glanced at Jess and shrugged. "Sorry."

Something in the cabin changed—although the lights hadn't flickered, it had seemed dark, and the air had felt cold and harsh. But as the man turned away, it all faded.

"Shit." It had been coming from *him.* Once more, she started backing away, but as her back came into contact with Vax's chest, she stopped. "He's . . . ah . . . a vampire?"

"Yeah. An ornery, evil one, at that. Just ignore him." Vax wrapped an arm around her in a gentle hug.

"Sound advice." Kelsey smirked a little and glanced towards her husband as he left the bathroom. "Too bad nobody gave it to me."

"Darling, nobody needed to give it to you. You already knew you should stay away," Malachi murmured, backing her up against the wall. He caged her in place with his arms and lowered his head to nuzzle her neck. "You just didn't listen to yourself."

"Malachi, dear, we do have a bit of problem here, might I remind you. Either contribute—or go get a room." Nessa glanced at them with a bored expression, as though she'd seen this show before.

Malachi murmured, "Oh, I'd love to get a room. What do you say, wife? Can we get a room?"

He got an elbow in his stomach. He grunted and stepped back, rubbing at his belly. "Fine, play with the strange-looking creature."

"She's not a creature, Malachi. She's a werewolf," Vax said.

The laughter and easy lust Jess had glimpsed in Mal's eyes faded, replaced by a cool, clinical expression. It was disconcerting. Very disconcerting. Vax didn't seem bothered by it, though. He stared at Malachi and repeated, "She's a werewolf."

"That's not like any werewolf I've ever seen, boy. And I've seen quite a few."

Vax grinned. "Yeah, old man. I imagine you have. So you ought to at least recognize the scent on her. Even if she does look a little . . . strange." Vax caressed Jess's back. He gave her a gentle smile—it looked so at odds on the harsh lines of his face. Vax moved into the bathroom and Jess held her breath, waiting for Dena's reaction.

She took a step closer. Then another. She kept walking until she stood in the bathroom doorway. Jess stared inside the bathroom, looking at Dena. The wolf just lay there. She was staring up at the ceiling, but there was an emptiness in her gaze, one that made Jess wonder whether Dena was seeing anything.

From behind them, Nessa spoke up. "It is safe, Vax. She

is not going to try to take another bite or swipe any time soon."

Looking back over her shoulder, Jess stared at the woman standing across the room. There was a weird look in Nessa's eyes. It made the bottom of Jess's belly feel like it was falling out from beneath her. *Dear God—what have I gotten into?*

It was weird. Chasing after the man who had killed Randi was a hell of a lot less unsettling than being surrounded by witches, werewolves, and vampires. Oh my.

As Vax joined Nessa, hovering over Dena's body, Jess looked at the other two in the room. Kelsey was standing to the side, watching everything with her mild golden eyes. There was an odd look in them, though—a contained one.

Jess's gaze slid over to the vampire.

He was an unnerving bastard, that was for sure. Memories of that gut-wrenching fear she had felt swam back up to taunt her, and she felt her spine stiffen as she stared at him. Being scared pissed her off.

A lot.

As though he knew what she was thinking, Malachi looked up at her, a sly grin curving his lips. "Vax, are you certain this pretty blonde needs to be here?"

Vax just grunted, a sound that could have meant a million things.

Malachi smiled a little wider. A cold chill raced down her spine. He might be on the side of the angels in this game, but Malachi was a very, *very* strange character. He came forward, moving with the same liquid grace as a jungle cat. A knot found its way into her throat, and Jess had a hard time breathing around it. His eyes were a deep, hypnotic blue—Jess wondered if this was how a bird felt when a cobra was preparing to strike.

"What are you doing messed up in this, madame?" he murmured as he moved a little closer. His voice was low, almost soothing. "There's power inside you. I can sense it, feel it lying inside your skull, but it is nothing that keeps you from living the life of a normal woman. Why are letting yourself get pulled into this world?"

There was something mesmerizing about his voice. About him. Jess had a weird urge to turn to Vax and ask him to take her back home. *Home.* Jess squeezed her eyes closed and reminded herself of what waited for her at home.

Nothing.

No family.

No sister relying on her. No sister to share pizza and gossip with. No sister to go see a movie with or watch as the Kentucky Wildcats got clobbered on national TV. Nothing.

Because of William Masters and Thomas Fitzpatrick. And they were going to pay for what they did to Randi.

"I have my reasons," she said. Her voice was stiff, stilted. She had a hard time forcing out the words, but she did manager it. That was something, considering how this dude made her feel like she was standing naked in front of her high school journalism class. Really, really exposed.

"Hmmm. Reasons. I see pain in your eyes. Such pretty green eyes. Such a pretty smile—there's little room for aught but pain and ugliness in our world. Is that where you want to be? Are you so certain this is what you want?" His voice was so seductive, and his words. She wanted very badly to leave it all behind.

Through the fog in her head, she had to force herself to think. Slowly, she shook her head. "You got a thing against green eyes or something?"

There was a soft laugh, and then Kelsey said, "It's not going to work on her, Malachi."

The woman's voice was like a cold splash of water. Jess felt as if she had just been bitch-slapped back into consciousness. Her eyes narrowed as she realized that the vampire had been trying to pull some kind of vamp mojo on her. "You son of a bitch."

Thick black lashes lowered, and he studied her with a hooded stare. "Yes. Remember that." As he spoke, he uncrossed his arms, letting them fall to his sides. As he did, she saw the words scrawled across his chest.

BITE ME.

In big, bold red letters.

Bloodred letters.

A faint, reluctant smile appeared on her face.

He turned away from her, and Jess started to pace restlessly around the room.

I T was almost comical, the look of stunned disbelief that came over Malachi's face. He had been standing in the bathroom, one hip propped against the rusted, dirty sink. He was standing a lot closer to the wolf-thing than Vax would have thought wise, and he wasn't paying much attention to her at all. Again, not too wise, in Vax's opinion.

But Malachi had done things a lot of people wouldn't consider wise, and he had come through all of them unscathed.

Very little surprised him.

Which made this that much more enjoyable.

If somebody had gotten hurt, Vax knew he wouldn't have been leaning back against the wall with a wide grin on his face. But since nobody had gotten hurt, he was going to enjoy every microsecond of this.

It wasn't every day somebody surprised Malachi enough to knock him on his big ass. A thunderous scowl came over his face as he rose to his feet. He crossed the distance between him and Dena in one giant step, one hand lifting. Whether he was going to grab her or hit her, Vax didn't know. But Mal never got close enough. He came to a dead stop a good three feet away from the tub, held back by something invisible to the naked eye.

Vax saw it, though. Witch sight gave the protective shield a faint, hazy glow. It was a containment barrier. Nothing in. Nothing out. It was what had kept Dena's fireball from hitting Mal, keeping it locked inside the shield. The were had ended up with singed fur and some nasty but superficial burns when her fire had, well, backfired, and ended up striking her in the torso, just a little to the right of her sternum.

"You'd think somebody as old as you would have learned some caution." Nessa came closer so that she could peer down at Dena and inspect the burns.

"Did it occur to you to warn us?" Malachi growled. Unless Vax was mistaken, there was a faint bit of color on Mal's otherwise pale face. As though the vampire just might be blushing.

Nessa just shrugged. "We all knew. And, well . . . you usually pick up on these things on your own." A grin tugged at her lips, and she didn't bother trying to hide it. "I wonder why you didn't this time."

Malachi snarled at her.

Vax suspected he knew why. Malachi saw the were and didn't bother looking for magick. Nessa had placed the shields over Dena's body the moment she had set foot inside the cabin. Vax had felt them and breathed a sigh of relief. He could contain Dena's magick, but not indefinitely. Nessa, though—that was a different story.

It was possible that Nessa's presence alone dampened the feel of anybody else's magick. Would explain why Mal didn't sense it. The cagey bastard was almost as sensitive to magick as any witch would be. Mal felt it now, though. Vax knew it by the look on his face. It was slowly bleeding from fury to confusion.

"This isna right," Malachi muttered.

Preoccupation had thickened Mal's accent. When the vampire wanted, he could speak with a complete lack of accent. But when he was distracted, angry, worried . . . the thick burr of Scotland came out.

The vampire's nostrils flared, and he breathed in slowly. "How in the hell am I seeing this? I *can't* be seeing this. It just isna possible." He planted his hands on his hips and stared at Dena as though she were some lab specimen.

And that probably wasn't too far off, Vax mused. He glanced at Jess, thinking about what she had told him, the little memory flash she had picked up from the were. A sy-ringe. A cell.

Then there was what he felt when he looked at this woman. She felt *wrong*. There was nothing natural about how she felt. Nothing.

There was a leaden weight in the pit of his stomach.

Vax glanced at Mal with sympathy. "Sorry, old man. You *are* seeing this."

"But this isna possible."

Vax lifted a shoulder. "Didn't think so, either." There was proof lying in the bathtub of just how possible it was. The *how* of it was slowly coming clear inside his head, and it only made the uneasiness crawling down his spine get worse.

A lot worse.

"Jess, I think maybe you need to tell them about what you picked up from Dena."

It didn't take her long. She explained in a flat monotone, as if she were some school kid giving a report on a book that hadn't interested her at all. She was nervous, though. He could tell. Whenever she was nervous, she had this bad habit of gritting her teeth, and when she finished speaking, she bit down so hard that Vax wouldn't have been surprised if the enamel cracked.

"What does this mean?" Malachi asked, shaking his head. "It makes no sense."

But it did. It was making a sickening sense to Vax. He looked at Nessa and saw nothing but worry in her dark blue eyes. "How does her power feel to you, Nessa?"

She shook her head. Moving her shoulders in a restless shrug, she said, "Not old. But not young, either. She has been practicing a while—there is nothing uncontrolled or chaotic about her power."

"Born with the power, or did she grow into it?" Some witches seemed to come out of the womb knowing magick. Not consciously, perhaps, but some of the witches that Vax had helped train before he left the school had been found levitating in their cribs or accidentally setting fire to their baby dolls in the middle of a tantrum.

For others, the power didn't come on them until they were in their teens. Some had it latent—the possibility of great power lurking inside them like a sleeping leviathan. The power might lie dormant for life, or it could came tearing out of them at some trauma.

"If I had to make a guess . . ." Nessa pursed her lips, studying with thoughtful eyes the woman under the shield. "I would say it came on her later in life. There is a great deal of rage inside her. It is linked with her power."

"Did she do this to herself?" Malachi asked quietly. "I don't see how, but what other explanation is there?" His dark eyes were troubled.

Nessa shook her head. "There is no possible way she could do this to herself with any sort of magick." Her voice was confident, as though she knew there was no possible way she could be wrong. Considering that she was pretty much the authority when it came to magick, her confidence was understandable.

"Not magick," Vax agreed. "Science. Is . . ." He paused, his voice trailing off as he tried to figure out how to put the question together. "Is it possible . . ."

Shit.

Kelsey had been curiously quiet through the entire discussion. She stood by the wall, her hands tucked inside her back pockets. She had been staring at Dena with enigmatic eyes, but now her gaze moved to Vax. There was a faint, humorless smile on her face.

"Is it possible to *make* creatures, outside of the bite, outside of the blood?" Kelsey offered quietly. "A way to pick and choose who becomes were, who becomes witch, who becomes vamp . . . or who gets a combination of the gifts."

Vax didn't like the look in her eyes. It was a bitter, unhappy knowledge—as if she already knew the answer to that question.

"What in the bloody hell are you talking about?" Still preoccupied with the woman lying in the tub, Mal didn't bother to look at his wife as he growled the question. "Attempting to build armies by Changing mortals into vamps or weres is something as old as time. It's a practice that has been around for ages, and it's usually unsuccessful. This, though—this is something new. I've never seen one like this."

"That's because she wasn't made a wolf through an attack. This was *done* to her."

That got Mal's attention. "Done how?"

She answered that with a shrug. "I don't know the specifics, but she was a witch first. This . . . was forced on her."

"Most attacks are forced." Vax folded his arms across his chest and studied Dena. Her misshapen body lay so still in the tub. With her strength draining away by the silver and her magick contained by Nessa's shields, she looked pathetic.

"Not like this one."

"Darling wife, you sound so certain," Malachi murmured. His dark blue eyes were unreadable, but the vibes coming off him weren't happy ones. The look on his face would have made sane people run for cover.

Of course, Vax had already suspected Kelsey's sanity, or lack thereof. After all, she had married the spooky bastard. As Malachi loomed over her, Kelsey stared up at him steadily. "Stop it with the intimidation tactics, pal." She jabbed him in the chest with an unpainted nail, her brows drawn low over her eyes. "That works all well and good on other people, but it doesn't work on me."

Mal reached up and closed a hand over her wrist. He lifted her hand to his lips and pressed a kiss to her palm. But he was still royally pissed. "You need to tell me what's going on, love. And later you can explain why you haven't said a single word about this."

Kelsey turned towards the misshapen werewolf. "That's the problem with taking a vampire as a mate. They get inside your head too easily."

She took a deep breath and closed her eyes. "The mystery of why we are different from mortals has intrigued people for millennia. For hundreds and hundreds of years, it was thought that we were cursed. Over the past century or so, those with a more scientific mindset have been looking for more rational answers."

Malachi shook his head. "There are no answers, Kelsey. We simply are what we are."

Kelsey smiled. She looked a little sad. "There are answers, Mal." She sighed, a soft, quiet sound. Her eyes roamed restlessly over the room, her expression troubled. "Some are desperate to discover them. To some extent, they have even found them."

As one, they all turned their heads towards the bathroom. "That is no answer," Vax said softly. "She is a sad, pathetic abomination."

Kelsey moved towards the bathroom. She didn't go inside, just peered around the corner. "Knowledge, just like any other power, can be used for good or evil, Vax. You know that as well as I." There was sympathy in Kelsey's gaze as she stared at Dena, but there was also practicality. "She is no innocent victim, though. She went along with this willingly."

"I tire of the doublespeak. Am I the only one in this wretched little cabin who hasn't a bloody clue what you are talking about?" Malachi demanded, his tone icy.

"I'm talking about an experiment. I think somebody experimented on her, trying to see if they could create a werewolf that also had the powers of a witch." Kelsey rubbed her hands up and down the outside of her arms, as if she were cold.

"Isn't possible." Mal's flat tone brooked no argument, but Kelsey just smirked at him.

"No? There are at least two Hunters who prove otherwise—Ben and Shadoe Cross. The two powers can be forced into one body. Hell, look at Leandra. It's just been our good luck that so far these creatures have been Hunters. It's just a matter of time, though. Sooner or later somebody like them will go feral. We'll have a hell of a problem stopping them. Apparently this man that Jessica is speaking of decided to speed up the process."

"Speed it up *how*?"

Now Kelsey looked a little nervous. She rubbed her palms down the front of her jeans and licked her lips. "I can't say for certain. But . . ." Her words died and she stopped, staring down at the floor. Her shoulders lifted and fell in a sigh; then they stiffened as though she were bracing herself. "One of the Hunters knows a physician. Dr. Samuel Radley." She paused and glanced at Nessa. "You know him. Or you did—before . . ."

"Before I died," Nessa offered in a flat voice.

From the corner of his eye, Vax could see Jess. Her eyes were wide, dark, and confused. But he didn't have time to explain, and even if he had, that was one story too bizarre for words.

Nessa reached up, tapping at her mouth with her index finger. Her fingernails were painted a wicked, bright shade of blue that almost matched her eyes. "Radley. Radley . . . oh, yes. He was the doctor who was attacked in New York City. How long ago was that?"

"Steven told me that he was attacked on New Year's Eve, 1899."

With a shake of her head, Nessa murmured, "My. More than a hundred years ago. He barely survived the Change. The vampire that attacked him took too much blood, left Radley too weak." Thoughtfully, Nessa said, "He wanted me to Change him back into a mortal. But it isn't possible."

Slowly, she turned. Head cocked, Nessa stared at Dena. "Or at least it shouldn't have been possible."

Kelsey said, "Radley has spent the past century trying to find a way. He has been studying what we are—all of us—trying to see if there is a way to undo it."

Most of what she said was too damned technical for Vax to follow—mumbo jumbo about chemicals in the brain, chemoreceptors, brain scans, and hormones. He didn't understand the medical jargon. He was, however, able to follow the basics.

There was something in their bodies—vamp, were, or witch—that made them what they were. Something tangible. Kelsey had met this physician and trusted him—he was indeed looking for a way to reverse the Change, or to kill a witch's magick without killing her.

"Why would somebody want to do that?" Mal demanded, prowling the room as though it was impossible to stand still. "Change what they are?"

Vax could think of quite a few reasons. But it was Nessa that answered. "Why? I could tell you why, my dear." For all her youthful looks, in that moment, Nessa looked every bit as old as she truly was. "Imagine having so much power inside you that your body cannot die. Even though it ages and you eventually grow old and weak and frail, imagine that power keeping you alive."

A tear slipped out of her eye as she added, "No matter how much you might wish for death." She didn't seem to notice that she was crying silently. "There have been many, many times when I would undo what I am, my friend. Without regrets."

She turned away and walked out, leaving them behind in silence. Finally Vax spoke first. He jabbed a thumb towards the bathroom and asked, "What does this have to do with *her*?"

Kelsey answered quietly, "Everything. If Radley can find ways to unmake us, then who is to say there isn't a doctor who has found a way to do just the opposite: create more?"

"Why?" Jess asked softly. She stood with her back to the wall, arms crossed over her chest.

Kelsey looked towards Jess, startled, as if she'd forgotten Jess was in the room. "There could be a million answers to that. Maybe just to see if he could. But it's probably a lot deeper and darker than that." She smiled bitterly and murmured, "Somebody wants to play God—making his own following, breeding his own army."

Fear wasn't something Vax felt very often. It just wasn't in his makeup. But as he turned his head and looked at Malachi, fear mingled with dread, turning his gut into a knot. "What if they found a vamp as old as you, Mal? Now add in Agnes's ability to control fire. Fire's the only thing that will kill you, man."

Mal just scowled and said, "Is not. Taking my head will do it just as easy as fire."

"But who would be quick enough to get in that close?" Vax shook his head. "Nobody." He looked at Kelsey. "He's a powerful bastard, and it's a damn good thing he's with us. We won't always be that lucky."

Kelsey cocked a brow. "Then that means you had better find the people who made her what she is. Now." She glanced towards the bathroom and said, "We'll take care of her."

"We will?" Malachi looked a little disgusted.

Vax said, "Well, you can always do the fieldwork. I'll take her back to Excelsior." With a bland smile, he added, "Hey, aren't you two still sort of on your honeymoon? Nothing like chasing after mad scientists to help fuel the flames, right?"

"I CANNOT believe you never spoke of this physician before, this Dr. Radley."

The room was wintry. Even the fire crackling away in the stone fireplace couldn't penetrate the frost that surrounded Malachi, pitching the entire room down to what felt like subarctic temperatures.

Oh, he was pissed.

Kelsey sauntered into the room, refusing to let the chill of his anger intimidate her. She had enough problems to worry about with the werewolf witch wannabe locked down in the basement. Basement. She pursed her lips. It was actually more like a dungeon.

After leaving Vax and Jessica Warren in the fishing cabin by the river, Malachi had taken himself and Kelsey across that river to this place. Malachi had known about the house. For all Kelsey knew, it belonged to her husband. He had places like this scattered across the States. Safe houses, he called them. Of course, instead of directing Vax here, he had sent him across the river to that smelly fishing cabin. Kelsey wasn't the least bit surprised. Malachi had a mean streak a mile wide in him, and he had issues with Vax. She wasn't overly worried about Vax. He'd lived in hellholes much worse than the small fifteen-by-fifteen cabin. She did feel a little sorry for Jessica Warren.

She was tempted to contact Vax and tell him about this house. He'd show up in a second, just to annoy Malachi. Both he and Jess would have decent beds to sleep in, instead of those small, miserable-looking cots.

Kelsey didn't, though. She was alone with her husband in this big, lovely house, and they apparently had something to discuss. She wasn't going to wuss out by inviting a couple of innocent bystanders into it.

Nessa had left—she hadn't said where she was going, and Kelsey hadn't bothered to ask. She had always been a bit . . . fey, but ever since the events of the past winter, Agnes Milcher had gone from fey to downright peculiar. She disappeared for weeks on end—one time she had been gone for three months. Kelsey was worried about her, but there was nothing to be done for it.

Nessa wouldn't ever be the woman she had once been.

Kelsey missed her friend. Even more, she hurt for Nessa. More than some, Kelsey understood why Radley was pursuing this. For people like Nessa. People who had been robbed of any chance of a normal life, of even the simplest of things, like spending your life with the man you loved.

Slowly, Kelsey turned and looked at Malachi. Dear God, how she loved him. He was her every waking thought; he was the dream when she fell asleep. Her entire reason for living. Losing him would destroy her so utterly, so completely. Agnes Milcher had been fifteen when she'd lost the love of her life, and she'd never again fallen in love.

Nearly five hundred years of loneliness. Yes. Kelsey understood. But Malachi didn't.

They hadn't been married even a year, but Kelsey knew the vampire pretty damn well. He was so used to intimidating people, he rarely noticed when he went into that mode. But she'd be damned if she'd let him intimidate her.

"You have nothing to say?"

She glanced over her shoulder at him as she opened the closet. "What do you want me to say? Yeah, somebody came to me about this physician. Yeah, I went and spoke with him. Yeah, I know about the tests he's running and I know that this has opened a can of worms that we probably shouldn't mess with. But the can is already open, and at least with Radley, we know what he's doing. He's a good man, Mal. He keeps us updated—"

"Us." His tone was silky, and saner people would probably have run for cover. His dark blue eyes glinted hard and cold.

Kelsey pursed her lips and studied him. What was he so miffed about? "Tobias and me." She tugged a cream-colored Aran sweater off the shelf and pulled it on, snuggling into it. Didn't completely eliminate the chill, but it helped a little. Absently, she freed her braid and combed through it with her fingers. "You see, when Radley asked to speak with the Council, *you* weren't around. I tried several times to get in touch with you—you might remember. I sent the message out with, oh, two or three different Hunters, and they were told to *fuck off, sod off,* or *stay the bloody hell away*." She deepened her voice and managed a fairly decent imitation of a Scottish burr, lowering her brows over her eyes and doing her best to look aloof, angry, and arrogant.

But nobody did aloof, angry, and arrogant quite as well as Malachi did. He stomped over and grabbed her by the front of her thick sweater and jerked her up onto her toes. "Then he isn't keeping *us* informed at all, is he, wife?"

"Don't tell me that you have your boxers in a twist because you didn't know about this," she said. She tried to arch away from him, but he just pulled her closer. "You're impossible!"

"I head the Council, Kelsey. You'd best remember that."

Okay, now she was getting pissed. "If you don't want

me to ram your balls into your throat, you're going to put me down. *Right* now."

It wasn't an empty threat. She really would do it. But before she could, he turned them both around, bracing Kelsey against the wall and leaning into her. "I've more pleasant things in mind for that part of my anatomy, pet. But not until this is settled."

Anger nearly melted away, but she was just a little too annoyed to give up on it so easily. Even if lust was settling in her belly, hot and liquid. She wanted to curl up against him, but at the same time she was mad enough to punch him in that straight, perfect nose.

Instead Kelsey stiffened her body. She couldn't push him, so she didn't bother. She settled on keeping her body as unyielding as a board while she glared at him. "Why don't you tell me what your problem with this is?"

"My *problem*? Bloody hell, is it so hard to understand? This man, this doctor, threatens all of us, yet you and Tobias made this decision to allow him to do this?" He looked down, staring at his hand, at the sweater bunched up inside his fist.

He looked as if he had forgotten how it came to be there, how he had her sweater clutched in his fist. Slowly, he uncurled his hand, and Kelsey felt the tension relax. Malachi backed away from her and turned away, scrubbing his hands over his face. "I'm sorry," he said quietly.

He sighed and shook his head. Softly, he said, "It's just . . . Kelsey, do you understand how dangerous this is?"

"Yes."

Malachi turned to look at her. "How can you possibly understand it, but *allow* it?" His expression was incredulous.

"I couldn't stop it. There is no 'allowing' about it. Radley came to us. He didn't have to. That right there proved to me that I could trust him." She shoved a hand through her hair. It tangled in the thick curls and she jerked lightly, concentrating on the slight pain instead of on her frustration. It didn't help. It didn't clear her mind at all.

Kelsey turned to look at Malachi, her voice pleading with him to understand. "Mal, even if we did attempt to keep him from his research, somebody else simply would have explored those same areas. And we might not have known about them."

Mal muttered something under his breath, something too low for her to hear. He stared out the window, but Kelsey suspected he wasn't seeing the mountains or the evening sky as it slowly changed from day to night. "Has he attempted this unmaking yet?"

"No. He isn't convinced it's safe. He won't try anything until he's certain it won't harm his patients."

"And how does he plan to find these patients? I cannot see him taking out an ad in the newspaper." His voice was flat, almost bored, but she wasn't convinced that the storm had passed. He was too unpredictable, even for her.

Still, the thought of a classified made Kelsey smile a little. *Looking for witches to participate in a dangerous, risky experiment that may or may not work. Could be deadly. Side effects unknown. Outcome questionable. Please respond to areyouinsane@huntermedical.edu.*

Oh, yeah. She could see it. Still smiling, Kelsey looked up at Mal and shook her head. "No. That wouldn't be the best way. But at least he isn't going to grab unsuspecting witches off the streets. He plans on asking for volunteers."

"Volunteers?" Malachi turned his head, staring at her.

He simply couldn't comprehend it.

Poor guy. He was getting surprise after surprise today— the man who usually couldn't be surprised. "Yeah. Volunteers."

"But what sane person would agree to this?" Malachi shook his head and turned away, staring again out the window.

He truly didn't understand it. Kelsey sighed and ran her hands over her hair, then curled them at the nape of her neck. "One who was miserable. Damn it, Mal. Look at Nessa. She lived five centuries. *Alone.* Completely alone. In love with a man that died when she was hardly more than a child. Do you think she lived all that time without once wishing that she had been normal? Free to live out her life as she chose, to die when she should? Even when her body finally let go, her power wouldn't let her. She's stuck here . . . again. In a young body, with all that power."

"Do you know how many people live because of Agnes Milcher?"

Sadness swamped Kelsey. "Hundreds. Maybe thousands. I can't imagine how many people she's saved. But she lost herself. She's been lost for five hundred years, and just when she had a chance of being at peace, that magick of hers yanked her back. Back into this life, back into this battle."

"This is the path that was chosen for her," Malachi said. He shook his head. His eyes were haunted. "I know it has been a hard one, but she is needed."

"She *was* needed. She should have been done." Moving over, Kelsey slipped her arms around his waist and rested her cheek on his chest. "Nessa doesn't have her soul mate waiting at the end of this road for her. She already had him and lost him. Can you imagine how much she much she is hurting? Haven't you ever wished you hadn't been chosen for this life?"

"No." He reached up, cupping his hand over the back of her neck.

"Not once?" Kelsey leaned back so she could see his face. She traced her fingers over his back. She couldn't feel the scars through the thermal cotton weave of his shirt, but she knew they were there. She knew how each mark looked, couldn't even begin to imagine the pain he had felt when those scars were still fresh. That had been two thousand years ago, give or take a few centuries. He spoke very little of his early life, but Kelsey knew he'd been a Roman slave before he had been Changed. He had landed in Scotland probably in the second or third century, although he didn't know exactly when.

Before he had been Changed, Malachi's life had been hell.

After he'd been Changed, his life had been empty.

"Two thousand years, and you've never once wished you'd been born the son of a Roman merchant? Grown up to become a soldier?"

"Not once." His fingers threaded into her hair and fisted there. His dark blue eyes stared into hers as he murmured, "Not for even one day. Not for even one second. Because every second, every day was just that much closer to you. Everything I have done has brought me here. Brought me to you. For you, I would have gone through a thousand years of slavery, ten millennia of solitude. If I had you waiting for me at the end of it all, it would have been worth it."

Kelsey felt her heart melt. She felt all gooey and syrupy inside, and when he lowered his face towards hers, she pushed up onto her toes and met him halfway. Their lips met, a slow, gentle kiss. When he pulled away, Kelsey wouldn't have been surprised if her legs had given out and she ended up in an ooey, gooey puddle right in front of his size-thirteens.

"Not one day," he repeated. "There is much in this life that has confused me, much that has left me angry, empty, even cold with terror and fear. But one thing I do know— all my life, everything I have ever done has led me to you. Undoing what I am would have broken that path. I might never have found you."

THE minute Dena had been taken off their hands, Vax had told Jess to get her stuff together. That took less than a minute.

Driving to the chain hotel off the I-64 near Evansville, Indiana, took nearly forty-five minutes. Jess dozed most of the drive, but when the car stopped right in front of the hotel, she had came awake. Seeing the hotel was like catching a glimpse of paradise.

A bathtub. A comfortable bed, not a cot. *Coffee* . . . It was past midnight, and the courtesy pot in the lobby was probably a few hours old, but she didn't care. She saw Vax looking at her with a faint grin on his face. So what if she had an addiction to coffee that was a little extreme.

Okay, maybe a lot extreme. One sip of the stale coffee cleared some of the cobwebs in her head, and the pounding inside her skull receded a little. After two more sips, she thought that maybe she'd be able to carry on a coherent conversation. Which was good. She needed to talk to Vax.

They checked into two adjoining rooms and the first thing she did was brew some fresh coffee. The second thing was taking the coffee into the bathroom where she stripped naked and climbed into the shower, coffee still in hand.

Ten minutes later, she felt a little more human. Clean clothes would have helped even more. She wore the same clothes she had put on that morning after her shower at the truck stop. One thing was certain: Tomorrow they were going to have to go someplace where she could grab a few changes of clothes.

Resisting the urge to look in the mirror, Jess walked over to the door that connected her room to Vax's. When it opened, Jess decided she might have to reevaluate the part about having a coherent conversation. Or even a coherent thought.

Vax stood there bare-chested, one hand resting on the doorknob. The light landed on his warm golden skin with a soft glow. Muscles rippled as he reached up and rested his other hand on the doorjamb. His thundercloud gaze dropped, lingering on her mouth before he met her eyes.

She shifted from one foot to the other, trying to remember why she had knocked. She had wanted to talk to him, right?

"Something wrong with the room?" he asked as she continued just to stand there.

Numb, she shook her head. "Ah, no. The room's fine. A Dumpster would probably be an improvement over that cabin." Vax reached up to scratch his chest, and Jess found herself staring at it. The skin under his hand was smooth and hairless, a warm, perfect shade of gold.

The black strip of rawhide around his neck had a small black stone hanging from it. A hole had been drilled through the flattened end, and he'd threaded the rawhide through so that he could wear it.

"Did you need something?"

Jess tried once more to remember why she'd wanted to talk to him. "Um, yes?" It sounded more like a question than like an answer.

As he sighed, his chest lifted and fell. "Maybe you should have drunk a little more coffee. You aren't making much sense." Then he stepped aside and said, "Come on in, if you want."

She did, still trying to remember what she had wanted to talk about. Talking was so not what she had in mind now.

He'd taken a shower, too. His room was the reverse of hers, the door to the bathroom on the right instead of the left, and she could still smell the scent of the hotel soap lingering in the air.

He had pulled his hair back from his face, and it was secured in a queue at the nape of his neck. Jess wanted to pull it loose. She wanted to comb her fingers through his hair, pull his mouth down to hers, and kiss him. Damn, but she wanted to feel his mouth on hers.

Wanted to feel his body on hers. She could all but see it, lying on that bed, his big body crushing her into the mattress, rubbing against her. . . . Jess spun away and wiped a hand across her mouth. She wasn't drooling. Yet.

Taking a deep breath, Jess tried to find something else to think about besides him. Not so easy. Like most hotel rooms, this one had that bland, sterile décor, uninspired prints on the wall, a blue and yellow patterned quilt on the bed.

There was a knife on the small stand beside the bed. Big and wicked-looking, the blade was slightly curved. The handle was a yellowed white. It looked like the fake bone handles she'd seen on some knives.

But she doubted this handle was fake.

"You look exhausted. You need some rest."

She jumped at the quiet sound of his voice. Turning her head, she gave him a faint smile. "I am exhausted. But I doubt I'll sleep."

He dropped into the single chair the room boasted. It was one of those hard ladder-backed numbers that was probably about as comfortable as it looked. He lounged in it like it was a solid gold throne. He draped one arm over the back of the chair and rested the other hand on the table. His fingers beat out a slow, rhythmic pattern. "Even if you can't sleep, you need to rest. Go soak in the tub or something. We'll leave in the morning."

"Leave," she repeated. Man, a bath . . . the idea did have its appeal. Filling up the tub with steaming hot water and soaking her aching body. But instead of leaving the room, she just continued to walk around restlessly.

Vax was frowning at her. "What's the problem?"

"Problem?" She realized she sounded like a drugged mynah bird. "No. There's no problem. And I already took a shower." She started to pace the room with long, quick strides, certain that if she moved around enough, maybe it would clear the lust from her system. He was still looking at her weirdly, so she forced a smile. "I must be more tired than I thought. Having a hard time thinking straight."

"Stress." Vax lifted a shoulder in a shrug. "This has been your whole life for a while now. You know, it's not too late for you to let it go."

Okay, now *that* cleared the cobwebs. Stopping in midstride, she turned and faced him. She ran her tongue across her lower lip and propped her hands on her hips. "Let it go," she repeated. More of the mynah bird thing. She didn't feel quite so drugged out, though. And the warm, mind-hazing lust was clearing up as well. She had a feeling she was heading in the direction of pissed. Very, very pissed off.

"Is this your subtle way of telling me that I should just go back home? Because *you* can handle it?" Jess asked, her voice low and furious. She wanted to yell. Wanted to scream at him.

"That's your choice." He lowered his lashes, staring at her with a hooded gaze.

"Over my dead body."

Straight black brows arched up, and he said, "Beg your pardon?"

Carefully and clearly, she said again, enunciating each syllable, "Over my dead body." The arrogant jerk, she fumed. Thinking he would leave her out of this. "I oughta break that perfect nose of yours. Fucking jerk."

He rocked back on his heels. "Okay. You want to tell me what the problem is?"

"You still think I should back off on this. Still think it's not my *problem*. You think you can ship me back home and you'll handle the dirty work. Bastard." She snarled at him, balling her hands into fists. One good hard punch on that carved jaw, and she'd feel a lot better. It might break her hand, but she'd feel better.

Vax stood up slowly. He had that patient, consoling tone in his voice. The sound of it just made her more furious. "Jess, you really shouldn't be involved in this, not any-more. You've done enough. I know where to look. Let me handle this now. It's just too dangerous."

"Dangerous. Gee, ya think? They *raped* my baby sister. They killed her. They threw her out like she was yesterday's trash, and all as a warning to me because they didn't like the questions I was asking. And you think I don't know they are dangerous?" She stomped over to him and pushed up onto her toes. She was still about three inches shorter than he was. Grabbing the black leather strip around his neck, she jerked him lower so that they were eye to eye. "I am *not* walking away from this until they have paid for what they did."

Vax reached up, closing one hand around her wrist. Not to pull her hand away, though. He just held her wrist, his thumb sweeping back and forth across the soft skin on the inside. "You can't be involved in this, Jess. These aren't just a couple of perverts. Bad enough if they were. But they aren't human. They won't be working alone. If only half of what Kelsey suspects is true, then we're all in trouble. You aren't prepared for this."

She narrowed her eyes. Without saying a word, she crossed the room and opened the door, stalking into her room. She could feel Vax watching her as she grabbed her gym bag out from under the bed and pulled it out. With barely restrained fury, she jerked the zipper down and reached inside. Jess wrapped her hand around the butt of the Browning. She pulled it out and jerked out the chamber, revealing one of the bullets.

It flashed in the light as she hurled it at Vax. Even to the naked eye, it didn't look like regular bullet. Those damn things had cost her an arm and a leg. The man who had sold them to her had said those bullets could bring down almost anything she might go hunting for. Or anybody. He'd smirked a little as he added that last part. He'd had a weird buzzing energy to him, that same weird kind of buzzing energy she'd felt around Dena.

Thinking back, Jess realized the dude had been some sort of shape-shifter. The bullets he'd sold her could bring down almost any creature imaginable.

Vax caught the bullet in midair and looked down at it. When he looked back up at her, he had an enigmatic look in his eyes. "Silver."

"Silver." She sneered at him. "You think I'm totally stupid? I may not be some all-powerful witch, but I am not just some helpless mortal. I knew there was something weird going on inside that club the very first time I got within a block of it. I could feel it. Feel *them*. I've known from the get-go that they weren't human."

"So you think a gun loaded with silver bullets is going to protect you?" With a lightning-quick speed that made her head spin, he crossed the distance that separated them. She retreated, but he followed, backing her up against the wall. "These people can move like the wind, darlin'. They make me look slow. You don't actually think you can hold on to that gun, do you?"

A faint smile appeared on Jess's lips. "The gun wouldn't be my only weapon." She concentrated hard, but never once took her eyes from his. As she saw the metal come into view, she said, "Why don't you turn around?"

He did, slowly.

That was when she saw his back. For a second, the blur of color didn't make sense to her eyes. Then she realized that his entire back, beginning just under his shoulder blades and disappearing under the waistband of his pants, was covered in tattoos. Feathers, to be exact. Finely detailed feathers, as though an artist had decided to use his back as a canvas.

She lifted her fingers to touch one of the feathers, but then she froze. His breath hissed out of him, and she slid out from behind him. The knife was pressing into his chest. Hard enough to pinch, not hard enough to draw blood.

"Leaving unguarded weapons around a telekinetic is a bad idea," she whispered.

Vax reached up and closed his hand around the hilt of his knife. She let it go, letting him take it out of the air. When he looked at her, she met his gaze head-on. "Nice trick. And somebody decides to knock you out? That pretty head of yours might seem hard as a rock. But it isn't."

"I know that. But I'm not the helpless little wallflower you seem to think. I may not be Mr. Indestructible, buddy, but I'm not helpless and I'm not stupid." She shoved her hair back from her face. As she did, she realized her hand was shaking. She clenched it into a fist, feeling her neatly clipped nails biting into her palm. She squeezed a little more tightly, hoping it might help.

It didn't. She was still furious. Scared to death, too, but that wasn't going to stop her. She took a deep breath and let it out slowly. When she thought she might be able to speak without screaming at him, she said, "I will *not* let this go. Not until it's over."

"And if it ends with you in a body bag?" A muscle jerked in his jaw, and his eyes darkened. His voice was rough.

"If that's the way it ends," Jess murmured. She turned away from him and started towards the bed. Then she stopped and looked down. She was still holding the gun. The Browning fit into her hand nicely. It was the reason she had chosen it. It was neither too big nor too small. She had gone to the shooting range routinely and could hit the bull's-eye every time.

She dreamed of putting a bullet between the eyes of the men who hurt Randi. It was weird to think of it. Jess had done a series on the dangers of guns. Her parents had hated them. Jess hadn't cared for them. But she would use this one to kill.

Suddenly unable to look at it, she tucked it back inside her gym bag. "You say you know how it hurts to lose somebody, Vax. I haven't just lost somebody. I've lost everybody. When Mom and Dad died, I promised I'd take care of Randi. I failed. She's gone. I don't have anybody now. Just getting through the day takes everything I have. How much worse could it be if I don't make it through this?"

She heard a soft sound behind her and then his hands closed over her upper arms. He pulled her back against him and wrapped his arms around her waist. "You sound like that's exactly what you want."

It bothered him. A lot. Vax held her close, breathing in the soft, clean scent of her hair. Words weren't something he usually wasted much time on, and right now that was bad. There had to be something he could say to make her understand how wrong this was. How dangerous.

Her hands covered his. She didn't cling to him, but she didn't push him away, either. "I wouldn't say that I want it—but it's not something I'm going run away from screaming, either."

"You know what they did to your sister. They'll do the same to you—worse. She was a warning. If they get their hands on you . . ." Involuntarily his own hands tightened. It took a conscious effort to make them loosen. Slowly, he turned her around and cupped her chin in his hand. Vax stroked his thumb back and forth across her cheek, aware of how soft, how delicate her skin was.

She was strong—he had seen the muscles flex as she ran away from the were, and he had felt the power when she decked him. He didn't have to see her in action to know she knew how to fight. But there was no way to understand the sheer power that a vampire had, the speed that came so easily to a shape-shifter. If she fell into their hands, they'd tear her apart.

His voice was gritty as he said, "I have enough trouble sleeping at night. If something happens to you, I may never sleep again. Let this go. I'll make them pay for what they did to her, I swear. But please . . ."

The thick fan of her lashes lifted, and Vax stared into her jewel-bright eyes. "I'm sorry. But I can't. They have to pay for what they did to her—I can't let this go. I *have* to do this. Or I'll never sleep again." She forced a weak smile. "Sleep isn't easy for me, either. Please, Vax . . ."

He felt the warm caress of air drift across his skin as she spoke. Felt his heart knot inside his chest. And he knew he couldn't tell her no. He should.

Dear God, he knew he should. And if she didn't willingly back away, he should force her. It would just take a few words, and Ms. Jessica Warren would find her tight little ass locked up in Excelsior. She'd be safe there.

Safe and secure.

And when the ferals that did this were dead, she'd be returned home.

But he couldn't do it.

Yes, he knew how much it hurt to lose somebody you loved. Knew that it was so much worse when grief was compounded by guilt. He'd been living with that kind of guilt for so long, he couldn't remember what life was like without its coloring his every waking moment.

Vax couldn't do that to her.

He closed his eyes. He draped his hands loosely around her neck, his thumbs resting just below the hollow of her throat. He could feel the pulse of life flowing through her.

All the years he had spent Hunting made it all too easy to imagine that life cut short. In a harsh voice, he said, "If you do this, then you don't do anything alone. You stay by my side, period. You understand me?"

In a mocking drawl, she said, "Yes, sir."

"Smart-ass," he muttered. Then he kissed her. Hard.

His hands molded to her skull and held her still. His thumbs pressed against her jaw, and when her mouth opened, he pushed inside, taking in as much of her as he could, as quickly as he could. Her hands came up, gripping his wrists. They stood there like that, touching only where their mouths and hands met on each other. Their bodies didn't touch. He couldn't feel the ragged rhythm of her breathing and he couldn't feel the long, sleek lines of her body.

He wanted to. Vax had wanted just that from the first time he had laid eyes on her. Wanted to feel her naked and sweaty under him. He lifted his head and stared at her through slitted eyes. Her face was flushed. Her lips were wet and swollen, and the soft green of her eyes had darkened to a deep, mysterious shade that made him think of the forest.

Slowly he let go, his hands sliding from her hair. He licked his lips and tasted her on them. "You stay safe," he whispered. His voice was ragged and hoarse. His body, as though sensing the coming frustration, started to scream at him. He wanted to grab her, yank her against him, rip off her clothes, and push her to the floor. Wanted it so badly, he was shaking with it.

But instead of reaching for her, he turned away. "Get to sleep. We leave early."

"Where are you going?"

Without looking at her, he said, "To bed."

"Wait."

He stopped in his tracks but didn't look at her. At least not right away. But a moment passed. Then another. Finally Vax turned around and looked at her. The second their eyes met, she reached for the zipper on her short

black jacket. She tugged it down and slipped it off. As it
slid down her arms, she glanced towards the bed. "There's
a bed in here."

Vax glanced at the bed in question. It was soft and feminine, and he suspected that she didn't like it at all. It was
a pity, because it suited her a lot more than she suspected.
He could imagine that long, pale body on that big bed, her
hair loose around her shoulders, her arms reaching for him.
"Yes. There's a bed. But the only way I'd want to get in
that bed would be if I was getting inside you as well."

Jess grinned. She reached for the hem of her close-
fitting tank and pulled it off. "Excellent—because that's
the way I'd prefer it, too."

But he barely heard a word she said. Under that tank top,
she was naked. She had small, high breasts. Her nipples
were a deep shade of pink, and as he stared at her, they
puckered and tightened. Vax realized his mouth was wa-
tering. He closed the distance between them with two
quick strides. He stopped in front of her and stooped just a
little as he slid an arm around her waist. When he straightened, her feet left the floor.

"Thought you didn't do casual." He stared into her face
as he spoke, even though he wanted to glance down,
wanted to see how her soft, pale flesh looked pressed up
against his. He didn't, though. At least not yet. One chance
to make sure she knew what she was doing.

A smile lifted the corners of her mouth. "Vax, 'casual' is
one word that doesn't describe you. At all." She leaned forward and pressed her lips to his jaw. "So where are you
going to sleep? My bed? Or yours?"

"Neither." He caught a fistful of her hair in his hand and
slowly wound it around his wrist. "We won't be doing
much sleeping."

"I hope not." Her wide grin vanished quickly, her lips
opening with a startled gasp as Vax pivoted and took two
steps. He pressed her up against the wall. Then he reached
down, grabbing one leg and pulling it up over his hip,
opening her. Vax pressed against her, feeling the heat of

her through the layers of clothing. He could smell her—sweet, hot, and female. The scent of her went straight to his head—and his cock. That scent was intoxicating. He could smell the soap and the shampoo she'd used, but under that was the subtle scent of woman.

He lowered his head. But instead of kissing her mouth, he ran his lips over her neck. Her breath hitched. When he reached the point where neck joined shoulder, he opened his mouth and bit down lightly. He let go of her waist, easing her to the floor. He slid his hands over her slim waist and up her rib cage, and cupped her breasts in his hands. They were small, soft, and delicate. He plumped one in his palm and pushed it high. Hunkering down, he caught one tight, beaded nipple between his teeth and sucked gently.

Then he pulled back a little, circling the crest with his tongue.

"Vax . . ."

Vax lifted his head, staring at her from under his lashes. Holding her gaze, he straightened and slid his hands inside the waistband of her pants. The snug black cotton clung to her slender curves, and he sank to his knees in front of her as he peeled them away.

Under the pants, she had on a pair of low-cut panties. Simple black cotton—black seemed to be the main color in her wardrobe. They dipped low over her hip bones, the cloth running between her thighs. He hooked his thumbs in the waistband and pulled them away, leaving her naked.

Lifting his gaze, he stared up at her. Then he pressed his mouth to her. She bucked against his mouth, and he closed his hands over her hips, holding her still.

He teased her, circling his tongue over her clit, caressing lightly over it, then retreating. She groaned, squirming against his grip as she tried to move closer. He muttered, "Be still."

She slammed her head back against the wall, a strangled groan falling from her lips. "Are you trying to drive me crazy?"

"I don't know. Maybe. Am I?" Then he pushed his tongue inside her.

The caress shattered her. He stroked in and out, pushing her closer and closer to the edge, and Jess was convinced that she was going to fly into a thousand pieces. Her knees buckled, her legs giving way under her. The only thing keeping her upright was the tight clasp of his hands around her hips. Jess braced her hands on his shoulders. Her fingers tangled in his raven black hair.

"Am I?" he repeated, lifting his mouth just a little. The hot caress of his breath was just one more teasing stroke, one more small push closer.

His words didn't make sense to her. She lifted her lashes and tried to focus on his face, but she couldn't focus on anything. Lights seemed too bright. The world felt like it was spinning around her, and nothing felt solid, nothing felt real. Nothing but the hard ridge of his shoulders under her palms and the heat of his hands clasping her hips. He asked again, but all she could do was shake her head and say, "What?"

He laughed and then pressed his mouth against her again. He licked her clit, teasing it with his tongue and then sucking on her. One hand left her hip. When he touched her between her thighs, she cried out. She rocked against him eagerly, but he didn't enter her. Instead he traced her folds with his fingertip with light little touches. Jess groaned his name and tried to move closer. He didn't let her. He just kept up those feathery caresses.

Each stroke of his tongue lashed through her like some fiery whip. He had her so swollen, so sensitive, so close to the edge, those gentle touches became a kind of erotic torture. She was caught on the edge, unable to go over but unable to ground herself, either.

Then he pushed a finger inside her.

At that, Jess exploded, slamming her head back into the wall and screaming his name. She bucked against him, her entire body arching. There was no end to it—just when she thought she might be able to breathe again, he moved, rising to his feet, one arm wrapped around her waist. Her feet left the floor and she lifted her knees, squeezing them around his hips.

His cock was trapped between their bodies. She had one fleeting second to feel him, hard and throbbing, and then he moved, easing back just a little. With his free hand, he guided his length between her thighs and held steady as he pressed against her. He was hot as fire, and as he filled her, she thought she was going to burn to death in the heat of him.

She wrapped her arms around his torso, sliding her hands up his sides. There were odd little ridges in the smooth skin, but she barely acknowledged them. She was aware of the muscles, the power, and the feel of his body rubbing against hers. The thick black silk of his hair fell around them both. Vax stared down at her as he pumped against her, and the eerie dark gray of his eyes shifted and swirled, going from deep, stormy gray to light silver.

He bussed her mouth with his, then skimmed his lips down, over her chin, along her jawline, down her neck. When his lips closed over her nipple, Jess cried out. That heat, consuming, erotic, and terrifying all at once. He tongued the rosy crest, pressed it up against the roof of his mouth, then suckled her.

Vax slid a hand down, smoothing it along the outside of her thigh, then back up, catching her behind her knee. On the other side, he mirrored the move, pushing her thighs open. Then he leaned into her. When he rotated his hips against hers, she felt every swollen, pulsating inch of his flesh. As he withdrew, she clenched around him in an effort to keep him from pulling away. She lifted her hips, trying to follow him, and he laughed. "Slow down. Are you always in such a hurry?"

Normally? Yeah. But even if she weren't, this was definitely something she would want to hurry. Not because she wanted it over, but because of what she could feel looming ahead of her. She could feel the thick shaft pulsing inside her, felt each subtle nuance of him as he slowly pulled out

and pumped back in. She could feel his hands, hard and calloused. She could hear the unsteady rhythm of his breathing. She could feel the heat of him, spreading over her
entire body like a blanket.

Jess had had lovers. Several of them.

But she didn't think she'd ever been this aware of anybody before.

He reached between their bodies, and she whimpered as
he brushed against her clit. He did it again and again. Jess
closed her eyes and held her breath, waiting for that next
light contact. It would send her screaming over the edge—
she knew it. She could all but feel the bliss that awaited
her.

But that light touch never came. She opened her eyes to
glare at him, only to find him smirking at her. "Such a
damned hurry," he teased. Vax straightened, holding her
against him as he moved to the bed. Without letting go, he
lay her down and bent over her. Vax nuzzled her neck, bit
her delicately on the ear. And all the while, he moved inside her, slow, teasingly shallow strokes that made her even
hungrier.

"Vax . . ." Oh, hell. Was that whimpery, breathy moan
actually *her*?

"Jess . . ." His voice was a low, silken caress.

Digging her nails into his shoulders, she started circling
her hips against his. Just a little more and she'd be there—

He didn't give her the chance, though. Vax dropped his
weight completely onto her, his big frame crushing her into
the bed. "You don't understand slow." He licked her neck
and then bit her gently. "Okay. We won't do slow this
time." He tensed over her and then slammed into her. Hot,
sweet pleasure exploded through her, her nerve endings
sizzling with each hard, deep stroke.

Her mind shut down and pure sensation took over. When
he caught her wrists and pinned them by her head, she let
him. His cock jerked inside her and Jess screamed into his
mouth. He swallowed it and kissed her harder. Using teeth
and tongue, he kissed his way down her chin, over her

neck. He nibbled on the fleshy part of one breast, just above the nipple, taking her to the edge of pleasure. Pain threatened, and she pressed herself harder against him.

The orgasm hit, starting low in her belly and spreading through her body with seismic intensity, each pulsating wave of pleasure lasting longer and longer. Jess keened his name. Her hands closed into fists, nails biting into her flesh.

She was blissfully, exhaustingly sated when he started to come, filling her with hot, pulsing jets. She started to drift off into darkness as he collapsed against her and let go of her wrists. Just before exhaustion took hold, she looped her arms around his shoulders.

Jess fell asleep smiling.

Less than an hour later, she woke up to feel his hands on her body. As he pulled her on top of him, he muttered, "Told you we wouldn't be sleeping much."

He was right.

CHAPTER 9

Vax almost always slept alone.

On the rare occurrences when he stayed all night with a woman, he woke before she did and left in silence. Not the nicest way to treat a lover, but too much time spent that close to a person tended to weigh too heavily on him, stretching his control to the breaking point.

Even somebody who didn't broadcast her emotions to the whole world was too much a strain. Close contact strengthened an Empathic connection, and you didn't get much closer than naked skin against naked skin.

But waking next to Jess was amazing.

Although he knew she was in turmoil, knew she was filled to the breaking point with pain, grief, and guilt, it was all contained. None of it leaked through her shields. He lay in the bed, sprawled facedown, and she was pressed against his side, one arm around his hips. Her lips were close to his shoulder blades. He could feel the soft, gentle rhythm of her breathing and her heartbeat.

It was—soothing. He couldn't think of a better word to describe it.

He'd had lovers before who were gifted, who knew how to shield, but they had been fellow Hunters. There was a decided lack of *restful* attributes among the Hunters. Even the Healers had to be warriors.

Sex had always been just that, a need to satisfy, a basic urge for satisfaction and on occasion for companionship. Hunters who didn't die young often faced long, lonely stretches of years, and they learned to take what pleasure they could where they could and not seek out more.

Long, peaceful moments of silence after making love to a woman were not something that had been placed before Vax often. Odd that he should find it here, with this woman. She was most definitely warrior material. She had so much fight inside her, so much anger. So much guilt.

He couldn't feel any of it, but he could see it in her eyes.

"You always think this hard when you wake up?"

Her voice was drowsy, and he lifted his head from the pillow so that he could look at her. Her eyes were still closed, but as he looked at her, her lashes lifted. She smiled sleepily at him before closing her eyes again. "Too early for you to be thinking so much."

"It's past eight." He didn't have to look at the clock to know what time it was. He had wanted to be gone by now, but they hadn't gone to sleep until after two. He wasn't going to complain, though. Even tired and worn-out as he was.

She just grunted. "Until I've had three or four cups of coffee, it's always early."

Vax laughed. He wouldn't mind a caffeine jolt himself. And some breakfast. His belly rumbled, and he amended that silent thought—a *big* breakfast.

She opened her eyes again, glaring at him. "You're still thinking."

Grinning, he lifted a brow at her. "What am I supposed to be doing?"

She blinked. "Go back to sleep?" She sounded hopeful.

"Can't." Six hours of sleep was a lot for him, and he wouldn't get any more for a while. And they did need to

get going. But he couldn't work up the interest to move.
She shifted beside him, and he felt the gentle press of her
breasts against his side. His cock stirred, and he decided he
did have an interest in moving, so long as the movement
ended with him on top of her, inside her. Just as he was getting ready to flip over and cover her, though, she pushed
herself onto her side. Out of the corner of his eye, he could
see where she was looking.

At the intricate tattoos on his back. She reached out,
brushing the tip of her finger along one of them. "You got
a thing for feathers?" she asked softly.

He grunted.

Jess slid him a sideways glance. "Is that grunt a way of
not answering my question?" Without waiting for an answer, she went on to trace another one. He didn't have to
see his back to know which one. It was the black one, the
one that looked as if a raging lunatic had carved it into his
flesh.

That wasn't too far off. After Cora had died, he had
parted ways with sanity. He'd sat in the ashes of Cora's fu-
neral pyre and used his magick to carve the design into his
flesh. Magick and rage didn't make for steady control, and
the tattoo was wicked long and ugly as hell.

As she traced her finger over one feather, Vax felt the
muscles in his back twitch. "Do these stand for anything?"

He was silent. He didn't want to answer that question.
But he couldn't keep quiet, either. Finally he said, "You
know much about Native culture?"

"No." As she answered, she traced the outline of another
feather. As her fingers brushed over his side, he twitched a
little. "You're ticklish."

"Am not." But he shifted away from her hand, rolling
onto his back. "Nobody knows who my parents were. It's
a possibility that one of my parents was Lakota. I was
found in Kansas City at a church when I was a baby. Probably just a couple of weeks old. They turned me over to the
orphanage." Closing his eyes, he remembered. None of his
memories from his childhood were clear—he'd long since

forgotten most of it. It was probably a good thing. The bits and pieces he did remember were blurs of hunger, pain, and cold.

"I lived in the orphanage for a while. I ran away a lot. People would bring me back. I don't know how old I was when I finally managed to get away for good. Lived on the streets. Picked pockets, gambled. Wasn't very good at the gambling. That started changing when I was a little older, eighteen . . . maybe nineteen. I started winning. I knew who had the good hands, who didn't."

"Empathy?" Jess asked.

"Yeah. Came into my gifts late. The Empathy came first. Wasn't too long before saloons started kicking me out. They were convinced I was somehow cheating."

Her hand had stilled on his back. Out of the corner of his eye, he saw the perplexed look on her face. "Saloon." She said it slowly, as though she was unfamiliar with the word.

He gave her a crooked grin. "Yeah, saloon. You know, dancing girls, whiskey, poker." His smile faded and he reached up, skimming his fingers over the ends of her hair. "I don't know how old I am, Jess. I was grown when the Hunters found me, talked me into joining them. That was in 1850."

Her jaw dropped. She blinked, opened and closed her mouth a couple of times, but never said anything. Her eyes had a vague, startled look to them. When she finally spoke, her voice was weak and thready. "1850?"

"Yes." He looked down and stared at the hand she had rested on his chest. He covered it with his as he sat up. "Then I only had a couple of feathers." With his free hand, he reached over his left shoulder. He could just barely touch the tip of that first feather. He couldn't see it, but he didn't have to. "As my Empathy grew stronger, I thought I was going crazy. One night, a woman was raped in the saloon where I was gambling—she was one of the whores, a young girl, just trying to feed her son. Some bastard raped her, practically tore her apart. I didn't know what was going on—all I could feel was her pain. I could taste her blood. I ran out of the saloon, trying to get away from it. Hid in an alley. God, I thought I was losing my mind. Then he came walking out of the saloon. He had her blood on his hands, and he was smiling."

Vax let go of Jess's hand and lifted his own, staring at them. "I killed him. When he walked by the place where I was hiding, I snapped. I grabbed him by the throat, hauled him into that alley, and killed him. I strangled him and I watched his face while he died. Then I ran."

Scrubbing his hands over his face, Vax took a deep breath. "I don't know what happened after that. I didn't ever want to see another person again. I think part of me hoped I'd die in the desert."

*W*HEN *he opened his eyes, he thought maybe he was dead.*

He'd spent enough time out in the desert with nothing to eat, nothing to drink. Had he finally died of thirst?

"No. You are not dead."

The words were stilted, spoken with a halting sort of cadence that Vax was familiar with. He turned his head and wasn't surprised to see an old Indian man sitting by the fire. Smoke spiraled upward, drifting through the small aperture in the top of the teepee.

As Vax watched, the Indian reached down beside him and lifted a gourd. "Here. You drink."

Vax didn't take it. "Where am I?"

Instead of answering, the Indian said something that Vax couldn't understand. But the words were lyrical, and deep inside, Vax felt something throb in response. The Indian repeated it and stared at Vax, as though waiting for some kind of answer. Then he shook his head, looking a little disgusted. "You talk like a white man. Dress like a white man. You do not even know our tongue."

"I am not—"

But he couldn't say it. Vax was Indian. Or at least half Indian. A half-breed didn't have a place in either world.

But at least when he lived among white people, he understood what they were saying.

"I can teach this to you."

Vax's heart skipped a beat. Then it started beating twice as fast. "Teach me what?"

"Our ways. Our words. Your ways. You may have white-man ways and white-man eyes, but you are not white man. You are Lakota. I feel this in you. You feel it, too." The old Indian pushed the water towards Vax once more. "You drink. You need your strength."

No. All he needed was a gun and a bullet. Or a knife. The bullet would be quicker, and he sort of liked the idea of blowing his brains out. That would sure as hell put an end to the weird images he kept getting. Feeling pain for no reason. Anger. Hurt. Fear.

"A bullet is not the answer."

"HE was reading your mind?" Jess asked as Vax fell silent. A psychic shaman. A lover who was almost two hundred years old. A vampire that was playing Dr. Frankenstein. This was all too bizarre for words.

"Two Stars was a thought senser more than a mind reader. He could pick up weird little bits here and there. It wasn't a powerful ability. But yeah."

"Thought sensing." Jess sighed. She put her head down, resting it on his chest. She could hear the slow, steady cadence of his heart under her ear. "And a shaman."

"More than that," Vax murmured. His voice sounded achingly sad. "He's the one who taught me how to control my gift enough to keep it from driving me crazy."

"Was he a witch?" Jess murmured. She wished she hadn't ever asked him anything. Somehow the tatts on his back were related to this shaman. However that was, it was something that made Vax sad. There was no taking back the question now, though.

"No. Not a witch. He was a shaman. He didn't truly understand a witch's magick. But he didn't need to understand the magick to help me learn to control my Empathy. Empathy makes a person able to experience the emotions of others. Shaman magick was similar, but shamans didn't feel the emotions of random people. They were connected to their lands, to their tribes."

"I didn't realize there was such a thing as shamanic magick. I thought shamans were more or less just medicine men, or wise men." She frowned up at him, but he wasn't looking at her. His gaze was on the ceiling over their heads, but she didn't think he was seeing anything but the past. "So were all shamans magick?"

"Are," Vax corrected, his tone almost absent. "There are still shamans. They're usually stuck on reservations damned far from the home of their peoples, but it doesn't make them any less. All shamans had to be wise men. There's no job description for being a shaman. They had to have the knowledge of the past, of their people. They had to have the ability to do their duties. But they didn't have to have the magick. The magick that connected them to the earth is rare.

"Two Stars was a powerful shaman. He was connected to the earth in ways that still amaze me, after all this time."

"You loved him."

A sad smile curved Vax's lips. "He was the closest thing to a father I've ever known. He didn't just save me from dying in the desert—he saved me from going insane. Yeah, I loved him. He was a good man." His next words came after a long pause. "He shouldn't have died like that."

Jess was almost afraid to ask. She wasn't much into history. Most of what she knew about Native Americans had come from school. Custer's Last Stand, Crazy Horse, Sitting Bull, and Wounded Knee—a lot of the stories had been whitewashed, she knew. Entire tribes had been wiped out by the invading armies. But as much as she didn't want to know, she asked anyway. "Died how? Who killed him?"

Rolling his head on the pillow, Vax stared at her. "Not a who. A what. There was a white family that had settled a few miles outside our hunting grounds. Nice people. The man and his wife respected Two Stars and the tribe. They traded with us. I remember their children came to the village once and played with our children. Then they got sick. The man came to Two Stars, begged for his help. Two Stars went. His kindness killed him—and half of our tribe. Chicken pox."

He jackknifed up into a sitting position and practically jumped out of bed, as though he couldn't stand to be still any more. "That man went to help a couple of kids, and he brought back a disease that killed more than a hundred people. My *family*. The only family I had ever known. Two Stars took me in and taught me how to control my gifts, but it was more than that. He gave me something I'd never had—a sense of history." He strode over to the window, staring out the window. "He gave me all of that— and when he lay dying, I couldn't do anything to ease his suffering."

She watched as he reached over his shoulder, touching his fingers to one feather. The tattoo lay just above his left shoulder blade. It was black, with ridged, raised lines—the ridges she had felt on his back during the night. "Two Stars had given me an eagle's feather—a sign of his affection for me. When the sickness spread through the village, I couldn't help heal any of them. My Healing gift has always been weak. But I could see the sickness. I saw it on him when he returned to the village that day, but I didn't realize what it was until it was too late. By then, warriors, women, and children had died. We had to burn everything, or more would die. I had to burn the gifts he gave me, including the feathers."

Jess rose from the bed and walked over behind him. She wrapped her arms around his waist and pressed her cheek to his back. She felt another raised line, and she shifted until she could reach up and cover it with her hand. "You did them yourself. The first one for Two Stars."

"For the only father I've ever known," he corrected, his voice hollow. "Nineteen children died in the village— because I wasn't good enough to save them. The blue feathers are for the children. The other ones are for the friends I've lost."

Jess closed her eyes. Dear God.

She hadn't counted them. Some were small; some were big. But there were dozens and dozens, possibly even more than a hundred. One in particular stood out in her mind, though. It lacked the smooth, delicate precision the other tattoos had. It was jerky, almost as if a child had scrawled it into Vax's flesh with a dull knife. She sought it out by touch, tracing it delicately. "And this one?"

The question had barely left her mouth when he pulled away. Suddenly remote and cool, he turned around and met her eyes. "That one is for my other failure."

And then he grabbed his pants from the floor and left her alone in the room.

M^Y *other failure.*

M   That sounded so . . . polite.

Failure didn't quite cover what had happened to Cora. He had failed to protect her. Failed to save her. The only thing he hadn't failed in had been her death. Oh, he had succeeded in that. He had killed her with his own hands, just like he had killed that man in Kansas City more than a century ago.

He hadn't choked the life out of her—no. He'd killed her by shoving a silver knife through her heart. He stood in the bathroom, staring at his reflection. All his strength, all his power—and in the end the only thing he could do for Cora was kill her.

"We can make it right, Vax. I know we can—you just have to help me."

Slowly he lifted his hands and stared at them. They were trembling. They had shaken almost unbearably as he pushed the knife into Cora's chest. They had shaken so hard, it was a miracle he had been able to do it at all.

You do not have to do this, Diego had told him repeatedly.

For a while, Vax had worked with Diego, a shape-shifter. The shifter had been a small, dark man who was deadly in both of his forms. He hadn't ever talked about his past, but there were rumors that he was descended from the Aztecs. Without even asking, Vax knew that Diego would have dealt with Cora—he would have ended her life swiftly and mercifully.

Vax hadn't let him, though. Ending her life would be the cross that Vax would bear for failing her. When Cora had disappeared, Vax had almost gone insane. It had taken nearly two weeks to find her, and by that time it was too late. The vampire that had kidnapped her had already Changed her. His taint had settled deep inside Cora, and the sweet, loving woman Vax had married had become feral. Little more than a killing machine.

Diego had tried to take the knife from Vax. Tried to send Vax away.

But if she was going to die because of his failure, then she'd die by his hand.

He could still remember the way she looked, hiding deep inside one of the numerous caves in the area around Carlsbad, in the Territory of New Mexico. There had been a miniscule fire flickering, giving him entirely too much light to see by.

He could have gone to his grave without seeing Cora like that. He would have gladly gouged his eyes out if it would undo the memory of how he had found her that night.

Blood had painted her mouth and chin a garish red. She'd fed sometime during the night, and by the looks of it, she'd drained whomever she'd fed from. Her lips were parted just enough for Vax to see the tips of newly emerged fangs.

She was alone in the cave.

Vax and Diego had already found the vampire that sired her. The feral had taken Cora from the bed she shared with her husband. He'd come silently one night while Diego and Vax were out Hunting, trailing after a rapist. The vampire had left but a torn nightgown and a few drops of blood and semen on the sheets.

Vax had hoped she'd survive the Change intact.

But after being raped by a feral vampire, sired by a feral vampire, Cora hadn't stood a chance.

With a hoarse cry, he spun away from the mirror, covering his face with his hands. It didn't block out the images, though. Didn't stop the memories from playing through his mind like a movie flashback.

It had been too much to hope that she wouldn't wake up.

As though she sensed his presence, her eyes had opened while he was still standing there, trying to make himself do what had to be done. She had leaped to her feet and rushed towards him, moving with inhuman speed. But she wasn't looking to hurt him. She had been crying.

"I knew you'd find me," she had whispered as she kissed him on his chin, his neck, all over his face. "I knew you'd find me. . . ."

"I'm sorry, Cora." He reached up, brushing her hair back from her face. He loved playing with her hair, combing through the thick curls, fisting his hands in it as he kissed her.

"Sorry?" She started to ask him why, but then she looked over his shoulder. He knew she understood the minute she saw Diego.

Eyes wide with terror, Cora jerked away. She held her hands in front of her naked body, trying to ward him off. "Vax, please. You can't do this."

He reached out, threading his hand through her red-gold curls one more time.

"Vax, please! You love me, remember?" As she pleaded with him, tears sparkled in her sky blue eyes. Her heart was racing—he could hear it.

"Yes. I do love you," he murmured. "Shhhh . . ." He lowered his lips and kissed away the tears streaming down her cheeks.

"We can make it right, Vax. I know we can—you just have to help me."

"I will." He tipped up her chin and kissed her gently before guiding her head to his chest. He held her with one arm.

With the other, he drew the silver knife from his waist. Am I really going to do this?

As though he were watching it happen to somebody else, he saw himself raise the knife. Watched as he drove it into Cora's smooth, silky back. She arched against him, screaming. A little puff of smoke escaped her lips, and the scream ended in abrupt silence.

"You did what you had to, my friend," Diego whispered. "This is not your fault."

Vax sat on the floor of the cave, holding his dead wife in his arms. "Yes, it is. I should have saved her."

T HE ugly, misshapen tattoo on his back seemed to be throbbing. Fiery pain licked along his flesh, as though somebody had just branded him. He had a sour taste in his mouth, and acid burned its way up his throat.

His words from earlier echoed in his mind.

Failure.

He turned and looked at his reflection in the mirror. Over the past ninety-plus years, he had been approached by more Council emissaries than he could count. Rejoin the Hunters. Come to Excelsior and teach. Join the Council itself.

Each time, he had refused. They couldn't get a reason out of him. Nothing more than a flat refusal.

But they should know the answer.

Those who had mattered most to him in life had suffered and died, and he hadn't been able to do a fucking thing to save them.

Vax Matthews was a damned failure.

L ESS than an hour after he'd left so abruptly, he came back in her room. Jess had an apology on her lips, but after seeing the look on his face, it died. He didn't want to hear it, she could tell just by looking at him.

"Time to go," he said. He grabbed her bag from the foot of the bed in one hand and with the other he closed his fingers around her upper arm and pulled her to the door. She gave the coffeepot a forlorn look and let him drag her out of the room.

Even though she'd actually gotten sleep, she was still so tired she felt stupid with it. She needed a little more caffeine, and now. But she didn't bother asking him to wait so she could pour a cup to go. He'd take off without her in a heartbeat, she knew it.

Why he was suddenly in such a hurry, she didn't know. It was close to ten in the morning and he was moving along like they had a plane to catch or something.

The hungry lover from last night was gone. She couldn't call him a gentle lover—her body ached too much to call him gentle. But it was the sweetest ache imaginable. She couldn't walk without remembering last night. In vivid detail.

She plodded along beside him down the dimly lit hall, trying not to think too much about her need for a caffeine fix. She almost lost that fight when she passed by the room right next to the elevator. Somebody was brewing coffee in there.

Vax slid her a look out of the corner of his eye. "I haven't checked out yet. You can get coffee downstairs while I do that. Stop scowling. You'll scare people."

"I'm really going to scare people if I don't get caffeine soon." She grumbled under her breath but followed him into the elevator.

She waited right by the doors and slid through them the second they started to open. Oh, yes. There was coffee. Hot, fresh, and strong enough to help clear up her fogged mind.

By the time she followed Vax out to the car, Jess felt human. She even relinquished the keys to her car and slid into the passenger seat without a complaint. As he took the driver's seat, she asked, "What do we do now?"

"Go back to Indianapolis. Find Dr. Frankenstein's lab. Destroy it."

He said it as though he were ticking each item off some invisible list. He started the car and pulled out of the parking lot. He hit the road and headed north. A few minutes later they were heading east, back the way they'd come late last night.

Vax hadn't so much as looked at her.

Jess didn't feel the need to always fill silence with useless chatter, but this quiet was making her uneasy. Vax wasn't just being quiet. He wasn't just not looking at her. He'd shut himself off completely.

Shouldn't have said anything, she thought dismally. Vax had started pulling back when she asked about the tatts on his back. She'd sensed it, seen the pain in his eyes, but instead of letting it go, she kept on pushing.

Then she had asked about *that* one, the big, ugly tatt that looked like it had been carved into his skin with a dull, rusty knife. There was a story behind that one that Jess wasn't sure she wanted to hear.

She felt like she was looking at a stranger and it hurt, because it was her own damn fault. If she had kept her mouth shut, maybe he wouldn't have pulled away so hard and fast.

There were a thousand other things she wanted to ask him, and a thousand things she wanted to say—almost all of them started with an apology that she knew he didn't want to hear. Instead, Jess just stared at the paper coffee cup. She finished off the rest of the coffee and put the cup in the console's holder.

"Any idea how we're going to find Frankenstein's lab?" she asked softly. She slouched down low in the leather seat and tucked her chin against her chest, exhausted and miserable.

"Yes." He drove with just one hand. The other arm rested along the car door, his fingers strumming out a beat.

Apparently he wasn't going to elaborate. "You feel like telling me how you're going to find it?"

This time he looked her way. It was just long enough for their eyes to meet; then he looked back at the road. "You're going to do it."

"Me?" Jess sat up and glared at him. "You know something I don't? Exactly how am I supposed to find it?"

"I'll help you with that." His voice was hard and flat, and for some reason it made her even more uncomfortable than she already was.

Nervous, she mumbled, "I don't think I much want your help."

"What was that?"

Jess closed her eyes. "I said I want some more sleep."

"I T's been four days. Dena is not coming back."
William stood with his back to the room, staring down through the security glass at the dance floor below. It was a one-way mirror. He could see out. Nobody could see in. William liked standing there and watching the figures gyrating below. When it got crowded like this and all the private rooms were reserved for more intimate parties, many of their patrons didn't bother waiting.

At last count, there had been eleven pairs of dancers getting it on. Well, one of them was two-on-one action instead of one-on-one. A cute young woman who had dyed her hair pink was sandwiched between two guys. William would have enjoyed it more if the bony-assed kid wasn't involved. He was blocking William's view of the girl.

The girl had a touch of magick ability. William really would have liked to bring her upstairs, have Thomas speak with her. She would have been a wonderful addition to the research. She was young, and the power was just barely beginning to spark inside her—the best kind, as far as he was concerned. She might fight it—it was better when they fought it.

William liked being involved in that part. When the chemicals were injected and the transition started, it made them burn. Drove them just a little crazy with fear. William liked playing with that fear. Liked seeing how far he could push them . . .

"Stop drooling over that one, Will. We aren't taking another woman even distantly connected to the club. We can't risk it."

William turned back to Thomas with a smile. "You worry too much. But relax. I know. We've already discussed this." He glanced towards the cute would-be witch and murmured, "Pity, though. She would have been fun."

Thomas shrugged. "I imagine. Bugger, Will, if you want her that badly, bring her up to one of the rooms. As long as she leaves alive and relatively unharmed, do what you want with her."

"Hmmm. She might object to what I want." Reaching inside his suit jacket, he withdrew a slim cigar case. He selected one, lit it, and took a deep drag.

"If she does, I'll handle her." Now Thomas smiled a little. "You're right. She does look like fun. I think I'll have Xeke speak with her. Invite her back to the upstairs rooms. Tomorrow, maybe. She'll need a bath."

The woman in question arched between to the two men. The soundproofed room kept them from picking up anything outside the room, but William imagined he could hear her screaming as she came. Very pretty—not all women looked so damned sexy when they peaked. "Have Xeke send flowers as well. Some champagne. Maybe a new dress."

He turned and saw that Thomas was looking at him weirdly. William just shrugged. "New dress. Flowers. Wine. If she's like most women, she'll primp a little. Soak in a nice hot bath for a while."

"Good thinking." Thomas's smile faded. "We still need to discuss Dena. I knew she wasn't ready to go out alone."

"You've sent someone to the reporter's house?"

Thomas nodded. He held a tumbler of whiskey in his hand, and he took a slow sip before looking back at William. "Dena was there. I sent Silas, and he could smell her. There was some blood. Some was human, but most of it was Dena's. There was somebody else there besides the woman." Thomas paused and took another sip. When he looked up, his eyes were dark and unreadable. The vampire was a bit worried about something.

"Do we have any idea who it was?" William asked.

A faint smiled appeared on Thomas's face. He lifted his glass in a salute. "Silas said it smelled like a witch. A man."

William snarled. Turning from the one-way mirror, he shook his head. "A witch suddenly shows up just when Dena would have eliminated our pest. I don't like it, Thomas." He started to pace as tension mounted in his body. He was acutely aware of the muscles coiling, shifting, stretching as he moved around the room. His skin itched. Fear had a way of tempting the wolf into trying to come out. William had his wolf under control, though. He wouldn't shift just because there might be a Hunter nosing around.

"Calm yourself, William." Thomas moved to the bar and splashed more whiskey into his glass. "Not all witches are Hunters. We already know the little sister was gifted. The reporter might well be. And birds of a feather . . ." He drank some whiskey and shrugged.

"Will flock together," William finished. He rolled his head back and forth, moved his shoulders restlessly. None of it eased the tension coiled in his muscles. Nothing except shifting would. "Perhaps you were right. We shouldn't have sent Dena out. At least not alone."

"I have been thinking about shutting down the lab. At least for a while. We could sell the club. Go elsewhere."

William turned and stared at Thomas. "No. There's no reason for that."

Thomas was still nursing his whiskey and paused with the glass almost to his lips. "I do think I'm probably just being cautious. However, I would rather be cautious and alive than careless and dead."

William shook his head. "It isn't being careless. If a Hunter moves in, we'll know. We'll have time to leave. It's not like we haven't prepared for a time when we might have to leave abruptly."

Thomas sighed. He dropped into his chair and leaned back. "And if we do not have time? Yes, I'll sense a vampire. As you would likely sense a shape-shifter. But what if they send a witch?" He cocked a brow and said, "You're still new to magick, Will. And it's a subtle ability. A good witch could hide herself from you until she was all but breathing down your neck."

William smiled confidently. "They wouldn't send anybody here alone, Thomas. We'll know." He closed his eyes, imagined he was shifting, clothes ripping as his body reformed itself. Running. "We've put too much into this to run just because of one lone witch."

HER temper was shot.

Jess had tried to understand why Vax had retreated so fast—whatever his failure had been, it had hurt him. A lot. She could see that. If he had just withdrawn emotionally, she could have tolerated that. It would have *sucked*, but she could have done it.

Yet after three hours on the road with nothing but that one cup of coffee from the hotel, she was at the end of her rope. He hadn't stopped once, not for food, not for a bathroom, and not for coffee. Every single question she'd asked had been met with either total silence or a bark.

So she'd overstepped her bounds, she got the point, but he didn't have to keep on snarling at her half the damn day. And now . . . She curled her lip as she climbed out of the car and stared up at the roadside motel where they had stopped.

It was inching close to two in the afternoon but there was plenty of daylight left. She almost asked him why they'd stopped, but before she could, he disappeared into the office. When he came back out, she didn't quite trust herself to say anything. Not until she had used the bathroom and gotten something to drink, something to eat.

She didn't get hungry too often—most often she had to make herself eat, but she usually didn't go so long without food. Jess couldn't remember the last time she'd eaten anything—she was pretty sure she hadn't eaten yesterday, so maybe dinner the night before? Had she eaten breakfast? She could have gone for a decent meal for once, but there wasn't any chance of that, not here.

"We're upstairs," he said as he grabbed her back. He still hadn't looked at her.

Fine. Be that way, she decided as she slammed the car door and spun on her heel. She stalked towards the stairs and took them two at a time, and he stayed at her back the entire way.

"So what crawled up your ass and died?"

Jess stopped in her tracks and turned to glare at Vax. "Excuse me?" She stomped down the hall and shoved him, planting her hand in the middle of his chest. "I know I pissed you off this morning, but give me a break. I didn't even have a chance to brush my teeth this morning, and I haven't had anything to eat in more than a day. You haven't answered a single question I've asked, and now you bring me to this fleabag? I don't even understand why in the hell we are here. Didn't we come to get a job done?"

She shoved against the metal railing and watched the posts move under her hand. The concrete was crumbling. No way the railing would hold up if anything heavier than a toddler fell against it. She didn't even want to think about how the room was going to look.

Vax looked at the railing and then back at her. His lashes drooped over his eyes, and he just shrugged. "We need some place to crash while we're looking for him. Might as well be here since you can't go home."

Jess propped her hands on her hips and drawled, "Gee, ya think? There's probably yellow tape and fingerprint dust all over my house. I've probably got cops wanting to talk with me. And there's no telling what my neighbors saw. But shit, *here*? You've been barking and growling at me all day. When you haven't been barking and growling, you've been ignoring me. And now I'm supposed to sleep in a hotel so damned dirty, I'll be afraid to pee here. Do you still want to know what—how did you put it? oh, yeah—*what crawled up my ass and died*?"

Vax just shrugged and said, "You want to bail, you can do it at any time." He didn't look like he gave a damn one way or the other.

Jess jabbed her index finger into his pectoral muscle so hard, it hurt her finger. "I'm not *bailing*. But if I do decide that I can't handle your shitty attitude, or your arrogance, or your moodiness, I'll just do what I planned to do all along. I'll go after William Masters myself."

Oh, finally. Something showed on his face.

His eyes narrowed down to slits as he reached up and closed his hand around her wrist. Vax squeezed lightly, careful not to hurt her. Her wrist looked fragile and pale caught in his hand.

He moved forward, using his body to crowd her up against the brick wall. In a soft, menacing voice, Vax said, "You'll damn well keep your skinny ass away from him unless I'm with you. You go nowhere without me, remember, blondie?"

"My skinny ass?" Jess repeated. Her brows arched upward and her mouth turned down in an angry sneer. "You know, you didn't seem to mind my skinny ass last night." She narrowed her eyes at him and added, "By the way, about last night—"

Vax shut down. He let go of her hand and stepped back. "Last night was a mistake. Shouldn't have happened."

Okay, she was not going to think about how much that hurt. She hadn't been able to think about much of anything else ever since it had happened. Stuck in the car with him, smelling that warm, sexy scent, reliving every last moment of the past night. She'd even let her thoughts get a little bit sappy. It had been a long time since she had felt a man's body pressed against hers while she slept. A long time since she had felt much more than a passing attraction—last night had definitely not been a passing attraction to her.

Jess didn't know what to think about last night. She didn't know how she should feel about it. She hadn't ever felt anything like the heat that had flared between them, but it had felt like so much more than that. Heat, as sweet as it could be, was superficial. It was there, and then it was gone.

Heat didn't rock her to her very core. Last night had.

She'd known it was a mistake. How could it be anything else? He was a Hunter, here for one purpose, and when he was finished, he'd be gone. But, still, hearing him voice it hurt. The sharp, twisting pain knifed through her.

It hurt. But she'd be damned if she let him see that.

"Well, gee. I'm so glad you decided that *now.*" Jess reached out and snatched the keycard from his hand. As she strode down the landing, she called out, "Me and my skinny ass will be in the room. *Without* you. You want a room, get your own."

After locking herself in the room, she turned on the lights and stared at the small, dingy space. She started towards the bed, but halfway there, she turned away. She finally curled up on the floor with her back pressed to the door. Arms wrapped around herself, she closed her eyes and worked very, very hard to think about absolutely nothing.

VAX watched as the door slammed shut behind Jess. He almost barged in on her. So what if she wanted to be left alone? He'd told her how it was going to be, and he . . .

He turned away from the door and shoved a hand through his hair. He had been acting like a bastard since that morning.

He could have taken the coward's way out and claimed it had to do with all her questions—she had unwittingly been digging into very old wounds, and it had hurt like hell.

But it went deeper than that. Her questions just reminded him of a promise he had made to himself ages ago. They had only known each other a few days, but even in that short span of time, Jess had worked her way under his skin, and he couldn't let that continue. Vax wasn't going to let her mean anything to him. It seemed as though almost everybody who mattered to him died. He lifted his hands to his face, pressing the heels of his palms against his eyes.

She was pissed off, and she had a damn good reason. Instead of treating her like a lover, he'd treated her like a stranger. It was safer for her in the long run. He knew that. But it was a damned shitty way to treat anybody, much less the first woman in decades who'd made him feel anything.

Silently, he walked over to the door. He laid a hand against it and opened his mouth to call out her name. He didn't, though.

He just waited there for the longest time. He lowered his shields, trying to pick up something from her, but there was nothing. She had locked herself down good and tight. *Sorry, Jess.* He mouthed it silently and then turned around, heading back to the car. They both needed clean clothes and food. He'd get those and later he'd try talking to her again, see if he couldn't get things back on an even keel.

L ESS than two hours later, he stood at the door and only wished it could be that easy. Jess's response to his knock had been *Go away*. He told her that he had some clothes for her and she ignored him. Food? The suggestion she gave him for that might not be anatomically impossible, but it sure as hell wouldn't be pleasant.

He was tempted to go to one of the vending machines for coffee and try to use some of that to coax her into opening the door. Instead, he went back to the office and paid for the room next to hers. He'd let her cool down a little more. Use that time to convince himself that distance was a good thing.

If she left the room, he'd hear her, and then—then . . .

"Then what?" he muttered to himself as he unlocked the door to his own room and stared inside. It was dank, dismal, and not particularly clean, but he didn't leave. Instead, he stepped inside and closed the door.

There was no *and then*. He needed to distance himself from her, and she sure as hell didn't need to spend any more time around him than necessary. She didn't realize it, but he was doing her a favor by pushing her away.

And if he kept telling himself that, maybe, come morning, he'd believe it. Maybe it wouldn't feel like he had just totally screwed up something important.

A ND then again, maybe not.
Vax woke up to the sound of a diesel engine roaring to life out in the truck parking lot behind the hotel. They had checked in a little past two p.m., and it hadn't been quite five when he'd had locked himself in the room next to Jess's. It was too close to nightfall for them to get much accomplished that night, and he didn't want to do it when Jess was still so pissed anyway.

If this was going to work, they both had to put what happened yesterday behind them. Otherwise, one or both of them were going to be distracted and that only led to bad, bad things in Vax's line of work.

So he had spent the whole damn night in the room, dozing off and on. Each time Jess moved around next door, he'd heard her. She'd left the room twice and he had opened his own door just enough to watch her walk down the hall to the vending area.

The second time, she'd seem him watching her. He'd opened the door a little wider and almost went out to her. But she had averted her eyes and hurried into her room, making it pretty damn clear she didn't want to talk to him.

Hopefully, she wasn't still so pissed off at him, but even if she was, they were going to have to deal with it. Although he had a feeling a night in this dump hadn't done anything to improve her mood. It sure hadn't done much for his, and he had reasons for coming here.

He lay on the still-made bed, arms crossed over his chest as he stared up at the ceiling. It was cracked, yellowed, and water-stained. The sad thing was, it was the nicest part of the entire damn room. The floors were soiled with food, drinks, and various body fluids. The smell was enough to make him sick even if he hadn't had a sensitive nose.

He climbed from the bed with a desperate urge to shower, but he already knew the shower was too disgusting to use. "Shit." He turned back and stared into the room. He decided he needed a swift kick in the ass.

He had a viable reason for picking a sleazebag hotel. He had paid cash for the rooms. Places like this would overlook little things like ID if you handed them a little extra cash. He had no idea if Masters and Fitzpatrick were looking for Jess, but it seemed likely. He wasn't going to risk it, and that meant staying out of the nicer hotel chains.

But he could have found something a little better than this. It was nothing short of a miracle that sirens hadn't woken him up at least once.

A faint sound from the room next door made him stand still. It wasn't Jess. She had the room on the other side. He could hear people moving around, though, heard somebody swear when an alarm clock went off and a couple more people bitching because the alarm woke them up as well.

If people were moving around, it was time for them to get out of here.

Vax had thought he couldn't feel much worse, but when Jess opened the door and he saw the bruised-looking circles under her eyes, he knew he'd been wrong. Guilt swam through his stomach.

She had splashed water on her face, probably in an effort to wake up. Her hair was slightly damp. She hadn't used the shower. He would have heard it if she had, and he suspected she'd had the same reaction to the bathroom as he had.

I'm sorry. He practiced the line silently and figured it was just a little too lame to let it go at that. *Sorry I'm a bastard and that I made you sleep in a hotel not fit for the living.* That was a little better, but before he could offer his apology, Jess pushed past him without a word.

He caught up with her as she started to descend the stairs. She didn't look at him once as she said, "I need a clean bathroom. Now. Give me my damn keys."

He did so silently, holding them in his palm. She snatched them without touching his hand, but when she would have turned away, Vax reached out. He didn't grab her, just touched his fingers lightly to her cheek. Her skin had a translucent look to it, she was so pale. The area under her eyes looked nearly black. He had a feeling she hadn't slept at all. "I'm sorry."

Her brows went up. "Really. For what? For staying a hotel too disgusting for words? I wouldn't let a corpse sleep here. Or for being a rotten bastard?"

Her words echoed his own thoughts so closely, it was unnerving. Vax murmured, "Both."

Jess studied him. She was just a little gratified to see that he didn't look as though he'd slept any better than she had. But then again, Jess hadn't slept, period. So even five minutes would have been better than what she had managed. "Does that mean you're going to act a little less like a bastard today?"

He looked away. When he kicked at the broken asphalt with a booted foot, she felt the corners of her mouth quiver in a smile. There was something pathetically cute about seeing a grown man looking so sheepish. "A little's about all I can promise."

"Fine." She shrugged and turned away. She considered seeing whether she could make him really grovel. That would be a sight, if she could manage it. But she didn't see him doing the grovel bit so easily.

"That's it?"

She glanced back at him and said, "That's what?"

"You lock yourself in there for, what . . ." He glanced towards the horizon, as though he were gauging the time. "Nearly sixteen hours, and that's all the hell you're going to give me?"

She'd looked at the clock on her way out and knew it was closer to seventeen hours, but who was counting? She glanced down at her clothes and plucked the shirt away from herself with a grimace. "I'm too hungry for hell. I don't want to mess with giving hell. I want a shower, clean clothes, coffee, and food. Then I might feel like giving you hell."

In response, he pushed a bag at her. Jess looked inside and, despite herself, she felt her heart melt just a little. She'd told herself she needed to follow his example and back off a little, but she didn't know if she could manage it.

The bag held clean clothes. Clean, new clothes that hadn't been washed yet, but she didn't give a damn. When she looked up at Vax, he jerked his head towards the room and said, "Go ahead and change."

"Ooooohhh no. There's a truck stop off the interstate, ten miles north of here. I want a shower before I put anything clean on." Clean clothes, a shower . . . Oh yeah, that was going to be heaven.

Plus, the truck stop had an adjacent Panera Bread. That meant coffee and a nice, fresh bagel.

By the time she finished in the shower, Vax was already sitting down and it looked like he'd demolished his breakfast already. After paying for coffee, a bagel, and an apple, she joined him at the table.

He didn't say anything, and she spent the next fifteen minutes filling her belly and fueling herself with two cups of coffee. By the time she'd finished, she felt human again.

She just might be able to make it through the day without killing the witch at her side.

Of course he also wasn't giving her those dark, sexy smiles that made her heart start doing a funny little cha-cha, either.

Vax sat across from her. In front of him there was a demolished soufflé, a half-eaten cheese bagel, an apple core, and a tall glass that had held milk. The man could put away food like nothing she'd ever seen. Curiousity got the better of her, and she asked, "You always eat like that?"

Vax looked away from an open copy of the *Star*. "Generally, no. I tend to eat more than that. Just not very hungry today."

All that, and he wasn't very hungry. "Exactly what do you define as hungry?"

He smiled. "Usually I'd want some pancakes, some bacon or sausage." He eyed her bagel. "Definitely something more substantial than a chewy piece of bread. And speaking of that chewy piece of bread, since you're done with it, we need to go."

Jess drained the rest of the coffee and stood up. "Let me get a refill." She also bought a bottle of water. On the way out, she swung by the restroom. She met Vax out in the car and wasn't surprised to see him sitting in the driver's seat again. "I guess I don't need to ask how you managed to get inside, do I?"

He just shrugged. "You're going to be too distracted to drive." If he hadn't had that no-nonsense, *I mean business* look on his face, Jess would have assumed he was talking about something a little more fun. But he did have that look.

A<small>ND</small> *distracted* was an understatement. Jess could feel the sweat rolling down her face and she wanted desperately to move, wanted a drink, wanted to *stop*. But Vax's low, hypnotic voice wouldn't let her. Every time she tried to pull back inside herself, his voice was there.

She hadn't ever put much stock in the powers of meditation, but then again, she hadn't ever witnessed them. Much less experienced them. It had taken less than four minutes for Vax to lull her into a deep meditative state. His voice guided her. She hadn't ever felt so attuned before. She could hear her heart beating. She could feel each and every breath moving in and out of her lungs.

But she sucked at the psychic bit. Totally sucked. Vax insisted that even a brief contact with Dena should be enough. *Something wrong happened to her. Happened to others. What happened to her goes against the laws of nature. Psychic skill doesn't work against nature. It works with it. If you focus, you'll be able to sense the wrong. You can feel it. You can find it.*

His words kept circling around in her head, and Jess blew out a harsh breath. *The hell I can.*

His hand tightened on her neck. "You're not focusing, Jess. Breathe in. Slow. Breathe out. Slow. In. Out."

"I'm not in labor," she snapped, trying to shrug his hand away. "I don't need a Lamaze coach." Vax suppressed a laugh. Jess slid him a dark look. "You think that's funny."

A smirk canted up the corners of his lips, and he shook his head. "No."

Jess took a deep breath. "Look, can we take a break? I'm hotter than hell, and I can't seem to breathe very well. Geez, who would have thought that meditating was so damned hard?"

Vax pulled his hand away and shrugged. "You're not focusing hard enough." He glanced in the rearview mirror and changed lanes.

"It's not that easy, pal. I keep hearing car horns, sirens." *You.*

She could hear him, smell him. How was she supposed to be able to concentrate when she couldn't quit thinking of him? She blew out a breath and propped her elbow on the car door. "It's just not that easy."

"I know."

He stopped the car and Jess looked around. They were in the parking lot of Circle Centre Mall. Under normal circumstances, she would have made a sarcastic remark about how the timing was all wrong for shopping. But she'd been wearing the same clothes for two days, and she was damn tired of it. "Oh, man. Clothes. I want. Gimme."

She closed her hand around the handle, but before she could open the door, the locks went down. She scowled at Vax.

"I bought you clothes."

Jess glanced down at the form-fitting black T-shirt and jeans. They were stiff and had that new-clothes smell, but she wasn't complaining. However, that bag hadn't included underwear. She needed a bra and she needed some panties. Right now, she was going without panties, which wasn't particularly comfortable with new jeans. The shirt was too form-fitting to *not* wear a bra, but if she had to wear her current one too much longer, she was going to burn the damn thing.

Patiently, she said, "You bought me jeans and a shirt. I need underwear. A bra."

His eyes dropped, lingered on her chest for a minute. Her body responded accordingly—her mouth went dry, her nipples peaked, and deep inside, she started to ache.

When he spoke, his voice was just a little hoarse. "We aren't here to shop. Once you get your focus, it's easy. And I can help you find your focus—if you trust me."

Jess looked longingly towards the stores. "Ten minutes? Please?"

Vax gave her that infamous narrow-eyed look. The one where his eyes resembled cold steel. "You signed on for this, Jess. We've got a job to do. It doesn't include shopping."

"Does it include us running around wearing the same bra for days on end and no underwear?"

At that, his eyes blazed. His gaze dropped, lower this time, and Jess flushed as she realized just where he was staring. Suddenly, the air in the car seemed to boil with the heat coming off him. He turned away and hit the button to unlock her door.

Jess hesitated and he slanted a look at her. "Get out now—or you might not be wearing pants in a minute."

VAX had to give her credit.

She didn't just make it fast.

As she came striding out of the mall, he kept thinking

about the fact that she'd been sitting next to him for the past couple hours, naked under the jeans.

His cock throbbed, and he glanced towards his lap. "Down, boy," he muttered. But his penis obviously had a mind of its own—just thinking of how she had looked after he'd made her scream out his name was enough. Now his body was determined to experience it again.

Uncomfortable, Vax shifted in the seat.

He'd guessed at her size when he'd bought her clothes, and he'd guessed just a little too well. The jeans outlined her long, slender legs like a second skin, and the shirt wasn't much better. It clung to her body, outlining each and every subtle curve. It ended about an inch above her blue jeans, and the bare skin between was smooth and pale. Vax knew just how soft and sweet her skin was. He could remember pressing his mouth to the shallow indentation of her navel, kissing lower and lower. . . . He decided he hadn't spent enough time on that, though. Another three or four hours might take the edge off. For now.

Jess climbed inside the car and tossed a green and white bag onto the floor along with a pink striped one. He recognized the pink one and had to suppress a groan as he thought about Jess and lingerie. The scent of her filled his head, though, making it damn hard to *not* think about her, lingerie or otherwise.

"You okay?"

A glance at the green and white bag explained why she smelled so good. She'd taken a couple of minutes to hit a bath shop. "You really know how to make good use of your time. Got any money left?"

Jess gave him a cheeky smile. "Hell, yes. End-of-the-season clearance." She pushed her hands through her hair and leaned back against the seat with a smile. "I feel a hundred times better. All right. Let's do this."

Vax had to give her credit. Once she decided to focus on something, she really focused. Within ten minutes, he had her a deep trancelike state. Reaching out, he took one limp hand from her lap and folded it in his. Vax pressed his palm to hers, watching her face. Her lashes didn't even flicker when he said, "It's time. You linked with Dena. You felt what had been done to her."

She flinched a little. "Dena felt wrong. On the inside."

"I know." He kept his voice soothing. Trances made people vulnerable, even to their own memories and thoughts. Her shields had kept her from feeling what Dena was feeling, but in a meditative state, with her shields lowered, Vax hoped he'd be able to strengthen the connection enough that Jess might be able to sense something.

Anything.

Dena hadn't been a willing volunteer. Or maybe she had started out that way and changed her mind. Whatever it was, there was strong emotion left over, and as Vax slid inside Jess's shields, he knew it was enough. Jess winced as if something hurt. "I feel it. Dirty. Wrong. They've hurt people."

Now the trying part was going to be using her tenuous connection as a compass.

By the time they had something solid, more than two hours had passed. Vax wished they could get a little closer, but he couldn't keep Jess under anymore. She wasn't going to be happy, either. She was sweat-soaked, and her clean new clothes were limp and wilted.

"This is it?"

Jess took a drink from the water bottle and stared in front of her. The gently rolling hills were a far cry from the urban sprawl of Indianapolis, but Jess knew where they were. They were actually not too far from her home. A few years ago, Whitten had been a rural community. It had become very popular over the past few years with urbanites who wanted to experience the "simple life" living forty-five minutes outside the city, and make the commute daily.

Real estate had skyrocketed, and where there were families, came more businesses. Whitten had turned into the modern-age version of a boomtown.

Jess looked at Vax. "This is the best we can do?" She rubbed her hands up and down her arms. "I'm exhausted. I feel like I ran a marathon. But we're done?"

"What we're doing isn't some exact science. You can't set a deadline on yourself and say that by the end of the day you'll have accomplished this, this, and that, Jess. You do what you can, with what you have, as fast as you can. And you did pretty damn good." The sun shining through the window did amazing things for him, glinting off his raven black hair, highlighting the planes and hollows of his face. The sight of him was enough to make her mouth go dry.

Jerking her mind back to the matter at hand, Jess leaned against the hood of the car and studied the main strip of Whitten, Indiana. There were steak houses, Tex-Mex chains, gas stations, and two department stores, and it looked like a third was in process. Just behind them was a sign announcing the availability of units in Whitten Crossing, a modern development for the modern professional. So far, it looked as though several attorneys and a doctor specializing in workplace injuries were the only occupants. She shook her head and said, "There is no way the lab Dena came from is around here. I screwed up."

Vax just smiled. "They aren't going to be advertising it, blondie. They don't give a damn about attracting the modern professional. And you didn't screw up. There's something here." He glanced towards her. "You look pretty steady."

She made a face. "I feel like hell. You could have warned me that this deal was going to make me feel like I went ten rounds." She rotated her neck as she spoke, trying to relieve some of the tension at the base of her skull.

"Why? You would still feel like this." He pushed off the car and moved closer, circling around so that he stood behind her.

When he reached up and cupped a hand over the back of her neck, Jess stiffened. Then he started to rub. It was as though the magick that pulsed in his veins also lived inside his hands. Little by little, each stroke eased the tension, and the ache in her skull started to subside.

A different one took up residence. Low in her belly, that ache spread and grew stronger with each brush of his hand. In a stilted voice, she said, "You ought to be careful about touching me, pal. What if I read something into it?"

"Like what?" He lowered his head and murmured into her ear, "Maybe you can read something into this." He slid a hand around her waist and pulled her back against him. He didn't rock against her, didn't even move, just stood there, his body pressing against hers, close, so close that there was no way she could miss feeling him.

His erection was huge. Jess just barely managed to swallow a whimper before it escaped her lips. "I can read all sorts of things into that." Hell. Her voice had that breathy, gasp-y thing going. Of course, it was amazing that she could even speak. She wanted to turn around and rub her body against his. Wanted to feel his hands on her again. But she wasn't going to.

There was no way in hell. He might not be the chilly stranger he had been yesterday, but she wasn't in any hurry for a repeat performance. Since he hadn't ever bothered to explain what the deal was, Jess figured keeping her distance was safer. Although it wasn't going to be easier.

"But I didn't like the way the story ended last time." She stiffened in his light embrace, refusing to wilt against him the way she wanted. She wanted to turn around and lean into him, press her lips to that hard, unyielding mouth. She wanted to strip out of her damp, uncomfortable clothes and then strip off his clothes so that there was nothing in the way when she climbed on top of him.

Instead she pulled away from him. "I wasn't expecting anything from you, Vax. I don't know if that's why you went and pulled the Mr. Hyde routine. I don't know what the problem was, but I'm not doing that again." Once she was a couple of feet away, she turned and faced him. "I told you that I wasn't into casual. I meant that. Yes, we had sex. Yes, it was my idea. I wasn't expecting wedding bells or anything. But I also wasn't expecting you to treat me like a leper, just because I asked some questions you didn't want to answer."

He closed the distance between them and reached out, catching a lock of her hair. He rubbed it back and forth between his thumb and forefinger as he stared at her. He had the most hypnotic gaze. His gray eyes glowed warm as he stared at her. That gaze gave her all sorts of wicked ideas.

Jess just couldn't forget how cold his eyes had looked just a day ago. So when he reached up and cupped her cheek, she stepped away. "I guess that means you're not in the mood for me to apologize, or try to explain . . ."

"You don't have to apologize or explain. But I don't plan on letting it happen again." She slipped around him and climbed into her car. "I'm worn out. I need some sleep."

CHAPTER 10

You didn't really expect any other response, did you?
    After he had been a total bastard, the last thing Jess was going to do was fall into bed with him. Well, she did fall into bed. Literally. And this bed was clean. Clean and comfortable, and they weren't going to get anyplace more secure than the hotel they were in. If Jess had any qualms about sharing a room, she kept them quiet.

The hotel was owned by a werewolf. Vax had made a phone call early that morning, and when his call was returned, he was given a name and address. The name was Elliott Winston, and the address took Vax to a hotel Elliott owned. He was old, even for a shifter. His hair had long since gone gunmetal gray, and his canny, suspicious eyes were set in a face as lined as a road map. But he was decent.

Vax took one look at the man and knew he could be trusted.

"This an official stay?" Elliott had asked in a raspy voice.

Vax had politely requested that it be unofficial. Elliott

had nodded and said, "So long as you pay, you can have a room as long as you need it. Unofficially, of course." Elliott's only request was that Vax give him a heads-up if shit was going to come in his direction. "Too old for it. Too tired for it. If it's going to come, I'll take a hike."

Vax had no intentions of the old man catching any trouble.

He did have to admit, though, he was pretty surprised the old man had been here as long as he had without trouble coming his way. This area was crawling with paranormal activity. The Council was going to have to get off its bureaucratic ass and get a Hunter out here on a permanent basis.

Just now, all this paranormal activity was going to come in handy. With so many shifters and low- to midlevel witches around, Vax wasn't going stand out so much as long as he didn't use his magick. Witches tended to have a better element of surprise when it came to tracking down ferals. They didn't come up high on the paranormal radar.

Jess wouldn't come up at all. He hoped. Until they knew what they were up against, they had to keep a low profile.

Even though it was only the afternoon, exhaustion pulled at him. He hadn't had a decent night's rest in days, and sleep was a sweet release just a few blinks away. If he stretched out on the bed and closed his eyes, he'd be under in minutes. It would be easy. Vax suspected he could actually sleep. But waking up in the same bed as Jess wasn't going to be wise. Although it would sure as hell be worth it.

"Stop thinking of it," he muttered. He pressed his fingers against to his eyelids and rubbed. But it didn't make it any easier to hold his eyes open. Finally he just gave in to it and let them close. Without looking, he reached with his left hand and snagged the back of the second chair, whipping it around in front of him. Then he stretched out his legs and propped his bare feet on the chair's seat.

Even though exhaustion was like a weight around his neck, his mind wasn't ready to shut down for sleep just yet.

Instead of fighting them, he went ahead and let his thoughts run their course. Come morning, they were going to find that lab. Thomas Fitzpatrick would be sleeping. The man was a vampire—Vax had no doubt about that. He'd spend the day underground, far from the sun. There was a good chance the lab itself was underground. Maybe in a recent construction, one that had a basement, privately owned. Jess might know some people who could help find such a place. Building anything left a paper trail: Trying to sidestep the rules that came with living among mortals was too risky. Neither side wanted to risk exposure—so that meant blending in and following the law of the land.

At least in the grand scheme of things. They drove; they owned businesses, some very lucrative ones, at that.

If he and Jess had to, they'd follow the paper trail. Or Vax would resort to less subtle means. He was debating on which method to better eliminate their asses when he finally fell asleep.

"WHAT is the matter with you?"

William looked up from his contemplation of the earth to find Fitzpatrick staring at him. "You need to feed," William muttered, and he rubbed a hand across his mouth. His belly rumbled in sympathy as he felt the vampire's hunger pangs.

"I intend to. But would you tell me why in the hell you are standing there staring at the dirt?" Thomas moved closer, but then he jumped back as William swiped out. His hand shifted from normal to a hooking claw, one that would have gutted Thomas if he had been standing close enough. By the time William's hand had completed the arc of the swing, it had shifted back to human form.

William's expression never changed. He continued to gaze at the ground with a raptured, intent look on his face. "The earth whispers. I've never heard it whisper so loud before."

Thomas looked up at the sky through the trees, checking

the moon. The full moon was still a few days away. But Thomas suspected the pull was affecting William in some weird way. The magick, perhaps. With every passing day, William's power had increased. But his control hadn't.

Interesting. All sorts of questions were clamoring in Thomas's mind. He wished he had William's chart with him. Thomas even started to reach for a pen to make a couple of notes, but he stopped. Now wasn't the time. Hunger was a ravenous beast inside him. He hadn't fed in far too long. His work tended to consume him, to blind him to anything and everything else. If he didn't feed soon, his hunger would rage out of control.

Thomas found uncontrollable impulses to be utterly distasteful.

"Try to finish up your study of the earth before sunrise. I have some questions for you, Will." He waited for some sort of response, but William just continued to stare at the ground.

Thomas wondered briefly what had William so obsessed. But he had his own obsessions urging him on. He couldn't take time to ponder William's.

William knew that Thomas was leaving. He didn't just hear him leave; he felt it. He felt each distinct footfall. Even when he could no longer hear Thomas, he felt him. William dragged his eyes away from the earth and stared at the trees. He couldn't even see Thomas. Yet he felt him.

This odd awareness had been with him for the past week, and it was growing stronger. He could feel air whistling through the branches. He could hear blades of grass rustling together. The sky seemed bluer, the earth richer—he had never felt so attuned to *life* before.

He thought perhaps the pleasure of ending a life would bring about a rush that would be almost orgasmic. William lifted his face to the sky and sought out the pale glow of the moon. It was nearly full. He could feel the power of it. The beauty. William had the urge to dance, as though the moon were singing to him and there was no way he could ignore its call.

Humming under his breath, William started to move to the moon's music. He danced his way out of the wooded area and stopped. His arms spread out wide, he turned in a slow circle, breathing in the scents of life, magick, and power. He'd spent most of his life blind. He hadn't ever truly felt anything until the magick opened his eyes, his ears . . . his soul.

His spine itched. Giving in to it, he fell to his knees and let free the animal inside. He welcomed the pain as his bones broke and realigned. His flesh rippled almost like it was melting, and when it took solid form again, there was fur instead of skin. The change ended with him on all fours. He threw back his head and howled to the sky.

In this form, with the magick pulsing through his system, he felt unstoppable. He could taste his victims. The pulse of life. The warmth of their blood. He could almost hear their screams. He wanted to hear them. On silent feet, he padded around the building. He could feel them inside. They would scream. They would fight. Some might hurt him. He would not mind the pain, but he wanted to feel it as their lives ended. If they fought hard enough, he would be deprived of that.

So instead of entering the building and following the familiar scents of magick, wolf, and vampire, he ran away. Outside the bright circle of lights, more life beckoned. The pulse of magick sang to him.

As he followed the call, he threw back his head and sang back to the moon.

Vax felt the scream. Heard it in his dreams. It ended in an abrupt, horrific spray of blood. He came struggling into wakefulness, scrubbing his hands over his face. The room was still dark. His limbs felt heavy, and his head wasn't much better.

Vax couldn't see. He rubbed his hands over his eyes, but it didn't help. All he could see was blood. It felt as if it were coating his body, thick, warm, and wet. But when he stumbled into the bathroom and hit the light, there was no blood on him.

Magick rolled through the air. Hot, potent, and foul. There was a satisfaction to it—as though some ravenous hunger had been sated. He could feel the wolf's satisfaction and, just faintly, a yearning for more. More pain. More bloodshed.

More blood . . . The wolf's greedy whisper echoed in Vax's head almost as if he stood before the creature. The taste of blood, metallic and salty-sweet, filled his mouth. He felt meat. Teeth tearing into meat, soft flesh ripping under his claws. Nausea boiled inside him, and he fell to his knees in front of the toilet and vomited. Even after he'd emptied his stomach, the heaves continued.

He knew she was there. He felt her watching him as he reached up and flushed the toilet. He collapsed back against it and stared at her. His vision kept trying to fade out, and Jess's face wasn't clear. Instead of her pale, narrow face, he saw a young woman, hardly more than a girl. Her skin was a smooth, dusky brown, and there was an innocence in her eyes that was rare nowadays.

Then the image changed—her innocence was gone. Her life was gone. Even her pretty, delicate looks were gone, mauled away.

Jess's voice came to him from far off, and then her hands touched him. Vax reached up, seizing her by the wrists and jerking her against him. His vision focused and he could finally see her face. She was pale, her eyes dark and terrified as she stared at him. But she wasn't afraid *of* him. As she leaned against him, he caught a faint flicker of emotion from her.

She was afraid for him. Vax let go of her wrists and wrapped his arms around her narrow waist. He pulled her close and buried his face between her breasts, unaware that he had started to rock himself and Jess back and forth.

"What's wrong, Vax?"

He shook his head, letting her presence soothe his raw emotions. Her shields were up, and it was as if being this close made him part of her shielding as well. Whatever he had picked up, whoever had been broadcasting, he couldn't feel it now. His mind was blissfully, wonderfully empty of everything but his own thoughts and feelings.

Her hands continued to stroke in aimless circles on his shoulders and back, and he let her. Let her soothe away some of the raw pain. He was going to have to deal with it soon enough. He'd have to find the girl. From there, he'd be able to track her killer. In his gut, Vax knew the trail would lead him to the men he and Jess had come to find.

The wolf had felt unnatural. Vax had sensed the magick within the beast and knew it was William Masters. The man he was here to find and stop had just killed another woman, practically right under his nose.

Guilt ate at him. Should he have pushed Jess harder? Her psychic gift was minimal. She had just managed to do some truly amazing things with it. But they had been close. He could all but sense them. This close—they'd been this close to finding the lab and the modern-day version of Dr. Frankenstein.

Gently, Vax eased Jess away from him. He stood up but had to slam a hand against the wall. His legs felt watery. He stiffened them and managed to stumble over to the sink. He reached out and turned the water on, staring at his hands. He was a little surprised to see they weren't soaked with blood. He felt like it stained him. He felt filthy with it.

Failure.

"What's wrong?" she asked again, her voice soft but insistent.

He looked up and saw her reflection staring at him. He almost didn't answer. He didn't want to. It was as if talking about it compounded his failure. But she had to know. Maybe, just maybe, she'd leave and let him handle this. His voice was rusty and tight and squeezing out words was just a little bit painful. "William Masters killed a woman last night."

Her face went as white as death. Her lashes flicked, and her eyes darkened to a deep green. Her tongue came out and she licked her lips. He could see her throat work as she swallowed, and then she blew out a slow, shaky breath. "How do you know?"

He looked down at his hands. He could still feel flesh ripping. As though he had been the one to plunge clawed hands into soft, unprotected skin, and tear. "I felt it."

"Oh, God." Her hands came up, but when she would have pressed herself against him, Vax jerked away. He bent over the sink and splashed ice-cold water on his face. Then he filled his mouth with water and swished it around a little before spitting it out. He could still taste the blood. He grabbed one of the toothbrushes Jess had bought and used what looked like half of the toothpaste. He could have polished his enamel off, and still he tasted blood.

On his way out of the bathroom, he grabbed one of the hand towels and scrubbed at his face.

"Vax—"

He stopped in his tracks, staring down at the faded blue carpet. She slid her hands around his waist. This time he didn't pull away. He wanted to turn around and bury his face in her hair, breathing in the clean, soft scent of her. Maybe it would overpower the scent of blood.

He didn't, though. He just stood there, stiff and still, as she murmured, "Are you okay?"

Even to his own ears, his laugh sounded hollow. "Okay? I just felt his pleasure as he killed a woman. She was practically a kid. So young. Had these big, innocent eyes. He raped her. He eviscerated her. And you want to know if I'm okay." Savagely, he pulled away. A couple of feet separated them when he turned around to glare at her. "I can see her face. I can hear her screams. And I can't stop myself from thinking, if I fuck up again, the next woman he murders is going to be you. But, hell. Yeah. I'm fine. Wonderful."

She took a step closer, and he held up a hand. "Stay away from me now, Jess. Just stay away."

She didn't. She took another step, and another, until she could reach out and link her fingers with his. Her palm pressed against his, and she lifted his hand, kissing the back of it. "This isn't your fault. You didn't make him what he is. You don't control the actions of others. Not his. And not mine."

Before he could say anything else, she rose onto her toes and pressed her lips to his. She slid her other hand around his neck, tugging him closer.

He didn't kiss her back. Jess didn't know how to respond to that, but she couldn't just pull away and leave him alone. Even if that was what he wanted, it wasn't what he needed.

Leaning her head back, she murmured again, "It's not your fault." She slid her hands down his chest, hooking her fingers in his belt loops and pulling him closer. His body felt cool. Too cool. She laid a hand against his chest, and the speed of his heart rate didn't make her feel any better. It was slamming away. With her hand lying over his heart, she looked up at him. His pupils were huge—they were so dilated, she could only see a thin rim of silvery gray around them.

Shock, maybe? She knew that seeing somebody die was a traumatic experience. Feeling somebody die? Been there, done that. Shock didn't even touch it. She cupped his cheek in her hand. "Vax . . ."

His hand was still cool when he reached up and closed it around her wrist. She could feel her pulse racing under his touch. Just that light touch . . . She tried to tug her wrist away, but he held on, lifting it to his lips. He pressed his mouth to the inside. Then he let go. "You don't want to touch me, Jess."

He turned away. For a second, she stood there, staring at the rich, vibrant colors that made up the feather tattoos on his back. Then she reached out and touched him. He stiffened, and then he spun around. Her breath left her lungs in a rush as he hauled her against him. His mouth came down on hers with bruising force, his tongue pushing past her lips, into her mouth.

He kissed as though he were trying to devour her. There was a desperation in every stroke, and it wasn't long before

Jess felt that same desperation. She arched against him with a moan and reached up, burying her hands in the black silk of his hair. She felt a harsh jerk, and there was a sound of ripping cloth. Cool air kissed her flesh as the scraps of her shirt fell to the floor. Vax's mouth left hers as he wrapped his hands around her waist. He boosted her up and closed his mouth around one distended nipple.

Jess groaned and tried to move closer. She couldn't get any closer unless she crawled inside him. That didn't keep her from trying. Jess wrapped her legs around his waist and rocked against him. There, separated by his jeans and her panties, she could feel the thick, throbbing length of his sex. He ripped away her panties and pushed two fingers inside her. Her head fell back. Through her lashes, she stared at the ceiling and struggled to breathe.

His head lifted, and she felt the strands of his hair caressing her flesh. "Look at me." The deep bass rumble of his voice made her shiver. But she didn't want to look at him. Even though she had her legs wrapped around him and she could feel the pulsations of his cock between her thighs, she couldn't look at him. It made her feel too exposed.

He slowed the rhythm of his fingers until he was just barely touching her. "Look at me," he whispered again.

Slowly she looked down at him. His eyes stared into hers, his mouth in a grim, unsmiling line. The room spun around them, and she shivered as he pressed her back up against a wall. "I told you that you didn't want to touch me," Vax muttered as he reached between them. The rasp of his zipper sounded unnaturally loud.

Hungry to feel him against her, she rocked her hips forward and he met her action with one of his own. One hand cupped around the back of her neck, drawing her closer. He didn't try to kiss her, though. His eyes stared into hers, and she could feel the warm brush of his breath against her face. She tried once more to close her eyes, but the hand at her neck tightened. "Open your eyes. I want to watch you."

Pillow talk wasn't her thing. Watching her lover wasn't her

thing. Staring into his eyes as he pumped into her did weird things to her insides. She felt hot, hungry, needy, shaky—and melting. She felt like she could melt against him.

"You're so soft." His lids drooped, turning his penetrating stare into a hooded, sexy gaze. "You're one dangerous woman, Jessica Warren." He bent his head and ran his tongue over her bottom lip; then he caught it between his teeth and tugged gently. "I don't like what you do to my head."

He pushed inside her, hot and throbbing. The entire time, he stared into her gaze. Her eyes were wide and unblinking. He could drown, staring into that gaze. He heard her breath hitch in her throat. Smiling a little, he rotated against her. The muscles in her sex grabbed at his cock, squeezing and caressing his flesh.

"Vax . . ." He bent his head as she moaned, catching the rest of the sound in his mouth. She tasted sweet, clean, and real—so alive. He needed that—needed to feel her and know she was alive and safe.

The dirty, ugly blood dreams had left him feeling stained, and he couldn't get enough of her. Every touch, every shared moan fanned the heat inside him, and the horror of death faded away just a little more. Until the blood and the screams and the death were no longer real to him. All that mattered was Jess, feeling her body move against his, listening to the soft screams.

"Come for me," he muttered. He canted her hips up and shifted so that he hit the stiff little peak of her clit. One stroke and she was arching up, pressing her breasts against him. Two strokes and she gave a breathless little scream. By the third, she was thrashing against him and shuddering her way through orgasm. The pulsating caress of her sex tightened around his cock, squeezing him closer and closer. Vax crushed his mouth to hers as he came.

"Whoa."

Slowly, he lowered her to the floor. They leaned against each other and stared. Finally Vax whispered, "I'm sorry."

Jess reached up and touched her fingers to his mouth. "Why? I'm not."

"We talked about this yesterday—you didn't want it."

She cuddled against him and wrapped her arms around his waist. "I did want it. I just don't like being ignored after."

Closing his eyes, he buried his face in her hair. It was soft and smelled of something feminine and faintly tropical. "You're not that easy to ignore, darlin'. I don't think I'll try that tactic again." He needed to hold her. Just hold her. He picked her up and carried her over to the bed. He braced his back against the headboard nailed to the wall. "So I don't need to apologize?"

Jess shook her head. "I'd rather you not."

H E felt drunk. Almost euphoric. For a mortal, she had packed one hell of a punch. William hadn't fed on her blood, but he could only imagine the kick such rich, ripe young blood would give. It was little wonder that vampires preferred their prey to be so young.

It was more of a wonder that William had waited so long to discover this unique pleasure. He stumbled into the wall as he turned the corner. Snickering a little, he managed to make it the rest of the way to his rooms without any more crashes. He opened the door and closed it behind him. He lurched towards his bedroom without turning on the lights.

Replete and tired, he had one goal in mind.

His bed.

William didn't make it out of the living room, though. Thomas's quiet voice stopped him just a few feet inside. "What were you thinking?"

"Thom?" William turned around but lost his balance. He fell into the wall and his head was spinning so rapidly, he just stayed there, letting the wall support his weight. He flicked on the light and stared into the dimly lit room. Thomas sat in the huge leather armchair by the door. He held a snifter of brandy in his hand, and as he lifted it to his lips, he stared at William.

"You reek of blood. Did you enjoy yourself?"

A foolish grin curved William's mouth, and he said, "I did, thanks. She screamed, Thom. Oh, she screamed." He closed his eyes, playing back the moments in his head and relishing each second.

"Yes. I know. Tell me, Will, have you gone mad?"

William didn't hear Thomas move. When the blow came from behind, it came with a speed and strength that sent William crashing to the floor. Like a bucket of icy water, the blow cleared his head. His eyes narrowed, and he stared up at Thomas.

Thomas crouched down in front of him and murmured, "Yes. She screamed. She screamed so loudly that the neighbors heard. They called the cops. Did you hear the sirens as you left? Or were you too drunk on her blood?"

William thought back, tried to remember. No. It had taken a few minutes to hear anything or even see anything. The adrenaline rush was all-consuming. So he hadn't heard the police. Unable to recall, he said, "No. I didn't hear anybody coming." Then he shrugged. "What the hell does it matter? Nobody saw me."

"They saw your victim." Thomas shook his head. "You stupid arse. I had thought that you had more sense than this. At the very least, the bloody mess you left behind is going to call too much attention. We do not need some bastard from the Council showing up practically on our doorstep to investigate some mysterious brutal murder." His pale brown eyes narrowed, and he reached out. William pulled back, but the vampire was stronger. Thomas hauled William toward him and whispered, "But worse, you risked exposing us all. Exposure now could cost me years of work. If that happens, I will slowly gut you."

William pulled back, and Thomas let him go. Shoving to his feet, he stared at Thomas. His emotions warred between outrage and fear. At least, he thought it was fear. William didn't remember fear very well. He was familiar with trepidation, but this disgusting fear couldn't be tolerated. "Don't threaten me, Thomas."

Thomas's voice was a silky menace. "Oh, my dear friend, I am not threatening you. Just warning you." He reached into his pocket and pulled out a syringe. "I have so many more things I want to explore. So many theories. One of them concerns sensory overload." The syringe was a fat one—it looked like one that would be used to give an injection to a horse. It was filled with a murky yellowish fluid. "This is the chemical we harvest from the witches. Actually, it's a synthetic one. I've been trying to develop this for some time now—finally succeeded. This is highly concentrated. Do you remember your transition? You started showing effects within days, and you were in miserable pain from the moment we started the dose. Well, *this* dose is more than a hundred times more powerful."

William stared at the syringe. For some odd reason, the sight of it filled him with dread. He started to shake. "I've already done the transition, Thom. I know all about it, remember?"

Thomas answered with a curious little humming sound. "You know all about it from *your* standpoint. What you don't seem to see is that this transition has affected your thinking. Until now, I hadn't realized just how much. I do not know whether there is too much power inside your body, or whether you haven't learned to control it appropriately. Of course, if you had listened to my advice and sought out training, perhaps we wouldn't be having this conversation."

Thomas tossed the syringe up into the air and caught it. He twirled it around in his fingers and stared at William with a smile. "I have this theory, my friend. It's possible to overload the senses. Magick is just another sense, after all. A highly refined, highly trained sense. But a sense nonetheless. And this theory of mine . . . well, you need just the right amount of the chemical to induce transition. Too little, and there is no change. Too much, and it will drive the patient insane, if he survives the transition. A massive bolus of the chemical, I believe, might induce a stroke."

William tore his gaze away from the syringe and looked at Thomas. He could remember how it had burned when Thomas had slid the needle under his skin and pushed the chemical into William's bloodstream. It had felt as though he were being shot up with a combination of acid, broken glass, and liquid fire—even more painful than the first time he had shifted.

The syringe Thomas used then had been less than half the size of the one he held now. Then, it had only been half full. Shape-shifters could take a lot of pain—their bodies became conditioned. Shifting was painful. They learned to accept pain; they learned to use it. They channeled it into their need to hunt, or they channeled it into sex.

But William had a breaking point. He suspected he'd meet that breaking point before Thomas injected even 2 ccs of the chemical. "What's the point of all of this, Thomas? So there's one less pathetic human bitch in the world?"

"Yes. One less pathetic bitch. And now there is a woman out there who was killed by something that can't possibly be human," Thomas murmured. He finally stopped toying with the syringe and tucked it back inside his pocket. Even though it was out of sight, William couldn't stop seeing it. "You risked us all."

He tried to brush it off. No human could be a threat to him. He knew that. But Thomas could be. Thomas could be a huge threat. William forced a smile. "Look, it's nearly the full moon. Latent effects of the transition are still manifesting—"

Thomas lifted a hand and shook his head. "Do not try to pacify me. Do not try to offer me trite excuses or lies. You fucked up. Be a man. Admit it. Or just keep your mouth closed. But do not try to pacify me." He finished off his whiskey and rose from his chair. He smoothed down his tie and brushed a few nonexistent wrinkles out of his suit.

William could smell blood on his partner. Thomas had hunted tonight. Rage curdled inside him. Thomas could hunt, yet he thought he had the right to come down on William for it. But he couldn't say anything. He couldn't forget the sight of that syringe.

A smiled curled Thomas's mouth. It was as if he knew exactly what William was thinking. He patted the syringe in his pocket and smiled at William. That smile made William's blood run cold. "If it doesn't kill you, William, it will leave you helpless. Useless. No good to anything or anybody. But I will not end your suffering. I'd rather you think of suffering, lying in a bed, trapping in the confines of your own body, for years and years on end. I'll make sure that I have pretty, young nurses on hand to give you a bath, to change your diaper, to wipe your nose when your immune system can no longer fight off the flu."

William knew fear. He knew it well. Before he'd become a werewolf, he had lived his life in fear. He woke up afraid. He worked afraid. He fell asleep afraid. He took more pills than a seventy-year-old man, but they didn't stop the tremor in his head. Then came that night, that night when everything in his life changed.

Shock, fear, and pain raced through his system as the wolf attacked. Teeth tore into him, and razor-sharp claws punched ragged gashes in his stomach. But when he'd emerged from the fevers of the Change, it was as if he'd left fear behind. It belonged to the pathetic, whining man he had been. He relished his new existence, his *fearless* existence.

But now fear tore into him. It turned his guts to slippery chunks of ice and locked a vise around his throat. He hated Thomas for it. Fear brought the wolf to the fore, and William barely felt it as the bones in his hands reshifted, forming themselves into wicked, hooking claws.

The smile on Thomas's face grew. "You going to strike me, pup?" Fangs slid down, protruding past his lips.

Fear shaped the world before him. As though William was looking at Thomas through tunnel vision, everything went fuzzy and dark. Everything except Thomas's face.

William heard a weird whistling sound and realized he was wheezing for air. A cold, clammy sweat trickled down his back. Tears blurred his vision. He couldn't think . . . couldn't think . . . With hands that shook, he reached up and rubbed his eyes.

It was during those few brief seconds when he had his eyes closed that William realized just how unnatural this was. He didn't feel fear like this. He didn't let it control him. Not anymore. A growl rumbled up out of his chest, and anger rushed through him in a torrent, washing away the fear. "You bastard. How dare you do this to me?" William roared. He struck out and watched as his claws carved four diagonal slices down Thomas' cheek. Blood welled, but even as it started to roll down his face, the lacerations were knitting themselves together.

"How dare I?" Thomas asked. He drew a handkerchief from inside his suit jacket and dabbed at the blood. "I could easily ask you the same question, you fool. You risked us all. You have let this new power go to your head, destroy your common sense. I simply gave you a reminder—you may feel indestructible, but you are not. None of us are."

MURDEROUS images didn't make for a restful sleep. But sleeping with Jess in his arms did. Vax woke up in the same position he had been in when he'd fallen asleep, his back pressed to the wooden headboard and his arms looped around her waist. He'd slept the whole night through, no nightmares. Jess was cuddled against him, her head on his shoulder, her chest rising and falling in a slow, steady rhythm.

She was alive. Safe, sound, and whole. Now he just had to keep her that way.

"You're doing it again." Jess's voice was sleepy, and when he looked down at her, her eyes were still closed. She opened them just long enough to look at him and smile, and then she snuggled closer. "Thinking too loud."

"I woke you up."

" 'S okay." A deep sighing breath escaped her, and she mumbled, "At least it will be if you get me coffee." She opened one eye and looked at him. "Get me coffee?"

He smiled a little. Lowering his head, he pressed a kiss to one narrow shoulder and whispered, "You probably bleed coffee, you know."

"Hmm. Eat, drink, breathe, and bleed it. Get me coffee?"

Vax climbed out of the bed and watched as she rolled onto her side and curled into a ball. "Yeah. I'll get you coffee." He swatted her naked ass gently as he added, "But you have to get up and get moving. Sun's rising. We need to find them today, and the sooner the better."

She yawned so loudly, he heard her jaw pop. After he started the coffee in the small in-room courtesy machine, he turned back to look at her. She sat back up in the bed and pushed her hair from her face before she wrapped the sheet around herself a little better. "Think we'll find them?"

As the rich scent of coffee filled the room, Vax shrugged. He leaned back against the wall and crossed his arms over his chest, pondering his answer. Finally he said in a low, quiet voice, "I think we will. We don't have any other choice."

Jess quirked a brow at him but didn't say anything.

She didn't need to. He could read the doubt all over her face, even though he couldn't feel anything coming off her. Vax rubbed his palms together and stared down at his hands. They had to find them. There wasn't any other alternative. Feeling the weight of her stare, he looked up. She sat in the tangled mess of sheets, surrounded by white sheets and blonde hair.

The sight of her hit him like a short arm jab straight to the solar plexus. A handful of days. That was all. They'd known each other just a handful of days, and she had managed to do what nobody else had done since he'd lost Cora. She had gotten under his skin. She had made herself matter to him.

Nothing could happen to her.

Vax couldn't do it again, lose a woman he cared about to the monsters. "We'll find them," he murmured, more to himself than anything else.

Behind him, the coffeepot made a weird gurgling sound and then it hissed. There were thick, heavy white mugs hanging on pegs attached to the wall. He took two and filled them. As he handed one to Jess, he sat on the edge of the bed and watched her take the first sip. She never waited until it cooled off, even a bit. Instead she hissed a little and took a second sip. She made a soft humming sound, and her eyes closed.

Vax laughed. "I've never met a woman who could make me hard just by drinking coffee," he murmured. "Not until you, at least." He reached up and brushed her hair back from her face, tucking a thick lock behind her ear. After a light kiss, he stood up and murmured, "We need to get going."

J ESS hadn't believed they would do it.

She hadn't believed *she* could do it.

But she had. Cold chills racked her body: She had a serious aversion to walking into the building that sprawled before her. It was a warehouse. Or at least it appeared on the surface to be a warehouse. The place gave her the creeps. Vax stood up, and she snarled at him. "They'll have security cameras, damn it."

He just grinned. "They don't work very well around magick."

"I'm not magick." She stared at the hand he held out to her, and looked around. She spotted two cameras on the first glance. They were still out of the cameras' range, for now. But if she put her hand in his and let him pull her closer to the warehouse, the cameras would catch them, alert anybody watching to their presence.

"I am. Come on." He gave her a gentle, cajoling smile and said, "Come on. Trust me."

Trust me. That was what it boiled down to—oh, the cameras would catch them. Jess didn't see how his being a witch could make the cameras not see him. But did she trust him to protect her inside those walls? That was the question. It was a whole new world inside those walls, and there were creatures within them that she wasn't able to stand against.

Jess blew out a breath and reached for Vax, linking her fingers with his. They started forward, and Jess stared at the cameras. But just before they would have stepped within the camera's viewing range, the little red light started flashing. There were sparks, and then she saw wisps of smoke drift from the camera. Her eyes widened as the same thing happened with the other camera.

They reached the door, and Jess looked at Vax. "How in the hell did you do that?"

He just laughed. "I told you the cameras wouldn't work around me. Technology and magick just don't mingle very well." He slid a hand up and down her back, moving it in slow, soothing circles. "You ready?"

Jess made a face. "Do I have any sort of choice?" The sun was starting to creep up on the horizon, and if anybody worked in this warehouse, then she and Vax needed to be out of sight before they showed up. Jess licked her dry lips and nodded. "Come on, let's do it." She took a step and then froze. "Speaking of *it,* exactly what is it we're doing?"

"Right now, just looking around." He tried the door, but it was locked.

Vax slid her an appraising look. Jess knew what he wanted before he even said anything. But she just gave him a sweet smile. "You worked mojo on the cameras. Do the same on the lock."

He gave her a disgruntled look. "I didn't work *mojo* on anything. Technology and magick don't mix well. I'm lucky—I can use a telephone, drive a car, and listen to electronics. But I've known people who can't even watch TV. There was this woman—she worked a job in the mortal world as a counselor. She usually had her own office, but they were remodeling and so she had a session in the computer lab. Every single computer crashed while she was in there. She never even touched them." He laid his hand on the doorknob and said, "I can use magick, but the more I use it, the worse it affects things around me. If their security system gets fried for no obvious reason, somebody will notice."

Without turning around, he reached behind himself and grasped her wrist, pulling her forward. He took his hand from the handle and replaced it with hers. "You, though, don't have that issue, do you?"

Jess stared down at the handle. Telekinesis worked more easily when she could see things, but she didn't have to. There was next to no weight to the lock. She felt the lightness of it as she unlocked it; there was a *snick,* and then the locks turned. "No. I don't have that issue." Although she sort of wished she did. She'd always been content with the ability she had. Moving things with her mind could come in handy. Could be a good weapon. But it suddenly seemed paltry. The unknown lay inside these doors, and she figured she'd have felt a lot more secure if she had something more in the way of firepower on her side.

Unconsciously she reached behind herself, touching the gun she had tucked inside her waistband. She closed her hand around the butt and almost pulled it out. But she made herself pull her hand away. She looked up and found Vax watching her. He held her gaze and reached up to cup her chin.

"I'll take care of you," he murmured. He pushed her hair back from her face, his fingers brushing against her cheek. Then his hand trailed down her arm and around her waist and then she felt him reach inside her waistband. He pulled out the gun and pushed it into her hand. "If it makes you feel better, carry it."

Jess forced a laugh. "Don't you know how many gunshot wounds happen every year? A lot of them are accidental. You want to be a statistic?"

Vax just bussed her mouth. "I won't be." He linked his

fingers with hers and led her inside. Jess swallowed. Her breathing was too fast. She could feel her heartbeat pounding—it beat against her ribs so hard that it almost hurt. Her ears were buzzing, and everything she saw seemed to take on a weird, surreal quality. Her body felt weightless.

"Breathe, Jess."

Air wheezed out of her in a rush. Hard hands pushed her back into the wall and she looked up. Blinking, she found herself staring at Vax. His eyes were stormy. His hands cupped her face. "Breathe."

Her eyes were too damn dark. Her skin was as white as a bedsheet. Vax didn't like it. He shook his head and muttered, "Let's get you out of here." He caught her hand in his, took the gun from the other one, and tucked it in his jeans. But when he went to pull her away from the wall, she wouldn't come. Jess shook her head and said, "No." She took a deep breath and expelled it in a rush. "I'm fine. I'm fine."

He didn't think she was. But her eyes weren't so dark now, and there was a little bit of color in her cheeks. "It's not too late to get you out of here. Not yet."

Jess gave him a faint smile. "Yes, it is. No turning back, Vax. At least not for me. I can handle it." His hand felt firm and strong in hers. She squeezed lightly. He squeezed back and then murmured, "Let's get to it."

The ground floor of the warehouse had a couple of roughed-in offices, but it didn't look as if they were being used at all. The desks were bare, there was nothing on the bookshelves—the entire area had a vacant feel to it. He found a stairwell, but it didn't go down, just up three floors. "I thought you said it would be underground," Jess whispered.

"It will be. There's another way down." But ten minutes of walking around just revealed two more stairwells and a utility elevator. Vax grumbled under his breath and started to retrace his steps. The warehouse had more cameras and each one had fizzled up into smoke before he got within thirty feet. "No monitors."

"What?"

Looking back at Jess, he said, "I haven't seen any security monitors. Eight cameras, and no locked rooms for employees only. Hell, this entire place looks untouched. It was like they moved the desks and furniture in as soon as the paint dried and never set foot back in here." The place wasn't vacant, though. He smelled them.

Blood. Soap. The faint, wild scent of werewolf. The cool, almost herbal scent he associated with vampires. And women. Even without shampoos, lotions, and perfumes, women smelled different from men. Softer and sweeter, and each woman smelled unique. Vax scented five different women.

The stronger scents belonged to the vampire and the werewolf. They were the ones moving around up here the most, and the most recently. Closing his eyes, he blocked out everything but the faint scent trail. The blood was human—he knew whose. The girl who had died during the night. The werewolf had had her blood on him when he came in here, and it was that scent that Vax locked on. He followed it into the centermost office. Most of the office space was large and open-aired, separated by fabric-covered partitions. But this small office was enclosed, insular. The blood trail came to a dead end right by the built-in bookcases.

"I don't believe it," he muttered. He turned slightly and looked at Jess. "A secret entry. This is a first for me." He cocked a brow. "Can you?"

CHAPTER 11

"BASTARD."

William rubbed a hand over the back of his mouth and tried to forget the bitter, nasty taste that fear had left. He'd seen Thomas in action. Thought he knew what the vampire was capable of. He had been wrong, wrong, wrong. Even though he knew that it had been Thomas's power causing the fear, feeling that fear pissed him off to no end.

He had paced the floor so many times, he wouldn't have been surprised to see tracks in the carpet. It felt as if the walls were closing in on him, but he couldn't seem to make himself leave the room. He wanted to, needed to. He wanted to run and feel the wind on his skin.

Maybe some bloodied flesh under his claws.

In the middle of the room, William came to an abrupt halt. That was exactly what he needed. Maybe not the blood. Not a good idea after last night. Had to lie low. Definitely had to lie low. With the rising sun, the murderous drive from last night had faded, and he knew that it had been too damn risky, what he had done. Way too risky. Stupid.

It was that sort of thing that led Hunters to the doorstep.
That was the last thing they needed right now. "Got to be
careful," William muttered. He nodded and repeated it.
"Be careful."

"It is a little too late for that, pup."

He turned. The sight of Thomas made his gut clench, but
he refused to acknowledge it. William didn't live in fear—
he wouldn't let himself develop an instinctive fear of some
fucking bloodsucker. "Shouldn't you be in your coffin?"

Thomas didn't smile. He came inside and made his way
to the bank of security monitors on the far side of
William's room. "You know, these do more good if you actually have them engaged." He turned them on. Most of the
cameras were trained on the labs on the level below, and
the images on the monitors were nothing remarkable. The
various subjects were sleeping or pacing their cells. One
camera was trained on the only cell that held more than
one person. This one contained the witches that Thomas
used to harvest the brain chemical. They were brain-dead,
but as long as their hearts beat, their bodies would live.
Lower brain function continued. The perfect donors.

But the remaining monitors showed nothing but black
and white bars flashing across the screens. The monitors
from outside and the ground level. Thomas slid William a
look and cocked his brow. "Perhaps if you had the screens
on, you might have seen something before they went
dead."

Unsure what Thomas was talking about, William just
shook his head. "Exactly what was I supposed to see?"

"The Hunter who just found the elevator down here,
perhaps?"

William heard the elevator as it started its descent. He
looked back at the bank of monitors. There was an odd little prickle low in his spine, and he hissed as recognition
tore through his body. Another witch. He could smell them
now. A man. A woman. Powerful magick. Very, very powerful magick.

William growled. Rage sizzled through his veins, and

then there was that disgusting, hated fear. The fear was fueled by some gut-deep knowledge. It was as if his recently acquired magickal sense had a measuring gauge, and when he held himself against this new witch, he came up lacking. He was lesser.

Lesser—my ass. Claws ripped through the tips of his fingers, and his hands shifted so rapidly, he never felt the discomfort that usually came with any sort of shift. "I'll show the bastard who the lesser one is." But when William started for the door, Thomas blocked him.

"Do not be any more a fool than you already are," Thomas said. William went around him, and Thomas backhanded him. "You rush out there without thought, and you are a dead man."

Through a haze of pain and fury, William pushed himself to his feet. He wiped the back of his clawed hand across his mouth. The smear of blood there was the last little spark—blood rage tore through him.

"You are an ignorant arse," Thomas said with a weary sigh. He reached inside his jacket.

William was already rushing him, leaping for him. Even though he saw the syringe in Thomas's hand, the fury and the bloodlust rode him too hard. He took Thomas down under him, and his own body weight pushed the thin needle inside. The drug hit fast, a shock to his system that was instantaneous. First there was a wave of weakness and dizziness. Then black dots closed in on his system. Shoving off of Thomas, he rolled away and stared down his torso. The needle had caught him in the abdomen, and only a scant bit of liquid was left inside the barrel of the syringe.

"What did you . . ." At least that was what he tried to say. It was more along the lines of *wah duh.*

"It's a sedative. An extremely strong one," Thomas offered. He stood up and nudged William's unprotected side. Then he followed with a harder kick. A wide smile spread across his mouth, revealing the tips of pointed white fangs. "You know, when I started this endeavor, I knew that I might at some point encounter fools like you. Individuals

that came through the transition with more power than
sense. That was why I manufactured this—do you know,
this particular narcotic is strong enough to put down three
elephants. Let's see how long it keeps you out. I think I
have a minimum of six hours. . . ."

Six hours was the last thing that William heard. Thomas
watched as William's eyeballs rolled up until just the bottom crescent of the iris showed in the whites of his eyes. A
tiny bit of saliva dribbled out the corner of his mouth, and
his heart beat more slowly with each passing second.
"Bloody fool," Thomas muttered.

The sound of footsteps drawing nearer had him stilling.
With no time to hide William, Thomas shifted into mist.
He passed through the walls, knowing that the Hunter
would sense him and, Thomas hoped, follow. It was too
much to hope for, though. The Hunter had little interest in
him.

It was the lab that the Hunter was searching for. Even if
William's fuckup last night hadn't happened, the Hunter
would have shown up on Thomas's proverbial doorstep. It
was the lab, and the subjects locked within, that had led the
Hunter here.

At least, Thomas had been operating under that
assumption.

The familiar blonde head gave him an unwanted surprise. Jessica Warren—Thomas snarled silently. His rage
at William kicked up, and he wished he had simply ripped
out the fool's heart instead of administering the enhanced
sedative. William should have killed the nosy, intrusive
bitch months ago. When she first appeared on the scene,
Thomas had known she would be trouble. He was so
wrapped up in his research, he had left William to manage
the day-to-day business of the club. For the most part
William had done an adequate job. Nate reported to
Thomas, keeping him abreast of William's management of
the club—and some of the more troublesome issues. Like
Jessica Warren.

William had been told to watch her, and if it looked as

though she would cause trouble, she was to be eliminated. *Before* the trouble started. Instead William had killed her sister. When she proved to be like a dog with a bone, William still hadn't been successful. Gave some serious credence to the theory, *If you want it done right, do it yourself.* Thomas should have killed Warren the very first time she showed that blonde head at Debach.

There was a curious little puzzle to her presence here. The tall man at her side was a stranger to Thomas, but Thomas could feel the power coming off the witch. After a century or so, the more powerful vampires developed a magickal sense. They learned to gauge a witch's power the same way they sensed the presence of another vampire or a powerful shifter.

What he sensed off the witch was exactly what he hadn't wanted to encounter. A powerful Hunter.

An inquisitive reporter could be made to disappear. Oh, there'd be questions asked; Thomas had no doubt of that. But there were ways to get rid of humans that wouldn't lead back to his door. Different story with Hunters. More so with witches. If this one disappeared, another witch could track him. They could connect this Hunter to the labs and therefore to Thomas.

All because some ignorant bitch wouldn't mind her own damn business.

Since they weren't going to be moved off their course, Thomas stopped trying. The door to the lab was hidden in the panels of the wall, but it wouldn't throw off either of them. Particularly not the Hunter. He'd found the passageway down here, after all. The woman jumped in surprise when Thomas solidified in front of them, but the Hunter had already drawn a blade from the sheath at his waist.

The familiar gleam of silver caught Thomas's eye, and he smiled at the witch. "Do you really think I'll let you close enough to use that?"

The man stepped forward, using his body to shield the woman. He waggled the knife and gave Thomas a taunting little smirk. "Do you really think you can keep me from it?

You're no fool, Thomas. You know what I am, why I'm here. You also know that we don't let the prey get away."

With a soft laugh, Thomas shook his head. "Why are you so convinced that I am the prey? It could well be you who doesn't live through this." Then he glanced at Jessica and smiled. "Or her."

He reached inside his jacket and withdrew a slender gold case. It was similar to a cigarette case, just a bit larger to accommodate the syringes. The murky yellow fluid wasn't as concentrated as the dose he had laid aside for William. For the trouble he had caused, William got something extra. But this dose would do the trick for the witch, possibly send his skills into meltdown. Or it would be enough to bring his nosy friend through the transition at an accelerated speed. That might be worth seeing.

There was something to her. Thomas hadn't been this close to her before. No way he could have known. Anticipation had him smiling. "You aren't normal, are you?" he murmured. "How intriguing."

"Jess. Leave."

"No, Jess." Thomas smiled at her and murmured, "Please stay. You know, if we both live through this, you had better run long and hard to hide her from me, Hunter. I've yet to have this experiment succeed on a mortal. But perhaps I was aiming too low. I wanted the average mortal, but I needed one like you, Jessica."

She stood behind the Hunter, her eyes wide and dark, her face pale. The Hunter said again, without looking away from Thomas, "Leave, Jessica."

"No, Jess. Stay, please. This is going to be so much fun." He flashed a syringe at Vax and murmured, "I'm going to have a hard time deciding whom to use this on. I have this theory—do you know that magick originates in the brain?"

Vax curled his lip. "Yeah, yeah, yeah, and you've found a way to duplicate whatever the hell it is that brings magick to a witch. Big. Fucking. Deal."

Thomas looked somewhat disappointed. "So you have it all figured out." He lifted the syringe and studied it. A faint smile appeared on his lips. "Yes, that is what I've done, but that's not what this dose is for. Although I think it would be fun to slide it into her neck and watch—will it kill her? Will she come through it with the strength of a demigoddess?" He looked at Jess like he would a smear under a microscope. Then he gave a dismissive shrug. "We shall have to see. But I'm more interested in what it will do to you, Hunter. Too much of what makes you witch may well make you little more than a weak, pathetic mortal. Some rewiring, so to speak."

That smile lingered on his lips as he looked back and forth between Vax and Jess. He tapped the syringe against his palm and murmured, "Which one, which one."

His eyes landed on Jess, giving her an idea of how a deer caught in the headlights felt. She suddenly understood why the damn things didn't run, even though they could feel death whispering its slippery, cold breath all over them. They didn't run because they couldn't. Terror clenched its fist around her chest and turned her legs to putty. The only way she stayed upright was by locking her knees.

She'd thought William was the big threat. But looking into Thomas's pale brown eyes, she had a bad feeling she was wrong. William was like a forest fire—destructive. But Thomas, a stiletto in the dark, just as deadly but so silent you'd never feel your death coming, and you'd have no chance to escape.

Under that intense, icy gaze, she backed up one step, then another. But she wouldn't let herself take that third step away. She was here for a reason.

He held her gaze as he rolled a syringe between his palms. Jess had seen three more tucked inside with it before he'd snapped the case closed. He lifted the syringe and smiled at her. "Perhaps, instead of letting William have her, I should have used this on your precious baby sister. What was she? . . . Oh, yes. An Empath. The transition is quite painful."

Jess started towards him, a snarl on her pretty, unpainted mouth. "You gutless son of a bitch. She was just a kid."

The Hunter wrapped his fingers around her arm, keeping her from coming any closer, and she turned on him, baring her teeth. "Let go of me, Vax."

"Vax . . . Vax . . ." Thomas narrowed his eyes, and then he smiled a wide, beaming smile that made shivers run down Jess's spine. "I've heard of you. My kind say that you lost your spine. Talk about gutless, Jessica. You should get to know your lover a little better. He killed his own wife."

Wife . . . Jess looked at Vax, but the stony set of his face told her everything. As though he could read her mind, his hand fell away. "Ahhh . . . I didn't think he would have told you," Thomas said, looking a little too pleased with himself. "I don't think I ever heard her name, Vax. Tell me, did it give you a rush, sticking that knife in her heart? She had just Changed. She would have been weak, not much of a fight there. Still, one dead vamp is one more dead vamp."

Thomas continued to talk, but nothing he was saying made much sense anymore. *Wife.* Okay, so Jess had known from the beginning that all they had was sex, but still— might have been nice to know about the wife part. Even more about the part where he had killed her.

Hard hands came up, wrapping around her upper arms. By the time she realized what Vax was going to do, he was already doing it. Jess went flying through the air and struck the wall. There was a blur in front of her. The blur was Thomas. He moved too quickly for her eyes to track. He had been coming for her, but Vax moved pretty quickly, too. Jess was out of harm's way, and Vax squared off with Thomas, catching the vampire around the waist and using a wrestling move that would done Kurt Angle proud. He flipped Thomas onto his back, jerked the syringe out of Thomas's hand, and hurled it to the ground. It hit the ground and erupted in flames. The flames didn't die down until the syringe was nothing more than a melting pile of plastic. Vax pinned the vampire and lifted his knife, but before he could use it, Thomas jammed a hand between them. He struck in the nose with the heel of his palm, and Jess heard bone crunch.

Blood exploded in a geyser, but it didn't slow Vax down. He didn't slow down when Thomas reared his head and struck Vax in the arm, catching the meaty part of the forearm and biting through skin and muscle. Thomas shook his head like a dog working a bone. Vax didn't make a sound. He shifted his grip on the hilt of the knife and then drove his fist into the vampire's throat. The vampire didn't have to breathe, but apparently vampires hated the sensation of choking as much as anybody. Thomas left go of Vax's arm, gagging. Blood and saliva flew out of his mouth.

Vax lifted the knife once more, but a blast from behind sent him flying. He landed on the floor beside Jess. He rolled to his feet in seconds, and he took Jess with him.

It was a good thing he was holding onto her, because what she saw in front of her was enough to make her want to run home, crawl under her bed, and hide. Her legs felt rubbery, and her guts seemed to go watery.

Smoke hung in the air, and there were little charred pieces of drywall and wood drifting down. And unless she was really seeing things, there was also metal melting.

Jess wondered if hell was anything like this. The heat was intense. She could feel it licking her flesh from thirty feet away. The thing standing in the doorway only added to the hellish imagery. It was big, and even uglier than Dena. Long, wicked fangs protruded out past his lips. He had a stunted muzzle, and his face looked grotesquely malformed. He threw back his head and howled. When he looked back at Jess, his mouth gaped in a bloodcurdling smile, thick strings of saliva dripping down.

And he wasn't alone. Her breath caught in her throat as another wolf creature appeared behind him. Another. Another . . . until they totaled seven. With murderous intent in their eyes, they started as a unit for Vax and Jess. Fire flew through the air, and Jess hissed, startled. Her gaze flew to Vax, and she watched as he lobbed another fireball towards the wolf-things.

An odd whooshing sound filled the room. It was so loud, it hurt Jess's ears. She clapped her hands over them and looked around, searching for the source. It was the fire. Vax hurled more fire at them, but each attempt had the same effect as the first. The whooshing sound was the noise the fire made as it hit the wolf-things and their bodies absorbed it.

Absorbed. Like a sponge absorbed water. "Son of a bitch," Vax muttered. Out of the corner of her eye, she saw Vax's reaction. It wasn't much, but considering that she had seen maybe three emotions—namely, lust, anger, and amusement—from him, the worried look in his eyes didn't bode well.

His gaze shifted from the menacing creatures in front of them to the ceiling above their heads, then down to the white tiled floor under their feet. "How much can you hold?" he asked quietly.

She knew he wasn't asking about her bench-pressing skills. "I don't know. Never put it to that much of a test. But I'll hold whatever I have to."

"When I say—catch it and aim it towards them." She never had a chance to ask what. His hand lifted, and although she couldn't see anything, she felt it. The earth rumbled beneath them; then it shifted and rolled. A gaping maw appeared in the tile, a tiny split that grew and grew until it had rent the entire floor straight down the middle.

Dust drifted from the ceiling, and then the crack in the earth spread upward, higher and higher until the crack climbed the wall and started to spread across the ceiling. Huge, jagged chunks of concrete and rock speared into open air. As bits and pieces of the building started to crumble, Vax shouted, "Now!"

Jess braced herself. It was a waste of time.

There was no way she could have prepared for the massive weight as broken pieces of rubble came crashing down. It was as if the weight of it came down on her skull, threatening to crush her. She shoved with all her might, sweat beading on her upper lip. The chunks of concrete hurtled through the air towards the lumbering atrocities. She saw the first three collapse, but then Vax grabbed her around the waist and hauled her towards the elevator.

She didn't fight him.

Maybe, just maybe, she wasn't as ready to die as she thought. Especially not at the hands of one of those things. Out of the corner of her eye, she saw the things pushing through the smoke, rubble, and fire. Her head screamed at her as she focused, but she didn't quit. There was an exposed pipe peeking through the ceiling. It was easier to move than the rocks had been, but she was exhausted and her control was shaky, so by the time she had used her mind to rip the pipe out of its moorings, she was sweating. She was in so much pain, she could hardly focus.

"Hurry," she gasped.

They made it to the elevator, and as the doors slid closed, Jess finished with the pipe. Fire exploded, and Jess lost consciousness to the sound of wolves howling.

Vax had been right. She handled herself well even when they were facing down something unimaginable. Something a little more than he had been prepared for. That was where he had fucked up. Going in there with nobody at his side but a telekinetic who had never seen battle—it had been so pathetically stupid. Criminally so.

Bad enough that he had almost gotten Jess killed. It was worse than that, though, because Jess would have been just the first if those hybrid shifters had gotten loose. He had put untold others at risk.

They were back in the hotel. Vax almost hadn't come here. But he couldn't drive around endlessly. He had to see how Jess was doing, and he had to think. He'd been thinking for the past three hours, and worried out of his mind over Jess.

She hadn't woken up.

He knew why. She'd overextended herself saving their necks. It wouldn't have been necessary if Vax hadn't been so damned stupid. He reached up and rubbed his eyes, feeling unbelievably weary.

THE phone rang on the table next to the bed, and he reached to pick it up without looking away from Jess's face. The low, quiet voice on the other end of the line sounded worried. "Look, Kelsey, I don't need you rushing out here to cluck over me. Just get Malachi and get over here. Talk to Jess. She'll fill you in."

Kelsey's voice was irritated. "Why don't *you* fill me in, big shot?"

Because I won't be here. He didn't say that aloud. "I don't have time right now." He was saved from having to make something up when Jess's lids started to flutter. "I have to go. Jess is waking up."

He hung up the phone and crouched down beside her. She groaned, and one hand came up, rubbing her temple. "Headache, huh?"

She rolled her head on the pillow and stared at him. "Oh, hell. A headache doesn't even describe it. I feel like my head is going to come off."

Vax skimmed his fingers over her forehead. "You overextended yourself. Pushed too hard. This is sort of a delayed reaction—almost as if you worked out way too much at the gym. It will take a few days to subside all the way. Rest helps."

"Yeah, like that's an option." She reached and wrapped her hand around his upper arm, using that to steady herself as she sat up. She weaved a little and groaned. "Holy shit."

"Lie back down, Jess."

She shook her head. "There's no time. Damn it, what are we going to do about those things?" She swung her legs over the edge of the bed, but every movement made her more and more pale. "Did you see them? It was almost like they ate the fire. And the concrete—some of those chunks probably weighed half a ton, and they didn't even slow down."

As determined as she was to rise, when it came time to actually stand, she made two tries before she finally gave up. When she looked up at him, Vax cocked a brow. "You done?"

She snarled at him. Vax leaned down and kissed the sexy little sneer before straightening. "I told you—it's going to be a few days before you feel like yourself, and at least a few more hours of rest before you can go anywhere." He tucked a strand of hair away from her face.

She acted as if she were going to smack his hand away, but instead she just wrapped her fingers around his wrist. She was pale; the dark circles under her eyes looked like bruises. Her voice shook a little when she said, "We don't have hours."

"No. We don't." He crouched down in front of her and sighed. He cupped her hands in his, rubbing his thumbs across the backs. Under the thin, delicate shield of her skin, he could see the fine network of veins. He could feel the fragile play of the small bones as she turned her hands over in his and linked their fingers. "I've called for help. They'll be here soon, but . . ."

Jess jerked away her hands and stared at him with disbelief all over her face. "No." She shook her head. "No. You *said* we'd do this together. I haven't gone and done something stupid. I didn't take off by myself to look for Masters, even though I wanted to. We're doing this together, damn it. I'm coming with you."

"No. You're not. You can't." He reached for her, but she recoiled. "Jess, you're too damn weak to walk. You can't defend yourself. And if I want to stop them before they hurt anybody, I can't slow down just to protect you."

"I won't ask you to." She stared at him with pleading eyes. "Please—damn it, you don't understand. I have to do this."

Finally he felt something from her. Her pain reached out to him, hammering at his shields and stinging him like a thousand angry hornets. The pain from overextending and her exhaustion had done what he couldn't do. They defeated her shields, allowing him to feel her every last emotion. The pain and exhaustion, her grief, rage, helplessness—and the determination.

The determination would fuel her. If he left her alone here, that determination would add to her anger, and it just might give her that last little desperate bit of strength she would need to walk out of this room. And Jess couldn't leave. She had to stay here, where she was safe.

"Don't you understand?" Tears welled in her eyes, making them gleam as she reached back out and took his hands. She squeezed them fiercely. Her voice cracked as she whispered, "Try to understand it. I have to do this."

Vax gently disengaged their hands. He reached up and threaded one hand through her hair. "I do understand." That light touch linked them, and he could read her. As he had thought, she was running on emotion and desperation. She was also weak. She'd hate him when this was over.

But she'd be alive.

She started to say something, and he brushed his lips over hers. "Shhhh." It was delicate, nerve-wracking work, forcing his way under the thin veil that separated unconscious thought from conscious action. Once he was there, though, it was a little easier. She was already so tired. All he had to do was coax that exhaustion to the forefront and . . .

She resisted. He could feel her body stiffening, and inside, she rejected the emotions he tried to force on her. Vax withdrew before she had a chance to figure out exactly what she was fighting. With grim eyes, he stared down at her. He was not going to let her leave this room.

He had only a few options. If he could cuff her to the bed, he would, but with her talent, she could probably undo the cuffs. Hitting her again wasn't an acceptable option. Even if it meant keeping her safe.

The only option left didn't exactly leave him feeling warm and cuddly, but it would work. His hand was still fisted in her hair—using his grip there, he angled her head back and took her mouth, rough and impatient. Her lips parted under his and he swallowed down her soft moan. Vax shifted forward, using the weight of his body to crush her back into the mattress. He pushed up her shirt, baring her breasts. The shirt caught under her arms, but that was fine.

He jerked at the clasp that held the cups of the bra closed. They fell aside, and Vax bent his head, catching one tight, swollen nipple in his mouth. Jess groaned and arched into him. She slid her hands down, working one in between them so that she could cup him through his jeans. Pleasure ricocheted through his system, guilt chasing hard on its heels. What he was getting ready to do was wrong—he wasn't going to let her give him any pleasure.

Catching her hands, he pushed them down by her head and muttered, "Hold still." He slid his way down her body, pressing a long line of kisses from her breasts down to her navel. The low-slung waistband of her jeans barred the rest of her from his view. Shoving himself to his knees, Vax reached out and freed the button. He lowered the zipper and then slid his hands inside. As he pushed the faded blue denim down her thighs, he held her gaze. After he'd stripped the jeans away, he bent and pressed a hot, open-mouthed kiss to the soft curls that covered her sex.

Jess whimpered and reached down, fisting her hands in his hair. She pressed up against him. The greedy, demanding motions of her hips were an erotic enticement that he couldn't resist, and one that he didn't want to. He kissed her again, stroking his tongue across her clit, circling around and around. He moved lower and plunged his tongue inside her, listening to her cry out his name.

He circled his tongue around her entrance, then nuzzled her clit. He rolled his eyes upward so he could look at her. He watched her face as he sucked on her clit, memorizing the way she looked, the way the flush tinted her cheeks pink and darkened her eyes.

He pushed his finger inside her sheath, pressing against the little notch there. She came apart in his arms, bucking her hips and screaming his name. As she came, Vax focused mentally and forced his way completely inside her subconscious. The exhaustion was stronger, weakening the hard, solid determination. He felt the last bit of her resistance fade, and when he pulled his mouth away, she collapsed bonelessly onto the mattress.

She blinked sleepily and lifted a hand towards him. Vax pressed a kiss to her palm before pushing back up onto his knees. He bent low over her body and kissed her, light and quick. She turned her mouth to his, trying to deepen the kiss, and he gave her one last push.

Her lids fluttered closed, and she fell asleep with a satisfied, sexy little smile. He stood up and grabbed the blanket, flicking it over her still form. His body screamed at him. His cock throbbed and ached. The need to lie down and force her back to wakefulness was strong. He wanted to rip his jeans off, tear away the shirt that was tangled under her arms, and cover her naked body with his. Ride her long and hard until exhaustion, *real* exhaustion, claimed them both.

Instead he turned away.

He had a job to do, and not much time to do it.

*I*s it worth it, baby?

Her mom's voice sounded muffled and distant. Jess had to strain to hear her. "It's worth it," she said out loud. "Randi is worth it. Worth anything."

I'm not talking about Randi, sweetheart. Randi is past your concern now. What comes of this doesn't matter to her. She just wants the same thing I do: you alive, safe, and happy.

Mom's voice sounded a little more real this time, a little more solid. Jess looked around for her, searching. She came up short when she realized where she was. What had happened to the hotel?

They were back in the little Canton cemetery, and her mom was sitting on her own tombstone, watching Jess with a sad, understanding smile. "It's okay, baby. Don't worry. I'm not a ghost or anything—well, not really."

Jess swallowed. She heard a funny clicking sound when she did it. "How do you know you're not a ghost?"

Leanne laughed. The sound was so familiar, so missed, that it made tears sting Jess's eyes. "I'd know, baby. I'm not haunting you, and I'm not trapped here. I just . . . I'm worried, baby. You're this close to finding it. Don't let it get away."

Confused, Jess shook her head. "Finding what? The only thing I've been looking for is the guys who killed Randi, and I found them. They're going to pay."

"I'm not talking about finding justice—or vengeance—but *life*. You put your life on hold when your father and I left you. Everything you did was for Randi. I'm so proud of what you did for her, but it's time to let her go. Time for you to live. You're so close, Jess. Is it worth losing the rest of your life over?"

Jess licked her lips. "You're not making any sense, Mom. I'm not going to die. Vax won't let that happen—he's a good man. Strong."

Leanne laughed softly. "Yeah, I know. I wondered if you did. He's it, Jess. Find him. Save him."

"Save him?" But Leanne was gone. Jess turned around, looking for her. "Mom? Mom?"

The only answer was a distant, faint voice. But it wasn't her mom.

Wake up, Jess. Come on, damn it—what the hell did he do?

K ELSEY sat back on her heels and covered her face. "Damn it, what did he do?"

Malachi peered over her shoulder and looked down at Jess's still, immobile features. "I would say that he made her sleep like the very devil."

"Yeah, but the question is, *why?* And *how?* Yeah, Empathy can be used to make somebody sleep—I've done it before—but it shouldn't be that hard to wake the person up. He didn't tell me a damn thing about what was going on, either. How are we supposed to help if we don't know what in the hell we're supposed to do?"

She fisted a hand in her hair and tugged a little, the gesture habitual. She reached out and tapped Jess on the cheek. Then she jerked back her hand and hissed under her breath. There was a huge well of pain inside Jessica Warren.

"I need more light."

She heard a couple of clicks as her husband moved through the room and turned on every lamp. "Kelsey."

"Not now," Kelsey said as she laid her palms alongside Jess's head.

"Yes, now. It would appear we do not have much time."

Her head whipped around, and she glared over her shoulder at Mal. "Then stop . . ." But her voice trailed off as she saw the note he held in his hand. She sighed and stood up. Foreboding settled in her belly like a hunk of lead. She took the note from Mal and read the short, brief sentence.

Tell her that I am sorry.

It wasn't signed. Kelsey recognized the heavy, broad scrawl, though. She had a bad feeling she knew why they'd been charged with passing on the message. "We have to wake her up," Malachi murmured. "I have a feeling he is in trouble."

"Vax *is* trouble." Kelsey laid down the note. Her fingers brushed against the dresser. A chill danced along her spine, followed by a whisper of wind. She turned her head and looked at the mirror. It was wobbly, just barely secured to the dresser. It also had one of the few common spells lying inside it. The foreboding only increased when she reached out and touched the mirror.

It was inactive spell, basically the witch's version of an answering machine. She could see Vax's face and hear his voice, but it was just an echo. She could talk to the mirror all she wanted, but it wasn't him.

That didn't stop her, though. "Vax, you stupid ass, what are you up to?"

"Kelsey." His eyes looked sad. "I'm going to assume that worthless husband of yours is around." He was quiet for a moment. His eyes slid to the side, as though he were looking at something outside his line of vision. "Jess overextended herself. She'll need to be healed before you can wake her up. She'll tell you where I am. I couldn't wait."

Kelsey snarled. "You could have *not* hidden your trail from me. I could have followed."

Almost as if he had anticipated her comment when he left the message spell, Vax smiled faintly. "You're probably gritting your teeth and wondering why I've wiped the trail clean, but it's to protect her. If you can follow me, so could somebody else. This way she's safe. Keep her that way."

He opened his mouth once more, but then he just closed it. Her eyes stared into his. Kelsey had the weirdest sensation that he actually could see her. "Bye, Kelsey. Malachi, take care of her."

As he turned away, fog rolled across the mirror's surface, and when it cleared, the mirror was once again nothing more than a mirror. With the message delivered, the spell was gone, as if it had never even been there.

"That sounded terribly final," Malachi murmured. He looked over Kelsey's shoulder towards Jess, and his face went grim. "Heal her and wake her up."

Under her breath, Kelsey said, "That was what I was trying to do." She crouched by the bed and linked her hands with Jess's. Now she knew why she hadn't been able to wake Jess up. Raw nerve endings, pain, and exhaustion had made it easy for Vax to work his way inside her subconscious—almost like a hypnotist. Once Kelsey had repaired the damage and pain caused when Jess overextended herself, the woman should be able to do the rest on her own.

The exhaustion Kelsey couldn't do much about, but she had a feeling she wouldn't have to.

Done, Kelsey withdrew her hands and sat back. Under her

closed lids, Jess's eyes were moving all around. She gave a
soft moan. Then she was silent for a moment. When her
lashes lifted, her eyes were blank, almost empty. Her forehead wrinkled, and Jess turned her head on the pillow to
stare at Kelsey. "What are you doing here? Where's Vax?"

Kelsey glanced over her shoulder at her husband, and
then she looked at back at Jess. "I was hoping you could
tell us."

W ALKING away from her might not have been the hardest thing he'd ever done, but it was pretty damned
close. He couldn't quite figure out why. Hell, he'd exe-
cuted his own wife. Had seen women and children run
down. Seen innocent people brutalized in ways that he
couldn't describe with simple words. And for some reason,
walking away from the bed had been almost impossible.
Each step seemed to cause razor-sharp shards to pierce his
heart, but it wasn't just the pain. He could handle pain. His
body didn't want to leave her—it was as if weights clung
to his legs, making each step slow and hesitant.

On his way out the door, he'd paused for just a second.
He had looked back and memorized the sight of her.

For the rest of his life, he'd remember how she looked,
lying on her back, her head resting on the pillow, face
turned towards the door. Her hand had been on the pillow,
palm up with her fingers curled in just a little. The rest of
his life could probably be measured in hours now, not
years.

She had looked peaceful. Safe. And if it was the last
thing he did, he was going to make sure she stayed safe. Of
course, from where he was standing right now, it was entirely possible that it just might be the last thing he did.

Masters was dead, as well as three more of the
grotesquely formed wolf creatures. He'd been the first one
Vax encountered on this little trip into hell, and he'd gone
down almost too easy. Vax didn't give a damn—he was all
for easy right now, considering how outnumbered he was.

He wasn't going to get any more easy ones, though. *You can do this,* he told himself. He had experience behind him, he had his knife, and he had silver nitrate. Enough of it was poison to any werecreature. He just hoped that would hold true for these hybrid creatures, too. After slicing and dicing his way through the gauntlet of fireballs and slashing claws, he had his chance to try.

Luck, God, or both were on his side this time around. He had to use up the only three vials of silver nitrate he had. He broke the seal and on each wolf-creature, he used his knife to cut a big, gaping hole inside them. Plunge the vial inside, jerk his hand out before the healing flesh sealed up around it.

The silver took a minute or so to pump through the body, so healing started pretty quickly. The vials, with their steady drips of poison, ended up sealed inside. The creatures' speedy healing ended up working against them. It had taken exactly seven minutes for the poison to eat away the tissue of the major blood vessels. A smaller dose might not have killed them at all, and it certainly wouldn't have killed them that fast.

Until now, Vax had figured the vials he carried around were overkill. He was glad he hadn't been too concerned with overkill. If he had brought along a dozen, give or take, he might have had a chance at walking out of here alive. Wasn't going to happen, though. He still had four wolves and a vamp to kill.

Masters had been the easy one. Didn't matter that he controlled fire if he didn't have utter and complete control over his magick. Masters had none. If Vax had to hazard a guess, he'd say that anytime Masters had worked to hone his skills, he worked on only one.

Fire wasn't the answer to everything. Self-healing, even the rudimentary skill nearly every witch had, was just as important as fire. Probably more. If Masters had bothered learning to refine the most basic of magicks, he probably could have healed the huge gash Vax had torn in his throat. Instead Masters had lain there bleeding out, too weak to fight back when Vax used his knife to destroy his heart.

It seemed though that would be the last easy one Vax had. Right now, he crouched behind an overturned table, sweating and so damned hot he could barely breathe.

Another fireball came hurtling through the air towards him. Before it could strike, Vax extended his power to absorb the fireball. Too many more, and he was going to spontaneously combust. Too damned hot in here.

But it was going to have to get even hotter. From the time he'd left this hellhole last night, he'd had a bad feeling how this was all going to play out.

"Come on out, Hunter. This is pointless."

Vax braced his back against the flat surface of the table and settled his weight a little more comfortably on the rubble-strewn floor. "I have to know. Why the hell do the bad guys always feel the need to strike up a conversation with the good guy? You got me pinned, cornered, and surrounded—doesn't get much clearer than that."

Fitzpatrick laughed. "You sound almost eager. Are you ready to die?"

There was an ominous crack from the ceiling, and Vax looked up. *"Shit."* The ceiling supports couldn't take much more. He rolled out of the way just as a huge chunk of plaster broke free.

"Be careful there. Will your ability to put out fires work if you are unconscious?"

"Oh, don't worry about me. I've got it—" A blast of wind arose, slamming into the table. Vax could either move with it or get the hell out of the way. He ended up crouching on the floor in the hall. The long, mostly empty hall. "I got it all under control."

A smoky haze filled the hall, and he coughed, trying to clear his lungs a little. He wasn't the only one coughing, either. He could hear the wolf-things struggling to breathe around the smoke, too. The only one who wasn't bothered by the smoke was the vampire. Fucking undead—they didn't have to breathe.

"Are you so certain? You're going to die, Hunter." Thomas Fitzpatrick's voice sounded a little less solid, and Vax swore under his breath. Too late to move, though. The vampire was suddenly there, his body solidifying from mist to solid. And he had something in his hand. Vax swung out with his foot, catching Fitzpatrick at his ankles and knocking him off his feet.

No time—

The words echoed through Vax's head as he rolled to his feet. The hell he didn't have time. He might well die here, but not yet. Not until he'd taken them—

Icy hot. Thomas reached up and patted Vax's face. Vax balled up his fist and swung, clipping the vampire with an uppercut that sent him flying backward. Then he wrapped his fingers around the barrel of the syringe sticking out of his chest. "Too late," Thomas said as he rubbed his jaw. He watched with a smug smile as Vax pulled it out. "It will take a few minutes to spread through your system, my friend; then you'll start getting weaker. A few days for the full effect. Assuming you can get out of here, that is. You'll go into a coma. You may or may not wake up. But regardless, you are no longer a witch."

Vax threw the syringe on the floor. It felt as though fiery claws were inside him, thousands of them, ripping through him. But he wasn't going under yet. Not yet. "A few minutes," he muttered. His heartbeat was racing like a damned racehorse. He could hardly breathe. The smoke was getting thicker. He saw a big, furred face over the vamp's shoulder.

Then two. Then three. Four

Was he seeing double? No. It was the other wolves. "What, you all here to make sure I don't get out?" he said. His tongue felt thick. He swallowed and started to say something else, but the smoke was getting to him and he ended up in a coughing fit.

"Actually, I think I will have them carry you out. You see, I've a mind to see if you survive. You're a stubborn one, aren't you? You might live through it. I'd like to see what comes of you."

"Talk, talk, talk," Vax mumbled. He closed his eyes and took a deep, calming breath. He did a quick mental assessment. It was all still there. For now. A smile spread across his lips. "I don't need a few minutes."

He struck out. Thomas's scream ended abruptly as his body exploded into flames.

"O H, no."
Jess climbed out of her car, staring in shock at the building in front of her. The smoke was so thick, she could hardly see the building. The heat was intense—a few years ago, Jess had been driving through Louisville, Kentucky, when a blaze went up near Churchill Downs. Wasn't every day a fire threatened the historic racetrack, so she had made a detour and done a few quick interviews, taken some pictures with the digital she kept in her trunk.

It had been a five-alarm blaze.

Up until now, Jess hadn't ever seen anything quite like it. But now the heat was so incredible, her skin felt burned. The fire seemed to have a life of its own. "Oh, my God . . . Vax," she whispered. She took off running, but she didn't make it even five feet. Big hands, hard as stone, wrapped around her arms. "Put me down, you bastard!"

"You cannot go in there," he whispered.

Jess struggled and screamed, "Vax is in there!"

"You cannot go in there," he repeated. "The fire will kill you."

"Vax . . ." Jess sobbed. *No.* She struggled harder. She had to get inside. Had to . . .

She didn't realize she was screaming it until a big, warm hand came up and cupped her face, and Malachi murmured, "You can't. I am so sorry."

"It won't kill me."

Like a drowning man catching a rope, Jess latched on to Kelsey's words with a desperate kind of hope.

"No." Malachi's voice was a low, threatening growl. "You will not, wife."

A faint smile canted her lips. "He's still alive in there, baby. I can't just leave him."

Malachi flung a hand towards the blazing inferno. "Nobody could be alive inside of that."

"A witch could. He's keeping the fire under control. I can feel it. He knows I can feel it. He needed me here so I could put it out when he was . . ." Kelsey's voice trailed off, and she shook her head. "There's no time for this, Malachi. He's alive. I can feel him."

The big vampire closed the distance between them and caught Kelsey's arms in his hands, dragging her up against him. "You will *not* go in. I shall go."

She shook her head. "You can't. Even for you, big guy, fire is deadly. The fire is spreading. Besides . . ." Her gaze slid to Jess, and Jess didn't have to be a mind reader to know what the witch was thinking. Malachi had to stay out to keep Jess under control.

Still, he wasn't letting it happen. Kelsey gave him a humorless smile and shook her head. "Sorry, baby. You know I have to." Right in front of them, Kelsey disappeared. Malachi's fingers closed around the empty air that had been her arms. His hands clenched into tight fists, and impotent anger carved deep lines into his face.

Jess saw a bitter, furious knowledge in his eyes. The ache in her heart spread.

Jess heard the wail of sirens in the distance. Squeezing her eyes closed, she started to pray silently. *Please . . . please . . . please . . .*

S MOKE choked her. Blinded her. Before she even tried to locate Vax, the first thing Kelsey did was absorb as much fire as she could. It was like eating the flames. Manipulating fire was as easy as breathing for her. Few knew it, but controlling the fire elements was her strongest gift. It had been the first gift to emerge when she was young, and it was the first she had learned to control.

She'd had no choice—as powerful as her ability to use

fire was, she was terrified of it. She'd had to learn to master that fear, and the gift, or it would have destroyed her. She'd been inside burning buildings before. Fire had marked her body. It had haunted her dreams every night for years. Even now, decades later, the nightmare slipped out of her subconscious when she least expected it, waking her in a cold sweat with a scream lodged in her throat, her flesh stinging as though she could feel the fiery kiss of flame on her skin.

Yeah, Kelsey was no stranger to it. But she hadn't ever dealt with anything like this. Around her, the flames eased back, and she forced a cool wind through the narrow hall. It pushed the smoke away for now. She hoped it would be long enough.

She heard screaming above the roar of the flames. Vax lay on the floor just a few feet away. So far the fire hadn't touched him, but if he kept forcing it to burn, he was going to burn with it. That was the whole point—Kelsey had figured that out the second they'd seen the smoke billowing out of the warehouse.

She had felt Vax's presence, and she had known he was alive. Just as she had known that Vax was keeping the fire burning because somehow those wolves were still alive. These weren't just wolves. She could scent the violent magick inside them—the magick would keep them alive for a little while longer.

Vax's face was a vivid shade of red, and his eyes were glowing manically. Panting, he looked at her. "Get out of here, Kelsey. I have to . . ." He broke off as a fit of coughing hit him. "Make sure they die." His gaze fell away, and she looked down to stare at the syringe on the floor. "He got me anyway. I'm over."

"No. You're not." She focused a little more, and the cooler bubble of air that surrounded her swelled, surrounding him. She dipped a hand inside her pocket and drew out the vials there. Silver nitrate: no good witch left home without it. There were four. She broke the seals and turned, hurling them towards the still-screaming wolves.

She gave a push with her magick to make sure the silver nitrate hit. The wolves were all burning—with that much exposed flesh, their bodies would absorb the silver that much more quickly.

One fell down dead before the vials even hit. "Let it go, Vax," Kelsey said. "Come on, buddy."

His lashes fluttered. They closed. Kelsey braced herself for the worst, but he didn't burst into flame in front of her. Thank God. She wasn't sure she could have lived with that image in her head. But the faint relief she felt died quickly. Vax hadn't extinguished the fire, for a reason—he had started it, and he would let it burn until he'd destroyed whatever he wanted destroyed. As long as it burned under his control, he could keep it from spreading.

But unconscious, he wasn't in control. "Shit."

Desperate, Kelsey dropped to her knees beside him. The concrete was hot and burned her skin through her jeans, but she gritted her teeth and blocked out the pain. Cupping his face in her hands, she pushed past his instinctive shields, trying to force him back into wakefulness.

There was a poison inside him. Something that was burning through him like acid. Kelsey didn't have time to try drawing it out—instead she just blocked it. It was an urgent move, blocking him from feeling the pain. "Damn it. You stubborn bastard, open your eyes."

She felt him. Knew he was aware of her. *Get out . . .* The words weren't said out loud, but she heard him nonetheless. *Get out, Kelsey.*

"Not without you, pal. You go, I go. And if you take me with you, Malachi will kill himself just to come after you and kick your ass from paradise and back," she said.

THEY were no longer alone. Fire trucks surrounded them, and Kelsey still wasn't there. Tears burned Jess's eyes, and sobs clawed their way up her throat. Spinning away, Jess moaned. Her legs wobbled under her, but when she would have fallen down, Malachi caught her.

"Shhhh. Don't give up so easily," Malachi murmured. But she didn't know whether he was trying to comfort her or himself.

Firefighters swarmed around them, trying to shove them back, but Malachi wasn't going anywhere. He was too big and too mean looking; plus the firefighters had their hands full. He kept an arm around Jess and they both stood there staring at the inferno. Minutes passed.

The firefighters seemed to be winning the battle. It didn't seem right that the huge fire was so easily contained. It didn't make sense. It should have spread, but it didn't. Jess didn't much give a damn, though.

She felt Malachi stiffen behind her. "Kelsey." His voice was harsh.

Unsure what to expect, prepared for the worst, Jess looked up at him. There was an agonized look in his eyes, and the bottom of Jess's stomach fell out.

Nononononono. She bit her lip to keep from screaming. Malachi didn't have to say anything. The torment on his face said it all.

Vax wasn't coming out. Neither was Kelsey.

She closed her eyes, an icy-cold numbness spreading through her. She welcomed it. It was better than the devastating pain that waited for her. Gone. Just like that. "He knew," Jess muttered, forcing the words out of her tight throat. She licked her lips and looked up at Malachi.

Except the vampire wasn't there.

Hell.

She searched the crowd for him, but it was a futile effort. She knew where he was—she just hoped that, in the chaos, nobody had seen him disappear into thin air. It was stifling hot, but she was freezing. Nerves and fear had turned her blood to ice, and she just couldn't get warm.

"He's gone." She scrubbed her hands over her eyes. Everything felt so surreal. Unfinished. Even saying the words out loud didn't seem to make it connect. "He's gone."

The ache in her heart spread, and she pressed her fist

against her lips as the sobs struggled free from the knot in her chest. The echo of her mother's words came back to haunt her. *Is it worth it?*

Jess just didn't know. Vax would have gotten Masters. Deep inside, she knew that. The sick, monstrous bastard was gone. But so was Vax, and she knew that ache was one more that she would have to live with every day. For the rest of her life. After only a couple of days, he had forced his way inside her heart, where she had sworn she'd never let anybody in. He'd done it anyway.

She hunched her shoulders, curling her body in. It didn't help. Grief spread, a physical pain that seemed to grow with every passing second.

There were some startled shouts. Downright shock. Quiet at first—Jess just blocked it out. But then it got louder and louder, and slowly she turned. This time, when her legs went out from under her, there was nobody there to catch her.

Inexplicably, the fire was practically extinguished. The charred, skeletal remains of the building were still smoking and dripping with water. It wasn't possible. Jess didn't know how it happened. A fire just didn't go that fast from a greedy monster that consumed everything to a smoky, smoldering mess of debris.

But as amazing as that was, it wasn't what held everybody's attention. What held their attention came stumbling out the door. Malachi first. There were some comical double takes as the firefighters who had tried to move Malachi back recognized him under the soot and smoke. He carried a limp, motionless body in his arms. The man Malachi held was so covered with ashes and soot, his flesh looked black.

Behind Malachi stood Kelsey. Her face was a painful, vivid shade of red, and her clothes were black.

Jess ran for them. Hands went to grab her and she shook them off, dodged those who would have blocked her way. She came to an abrupt stop, staring at Vax's face as numbness spread through her. She was afraid to ask. Afraid to let herself feel anything: hope, fear . . . anything.

"He's alive." Kelsey said it in a soft, raspy voice. Her face was so red—even her eyelids looked red. Sunburned, almost. She weaved back and forth on her feet.

A couple of paramedics gathered around them, but Kelsey wouldn't leave Mal's side. She gave Jess a pleading look, but Jess never saw it. As paramedics took Vax from Malachi, Jess followed them. Their bodies blocked her from him, and she forced her way through, ignoring everything they said and did.

She had to see for herself. Had to.

She reached out and touched his wrist. Her eyes closed as she felt the strong, steady pulse under her fingers. Relief flooded her, swamping the tension and adrenaline that had been keeping her upright. She stood and tried to take a step away, letting the paramedics do their job.

Except she only made it two steps.

"THAT wasn't exactly the kind of distraction I was looking for."

Jess jumped as the voice came out of nowhere. She looked up and saw Kelsey standing by Vax's bed. Pain streaked through Jess's head and she winced, touching the tender laceration at the base of her skull. "Don't ever pass out in front of paramedics," she warned. "They don't like it."

A humorous smile appeared on Kelsey's lips. "I'll remember that. But while they were fussing over you two, it gave Mal and me a chance to slip away. Have you spoken with the police?"

Jess nodded. "Yeah. I don't know who you are or where you came from. I was supposed to be meeting a source, somebody who had leads on the recent kidnappings. Vax was supposed to meet me there, backup type of thing, but I couldn't find him when I got there." She forced a smile. "I know how to fabricate a believable alibi."

Then she looked down at her hands. "They won't tell me anything. Privacy, yadda yadda, and all."

There was a look in the witch's eyes that Jess didn't like. Kelsey reached out and touched a hand to Vax's face. He had an ashen look to his skin, and he lay on the bed as still as death. So far Jess had been kicked out of the room four different times as various doctors examined him.

The last one had been a neurosurgeon, and he'd had a weird look in his eyes, his mouth set in a grim line as he left the exam room.

Jess had hoped that maybe Kelsey could tell her something, but apparently Jess was just going to be kept in the dark. Kelsey pressed fingertips to his temple. Vax never moved. Kelsey stood silent and still for a moment, but when she looked at Jess, the nasty little knot of dread in Jess's belly got worse.

"He'll be fine. Mostly." Kelsey looked away evasively and turned as if she were going to leave.

"Don't you *dare* leave," Jess snarled, reaching out and clamping a hand around the woman's wrist. She dug in her fingers. "What is going on? You know something. I can see it in your eyes."

An unhappy smile curved Kelsey's lips. "Yeah," she muttered, her voice flat, almost bitter. "Yeah, I know something. But you'll have to talk to him."

"And where can I find him?"

Kelsey blinked. "Here?"

Glaring at her, Jess said, "It's not like he can *stay* here. When are you all going to get him out of here? Where are you taking him?"

The witch did a nervous little shuffle with her feet, her eyes looking everywhere but at Jess. Finally she turned to Jess and said, "He's not going anywhere. At least not until he can walk out of here on his own. And that will be a few days."

"But . . ." Jess let go of Kelsey's wrist and looked back at Vax. "What's going on?" She reached out, skimming the tips of her fingers over his jawline. Just recently there had been a bruise. She'd put it on him. She'd seen the dark shadow of it. It had been gone in less than a day.

If he could heal that quickly, then how could they leave him in the hospital? More, if he could heal that quickly, why did he need to be in a hospital, and why wasn't he waking up? "I need to know what's going on." Something was wrong. She felt it in her gut.

Shaking her head, Kelsey said, "No. You got questions? Yeah. Me, too. I've got a couple dozen questions easy. But I can't answer them for you." She turned away, but then looked back at Jess. "Thank you for covering for the two of us. The last thing we need is to get pulled into an arson investigation. Now, if you'll excuse me, I have to go and strangle my husband."

Kelsey hated leaving. She really did, but it was the only way. Kelsey focused on her husband and let the magick carry her away. Jess didn't look away from Vax again. Kelsey's heart broke a little, but she didn't have any certain answers for the other woman, and for all her suppositions, it wasn't her place to explain what she thought had happened while Vax was down in that fiery hellhole.

When Kelsey opened her eyes, she was back in a small, cramped hotel room. It wasn't a nice one, but it was close to the hospital and that was what counted. From the window, they could see the sprawling medical campus. Kelsey hated leaving Vax there. But she couldn't get him out without attracting a hell of a lot of attention, and after the fire, they couldn't risk it. They had to get a few Hunters out here, preferably some who had medical experience and the ability to blend in with mortal society.

"Strangle me for what?"

Rolling her eyes, Kelsey turned around and demanded, "Do you have to constantly eavesdrop?"

Malachi lifted a big shoulder. "No. I just enjoy it so." He reached out and traced the upper curve of her lip. "Now, why are you strangling me this time?"

Curling her hand into a fist, Kelsey slugged him in his belly. It was a lot like hitting a brick wall, but it sure was therapeutic. "What the hell were you thinking, going in there?"

A red brow lifted. "I was thinking that my wife was in

there. So was a man I consider a friend. Did you really think I'd just keep waiting outside where it was nice and safe?"

"And flame-free?" She curled her lip in a sneer. "Gee, how stupid of me, thinking it was best that you stay someplace where you weren't risking turning into a pile of ash."

Jerking her against him, Malachi lowered his head and kissed her, quick and rough. "For once we agree."

Lust and love warmed her body as she stared up at him. "You big jerk."

"Hmmmm." He kissed her again, slower this time, tracing her lips with his tongue before pushing it into her mouth. His hands skimmed down her sides and then he pressed them against her back, flattening them and aligning their bodies. She felt the hard, heavy ridge of his cock against her belly.

By the time he lifted his head this time, she was breathless and whimpering, ready to strip both of them naked and jump on him. She might have done it, too, but Malachi eased back just a little. "How is he?"

Unsure how to answer that, she shook her head. "I honestly don't know, Malachi." Slowly, she turned in his arms. They would have to leave soon. They hadn't actually paid for the room. Malachi had shifted to mist and re-formed inside one of the vacant rooms and opened it from the inside. Kelsey was exhausted and would have loved some rest, but they couldn't stay.

Too many people had seen both of them, and there were going to be a lot of questions about the fire.

"Should we get him out?"

Kelsey sighed. She'd asked herself that question probably ten times now, and each time the answer was the same. She wanted to get Vax out of there, save him the hassle of a thousand questions, but too many people had seen him. The way he looked, he wasn't the kind of man people forgot about. If he disappeared, there was a good chance that his face would show up on a "wanted" list in connection with the fire.

That wouldn't be a good way to start his new life. Besides, he did need medical care.

"He's too sick to move right now," she hedged. Part of her still hoped that she hadn't sensed what she had. Or, rather, a distinct emptiness. "He needs medical care."

"Is there some reason you can't heal him? Or a reason he can't heal himself?"

Unhappy, Kelsey looked up at Malachi. "Yeah. There is."

JESS stared at their joined hands. He had a thousand little monitors hooked up to him, and she had gotten used to the monotonous beeping. Every so often, a nurse would come in, check the readouts, and leave, all without saying much of anything.

He'd had an EEG, a CT scan, an EKG, an MRI, and a PET scan. Jess didn't know what all of those tests were, or what they were for, but she had figured out one thing: The doctors saw some things on those tests that bothered them.

"You need to wake up."

She looked at his face while she spoke, but there was no sign that he heard her. She swallowed around the knot in her throat and kept on talking. "I didn't want this, you know. I didn't want you getting involved. I didn't want anybody else getting hurt. I didn't. . . ." Jess closed her eyes and whispered softly, "I didn't want to care about you."

She thought back to the first time she had seen him and realized it hadn't been even a week. Five days. Five nights. One of those nights had been easily one of the best nights of her entire life. But that was it. A handful of days. Six days ago, she hadn't even known him, and now she couldn't imagine a world without him in it.

"Wake up." She whispered it softly as tears fell down her cheeks. "I can't . . . Damn it, Vax. I can't lose somebody I love again. I don't care if you don't love me. I can deal with that. God knows I never set out to fall for you like this. You don't have to love me. You don't have to ever even see me again. You just have to live."

Still no answer.

Jess lowered her head to the bed and cried quietly.

CHAPTER 12

IT hurt his heart, watching her. Jess sat at his bedside, her head resting on the bed and her shoulders trembling as she sobbed. He could hear her crying. God help him, it hurt.

He was ready for this to be over. These weird dreams, these weird flashes, he just wanted all of it over. The strange dreams plaguing him weren't really dreams. Vax knew that, even though he didn't exactly understand how it was happening. His body was lying there practically lifeless. Try as he might, he couldn't make himself wake up.

He was stuck, completely stuck. He didn't know why, and he didn't know how to get *un*stuck. One thing was certain: Staying here like this, watching her cry, was going to break what little heart he had left. "You don't love me." He spoke to Jess even though he knew she couldn't hear him.

"I think she does."

There had been a time when the sound of that familiar voice would have made Vax either sick with guilt or sick with longing. Now it just filled him with a distant sense of regret. He turned and watched as Cora stepped up to his side. She stared at him with her pretty blue eyes, so sad.

He was hardly able to believe that she was there, standing in front of him—whole, healthy, and blissfully, completely human.

"I should have saved you," he murmured as he reached out and brushed Cora's red-gold curls back from her face.

"Vax, you did save me. I knew what I had done—what I would have done. I wanted to stop. I couldn't. If you hadn't . . ." Her voice trailed off, and she paused. Closing her eyes, she whispered, "I couldn't have spent eternity dealing with that, Vax. You know that."

"It was my fault—"

Cora pressed her fingers to his mouth. "No, darling. No, it's not your fault. It was just meant to happen this way." She was silent for a moment. She combed the tips of her fingers through his hair the way she had done when they'd fallen in love and gotten married. She skimmed her fingers down the line of his jaw. "I loved you so much. I do not know if I ever told you just how much I loved you. You were my entire world."

In a rusty voice, he murmured, "And you were mine."

A bittersweet smile curled her lips. "I know. And I have been for too long. But not anymore." She swallowed, and when she continued, her voice was halting and reluctant. "It is time to let me go, Vax. My time here is over. Let me go. Let me move on."

"How?" Vax shook his head. "I don't know how."

Cora smiled. "You can start by waking up. And tell her that you love her." She looked at Jess and smiled. "I like her." Then she was gone.

Tell her I love her. Yeah, like he was going to do that.

S HE was dreaming.

Jess had to be dreaming. She could feel him playing with the ends of her hair, and she was terrified that if she moved, she would wake up. She'd find him lying still as death in that damned hospital bed, the monitors beeping away, tubes running every which way as they pumped food, liquids, and medicine into his system.

But she had to turn her head. She had to look at him. Slowly, she looked up. She braced herself, knowing she was going to wake up. But she didn't. Or maybe she really was awake. Maybe *he* really was awake.

"Oh, God."

He smiled, a weak shadow of his real smile. "Do I look as bad as you do?"

She gave a watery laugh. "Worse." Relief escaped in a harsh, painful sob, and she caught his hand, pressing it to her cheek. "I can't believe you're awake."

"How long has it been?"

Jess swallowed. "A week." A long, agonizing, painful week, when she thought she was going to go insane. "A very, very long week."

His lashes drooped closed. "How long you been here?"

Jess just shrugged. She left only when the nurses threatened to kick her out. Then she'd make the forty-five minute drive back home, shower, crash for a couple of hours, and get up so that she could be back here again. After the first time home, she almost didn't go back.

The police tape hadn't stopped her from going inside, but the cops weren't overly pleased with her for doing so. Or with the story she fabricated. But they couldn't exactly prove otherwise. So the official report was that somebody broke into her house and threatened her about one of her ongoing investigations. She'd kept it nice and vague, and after repeating the same line over and over, the police finally eased up a little.

The windows were being repaired today, and sooner or later she was going to have a lot of cleaning up to do, but none of that mattered. Not a bit, not now.

"You need to go home and rest," Vax said. His voice was hoarse and there was a distance in it that bothered her.

"I just . . ." She licked her lips and forced a smile. "I wanted to be here when you woke up."

"You were." He still had his eyes closed. "That was sweet of you."

Sweet? Something was wrong here. Something was off. He was right there, but Jess felt as though they were standing miles apart. "Vax . . ."

"You have a life to get back to, Jess. It's time you did."

"A life?" she repeated. *A life—how in the hell am I supposed to do that?* Jess had kind of hoped . . . No. She wasn't even going to let herself think about what she had hoped for. It was so obviously not going to happen. She felt a little numb inside as she asked, "But what about you? You don't have family here. You've been pretty sick. You need someone with you."

Now he opened his eyes. There was a cool, cynical smile on his lips as he said, "I don't need someone, Jess. I don't need anyone. Go on home now."

Jess swallowed. Okay. That hurt. No, she hadn't expected forever or anything from him. Circumstances had thrown them together, and chances were, that was the only reason he'd shown any kind of interest in her. In the normal world, whatever that was, he wouldn't ever have wanted her. But, still—she had expected a little more than this cool dismissal. "Vax—"

"What?" His voice was hard and flat as he said, "What the hell do you want? Job's done. I'll heal up and go home. You go back to your life. Figure out whatever the hell you are going to do with the rest of it."

"My life?" she repeated. Tears stung her eyes, and she stood up slowly. She was pissed. The hurt was still there, but now she was pissed. She wasn't sure exactly why, but pissed off and hurting was a lot better than just hurting. "You're going to heal up, go home, and I'm just supposed to get on with my life. You want to tell me how the hell I'm supposed to do that?"

"It's your life. You figure it out."

Ouch. Jess clenched her jaw. It was either that or start screaming at him. "You're a cold bastard, Vax. I hadn't realized that until now."

"What do you want, Jess?" He gripped the neckline of the hospital gown and jerked. The snaps came free, and he let it fall to his lap. He looked down at his chest and started plucking off the tubes and probes attached to his body. The little pads for the EKG, the IV, all of them. The machines started beeping, and two nurses came rushing in. Vax gave them a steely glare and said, "Get out."

They stopped dead in their tracks and looked at each other. Neither of them was as stupid as Jess: They did the smart thing and left. Jess tucked her hands into the back pockets of her jeans and stared at Vax. She gave him a catty smile and said, "Gee, can I help you with the catheter?"

He just stared at her. "What do you want?" He gave her a derisive, mocking smile and said, "Please don't tell me you were looking for some kind of happily-ever-after. It was sex, blondie. We had sex. No big deal."

"You also nearly died." Jess swallowed and turned her head. She didn't want him to see how close she was to crying. "You also saved my life. You made me a promise and you kept it. You also made me a promise and you broke it when you fucked me senseless and then used your damned magick on me to keep me asleep while you snuck off to go take care of things. Apparently I'm just a weak, helpless woman and I would have gotten in your way."

"Jess—"

"Kiss my ass, Vax. I'm not done. You damn near died. I don't understand how that happened. Witches are supposed to heal fast, aren't they? But you almost fucking died! You went into that place knowing exactly what you were going to do, and if Kelsey hadn't saved your ass, you would have died." She looked back at him. "You went in there, *knowing that.*"

"Hoping for it," he said lazily. He shrugged and said, "So what? I've had a good run. Would have been a great way to go out, blaze of glory and all."

"I don't believe that you want to die." Jess shook her head and said it again. "I don't." If he had wanted to die, he would have done just that. His injuries had been bad enough and he'd been weak enough from the smoke inhalation that if he'd wanted to die, he would have. Instead he had fought to live.

"I don't care if you believe it or not, blondie." He closed his eyes. "Go on back to your life, Jess. It's done. Job over."

Jess couldn't make herself leave. She didn't know why. She wasn't much into the pain scene, and God knew this was about as painful as things could get without any physical injury being inflicted. She felt as though he had ripped out her heart and wadded it up in his fist before stomping it into the ground. "Job over."

"You keep repeating things. Do I need to talk louder, or what?" His lashes lifted, and he looked at her with flat eyes. "I came here to do a job. It's done. Why's that so hard for you to comprehend?" He studied her and then started to smirk. "I didn't figure you for the type to romanticize things, Jess. You've known me, what, a week?"

"Less."

"Less. And there you are giving me moon eyes. You're wasting your time, baby. There's no star-crossed-lover deal going on here. No happily-ever-after. We had sex. We caught the bad guy. You didn't do too bad, either. Now it's done. It's over." He closed his eyes again and shifted around a little on the bed. "Go home, Jessica."

This time she did.

H E watched as she walked away. He could hear each soft footstep, and each one of them felt as if he were gouging a knife into his chest.

"Kind of harsh, weren't you?"

It was going to take some getting used to, not being able to sense her. Sense any magick. He glanced over his shoulder and watched as Kelsey separated herself from the shadows. "Why did you do that, Vax?" she asked softly. "And don't lie to me. Don't forget that I can feel what you're feeling."

"She thinks she loves me," he said quietly.

"You didn't lose your Empathy, Vax. You may not be a witch anymore, but you didn't lose that. You know how she felt."

"I know she's convinced herself that she loves me. People do that, Kelsey. They go through hell, and then when it's over, they convince themselves of the strangest things. Women get raped and then blame themselves. Kids get beaten and they think they did something wrong—"

"And you two stopped a couple of killers and she fell in love with you. Just like you're falling in love with her. It's not the same thing, Vax. You know it."

He tried to sit up, but he was still too weak. Instead, he found the button to raise the head of the bed, and jammed it. It worked too damn slow, but finally he could see into Kelsey's eyes without straining his neck. "What I know is that I'm not the man I was a week ago. I don't know who or what I am. But if she does love me, then she loves *that* man. I'm not him anymore." He stared down at his hands and focused, but nothing happened.

No fire. Nothing.

"I'm not the same man."

"Bullshit." Kelsey said it firmly. She reached out and covered his hands with hers. "The magick didn't make you, Vax. *You* made you. All the things you've done with your life—the magick made them easier, but it was you who did them. It was you who saved lives. It was you who saved people. The magick was just your tool. It isn't you."

He felt the heat emanating from her hands, and even though he couldn't feel the pulse and flow of magick anymore, he knew what she was doing. He tried to jerk away, but Kelsey tightened her hands. It was pathetic, realizing he wasn't strong enough right now to pull away from the skinny, mouthy witch. "I don't want healing."

"Tough. I know you. You're going to sneak out of here the second you can walk, and you'll head home. I don't want you collapsing on the roadside, pal." She stayed in front of him for a few minutes and finally the heat faded.

She lingered there for a moment, staring at him. "I know this wasn't what you planned on. I don't know if you went in there with some weird suicide quest going on in your head, or what. I can't imagine what you're feeling right now, or what you're going to feel tomorrow or the day after. But you've got years left in front of you. That much I do know. And if you leave it like this with her, you're going to regret it. Every day. For the rest of your life."

She stepped back, and Vax watched as she disappeared. She was right. He was going to regret it. But he already knew that. It didn't change anything.

He heard something from the hall and looked up. The nurses were back, peering at him through the door. Probably figured he was talking to himself, and they were trying to decide whether they needed to order a psychiatric consult. He smiled bitterly. Wouldn't be a bad idea, except it was a little too late in coming. He lay in the bed, even though, thanks to Kelsey, he had the energy to stand up now.

The catheter brushed against his thigh, and he lifted the sheet, staring down at it. The hospital gown was still tangled around his waist, and he grabbed it and jerked it free. Throwing the johnny to the ground, he stared at the catheter.

Finally he looked up at the doorway. Both nurses were still there. Cocking a brow, he said, "Either of you going to take this out?"

H E made it to Nebraska.

He was tired as hell. Maybe that's what it was. When he had left the hospital, he knew it was the right thing to do. But the farther he got from Jess, the harder it was to keep convincing himself of that. So he was tired, and it weakened his resolve. Sounded like as good an excuse as any, he figured. A lot better than the fact that he just couldn't let it end this way. A lot better than admitting just how right Kelsey had been. Yeah, he been prepared for regrets. He'd regretted it even as he'd been pushing her away, and he knew he'd have to deal with it.

But Vax hadn't planned on it hurting like this, lingering with him, riding his back like some hell-born monkey.

He couldn't keep going. He wasn't going to go back and beg for forgiveness, plead with her to take him back. Hell, they'd never really had each other, so how could one of them take the other back?

Vax did have to tell her he was sorry, though. Maybe explain why he had ended it like that. Yeah. Good idea. Smooth things over, apologize, say whatever he had to say to ease the pain he'd put in her eyes. It wasn't going to completely erase the ache in his heart, but maybe he'd sleep.

The drive took too damn long. Way too long. He tried not to think about how he could have done this a few weeks ago. He'd never fly again, not unless he was in a plane. Vax didn't really care for planes.

By the time he reached Indianapolis, he'd gone nearly twenty-four hours without sleep. He was punch-drunk with exhaustion, and nervous. Nervous—it was weird, but Vax couldn't remember the last time he'd been nervous. Had nothing to do with the magick, though.

Had to do with the fact that he was standing at Jessica Warren's front door, freezing his ass off and too aware of the fact that he probably wasn't going to make it inside, not if he knocked. So maybe he shouldn't knock. Vax looked behind him. It was quiet on the street, and late, pushing eleven o'clock. The lights in Jess's house were out, although he knew she was there. Sleeping, deep and dreamless. He could sense her. At least that much hadn't changed.

He had a feeling that if he knocked, she wouldn't let him in. Vax wasn't leaving until he said what he had come here to say.

After one last look at the door, he went to his bike and retrieved a small black case from the leather pack strapped to the back. More often than not, when Vax had needed to get inside someplace, he'd used magick. But that hadn't always been possible. Any Hunter worth the name knew how to break into places. Vax might not be much of a Hunter anymore, but he figured he could still do the breaking-and-entering bit easily enough.

He kept his senses wide open as he worked. It was weird having to rely on the five human senses again. He heard a car coming, and just as it turned onto Jess's street, he heard the final little *snick*. He grabbed his tools and opened the door, closing it gently just as the car passed by her house. He didn't bother packing away the lock picks. Jess was still asleep, but he wasn't going to count on her staying that way. If she woke up before he got into her bedroom, she was likely to call the cops. He imagined that seeing him get his ass thrown in jail would be sweet revenge.

Jess didn't wake up, though. He stood in the doorway to her room, staring at her in the dark. She lay on her side, one hand drawn up. Pale blonde hair lay in a tangle around her shoulders. The moonlight streaming in turned the blonde strands to silver.

She wore a top with skinny straps, and it clung to her slender form. She sighed in her sleep and Vax tensed, waiting for her to oepn her eyes. All she did was roll over. One hand reached out, as though she were reaching for something. Or someone. His heart knotted as her fingers closed into a tight fist and she sighed again, a sad, broken little sound.

Silently he crossed the room. Should he wake her up? Let her sleep? There were bruised-looking shaodws under her eyes. She didn't take very good care of herself. It had been months since she'd had a decent night's sleep. With that on top of the hell she'd gone through recently, she had to be exhausted.

The considerate thing to do would be to leave. Come back in the morning and talk to her then. But Vax hadn't ever bothered much with doing the considerate thing. Why start now?

Instead of leaving, he took his jacket off and crossed the room. All he was going to do was lie down beside her, watch her sleep. That was all. He wouldn't even touch her.

But the second he lay down, she cuddled up against him. Her fisted hand unclenched and slid across his chest, resting just above his heart. He tensed, and swore silently. Okay, so maybe this wasn't a good idea.

There was no way in hell, though, that he was going to move. She'd take care of that herself as soon as she woke up. Most likely this would be the last chance he had to touch her, or at least to have her touch him. He wasn't going to miss a second of it. If that made him more of a bastard than he already was, he could live with that.

Need, a low-level burn whenever he was near her, pulsed and flared, but he throttled it into submission. Jess sighed and tried to squirm a little closer, rubbing her cheek against his chest. Through the cotton of his T-shirt, he could feel the warmth of her skin, and he muffled a groan. This was going to be both heaven and hell. And if she didn't wake up, it was going to be a long-ass night, too.

Surprisingly enough, though, he felt sleep weighing down on him. Too heavily to fight, in fact. He felt his eyes closing. With Jess, soft and warm, pressed up against him, he stopped fighting it. A few minutes. Just a few . . .

JESS was dreaming. She knew she was dreaming. She knew she needed to make herself wake up. The last thing she needed was to have another dream centered around *him*. But he felt so good against her, so right. Cotton bunched under her hands as she pushed his shirt up. She pressed her lips to his chest and felt his heart pounding with a fast, erratic beat. She wanted to see him. If she looked at him, would she wake up?

It was a risk she had to take, because *not* looking at him just didn't seem possible. She lifted her lashes and stared at him. Jess held her breath, waiting for something bad to happen. He'd disappear. She'd wake up.

Neither happened. Instead his hands closed over her bare hips and pulled her against him. The heat of his body was a sweet, erotic pleasure against her own, and for a second she wondered at how real this particular dream seemed to be. Was he . . . No. The arms around her felt sure and strong. It was a dream, had to be. Vax was still in the hospital and would be for a while yet.

Good. She was too damn pissed to deal with him in reality. And she was hurt. But in a dream? Oh, yeah. That was all good. She bent her head and pressed her lips to his. Her hair fell around them like a curtain, cutting off the rest of the world. Then Vax slid a hand into her hair, using it to anchor her head as he pushed inside her mouth, kissing her as though he was as starved for her as she was for him.

Not possible . . . Another sign she was dreaming. In reality he hadn't given a damn about her, not once he'd done his fucking job. Fury blistered through her, even here. She bit his lip as she tried to move closer. His hands moved gently over her as though he wanted to soothe the rage she felt. But Jess wasn't in the mood to be soothed. She wanted to get as close as she could, wanted to take him deep inside and never let go, never wake up—and at the same time she wanted him to hurt.

She reached between them, jerking at his jeans. The silver buckle felt oddly cool against her hands, and it resisted. She kept fumbling with it until she freed it, and then she went to work on his jeans. As she lowered the zipper, he groaned against her lips. His hand tightened on her hair, and Jess pulled away. When he reached for her, she evaded his hands, moving down his body until she could take him in her mouth. He bucked against her. She raked her teeth gently over the thick head of his cock and sucked on him.

"Fuck, Jess . . ." It was the first thing he'd said. No sweet, tender words, no soft apology, just those two guttural words. He arched up against her, pushing his length farther inside her mouth. Jess took as much as she could, and then she slid back up. She stared up at him through her lashes.

The words he'd said to her in the hospital came back to haunt her. *It was sex, blondie.* She lifted herself and looked down at him, snarling a little. *Sex. Just sex . . .* She crawled back up his body and rubbed herself against him. Through the thin silk of her panties, she could feel him. Thick, hard, and full, throbbing against her. She pushed herself up, bracing her weight with one hand on his chest and using the other to catch her panties and pull them aside. She took him inside with one quick, hard stroke, and fell into a fast, furious rhythm.

His hands went to her hips, trying to slow her down. She didn't want slow. "Easy, Jess. Slow down a little," he whispered against her lips. He touched gently, spoke gently. He slid his hands up her back, over her neck, before he cupped her face and pressed a soft kiss to her lips.

Soft and sweet—here, lost in a dream that should be *hers,* and he was trying to be in control. Acting like he wanted to make love to her. Such a damn joke. "You want slow, go find some stupid bimbo and pretend to make love to her," she said. "This is just sex—no reason to take it slow and easy."

Part of her realized now that she wasn't dreaming. But she didn't want to acknowledge that. Just as she didn't want to acknowledge the pain simmering deep inside. Acknowledging it would be throwing a match inside a gas tank. It would explode inside her and consume her.

He tensed below her, his lashes dropping low over his eyes, shielding them. Then he moved, slipping his arms around her and locking her tight against him. He rolled, putting her body under his and catching her wrists, pinning them down by her head. His hands were gentle but unrelenting, and she couldn't break free. His weight crushed her into the mattress, and she could feel him pulsating inside her. She rocked her hips upward, and he swore.

"Damn it, Jess . . . Slow down. I didn't plan on this. . . ."

Hell, no. He hadn't planned on this. Sleep a few minutes, and then he'd wake up and get out of bed before she awoke. Instead he woke up with his dick in her mouth while she stared up at him with fury in her eyes. The fury he could have handled. He'd earned it. But the pain there was eating at him, and he couldn't bear it. He lowered his head and kissed her. She turned away, and instead of trying to follow her mouth with his, he kissed her neck.

At the same time, he started to rock gently against her. She kept up that mad little shimmy with her hips, trying to take him deeper, harder, and faster, but he wasn't going to do it. He'd done a damn good job of convincing her that he'd just fucked her because she was handy, and now he had to undo that damage. Words alone weren't going to do it. Even thought he wanted to give in and take her with hard, quick greed, he wasn't going to.

Propping himself up on his elbows, he released her wrists and cupped her face once more. "I love how you taste," he whispered against her lips. She kept her mouth shut, but he wasn't going to let that stop him. He traced the seam of her lips with his tongue. Her mouth softened just a little, for just a second, and then she jerked her head away again. "And the smell of you," he murmured, burying his face in the crook of her neck. He rolled his hips against hers. She clenched around him, and he heard that quick, unsteady gasp leave her lips. "And I love how you feel." He traced a hand down her side, pausing at the covered curve of her breast. The silky material of her chemise was little obstacle, but it was in the way. He wished she were naked, completely naked in his arms, but he didn't want to risk pulling away long enough to fix that. "Soft, strong . . ."

Vax shifted his weight until he could slip a hand between them. He circled his fingers over the tight knot of her clit. "Wet—tight." So damned tight. He groaned as the muscles in her pussy flexed around him. Her hands came up, resting on his shoulders, hesitantly at first and then firmly. One hand slid over his shoulder, fisting in his hair. When he went to kiss her again, she sighed against his lips and opened her mouth, letting him inside.

He wrapped his arms around her and had to fight against pounding himself into her now that she'd relaxed a little. Instead he kept up that slow, almost lazy rhythm. As though he'd be content to do nothing but make love to her for the rest of the night and into the morning. Yeah, that would suit him to a T, but there was no way he could make this last much longer.

Her breathing hitched. He felt her stiffen under him, felt her clench around him as she moved closer and closer to orgasm. "That's it, Jess," he muttered against her mouth. "Come for me—let me feel it again."

She climaxed with a gasp, and he captured that soft, broken sound with his lips, riding her through the orgasm until she stopped bucking and thrashing under him. Her hand stroked down his sides, stopping at where his jeans rested just below his hips. He gritted his teeth and pulled away. His cock ached and throbbed, and his body screamed at him to climb back on top of her, push inside her, and fuck her until he exploded.

He wasn't going to, though.

It took some doing to zip his jeans up over himself. He was hard, pulsing, and wet from her, and shoving his rigid flesh back inside his jeans was a little piece of hell. Jess lay on the bed, unmoving. She stared at him with dark, shuttered eyes, and he shifted until he could lie down and pull her against him. "I didn't come for that," he said softly. "I don't expect you to believe me, but it's a fact."

Her voice was remote as she responded, "Well, then why did you come?"

For the longest time, he wasn't sure how to answer. He knew what he *wanted* to say. But he didn't have the right to say it, and not just because he'd hurt her before. He'd meant what he'd said to Kelsey at the hospital. Even if Jess did think she was falling in love with him, it couldn't work.

He couldn't think of anything that could describe his sudden descent from witch to mortal man. But even if it hadn't happened and he was still a witch, he knew it wouldn't work.

He couldn't fit into her life here, and beyond that, he didn't know what the hell he was supposed to do with his own. He recalled what he'd said to her, and wondered if maybe those words were directed more at himself than at her.

Let me go, Cora had said. Vax had meant it when he'd told her that he didn't know how. Guilt over his dead wife had been his companion for nearly a century. *Let me go. And tell her you love her.*

It wasn't that easy. It couldn't be that easy.

"Did you know I was married?"

She tensed against him, and then she jerked back. She sat up and stared down at him, and then she rolled away, getting off the bed as though she couldn't move away from him fast enough. *"What?"* she demanded.

Slowly Vax sat up and climbed out of the bed. She was pissed. He didn't have to be an Empath to sense that. He might be a little dense, but he wasn't totally stupid, so instead of going after her, he just stood by the bed and repeated what he'd said.

Her reaction wasn't exactly what he'd been prepared for. She crossed the room and balled up her hand. He saw the punch coming, but not soon enough to evade it. His preternatural speed was gone, yet another thing he was going to have to adjust to. His head snapped with the force of her blow, and blood flooded his mouth. Gingerly, Vax probed the cut on the inside of his cheek with his tongue. "Feel better?"

"No, I don't, you son of a bitch. *You're fucking married?"*

Maybe he was totally stupid, Vax decided. The reason for her fury finally penetrated, and he couldn't help but smile a little.

"You think this is funny, you prick?" She swung at him again, but this time he evaded it. He caught her clenched fist and lifted it to his mouth, kissing the back of her hand.

"No. No, Jess, I don't think it's at all funny. Maybe I wasn't clear enough. I *was* married. A long time ago." He let go of her hand and turned away, staring out the window. All the houses seemed to crowd in on him. Now that he was awake and aware, he could feel the presence of others. If he relaxed his shields even a little, the thoughts and dreams and emotions of all those sleeping people would crowd in on his mind. Losing his magick had weakened his shields. Vax didn't think he'd ever felt this exposed, this raw and open before.

Turning away from the window, he leaned back against the wall and looked at Jess. She was staring at him, still furious. Still enraged. So fucking beautiful, it made his heart hurt just looking at her. "She died before you were even born."

Jess opened her mouth to say something. Then she closed it without saying a word. A thoughtful look crossed her face, and she whispered, "Fitzpatrick—he said you had a wife."

"Yeah." Vax had all but forgotten that.

"He also said you killed her," Jess added. She turned away from him, her movements tense and jerky as she strode to the wardrobe across the room. As she opened it, she said, "How did she really die?"

"He wasn't lying, Jess. I killed her."

At those flat, emotionless words, shock rippled through Jess. The jeans she had pulled out of the wardrobe fell from numb fingers, and she never even noticed. Slowly, she looked back at him and asked, "You're not serious . . . are you?"

Instead of answering her, Vax asked, "Did Kelsey tell you . . . tell you what's happened with me?"

Jess blew out a breath and stared at him. Okay, so was he going to answer her or not? Getting answers out of him was like pulling teeth. But instead of demanding he explain what the hell he'd meant when he said *I killed her,* she answered his question. "No, but I figured it out when you didn't Heal like you should. Somebody pumped you full of that poison, didn't they? You're human now." She cocked her head, studying his face closely. Her ability to sense emotions was seriously limited, although she was getting better at reading him. But she couldn't decide one way or another how he felt about this new change in his life. "You okay with that?"

Vax snorted. It was the same derisive, cynical sound

she'd heard from him on a regular basis. Amazing how sarcasm could be such an endearing quality. "Don't have much choice in the matter, do I? Would you believe it, though? Being normal was really all I ever wanted."

"You wanted your wife. You loved her." He didn't have to say it. She could tell. Jess wondered what had happened to her—he couldn't have killed her, though. Jess couldn't believe that.

"Yes." He nodded, his eyes staring into nothingness.

Okay. Jess swallowed against the knot in her throat. His coming here didn't necessarily have to mean much of anything. He'd been a jerk on purpose. She was figuring that part out, and she was pretty sure she knew why he was here. He felt guilty for being an ass, and he wanted to smooth things over. Fine. She could let him. Jess wasn't going to pine away over a man who was still pining for his dead wife. But she wasn't going to let him take his sweet time getting this over with. She wanted it done and over and him out of here so that she could indulge in a good old-fashioned crying jag. Then she'd get to work on getting over him. It would be harder, though, now that she knew she hadn't been so totally wrong about him.

He wasn't the ass she'd been telling herself for the past day and a half that he was. He was a proud, arrogant, *good* man, one worth loving. An ass wouldn't have felt guilt. Vax did. Maybe he even cared about her. He just couldn't love her back.

"What happened with your wife, Vax?"

Gently, he repeated, "I killed her, Jess." His eyes were carefully blank, but she sensed something inside him. Guilt. Pain. A weird sort of acceptance. "I was out Hunting. A vampire came. Kidnapped her. Changed her. Not everybody goes through the Change intact. Cora didn't."

Oh, God. She licked her lips and moved a little closer. Okay, now things were making even more sense. She didn't like the way the puzzle was looking, either.

He glanced at her. That thick, raven black hair shrouded his features as he quickly looked back at the ground. "I'd never loved anybody the way I loved her. And I totally fucked that up, Jess."

"How?"

He shrugged and started to pace the room. Even if his magick was gone, nothing had changed. There was something vital about him. It was as if he carried a light inside him, and when he was near her, she felt warmed from it. When he left, she'd go cold, and her world was going to be a lot darker.

"I didn't protect her. I couldn't save her. A feral vamp stole her from me, raped her, killed her, and turned her into a vamp, and she went mad. Went feral. She had killed people. And I knew she wouldn't stop until she died. She couldn't stop." His voice was emotionless. But it just made the pain in his eyes that much more intense. "So I killed her. It took me two weeks to find her. When I did, she asked me to save her. Told me we could make everything fine. I kissed her. Then I shoved a knife in her heart."

Jess moved closer, and he lifted his head to look at her. As their gazes met, a tear rolled down his face. "You saved her, then. You saved her the only way you could." She reached up and laid a hand over his chest. "In here, part of you knows that. You just have to let it go. Forgive yourself."

She pushed up on her toes and kissed him gently. "Stop feeling so guilty. Forgive yourself and let it go." She went to turn away, but he caught hold of her shoulders. He bent his head, looking into her eyes. His hair fell around him, and Jess couldn't resist closing her hand around a fistful of it. She loved his hair, just fucking loved it.

"What about you?" he murmured. He slid his hands down her arms and then pulled her against him, locking his arms around her waist. "Can you forgive me?"

She could do that. A few minutes ago, hell no. Punching him had helped, even if she had hit him over the wrong thing. She forced herself to smile at him. "Yeah. I can do that. We'll chalk it up to you having a really rough day. Week." *Life.* But she kept that last part to herself. She had a feeling that if he knew how much she hurt for him now, he wouldn't like it all.

She leaned in and kissed him. Slow and gentle, trying to commit to memory every last thing about him, the way he tasted, the way he felt against her, that warm, sexy scent of his. "Consider yourself forgiven. But it wasn't bad advice, pal. I need to get on with my life. And so do you." She kissed him one last time, quick and light, and then she disengaged herself from his arms and stepped away.

"That's what I'm doing." He came up behind her when she would have bent over to grab the jeans she'd dropped earlier. "That's why I'm here." He brushed her hair aside. "You know, I really have no clue how to go about it. Nothing's the same anymore. I'm not sure what I'm supposed to do."

She stepped away from him again. Vax didn't like how easily she kept moving away. At least her eyes weren't glinting with anger and pain. But the shuttered look in them wasn't much better. She gave him a bright, easy smile—one that was completely false—as she said, "After all this time, you shouldn't have to do anything because you're supposed to. Go do what you want." Her smile gentled a little. Looked a little more real. "Go on. You've earned it."

"Earned it." He laughed at that and shook his head. Then he reconsidered. Had he earned it? Vax didn't know. But maybe. Just maybe. He realized though, that he didn't want to go back to his old life. Not the one before he'd met Jess, and not the one before he'd lost Cora. Even if he could. Vax was done with that life, with both of those lives—and he was *glad*.

It was over for him. He'd told Jess to go find some sort of normal life, but he was going to find one, too. One that didn't involve reinventing himself every other decade. One that didn't involve his moving around nonstop so that people never saw him long enough to wonder why he didn't age. And he hoped it would be one that involved her.

"Come here," he murmured. He reached out and caught her wrist, pulling her right up against his chest.

"Vax . . ." She pushed away from him, or tried to. This time he didn't let her. Something flashed in her eyes. Looked sort of like desperation. *Now why would you be so desperate to get away from me, baby?* he wondered. If she was still pissed, he could have attributed it to that, but she wasn't mad. What he sensed coming off her was pretty far from mad. It was chaotic and confused, and Vax wasn't sure he was ready to delve into that mess of emotion.

At least not until he was a little more sure. He spun them around and pinned her back against the wall.

"Damn it, Vax," she swore, but there wasn't any fury in her voice. She acted like she was going to push him away, but her fingers dug into his shirt and tugged him closer. "What are you doing?"

He lowered his mouth and murmured against her lips, "I'm doing what I want. Exactly as you said. What I want is to kiss you. For the next few hours. Then I'm going to strip you naked and make love to you for the next day. Maybe the next two."

"Vax, look, you said it yourself. I need to find a life. I can't . . ." She gasped for air, and then she moaned against his lips as he kissed her harder. When he stopped, she muttered, "I can't move past this until I let go of you. You were right. Maybe I did start fantasizing about something more, some stupid happily-ever-after. My mistake. Just . . ."

"No. It was mine. I wasn't right. You don't need to find a life and move on. You've already got one. . . ." He let go of one wrist and reached up, cradling her cheek in his palm. He rubbed his thumb back and forth over her lip. "With me, if you'll take me back."

"Take you back?" she repeated, her voice faint. "Vax, you weren't ever mine to being with."

He laughed and kissed her again. This time she didn't try to turn away. That was a start, right? "I heard you, you know."

Blood rushed to her face. She hoped she didn't sound as nervous as she felt. "Heard me when?"

"When you were talking to me at the hospital. I heard what you said. Every word." He stared at her, his dark gray eyes so focused, so intent. "I knew when you weren't there. I could feel your absence. When you were there, I knew."

"Everything?"

His lids drooped. "Yeah. I heard everything."

Oh, now, wasn't that just wonderful? she thought bitterly as she recalled how she'd laid herself bare while he was unconscious. Jess wrapped her arms around herself tightly as though that would keep her pain and humiliation trapped inside instead of their spilling out. "I thought you were going to die. Maybe I got a little emotional."

"Don't." His voice was harsh. "I may not be a witch anymore, but nothing's wrong with my Empathy. You're lying to me. I know it. I can feel it." He leaned down and muttered against her ear, "I also know *why* you're lying."

She glanced up at him and then looked away. "Look, Vax, I don't . . ."

"Don't what? Don't want me? Don't lie to me, Jess. I was wrong. I fucked up. I'm not going to lie and say that I didn't mean to hurt you. I did—I thought it was for the best."

"For the best," she repeated slowly. "I don't see how in the hell your being cruel could possibly be for the best."

"I thought it could—if it saved us from hurting each other later on. But I was wrong to think that. I was wrong to try and take the choice away from you." He threaded a hand through her hair and forced her to look at him. "You said you loved me. How is that possible? You hardly know me."

She had a flippant reply—she opened her mouth to say it. She *wanted* to say it. She wanted to see just a little bit of her own pain reflected in his eyes. But she couldn't. "I don't know. I just . . ." She turned away, blinking away the tears burning her eyes. "Do you know, I haven't really let myself feel anything since my parents died. I mean, I loved

Randi. But she was already part of me. Part of my life. Part of my heart. But I haven't let anybody else in. I haven't let anybody make me feel anything. But you—I couldn't control it. Even from day one. I don't know if I believe in destiny or anything like that, but I do know that you made yourself matter to me."

"Matter to you. Is that the same thing as love?" Vax asked as he eased a little bit closer.

Jess hedged. "I don't know."

"Yeah, you do. You already said it once. You're just afraid to tell me again." He kissed her again, and this time Jess didn't pull away. "I don't blame you. I hurt you, and I'm sorry for it. But—" His lashes drooped, shielding his eyes. "I didn't think I was the same man I was when I walked into that building."

"Not being a witch doesn't change you, Vax."

He shrugged. "I thought maybe it did. I was wrong, though. I walked into that building knowing that I loved you. And I came back here tonight for the same reason." He pulled her against him, held her close for a moment. She reached for him, but before she could wrap her arms around him, he stepped back. Turned away from her.

Jess watched as he picked up his jacket. "I want you to think about it. Think about you and me. I think it could work," he said. "Will you do that?"

He didn't wait for an answer as he turned around and walked away.

He was halfway down the hall before Jess figured it out. When she did, she couldn't figure out whether she was mad or giddy. He'd walked away because he thought she'd fallen in love with a witch. "You stupid jerk!" She shouted it at him so loudly that it hurt her throat. "You arrogant, stupid, brainless . . ." She sputtered, running out of insults, and finally just settled on, *"Man!"*

He turned around, staring at her with shuttered eyes.

"You want me to think about it?" she snarled. "I can't believe this. You insult me. You make me feel like an idiot, and for *what*?" She shook her head again and glared at him. "You are a jerk."

"You've said that."

Jess snarled at him. "Did I already say that? Okay, here's something new." She balled up her fist and slugged him in the gut. The startled *oomph* made it worth the pain that shot up her forearm.

"I've got a news flash for you, slick. I didn't fall in love with a witch. I fell in love with *you*. Or at least I thought I did. But that was before I realized how phenomenally stupid you are." She spun away from him and headed back towards her bedroom.

Two brawny arms slid around her waist and lifted her off her feet. "Maybe I am stupid. Does that mean you don't have to think about it?"

Jess sniffed. She struggled to get away from him, but he wasn't putting her down. "Let go of me."

"I tried that once. I didn't like it. Tell me you love me," he ordered. He accompanied it with a soft, gentle kiss to her neck. "Or do you need to hit me again first?"

"I don't know. I think I ought to hit you a few more times." He raked his teeth over her neck, and she shivered. "I think maybe I *could* love you. But you're still a stupid jerk."

"I know. Would you feel better if I said maybe I think I could love you first?"

"Too late. I already said it." She tugged lightly on his hands, and this time he sat her down but didn't let go. She had just enough room to turn around, but she wasn't so certain that was an improvement. Now, instead of feeling the hard, long length of his body against her back, she felt him pressed all against her front, staring down at her. His eyes were so dark a gray that they were nearly black, and his gaze kept drifting to her mouth.

"How is this going to work?" she asked quietly.

He grinned at her. She felt the thick, steely length of his cock nudging into her belly. "I have an idea or two." His hands rubbed up and down her arms, warming her chilled flesh. "Let's go back to bed, and I'll tell you all about them."

She rolled her eyes. "I know how that works. I'm talking about us. Is there an us?"

Tracing her lips with his fingertips, he said, "I think there is." But the humor and heat in his gaze faded. "Do you want there to be an us?" Slowly, he let go and turned away from her. "I don't know where I'm going now, Jess. I can't be a Hunter." He looked around, staring out the window. The next house was maybe fifteen feet away. "And I don't belong in a place like this. I can't live in the city. I can't . . ." Vax trailed off.

"Oddly enough, I don't think I ever saw you living in a city. Tell me something—you honestly think the two of us could work?"

His lashes lifted, and Jess felt a tremor deep inside. His eyes—they were glowing. His hands cradled her face, and his lips covered hers in a deep, hungry kiss. "Yeah. I think we could. Hell, screw that. I *know* we could," he muttered, pulling away just long enough to whisper in her ear, and then he was kissing her again.

By the time he pulled away again, she was breathless. "Well, maybe you can't live in the city. I don't think I have to." She smiled up at him. "You know, somebody told me a few days ago that I needed to get back to life. That I needed to find one. Maybe this isn't the best place to do that."

"You'd live in Montana?" He crooked a grin at her. "Have you ever been to Montana? My ranch is in the middle of nowhere. Nothing to do. Nothing."

With a wicked grin, she ran the back of her hand down his fly. "I wouldn't say nothing. Besides, I've had enough excitement to last me quite a while."

He caught her hand, pressing a kiss to her palm as he wrapped his other arm around her waist and hauled her against him. "So you want to come and play ranch hand, is that it?"

Jess snorted. "As if. No. I don't want to play ranch hand." She rose on her toes and pressed her lips to his. She lifted her head and smiled up at him. "You know, I've always had this idea in the back of my mind. Mom always told me I had a wild imagination. Maybe I should try writing a book."

Turn the page for a preview of

Through the Veil
by Shiloh Walker

Coming soon from Berkley Sensation!

It's said that a warrior will come. Like a wraith . . . living not in our world . . . not in hers.

The demons can't find her. She doesn't exist to them. But she doesn't exist to us either.

They can't destroy.

She can save us. But she can also destroy us. Because she doesn't seem to realize we are here.

Hᴇʀ body ached.

It wasn't anything new. Although Lee was only twenty-eight years old, she already felt ancient. Exhausted even upon awakening, with stiff, aching joints, and bruises that seemed to appear out of nowhere.

Rising from the bed, she tried to hold together the fragile wisps of the dream, but as always, it faded away, out of reach, out of mind. *He* faded away.

She didn't know his face. But each night he came to her, she found him again, those eyes moving like hands over her body—hungry, frustrated.

He had yelled at her.

Scowling, Lee stalked into the bathroom, turning the hot water on full blast before turning to tug off her T-shirt. He wasn't real.

He *wasn't*, her mind insisted, even though something inside her heart argued.

Her reflection caught her eye and she stilled, fighting the impulse to turn and look. Damn it, she was going to take all the mirrors down. She couldn't *not* look when the mirrors were there.

But every time she saw a bruise, a chill ran through her.

It was no different this time.

Her eye was black, swollen, raw looking.

It had been fine last night. And today she looked like she had a bruise that had been healing for days. Her mouth trembled as she tried to make sense of what she was looking at.

The doctors had tried to tell her she was doing it to herself. They had even done a sleep study and watched her all night long to determine what caused the bruising.

The study had revealed nothing.

And everything.

For when she walked out of the room where they had monitored her body all night, her ankle was swollen, twisted, and discolored. It had been fine the night before.

The tape of the study had shown her lying quietly on the narrow bunk, never once rising in the night. The only weird thing was a blip in the middle of the tape that lasted no more than a few eyeblinks. For that one period, the bed was empty. But she hadn't gotten out of the bed. The probes and lines weren't long enough to allow her to leave it without one of the attendants disconnecting them.

And they hadn't done it.

Odder still, an attendant had been in the room during the blip. They could see him at the edge of the screen. But he'd never seen her move.

She hadn't done any more studies after that. Even though the doctors tried to urge her to, it had simply unsettled her too much. So no more studies. She'd just deal with looking like the loser of a boxing match.

Leaning forward, she probed her eye, touching it gently, wincing at the tender flesh she encountered under her fingers. The iris looked fine. Maybe a little bloodshot. But her eyes were always bloodshot.

There was another bruise on her knee, like she had fallen down. The flesh was sensitive there, too. But those were the only injuries. A rather light night, actually. Lee knew from experience, though, that that wasn't necessarily a good thing.

Turning away from her reflection, she climbed into the shower. Shower . . . then caffeine. With caffeine, she could face almost anything.

THROUGH the veil, Kalen could see her. Stubborn little bitch. He could still faintly smell the sweet scent of her skin, the satin texture of it, the silk of her hair. The vivid bruise on her face infuriated him, even though her rapid ability to heal was already lessening the vivid color and the swelling.

The *mortig* demon that had attacked her was dead. Dust in the wind. Not that Kalen had anything to do with it.

Lee had taken damn good care of it herself. She was good at that. Always had been. Scowling, he wondered if maybe she was a little *too* good at it. Good at taking care of herself, good at rationalizing away problems, good at everything.

Clenching his jaw, he turned away from the veil and prepared himself to face the coming day without her. It was a frightening thought. But it always had been.

One never knew what the day might bring. Not in this world. The barrier that kept the demons back during the day was getting weaker and weaker. There had been a time when he had gone weeks facing the things only at night. Now the things dared to come out not just at night—but all the time.

Sooner or later, Kalen would end up facing one he couldn't fight off.

Facing another day without her—because until she was ready to accept reality, not *her* idea of what reality was, every day was entirely too likely to be his last.

LEE stared with focused intent as she wielded the stylus, watching as the image took on life and color.

It was a man.

A strong jaw, silver eyes, long hair that blew in the wind, staring out over a land that looked barren and desolate. There was something starkly beautiful about it, though. Like it had once been so lovely, it could bring a tear to the eye.

He was crouched on a jagged outcropping, wearing a coat the blew in the wind around a lithe, powerful body, tensed and ready. . . . She added more color to his hair, a silvery sheen to the dense black. Then she added more definition to the muscles that rippled along his arms.

Lee worked in a daze. Once she finished with the man, she added to the background, working with the sky, the clouds, drawing in shades of creatures so monstrous they would have given her nightmares, if she were prone to them. In her mind, they already had names. *Mortig* demons. *Vierom* wraiths. *Wasso* minions.

Battles raged in her mind as she worked. Hissing calls, furious shouts, the sounds of metal clashing, the hum of laser weapons slicing through flesh. She could almost smell the scent of burnt flesh.

No battles now, though. The battles had already been fought.

Now he rested. Now he prepared.

Now he waited . . . waited for her.

I'm getting tired of waiting, Lee. . . . We need you. . . .

Then silence fell and she heard him, like he was whispering into her ear from just over her shoulder. *How much longer will you hide from what you are?*

Lee snorted. "Just because I don't think you are real doesn't mean I am hiding," she muttered as she saved the work. Standing up, she wavered a little, her knees weak and shaky as though she had just run a mile. *Or fought a battle.* Pressing a hand to her temple, she laughed shakily and muttered, *You're losing your mind, chick.*

Actually, you're more sane now than usual, Lee. When are you going to stop fighting the truth, pet?

Lee ran her tongue around the inside of her cheek as she

started across her studio. "I'm hearing things," she muttered, shaking her head. "Man, I need a break. A vacation. Drugs. Something."

You need to stop being so blind, Lee.

"Damn it!" she shouted, spinning around. That voice sounded so real . . . Holy shit.

It was him.

The man from the picture.

He was standing right there.

In her studio.

With hair that flowed to broad, rock-hard shoulders, eyes the color of pewter, and a coat like Jack the Ripper would have worn. He had what looked like a sword hilt peeking over one massive shoulder, and hair that was raven-wing black.

But he was also transparent.

Lee pressed one hand to her mouth as black dots started to dance before her eyes. His teeth appeared as he grinned at her, a sensual twist of his lips before he faded away.

She managed to whisper, "Oh, hell," before she hit the ground.

Long moments later, Lee groaned, forcing her lids to lift, a throbbing settling right behind her brow as she sat up. With her hands on the ground, she stiffened her arms and forced her weight up, swearing as the world spun in dizzying circles around her. "Whoa . . . what in the hell . . ."

An image of that man danced before her eyes. "For crying out loud," she muttered, pressing a hand to her temple. Damn it. "Working too hard."

He looked too real.

There was a life to him that was unlike anything she had ever created in her life. Everything, from the texture of his hair, the color of his eyes, to the demons that surrounded him.

She got to her feet, locking her knees when her legs wobbled underneath her. Lee rubbed her gritty eyes, trying to figure out how she had ended up on the floor. She needed to go to bed. But dreams chased her too vividly there. And his image, that mocking grin, seemed to taunt her every time she closed her eyes.

"I'm losing my mind," she muttered.

Pressing the tips of her fingers to her eyes, she shut her computer down and left her studio. "That's it. I'm done for the day."

KALEN watched with a faint smile as she walked away, shaking her head and rubbing the goose egg that was no doubt forming.

She'd seen him.

He'd seen the shock in her eyes, felt her gaze connect with his . . . *At last* . . . She was already rationalizing it away, but for once he had managed to breach her conscious mind.

Maybe tonight they would speak of something more than the battle against Anqar.

Hours later, Kalen muttered to himself, "And perhaps kittens will fly."

Lee stood at the front line of the encampment that had been set right at the city limits. Much of the city had fallen to ruins, but the inhabitants of New Angeles were determined not one more square foot of their land would be given to denizens of the demon realm.

They followed their leaders, Kalen Envren and Lee, with a blind, fearless devotion that was almost slavish.

They didn't know her last name. They didn't know where she lived. They didn't know where she came from. Nothing more than her first name and that she fought like a woman possessed, and that when she was in the battle, the battle was likely to be won.

That was all they knew.

Yes, that blind, slavish devotion was a bit disturbing. Even more so, considering that not one of them had ever seen the woman by the light of day.

Not even Kalen.

He had known Lee for more than twenty years. She had

appeared out of the darkness when she had been hardly more than a baby, a chubby, cherubic little thing with big, angelic blue eyes and dimpled cheeks, her curling hair pulled into a ponytail high on her little head as she pushed a meat-filled sandwich into his bony hands, whispering, "You're making my tummy hurt."

He'd been so hungry.

Starving. Locked in the basement of the house where the *mortig* demons had set up camp, he had been waiting for death. Or possession. A boy of ten was ripe for them, a good prize—especially one weakened by days on end of abuse, starvation, and fear.

She'd fed him that night, freed him two nights later.

He hadn't seen her for three years. When he had seen her the next night, he had been fighting in a rebel army just outside of Orleans. Even though she had grown up a little, he still recognized her as the child who had freed him from the little hell in his prison in New Angeles.

"What's your name?" she had asked. Sitting on the crypt, she had sat swinging her feet, that dimpled smile exactly as he had remembered it.

"Kalenes Envren."

Her brow had puckered. "Kalenes Envren?" She'd frowned a little. "Kalenes almost sounds like a girl." Her giggle had made him flush and she had pursed her lips as she studied him a little longer. "I like it . . . I think. Ya know what? I think Kalen sounds better."

He'd called himself Kalen from that point on. And he didn't see her again for three years, when he went from participating in a rebel army to leading one. And she saved his life, pulling him out of the way when his lieutenant would have slashed his throat from behind.

After that, Lee had started fighting, not just sliding in and out of his life like a wraith, but fighting like some warrior angel.

Now he led the army, and she served at his side, appearing out of the night like a shadow, full of whispered secrets and magicks that had, at times, destroyed entire armies of

demons. And when she came out of the darkness, it was
often with a plan fully formed that would help defeat some
small faction or free a captured rebel.

The woman should be leading this army. Damn it, he was
a soldier, he wanted to be out there *fighting*, not issuing orders and playing the diplomat with fellow rebel leaders.

Crouched on the twisted outcropping of rock, Kalen
watched as she issued orders to the rebel soldiers with
ease, the sunny banner of her curls gleaming in the false
light as she shook her head in response to a question.

This had to stop.

They couldn't keep fighting this war only at night. The
demons were stronger then. If they fought during the day,
they'd not just keep them at bay but beat them back. *Win.*

But until she opened her eyes . . .

The screams painted the night like blood. Hot, vivid
washes of it. Kalen jerked to his feet, grabbing the plasma
assault rifle from the ground and slinging it over his shoulder. His feet moved silently over the uneven ground as he
moved closer to the source of the turmoil. Too many
screams. Too much of it.

"I don't like this."

He closed his eyes as Lee slid out of the darkness like a
wraith. Her hair gleamed like silver in the darkness of the
night; her blue eyes were colorless. "You heard the
screaming," he said flatly.

Her lips flattened. "The very dead heard the screaming,"
she whispered.

They slowed to a halt, and he heard the soft whimper
that rose in her throat before she could stop it. As powerful as she was, she was still a woman. Her heart was still
soft. Hell, seeing all this death made his heart hurt. Clenching his jaw, he drew the rifle from over his shoulder and
leveled it at the *jorniak* demon that was still feasting in the
middle of the death and devastation.

Lee lifted her hand and the pure silver energy that flowed
from it was the same as the laser of Kalen's plasma rifle.

The *jorniak* demon screamed, the hissing quality of it's death noises making their skin crawl, while the stench of his blood made their eyes water. *Jorniaks* never really stank, unless they bled. Once they bled, the smell of them was enough to make you want to puke.

Kalen's bolt had gone through one of the demon's three lungs, enough to hurt him—enough to keep the male from running very far. Kalen liked to ask questions.

Lee's bolt had killed him.

Sometimes Lee's anger got the better of her. Maybe actually leading the army wasn't the wisest course of action for her. She acted first and asked questions later. Kalen had learned the value of asking questions.

But he understood why she had destroyed the thing. This small unit had basically been a hospital on wheels. A few soldiers, but most of the dead were doctors, nurses, and medics. They were harmless, all of them.

"He killed them all, Kalen."

With harsh, jerking motions, he shoved his plasma rifle into the harness on his back, the fury burning in his gut. But at the low, rough sound of her voice, he turned to look at her, a fist closing around his heart. There were tears sparkling in her cerulean eyes.

Lee didn't cry.

"Damn it, how much longer do we have to keep doing this?" she rasped as a tear spilled over and trickled down an ivory cheek.

Kalen cupped his hand over her neck, drawing her against him, his body jumping to life as her sleek curves came into contact with his tensed muscles. "Until we win, darlin'. Until we win," he replied.

A shudder wracked her body and then she sighed, catching her breath. He gritted his teeth as he felt the soft push of her breasts against his chest. Before his control shattered, though, she stepped away, turning from the destruction and death that lay before them. Kalen watched as she shoved a shaking hand through her hair.

She hated being stared at. She slid him a nervous look and then jerked her eyes away. Kalen sighed, turning away, forcing himself to walk into the splattered circle of blood.

Akira was dead. She had been a twenty-one-year-old medic that Kalen had known since she was a kid. A tic throbbed in his jaw as he studied the gore that had been her once-pretty face. Her eye was missing, as was half her cheek, the glint of bone gleaming white in the moonlight. Blood shone wetly; her throat was a wet, open wound.

At least she had died quickly.

And most likely first.

Although Akira had been a medic, she was also a tele-kinetic. If she hadn't died fast, and first, she could have called for help. Magick and powers of any sort were rare among anybody in the health care field. They tended to be rather grounded. The gruesome things they saw in their line of work tended to be too brutal for any Empath to deal with.

He reached out, gently closing Akira's one remaining eye, his gut clenching at the already cold feel of her skin. Damn it, she had been fine just a few hours ago.

Rage boiled inside his heart as he straightened up and counted every last body.

Five of them.

Five friends dead. And Akira was hardly more than a kid. Blood roared in his ears, while reality seemed to freeze in front of him.

This could all stop.

Lee could help them stop it.

It was within her power.

She moved in the shadows of their world, fighting while the demons came out, prowling in the night. But if she would walk in the light, when the demons were weakened, they could mount enough power to eradicate them.

Lee was the soldier of light, their chosen one.

But she ignored all his whispers, all their pleas to open her eyes and come. And they continued to die.

Woodenly, he turned and faced her, feeling his heart in

his throat, the bitter taste of anger in his mouth. "How long will you hide, Lee?"

She lifted her head and a breeze blew by, blowing long strands of her silken hair across her face, hiding everything from him but those azure eyes. For long moments she stared at him, unmoving.

Kalen moved to her, the thick soles of his combat boots thudding dully on the rubble-strewn ground. It was thick with garbage, dirt, medical supplies . . . and things he'd rather not think about. He paused by the carcass of the senior medical officer, knelt down, and stared into the man's wizened, old face. "Godspeed, Jacob," he whispered. Kalen blew out a tired breath and ran a hand down his face before snagging a blanket from the rubble and drawing it over Jacob's body. Then he rose and met Lee's gaze over the distance that separated them.

Purpose filled his eyes, his gut, his steps as he moved to her, hands curled into loose fists. Kalen saw the trepidation enter her eyes, watched as her throat moved, the fragile skin shifting, betraying the nerves he suspected she was suddenly feeling.

Her nerves rarely showed in her eyes.

That was one of the reasons she was such an amazing warrior.

Lee was amazing. Plain and simple. Her instincts were nothing short of phenomenal. She knew where clutches of demons hid, led the armies to them with unerring skill, demolished them with bursts of magickal power that kept their people safe and didn't cost them anything in way of supplies. But she never stayed.

She never risked herself for anything longer than a few hours a night, a few nights a week. Weeks would go by when she wasn't seen at all.

And it cost them lives.

Because people depended on her.

And she had proved time and again she would only come when she couldn't stay away any longer. Her conscious self didn't even know what was going on. She hid behind the veil of her memory, safe inside her normal world where demons didn't exist, where everything was safeness, security, and light.

And here, in this darker reality, where things existed whether she liked it or not, she could join them, save lives. . . . But she refused.

Closing the distance between them, he loomed over her, staring down into a face he knew almost as well as his own. "When are you going to open your eyes, Lee?"

She blinked. He could see the tension that suddenly tightened her body and stiffened her shoulders, drawing her back ramrod straight. Tiny little lines fanned out from her eyes. Her lashes lowered, the spiky little fans hooding her eyes and shielding her gaze from him as she murmured, "What do you mean, Kalen?"

"When are you going to come into the open? Join us? We're dying while we wait for you," he growled, reaching and closing firm, unyielding hands around her upper arms as he drew her closer to him.

"I've been fighting with you for more than fifteen years—since I was a kid, Kalen. What more do you want?" she demanded. "I gave you my childhood."

"I want you to join us. Not just to fight when you can't hide anymore. What do you do when you're not here? Where do you live? What is your home? What is your *name*?"

With every harsh question, he watched her flinch. Even here, she couldn't answer. Even when she was here in her subconscious dreams, she was too afraid. With a rough, disbelieving laugh, he let her go and turned away, reaching to wrap a hand around the cable of his thick hair.

"You come and go like a shadow in the night, Lee. You're like flash fire, baby," he whispered. "Just as reliable. Just as hot. Just as deadly. You can cause a hell of a lot of damage to the demon realm, sweetheart. But too many of our people want to depend on you to always be there. People have launched entire campaigns thinking that at the critical moment you will come and pull off a miracle. When they've been right, it's been amazing. But when they've been wrong . . . it's been too devastating for words. I can't let them depend on you anymore. *I* can't depend on you."

Turning back to face her, he felt a hollow ache settle in his heart. "You belong in my world. I know this—in my gut. You know it, you always have. Otherwise you wouldn't keep coming here. The prophecy tells of a woman who will come and lead us out of the hold the demons have on our world."

Kalen plunged his hands through his hair, fisting them, resisting the urge to tear out hunks of hair, anything to relieve the building pain and frustration inside him. They needed to end this. They had to find a way to unite and drive back the monsters into the Under Realm. But they had to band together to do it, and they couldn't, not continuing on as they were.

A sudden surge of weariness flooded him and he had to fight to stay on his feet. All the fighting, endless, seemingly useless fighting . . . Inches gained only to lose yards on the next front. Staring into the sky, he studied the flickering lights of the auroras. They had once been much brighter, so beautiful it made the soul hurt just to look at them.

But the smoke, the fumes from the ever-present burning of the fire bearing the demons—and pollution from the more noxious demons—had clouded the skies until the sun was little more than a hazy, bright circle behind the smog.

Kalen couldn't remember the last time he had seen stars.

His world was falling apart. His people were being killed to extinction.

"Lee, are you ever going to open your eyes?"

"Kalen—"

Cutting his eyes to her, he whispered silkily, "Don't. Just—don't, Lee." Crossing over to her, he cupped her face in his hand, tightening his hold when she tried to jerk her face away. "You aren't here every day. You haven't been the one to go into a safe haven and find entire families slaughtered, wiped out, from the elders to the babies. You haven't had to comfort friends as they've had to watch the women they love slowly go insane because they were raped by *wasso* minions.

"You live there, in your reflection of this world, safe and secure, blind to what happens here. Except for your dreams, where you can't block us out. And then you come and you go—always when you're needed the most to save our throats right in the nick of time. But never when *I* need you the most. Never. Not once have you come for me. Not for us. Always for you, because you can't resist that nagging in your gut."

"Damn it, I've saved your fine ass a number of times," she sneered, jabbing him in the chest with a nail she painted the color of *junyai* rubies. "Your life. This army. All of you."

"Yes. Because something disturbed you while you were asleep in your world. Damn it, I know what's going on. *You* know. If you'd just open your eyes . . . part of you has always known," he whispered passionately. The wind started to kick up and his hair blew around them like a cloak, winding around her slim shoulders as he moved closer, nudging her toes with his.

"Known *what*?" she demanded, rising onto her toes so that she was snarling into his face.

Her mouth was just a breath away from his . . . just one breath . . . Kalen could almost taste her, taste her fury, her fear, the hunger she tried so hard to hide. He laughed softly, releasing her chin to stroke his fingers over her eyes. "Known what you are. You're no mortal woman. You're magick. You're power. . . . You're a warrior and you belong here. You see things in your mundane world that other people don't see, but you block them out. You feel things, hear things, sense things. . . . You are like a wraith in that world. A mere shadow of your true self. When are you going to come *home*? Come to us? Fight with us?"

"I fight with you all the time," she whispered, her lips trembling, tears welling in her eyes as she stared at him, hands clenched into tight fists at her sides. "You act like I'm in some other world, but I am *right here*."

"You still don't know, do you?" he whispered, shaking his head. "Still. Lee . . . you *are* here. Part of you. Part of you lingers there. But you're nothing but a shadow of yourself in either world. And you have to open your eyes and start seeing *your* reality instead of the one somebody created for you. Otherwise you'll remain in the shadows."

Lee gritted her teeth, a tiny shriek of frustrated anger slipping from behind them as she spun away and punched her fist into a ruined wall. "Damn it, what in the hell are you talking about? You always talk in riddles, you overgrown, self-righteous, hypocritical *bastard*!" she shrieked.

He said her name softly and waited until she turned around to glare at him before he asked quietly, "Where do you go when you aren't here? Do you know?"

A blank look entered her eyes, one he'd seen before. He often tried to probe her mind—sometimes she deflected, but sometimes he knew she honestly didn't know. Her face turned mutinous, a line forming between her eyes, that lush pink mouth puckering into a sullen, sexy little scowl. "What does that have to do with anything?" she demanded, tossing her head, throwing the blond wisps of her curls out of her eyes.

With a tired sigh, Kalen rubbed his forehead. "You don't know, do you? Damn it, Lee, doesn't that strike you as pretty fucking weird, that you don't *know* where you go in between flitting in and out of my life?" he demanded, flinging a hand in her direction before he let it fall limply to his side. She just stared at him, her lids flickering, her eyes glittering like diamonds in the faint light.

"You can't tell me that you remember anything about what you did yesterday, can you?" he asked. *Damn it, prove me wrong . . . prove me wrong!* It would be so much easier if she was just some elusive witch from the mountains. From anywhere—so long as she lived in this world.

But he already knew the truth.

Their warrior wouldn't come from their land.

And if she refused to believe, they were done for.

When she remained silent, he felt something inside him die. "You can't," he answered for her. "Because you don't remember."

Something broke open inside him and he lunged for her, drawing his blade from the sheath at his hip, grabbing her forearm. She shrieked and shoved at him, startled. He could feel the fire of her magick as she pressed her hands against his chest. One pressed against the dull sheen on his metal plate jacket that he hadn't zipped up. But the other landed on his chest, just a little off center. Above his heart.

Gripping her left hand, he wrenched her palm away from his chest, smelling the scorched scent of burnt skin as he pinned her arm down. With teeth gritted against the pain, he took magicked blade she had given him long ago and sliced a shallow mark into her arm, his heart bleeding as he heard her soft gasp of pain. "*Explain that . . . when you wake in the morning. Explain your bruises away however you will. But it will be harder to explain a knife cut.*"

Rolling away from her, he stormed off, feeling sick in his gut for what he had done. Kalen closed his eyes, fighting the urge to scream and rail at her. It wouldn't do any good. She hadn't listened to him in all this time.

She wouldn't listen now.

"Leave, Lee. Leave and don't come back. We'll fight this war without you."

And if she kept coming back, he would end up doing something that would destroy them both.